ex–Cottagers
in Love

ex-Cottagers in Love

A NOVEL

J. M. Kearns

KEY PORTER BOOKS

Library and Archives Canada Cataloguing in Publication

Kearns, J. M. (J. Michael)
    Ex-cottagers in love / J. Michael Kearns.

ISBN 978-1-55470-000-4

    I. Title.

PS3611.E27E93 2008   813'.6   C2007-905487-0

ONTARIO ARTS COUNCIL
CONSEIL DES ARTS DE L'ONTARIO

The publisher gratefully acknowledges the support of the Canada Council for the Arts and the Ontario Arts Council for its publishing program. We acknowledge the support of the Government of Ontario through the Ontario Media Development Corporation's Ontario Book Initiative.

We acknowledge the financial support of the Government of Canada through the Book Publishing Industry Development Program (BPIDP) for our publishing activities.

The quote from Bob Dylan's song "Dear Landlord" is reprinted by kind permission; Copyright © 1968; renewed 1996 Dwarf Music. All rights reserved. International copyright secured.

The quote from Virginia Woolf's *To The Lighthouse* is reprinted by kind permission of The Society of Authors as the Literary Representative of the Estate of Virginia Woolf.

The concluding lines from "On Raglan Road" by Patrick Kavanagh are reprinted from *Collected Poems*, edited by Antoinette Quinn (Allen Lane, 2004), by kind permission of the Trustees of the Estate of the late Katherine B. Kavanagh, through the Jonathan Williams Literary Agency.

The author gratefully acknowledges that portions of this book were written with the support of a Canada Council Explorations Grant.

Key Porter Books Limited
Six Adelaide Street East, Tenth Floor
Toronto, Ontario
Canada M5C 1H6

www.jmkearns.com

www.keyporter.com

Text design: Martin Gould
Electronic formatting: Alison Carr

Printed and bound in Canada

08 09 10 11 12 5 4 3 2 1

"Anyone can fill his life up
With things he can see but he just cannot touch."

— Bob Dylan, "Dear Landlord"

"The faintest light was on her face, as if the glow of Minta
opposite, some excitement, some anticipation of happiness
was reflected in her, as if the sun of the love of men and women
rose over the rim of the table-cloth, and without knowing what it
was she bent towards it and greeted it."

— Virginia Woolf, *To the Lighthouse*

"That I had wooed not as I should a creature made of clay —
When the angel woos the clay he'd lose his wings at the dawn of day."

— Patrick Kavanagh, "On Raglan Road"

To R.

BOOK ONE

The cottage

I

The homemade lamp

HER ARMS WERE A LITTLE TOO LONG.

I noticed that right away, when Maggie Taylor walked into the law firm where I supervised some bedraggled paralegals in an office tower in downtown L.A. I had already heard about her from Zeke Weiss, a sixtyish guy who was supposedly on my team but who spent most of his workday like some rambling mendicant, sharing his salty thoughts with friends whose cubicles were scattered all over the fifteen floors occupied by Sarronick & Beatty ("SOB" to its intimates).

This was in 1984. George Orwell had predicted dire things for this year, and my being stranded in a huge law firm like SOB seemed to bear him out. I had come to L.A. in 1977 because some of my favourite music had been made there, by people like Brian Wilson and Jackson Browne. Bitten by the songwriting virus as a grad student in Toronto, I had hung on long enough to finish a PhD and then left my home and native land for the great US of A, a hitchhiker with a knapsack and a guitar. My years in Los Angeles began auspiciously with a live audition at Elektra/Asylum Records, and then went quickly downhill. I ended up doing the thing I had promised myself I would never do—working in law. Even worse, I wasn't an attorney like my father and grandfather in Calvan,

Ontario; no, at age thirty-seven I was a mere paralegal, and had
been for five years.

Anyway, Zeke the litigation assistant had told me he had a
girlfriend who was a lot younger than him, and who was beautiful and Italian and liked Peter, Paul, and Mary and other
obsolete folkies who hadn't been seen for years. Since I was well
on my way to being an old folkie myself, I thought this counted
in her favour.

Then Zeke got Maggie hired by my fearsome supervisor
Cynthia. Cynthia—who was a slender, distant brunette with
haunting brown eyes and with whom most of the male paralegals
were in love—had once authored a memo about me called
"Towards the Improvement of David Moore" when I was literally
caught napping, behind a desk in an empty office on the fortieth
floor. I astonished her by firing back an incisive memo called
"Why Improvement Is Not Called for in this Case." Let me
expand on this briefly, for it will be on the exam. In my memo I
explained that some people *need* naps, and that I had *always*
needed them. I could remember as a schoolboy the torture of
trying to pretend I was awake in trigonometry class, which came
right after lunch, and the grogginess that would persist for most
of the afternoon if I didn't nod off for a moment. Even my
lawyer father, in the days when Canadian professionals were
allowed to come home at noon and have something called "dinner," used to lean back in his blue chair in the living room after
that meal and fall asleep for ten minutes, before returning
refreshed to "the office." Was there any moral or legal reason why
a responsible employee should not have the right to a short sleep
when needed? A short sleep that would increase productivity?

You may say that I must have been hypoglycaemic or dia-
betic, but I had had all the tests and everything was normal. It
seemed that this was a natural condition approved by God, and
that I needed to manage it.

And in fact I eventually found a little park down the street from the law firm, where I would, on favourable days and on my own time, lie down under a tree after lunch, with a jacket as my pillow. I think I had a vague hope that one day I would spot a few other bureaucratic types splayed out on the grass, and we would nod the secret nod to each other and realize that we were members of a fraternity—not lazy or perverted and not alone, we were just different. Then the League of Nappers would arise and fight for our dignity.

Back to our story. The scary Cynthia hired Zeke's friend Maggie, and one spring day in Orwell's year she walked into my life and my room and my team.

Her arms were a little too long, yes. But other than that she was perfect. She was Sophia Loren with glasses, and my ideal woman was Sophia Loren crossed with Virginia Woolf.

The Virginia Woolf part would take longer to determine, as you'll see. But the Sophia Loren part was fully resolved in the first minute. I had loved that astonishing actress since I was a pimply undergraduate at the U. of Toronto masturbating in the shower after seeing her strip for Marcello Mastroianni in *Yesterday, Today, and Tomorrow*. My precocious roommate Adrian had assured me that reaching orgasm upstream against a torrent of hot water was truly reaching orgasm, and the image of Ms. Loren did not fail to prove that out.

This woman who now appeared before me, this Maggie Taylor who had been dating my ageing supervisee for years, this revelation of how little words can prepare you for the actual sight of someone—this twenty-nine-year-old woman had finer features than Sophia Loren, and a more introspective air. Yet she had a similar cat-like quality of face. Her eyes were large and grey, and flashed with something impudent. Her figure was a dramatic hourglass. I could hardly look at her, and she seemed to notice that.

It was love at first sight. Or what is often called love. I knew clearly, as Zeke introduced us, that I wanted to divest him of

her. I thought, *this woman has to be mine*. Then she spoke and she
had a high voice like a bird and its delicacy made me think
my not-overly-macho maleness might still be equal to the
challenge.

I had to train Maggie on how to review boxes of documents,
to find the ones that could help (or hurt) our case. She would sit
beside me at my desk. My team was arrayed in a horseshoe in a
large irregular room paved with linoleum. There was no privacy:
seven of us were in each other's faces all day, and one of the seven
was Zeke, her boyfriend. So Maggie would sit beside me and I
would try to explain obscure clauses in the insurance policies
which our client had foolishly sold to marauding corporations,
and she would look me in the eyes and we would start giggling.

I was never sure what was funny: maybe our genes were
sharing some delicious banter. But two things were quickly
clear. She was very smart, and she didn't give a shit about corporate liability. This forced me to be the Solemn One, a role
that seemed to delight her, because her nearness rendered my
performance so unconvincing. Eventually we got through the
training and she began to work in a small alcove in the corner,
and I was able to recover some of my concentration.

I had a lamp on my desk that was the one beacon of incan-
descence in a fluorescent sea. It was a lamp I had built myself.
I am not a carpenter and owned few tools, but with a saw and
hammer I had roughly fashioned it out of pine. It had a circular base, a square stem, and an unlikely scalloped shade I had
bought at a classy lighting store. The electric cord left the stem
about halfway down and headed off in search of an outlet. It
was, frankly, an eyesore, and Maggie liked to mock it, but to me
it represented some kind of rebellion against the corporate
ambience. Then one morning when Zeke was away on vacation
for a week, Maggie came over and asked me if I would make a
lamp like that for her. I was shocked: this was the first inviting
thing she had ever said to me.

So I did what any lusty lampmaker would do: I asked her out to dinner.

On a coolish August evening, Maggie swept into my crummy rental house in Eagle Rock and she was wearing a black cape.

She took off her cape and stood in my front room and looked at the lamp I was assembling on a card table, and I stared at her. Now you may be wondering what she was wearing. Like many men I am more affected by wardrobe than observant about it, and I certainly don't know the technical lingo. But I'll try to give some impressions. She had on an elegant plum-coloured dress; the front had a pattern on it—embroidery? or is it brocade? It had a high waistline that made it hug her form, and the skirt was long. She looked like a queen, like the queen of anything I cared about. Her hair was pulled up in a sort of bun with many tresses coming down in wonderful ways. I couldn't believe she was my date.

She looked at the lamp. She said, "There are no pencil marks on it."

I said, "I'm trying to do this one better. I sanded it clean, after I sawed it."

She said, "But I like the one at work. It shows its own process."

Then she picked up my guitar, a 1962 Gibson J-45 that a Toronto friend had given me because I could play it and he couldn't. She said, "This is beautiful. Can I hear it?"

I said, "Maybe I can play it for you later."

So we went on our first date.

Which was also our last, for three years.

Ominously, she had invited two people from SOB to join us, two paralegals from down the hall who had known me quite a while and had, in the short time she'd been at the firm, taken her under their wing. This compromised the situation already, because Sandra and Bill were very protective of Maggie and very sceptical of my credentials as a lover—not to mention that they adored Zeke and were adamantly loyal to him. Why were they wary of me? Well, *they* would have claimed that they could tell I was a commitment-phobic despoiler of female hearts, based on almost no evidence (that they knew about); but *my* theory was that they had more than earned their supervisor status (they'd both gone to law school and Bill had passed the bar), whereas I, who had also risen to Coordinator, was squeaking by on native ability and no legal training other than growing up in my dad's house. As for Maggie, perhaps because of her high voice and pretty features, they took her to be an angel: innocent, sweet, and vulnerable to molestation.

Nevertheless, when the two of us sailed into the Westside Café on Santa Monica Boulevard, Maggie and I had the unmistakable vibe of an item, and our waiting friends were swamped by the sheer glamour of us—or so it seemed to me. The beef tournedos was superb, the conversation scintillating, and I thought we were truly launched. On the way home she not only asked me to drive but pretty much admitted that her days with Zeke were numbered, even though he still reminded her of Woody Allen; and we started to share stories about our pasts. We talked about childhood summers and she said her family liked to take road trips. I said we went to the cottage. After I translated that into American, I told her that my parents were lately threatening to sell our cottage—I didn't really know why—but I certainly wasn't in a position to buy it. She flashed me a feeling look.

About eleven P.M. I parked her Chevy Malibu on my street and we got out of the car.

I took her shoulders in my hands and looked at her lips.

She said, "Please. I really can't."

I said, "Are you sure?"

I could already taste her kiss; I *knew* it was meant to be.

She said, "I'm sorry. This was really fun, let's not spoil it."

She drove away and I went into my cheap little house and found a two-by-four that was leaning against a wall and swung it as hard as I could against a doorjamb and the doorjamb cracked.

And that was it for three years, except that I was in love with a person I supervised and I had to see her every day and Zeke had her and I didn't. All because she was too dishonest to admit what I thought I knew, or maybe too damn loyal to a faded love.

After a while she was assigned to a different case, but before that happened there were two revealing incidents that I should mention. Clues to the Maggie character, signs that I might be better off without her, after all. One was when my boss Cynthia and I decided we needed a person to specialize in the computer side of our pretrial research. We thought that person should be Maggie. We asked her and she turned us down. It would have meant new training, advancement, prestige, eventually more money. She turned us down, and went back to reading dusty documents.

Then one morning I was walking the half-mile from my parking spot to our building on Flower Street and I saw a woman walking, about a hundred feet ahead of me. She had thick brown hair, good shoulders, and fine ankles—that's all I could see. Something about the look of her was utterly foreign to me, yet I found myself thinking, *why can't I meet someone like that? What a beautiful creature.* When she got to our building she turned to greet someone and I saw that it was Maggie. Later that day I ran across her in an attorney's office; she was rifling through a box on the floor. I went in and stood there and said, "When are we going to start dating?"

She never got up; just knelt on the floor and pursed her lips and said, "You know Dave, this is hard to say but there really isn't an attraction."

"Okay," I said, and I got out of there, and my heart felt like a dead weight inside me.

The thing is, she was *lying*.

2

A literary exchange

CUT TO 1987.

A lot of things had changed in three years. The case I was working on had gone to trial in San Francisco, so in early 1986 I had set up a satellite office there for four attorneys and a handpicked team of paralegals. The latter were mostly recent hires by me. The best of them—and they were very good— included a soft-spoken Filipina named Pam, a big beautiful black woman named Brenda, and a perky all-American cheerleader type named Sharon. Oh, and there were a couple of dudes who were less useful but fun to drink with. We were all living in the City for the duration of the trial and it was a sweet gig. It was Reagan's crazy 80s and our profligate client was happy to pay for lavish apartments, taxis, any restaurants we might want to frequent, and a special stipend for the "hardship" of temporary relocation.

It would have been a wonderful time to be in love, so of course I had nothing going on romantically. What I did have was a lot of gourmet dinners in North Beach with lucky paralegals and two young attorneys who liked to parade their knowledge of wine.

Maggie was working on another case which regularly took

her to San Francisco, but I never saw her. What I didn't know was that she had struck up an intense friendship with Pam, Brenda, and Sharon, the heart of my trial team; they had formed a madcap quartet who got tipsy and had a lot of laughs together in their own haunts by the Bay. Maggie had also lost twenty pounds that mattered a lot to her, and she had finally broken up with Zeke.

The first I heard of any of this was when Brenda mentioned casually to me that Maggie wouldn't mind if I contacted her. I had thought that door to my heart was solidly sealed, but it didn't take long to open again.

Messages were passed back and forth and without a single direct phone call, we had a date.

Our second date. This one turned out better.

We met at Basta Pasta, my favourite restaurant in North Beach, on a side street up from Columbus. Maggie walked in and found me at a table by the window. Her wavy hair was wet and her glasses were fogged. She wiped the glasses, then doffed her raincoat. For me, the moments when Maggie took anything off were sublime theatre—they engaged me on any number of levels, from the spiritual to the carnal—and this one was no exception.

She sat somewhat carefully in the chair opposite me and I saw that for this occasion she had worn a carmine shawl that was woven like a tight spider web. Under it was a long-sleeved black leotard (and yes, a skirt of some sort). How she had chosen that leotard I did not know: she couldn't have realized how unfair it was. Anyway I was faced with her very pale skin set off against black silk, or whatever that material is, and I was gripped by weakness too delightful to disclose.

So, manfully, I focused on her fine grey eyes. Which were glassy.

And what was I wearing, you ask. On this day I had on blue jeans and a dark T-shirt, and over the T-shirt a long-sleeved

shirt with a subtle olive plaid. I tended to splurge on shirts. I
chose nice ones; they were my outer layer and I wore them a
little large.

"Do you want a drink?" I said.

"I think I'm already drunk. We had margaritas at
Brenda's."

"I didn't know you drank."

"I don't!"

I ordered the Pasta del Giorno to get us started, and a bottle
of Chianti Ruffino. It soon emerged that Maggie really was
drunk, and that made the conversation much less filtered than
it might have been. Instead of an awkward dance, we engaged in
a stream of confessions.

The best one emerged from an odd literary exchange.

"What is your favourite book?" she said. "Oh, I don't care
what it is. Mine is *Pride and Prejudice*."

"You don't want to know what mine is?"

"If you must."

"I like *To the Lighthouse*," I said.

"Virginia Woolf. Wasn't she real stuffy?"

"People think that. She was an intellectual, but she was very
unstuffy. And this is the book where she found her form. It's
amazing, it feels like actual life; it's funny and sad and it's a
fucking thriller."

"No—a thriller?"

"I thought so. I read it the summer before my fourth year.
I was in a library in Vancouver, in a big reading room, the sun
coming in. My friend Adrian came to collect me and I told
him, 'Go away, I have to read more of this!' It was white knuckle
time."

She laughed. "What was so thrilling?"

"I don't know. I had felt like a freak for ages, felt that
nobody was like me, then all of a sudden I read her first page
and there it was. Life as I knew it. I wasn't alone."

"Okay, now can we get back to me? I'm going somewhere with this point."

She gripped the table with both hands and I saw that she was unsteady. I asked her if an espresso might help and she said yes. I moved the wine bottle away from her.

The espresso came and she sipped it carefully. "The room has stopped spinning," she said. "Do you know the plot of *Pride and Prejudice*?"

"Sure. English lit was my minor."

"But do you *know* it?"

"Let's see, it's about Elizabeth something, this guy doesn't want to love her but he does."

"That is so skewed! It's about her hating him, even though she is hugely attracted to him. She thinks Darcy is a bad person, she refuses his proposal . . . and then all hell breaks loose."

"Alright."

The waiter came and we ordered the excellent Chicken Toscana. And then Maggie told me that the same story was happening to her: it was playing itself out even as we spoke. The same plot as Austen's.

"I was convinced you were a bad person," she said, "even though I was attracted to you."

"You were? I knew it. Wait—why was I a bad person?"

"You were too serious about your stupid job. I overlooked a document once and you totally lost it. You were rude. And Bill and Sandra told me to watch out for you."

"They don't even know me."

"They said you dumped a nice girl in 1981. Bill said he didn't trust you. You were arrogant."

"Jeez. Now I wonder why you're here."

"Take it easy, Musk. I didn't totally believe them. It was partly me. I wasn't ready."

She smiled and I thought, *this night I am going to get that kiss.*

Then I realized what I had just heard. "Did you call me Musk?" I said.

She laughed. "Yeah, it's our nickname for you."

"From Muskoka?"

"Muskoka? No, we have crushes on certain guys and we call them the Four Musketeers, and you're one of them."

"Who has crushes?" I said.

"Pam and Sharon and Brenda—and me."

"My team."

"That's what I'm trying to explain to you. Pam told me she had this great supervisor, who took time to explain things to her and always thanked her. David Moore. She didn't know I knew you; Sharon didn't either. Sharon said you put her in charge of a special 'swat team' project and she was amazed you thought she could do it. Then she pulled it off. It was just like when Lizzie Bennet visits Pemberley!"

"Pemberley . . ."

"You know—Darcy's estate. She hears good things from his housekeeper, who adores him."

"I can't believe this."

"It gets better. You know how tough Brenda is: the people she makes fun of are the ones she really likes. Well, she's always making fun of you."

I was misting up—probably the wine.

The confidences continued to flow. She told me what had happened with Zeke: she just knew it was time to move on, and he didn't disagree. I told her how bitter I had been when she turned me down, how elated I had been on our first date.

I said, "I have to ask you. Why did you stay with him for so long?"

She said, "Because he was safe. I trusted him."

"You trusted him?"

"Not to harm me."

We finished dinner and walked down Columbus in a light

rain, and after a few blocks she said she might be sick, and I hurried her into a little church and waited on the steps.

She was shaken up on the play and I put my arm around her and got her into a taxi and took her back to Brenda's place. The kiss had to wait.

She was never called back to San Francisco. My trial wrapped up and by January I was back in L.A., on a new case with a new attorney in charge. It was 1988, the year of this story.

The good news was that at last Maggie and I began to see each other. The bad news was that my life as a paralegal took a great fall. My new boss was a burly brute who treated me like a servant; I was moved into an office of my own but it was tiny and windowless; and the new case was a mess.

My job was starting to suck, but my personal life seemed to be on the rise.

3

David Lynch

MAGGIE AND I WERE BOTH SEXUALLY EXPERIENCED, BUT sometimes with a new person you have to lose your virginity all over again.

We got pretty good at necking. We would stop in our favourite Mexican restaurant on Sunset, or in a seedy Chinese place called the New Moon, east of downtown. We would sit in a booth and I would slip my hand under her dress and feel her bare thigh. Like an embryo that relives the stages of evolution from tadpole to human, our sexual journey seemed now to have reached the teenage years. We would kiss for hours, dizzy on Mai Tais or Coronas, then stagger down the street in a haze of satisfaction, not needing to go any further.

The first time we slept together, crazily enough, was at Zeke's place, and all we did was sleep. Maggie was keeping an eye on his apartment near MacArthur Park while he was on a document production in Modesto, and it was near the movie theatre where we had just seen *Wall Street*, so we stopped by to check on things. We were tired and didn't feel comfortable about going in the bedroom, so we lay down on a couch. We put our arms around each other and it was as if we were dancing cheek to cheek, horizontally. We awoke in the dawn and neither of us had moved a limb, so natural was it for us to be entwined like that.

Still I needed something to push me off the ledge of love, into the chasm of lust. She was too beautiful to me. Or maybe I was buying into that angel quality.

As it turned out, it would be David Lynch who rode to my rescue.

It happened like this. One Saturday night in March, Maggie came to my new place to watch a video. With cash from my stint in San Francisco I'd been able to swing the deposit on a better rental, on a nice street in Pasadena up near the mountains. It was a one-storey house, four rooms and a bath, with a driveway of its own, rimmed with bougainvillea. I was still deep in debt, but I had a better view.

We sat on my couch and had a drink before the movie.

"I listened to that cassette you gave me," Maggie said. "I have some thoughts on it."

She had asked to hear what I was doing as a songwriter— after all, that's what I claimed I was, and I had recording equipment in my other front room, into which most of my debt was sunk. I wasn't sure my ego was ready for what she might say, but I gave her the go ahead.

"Well first, I don't understand why these are all country songs," she said. "Is that what you do?"

"Not exactly. It's just that a lot of country singers don't write their own stuff. So they need songs."

"You're trying to get someone else to record your material."

"Right. I mean, most of my songs are not country at all, but I'm trying to get some income out of this."

She narrowed her eyes. "I don't know how to say this, Musk, but I'm not sure this tape is making it. Have you sent it to anyone?"

I explained that that wasn't as simple as it sounded; contacts in Nashville were hard to come by—and I was still trying to perfect the recordings.

"Maybe that's wise."

"The tape is that bad?"

"I'm not saying it's bad—some of the lyrics are really good, I like the tunes . . . it's the singing."

"Oh god. You hate my voice."

"I don't hate it. I'm just not sure it works for country."

I was silent and she said, "I don't know what I'm talking about. I don't even listen to country. It's good. If it was just a little more . . . lively."

"Lively?"

"I don't know. You don't always sound like you *mean* it. I'd like to hear your Dave songs—your real stuff."

I was an inch from falling into a very depressed place, and I knew I would not be any fun at all once I got there.

I said maybe we should watch the film.

She said, "I've hurt your feelings."

I slid the video in. It was a very strange movie we had both wanted to see, called *Eraserhead*, that David Lynch had made a decade earlier, featuring a mutant baby in an industrial waste-land. It had odd noises and freaky visuals and with all the lights off, it lit my room a corpse-like blue.

About twenty minutes into the movie I turned to Maggie. The silence between us had allowed me to recover my equilib-rium, and I had developed a cold, vengeful design on her. I began to unbutton her blouse and then got impatient and yanked it the rest of the way open. I pushed her down on the couch and dragged her skirt off. The TV made sucking noises and she looked up at me in a detached way, as if I was just part of the movie. I started to kiss and bite her thigh and then I went inside her and held my torso up at arm's length, pleased by the lurid glow of her breasts.

It seemed we had graduated into lust. We went slow, things happened on-screen and sometimes I would catch us both looking at them.

We were a team.

And later, after the main character's head exploded and other fun things brought the movie to a close, we laughed. I drank a beer and sat back, feeling free and easy. When she returned from the bathroom I was strumming my guitar.

The muted TV was still our only light. Maggie sat down at the other end of the couch and took a swig of my beer, and I started to play a song that came to mind. It was one of the first songs I'd ever written, composed fifteen years earlier. It concerned the demise of . . . me. I guess it was a casualty report from the last time I had really risked my heart. Her name had been Pamela, and most of what I knew about love I had learned from her. She had scared me pretty bad. I had been in her grip like no one before or since—addicted, committed—yet the whole year we'd been together, a feeling of sadness had plagued me. She'd never had an interest in my intellect, so all I had to hold her with was the rest of me—and it hadn't been enough.

The intro was fingerpicked. It moved sadly between D minor and G seventh, in a way that made a hypnotic little riff. I started singing the first verse:

I made my move
It was too late
Don't cry for me
When I'm gone away
At all . . .

Maggie sat up straight. "Sing that into your tape recorder," she said.

"What—now?"

She insisted, so in the next room I switched on my equipment and pulled two mics into position. Maggie sat in the corner, facing me.

"Sing it right to me," she said.

After one false start I sang the song through. Like some of
the Joni and Neil songs I had loved back then, it was not a "correctly" constructed song. It had no chorus and the title line
only happened at the end.

I think I'll go
A mile or two
And lay me down
In the lake so blue
The sun will find
My seaweed mind
And you can ride me again.

"It's called Seaweed Mind," I said.
"I like it," she said. "Let's play it back."
I didn't want to. The song had felt fresh; it had regained its
meaning for me because I was hearing it through her ears. But
I didn't want to test it yet—didn't want to push my luck.
So we got into bed.
In the dark I said, "So—what do you want out of *your* life?"
"I don't know. I wanted to act once . . ."
"You wanted to act? Did you, ever?"
"I'll tell you another time."
She put a leg across me and brushed my lips with hers. It
was immediately clear that our bodies wanted more.
This time I was lazy and she made sweet work of me.

4

Not a cabin

MAYBE MAGGIE NEVER SHOULD HAVE AGREED TO GO TO Muskoka. Maybe that's where she went wrong.

We had talked about taking some time off and going somewhere; we had both accumulated lots of paid vacation in the last couple of years. Maggie's idea of a holiday was a nice hotel near shows and galleries; her idea of nature was a motel pool on the way to a big city.

And that would have been fine with me, but one July weekend we were sitting in my kitchen and the phone rang. It was my sister Susan calling from Calvan, Ontario. I was pretty bad about keeping up with my brother and two sisters and their four children, all of whom were in Ontario. But Susan was faithful and every few months I would hear from her, and would learn about the nephew and niece whose lives I was missing out on. She never asked much about me—apparently no one in Canada could get their mind around my life in L.A. I was just a satellite, anyway; my sisters were the ones with children, so I orbited around them. She did know I was seeing a new person named Maggie; I had told her that when she called in May.

We exchanged pleasantries and then Susan said she had a surprise.

"I've rented a cottage on Bayne Island, for the last two weeks of August," she said.

My spine tingled.

My parents had made good on their threat to sell the Moore family cottage; this had happened in October '84, not long after my first date with Maggie, and was another disaster that I blamed on the Orwell curse. It was now 1988 and I had managed not to think much about losing access to my favourite place in the world; but the sick fact still sat in my heart—and now here was my little sister saying she could take us back there.

"It's right on Bayne Island?" I said.

"Right on the big bay," she said.

"And it's a rental?"

"Some friends in Calvan own it. It's a gorgeous place; you'll remember it when you see it. Over beyond Heron Point. Big wraparound porch."

"I think I do!" I said.

Maggie had caught the sense of this exchange and was waving her hands in a manner between caution and protest.

Susan said, "You don't have to decide now, but I'll need to know soon."

I said, "That's okay, I know what the answer is going to be. We're in."

I got off the phone and then faced a tribunal of one.

I drew the shrewd conclusion that Maggie was angrier about my making a commitment without consulting her, than about the actual plan. This may have been incorrect.

"I want us to have time alone together, away from work, away from everything," she said.

"We'll have lots of time alone. This is just too huge to refuse." I tried to explain to her what the ramifications were, how I had felt cut off from my family ever since I had come to L.A., how I had only been back for one Christmas—my nephew George was eight then, now he was thirteen. And Muskoka, I

hadn't been there for more than a decade. The spot I loved the
best.

"I feel grounded there," I said. "It puts everything else in
perspective."

"It's just a cabin, isn't it? On a lake."

"Oh no," I laughed. "It isn't just a cabin, not a cabin at all.
It's a *cottage*."

5

The tin boat

WE WERE ON THE ROAD TO MUSKOKA.

After the long Monday flight to Toronto we had ridden the airport shuttle to Calvan, my hometown an hour away, now grown to a city of one hundred thousand souls. We stayed in a motel south of the city. There the noisy pipes wouldn't let us sleep, so we took Polaroids of ourselves in various stages of undress and finally lapsed into a coma. The next morning we picked up my sister's Toyota, which had been cleverly left for us at my parents' house, and hit the highway after a short visit with them.

Maggie gave me her take on my parents. She thought Irene, my mother, had been a bit bitchy at first, as if she didn't need any more Girlfriends of Dave added to her list.

"Then she seemed sceptical of the game plan," Maggie said, "which was basically driving a car up to a lake."

"Yeah, how do you question that?"

"Your dad, though, he was a sweetheart. You had made him sound so stern and scary."

"He wasn't?"

"Naw, he struck me as an old-school gentleman, sort of fading, you can see it in this Polaroid."

As we drove north through a great deal of farmland, I

tried to clue Maggie in on the unique phenomenon of the
Canadian cottage. It's like a dual lifestyle, I told her. A split
personality. Most of the year we Ontarians are stuck in cities
and towns in the southern part of the province, like Toronto
and Calvan and dozens of others. We develop thick coats and
we plod through the creaky snow. But in the summertime we
change. Our fur drops off and we start to extrude fins and
just in time we get into cars and migrate north, to the lakes
and rivers of the Canadian Shield. There we live an amphibian
life, divided between the water and the cottage. Of course,
there's more to it than that. There is a meaning to it, a
mystical significance that can't be conveyed unless you've
experienced it.

We passed Barrie and started seeing less farmland and
more trees.

"Does the sun ever come out in Ontario?" Maggie asked.

I had to admit that the view from the 400 wasn't exactly awe-
inspiring, especially on a drizzly day. But then, freeways seem
to create a margin of boredom in any land they pass through.

We crossed the Severn River and the land became notice-
ably more rugged. We had been on the road for three hours.
We were getting close.

"Up ahead, that looks almost urban," Maggie said, with longing in her voice. "Is that a town?"

"Yes it is. It's Bracebridge," I said.

But I made a left, away from the object of her desire. Now
we were on a two-lane road, hugging the curves of a river that
ran green and grey in the afternoon.

"This is the Muskoka River," I said grandly. "It leads to
Lake Muskoka."

"Those look like suburban houses," Maggie said. "Are they
cottages?"

"No, that's just the edge of Bracebridge. It spills along the river."

I was in a state of elation—in fact I was a little shaky. The woman of my dreams was beside me on the car seat and I was about to reconnect with a beloved sister and a mystic place.

You know that feeling you sometimes get, that you have gone astray but there's still time to get back on course if you could just see what that course once was? As we drove towards the lake I had that sense, that a window was about to open on a life I could still lead. I had just turned forty-one, but maybe it wasn't too late for me. I knew there was a lot wrong with my existence in L.A., but if there was ever a place to reset your compass, this was it.

"Brief me about your sister's family," Maggie said. "What are they called again?"

"The Stones. Like the rock group."

"Are they anything like them?"

I laughed. "They are the opposite. Very respectable."

"Boring?"

"No! Susan is big hearted, likes to surprise people, good mother. Ed . . . tries hard. Nice man."

"How do you know she's a good mother?"

"She was very good with her dolls when she was a kid."

"How old is she?"

"I guess she's . . . thirty-six. And he's in his late thirties."

"So I'm the youngest and you're the oldest. Isn't he a minister?"

"Yes . . ."

"Doesn't that bother you? You don't believe in that stuff."

"It works for him."

I made a left next to a sheer rock face with pines clinging to it. We'd been seeing this kind of thing for the last hour—as if the bones of the land were protruding. We passed a small farm, the kind of discouraging place that was given to Irish settlers in the last century, before they realized that the soil was too thin and the landscape had other virtues.

We came out of thick woods and a small lake appeared on our right.

"Is that it?" Maggie said. Now *she* sounded nervous.

"No, that's Portal Lake. It connects to Lake Muskoka."

I gunned the Toyota up the last hill and we passed through the gravel parking area, filled with cars. Beside it was a field of wildflowers, sloping to a maple grove. My whole life I had never looked at that field without thinking: *picnic spot.*

"Nice meadow," Maggie said.

And then we reached the crest of the hill and it lay below us. The grey, choppy lake of my lost youth, looking like some dramatic canvas by Goya.

I had to attend to my driving on the steep slope down to the marina. At the bottom a big pier rose like a rampart out of the water, boats clustered at its base. Beyond was a maze of smaller docks.

Thinking I would impress Maggie, I pulled the car right onto the pier.

I turned to her and she produced a doubtful smile.

"It looks better than this usually," I said. "It's overcast right now."

"It's interesting," she said. "I like that you can hardly see the other side of the lake."

"Right on."

"So what do we do now?"

"I think we have to get out of the car." Surprising even myself I reached over and caught her in a hug, tears in my eyes. She looked at me as one would look at a puzzling new crossword.

I leapt out of the car and stood upon the strand.

"I think it's going to rain," I said.

Maggie got out and examined the lake suspiciously. I think she was gathering that the innocent-looking whitecaps in the

distance were actually the same large waves that were crashing
against the dock. Then fortunately she was distracted.

"Dave," she said. "I just saw a heron take off from that
flagpole."

I was taking stuff out of the trunk. "No kidding," I said.

We got all the luggage and groceries onto the ground, then
dragged them down to a smaller dock at water level.

I stood there holding a bag of tomatoes. Everything was so
familiar: the muddy water by the dock, the smell of gasoline
and fish, the look of the west wind coming straight across the
channel. I couldn't quite believe this place had held firm for
years while I had neglected it. The shapes of land and lake were
still the same.

Drops fell on us and I ran to the phone booth to call Susan.

Back in the car we sat listening to the rain. "I think maybe
we unloaded too soon," Maggie said.

I put the wipers on and noticed that the island, which Maggie
had taken to be the other side of the lake, was no longer visible.

I stared out at the water, and after a while I saw a speck of grey.

"There he is." I pointed. "There."

"You have to be kidding. That's a boat?"

In a couple of minutes we could make out the motorboat
shape, one figure in the back. I had never gotten to know Ed
that well, but as I saw him coming, my heart went out to him.
My family knew how to cross a choppy lake in the rain in a little
outboard, and he was one of us.

I waved him in and tied the bow, as Maggie held the stern
rope. Ed threw his cowl off and we saw the bald head and the
crinkled smile. His deep-set eyes held great warmth: they were
like lanterns darkened by their own smoke. He looked over
forty, which I liked to think wasn't true of me. But there was
plenty of juice in his handshake.

"Dave," he said. "How are you? Sorry about this weather."

"No problem."

"It's been like this since Saturday. A lot of wind and rain. You must be Maggie. I'm Ed Stone."

"Hi Ed."

He handed us slickers, yellow like his.

"I've heard . . . actually I haven't heard very much about you, Maggie," Ed said. "I'm thinking you're new."

She raised an eyebrow.

"That came out wrong," he said.

"Actually, she isn't," I said. "I fell for her four years ago. It just took her a while to get around to me."

"Good things are worth waiting for," Ed said, beaming at Maggie.

"I am new *here*," she told him, "and I would like to give you this rope."

It was a hairy ride.

We were in a sixteen-foot tin boat with a small outboard motor—it had been my father's auxiliary boat—and we were on rough seas. Maggie sat in the back with Ed, and I perched in the bow, facing them like a figurehead in denial.

A curtain of heavy rain swept across our path, and the waves hit me from behind. The water was cold. A big crest doused me and I yelped.

"I'm glad he's up front," Ed said. His tenor voice eased through the storm on its own wavelength. "You got here yesterday— from L.A.?" he asked, acting as if this was a perfectly natural place to converse.

"Right, Monday," Maggie shouted.

There was a flash of lightning that briefly showed us the whole lake, tilted at a crazy angle. Maggie yelled my name and then a crack of thunder shook the boat.

"We're below sea level," she shouted, clutching Ed's arm.

He put his hand on her knee. "It's okay, we're doing fine. That was miles away."

We smacked and chopped our way across the channel, then

finally passed a small island and entered a big bay. The waves were now just wrinkles on the water. I looked off to starboard and the shore was in mist. "Over there—our old cottage," I said.

"You can't see it," I added helpfully.

Ed steered left into a cove. I turned my head and I saw our destination straight ahead, glowing like a stage set.

6

A quick nap

As Ed slowed the engine for our final approach, I was hit by a stab of cottage envy. This was a fancy place, and some other family still owned it. Up from the shore about forty feet, it was classic Muskoka: mansion-like, two-storey, with a big veranda and ornate eaves. I had seen it before from a boat, but I'd never had to experience it. Maybe this was good news in one way: a place like this might suit Maggie better than our plain old cottage would have.

We pulled alongside the dock and I could see relatives mustering on the porch.

The first to reach us was a young teenager with dark blond hair.

"George," I said. "You're not eight."

"Hi," he said. There was still some boy there, but it was overlaid with the awkward solemnity of early adolescence.

"This is Maggie—George," Ed said.

Maggie stood up in the boat. The dock was tantalizingly close. "Hi George," she said. "I hope to join you soon."

A smile lighted on the kid's face and then flew away. He reached for her hand and she stepped onto the dock.

In the light rain we carried groceries up the slippery rock

steps. George led the way, followed by Maggie. On the porch were two more people with some of my DNA in them.

My sister Susan, greeting Maggie now, was changed too. Her auburn hair, once luxuriant, was in that practical short style that moms seem to default to. Her smile was pretty as ever, but it had more flint in it. She looked haggard.

"We're the dry ones," she said to Maggie. "We guard the fort. This is Alicia."

The little sweetheart standing beside her looked about eight, and had her mother's blue eyes and long curly hair, but its blonde color that must have come from Ed's side of the gene pool. She was decked out for the occasion in a dress and plastic Cinderella jewellery.

Then Susan looked at me and her smile turned back the clock. It sparkled with sly knowledge, as if this whole thing was a prank she was perpetrating. I hoped it would succeed.

Alicia led us inside and we got a sense of the place: a great room with old chairs and a fireplace, a big farmhousy kitchen, stairs going up in the corner. George put another cedar log on the fire. Susan and Ed watched us, beaming.

Maggie looked agreeably surprised.

Maybe it was the cedar smell, I don't know. But suddenly I hit the wall. All I wanted was to lie down for a while and get my bearings. I was groggy and blank. I didn't feel equal to any of this—wasn't ready for these parents and their unfamiliar children.

Then the bell tolled, and it tolled for us.

"Ed will show you where the guest cabin is," Susan said. "Dinner is at seven."

Carrying our luggage, we followed Ed down a soaked path. It was almost dark and we had to steer by his yellow raincoat.

"I thought you said no cabins, only cottages," Maggie whispered to me.

But it *was* a cabin, with two rooms, unfinished wood

everywhere, and spider webs in the rafters. The first room had bare lightbulbs and a lot of wire hangers. We let our suitcases drop.

The second room was better: it had actual beds in it—narrow metal beds, admittedly, but a nice old dresser between them and windows looking out on the lake. And a chamber pot on the floor.

"Is that . . . ?" Maggie said.

"There is a bathroom," Ed said. "And a bathtub. They're in the main cottage—fully available to you, of course."

"Of course." Maggie sank onto one of the beds. It creaked.

"I'll leave you here to get settled," Ed said. He hurried out. I sat on the other bed. It creaked too.

"I am bushed," I said.

"Why did you agree to the cabin?" Maggie said. "We should have fought it, right away. Now it'll be harder to win."

I laughed. "We're not gonna kick them out of the main cottage," I said. "This is nice."

"Dave, I don't do chamber pots. This is madness!"

"It's kind of secluded, don't you think?"

"We're in the fucking woods. There are spiders."

"I'll tell you what," I said, "you lay out your stuff in the other room. I am feeling really ropey. If I can get a quick nap, I will rise up and fight for you against spiders and humans."

"*Ropey*? Is that a Canadian word?" She shook her head but she retreated into the other room and unbuckled a suitcase.

Okay, I'll admit that maybe I should have explained to her what this napping business was all about. I should have sat her down and told her about my boss Cynthia's evil memo and my response, about my lifelong search for refuge and my longing for allies. I could even have unfurled my hypothesis that it was dreaming, not sleeping, that did the trick for catnappers like me. But it's not easy at the best of times to convey a disability to those who don't suffer from it; and the moment when sleep offers itself is no time to talk theory. You have to grab that chance.

I lay on the bed and adjusted a pillow. I turned on my side towards the wall and got in the fetal posture that always worked, a sort of contained tension. I was all weak and racing now, but if I could just go under for a couple of minutes, my heart and lungs would reset themselves and it would be a new ballgame. The glare would fade and I would be able to process all this new data, would be able to bond with the people I was supposed to love.

I jerked a couple of times and then felt myself sinking into an image of moving highway.

But something crashed. I turned over and Maggie was there, holding a drawer from the dresser.

"Maggie . . ."

"It fell out. I'm unpacking. My birth control pills go in this drawer."

"Shit. I was nearly under."

"Sorry. Go back to sleep. I'm done."

"But I can't now. You made sure of that."

Slowly I sat up, rubbing my forehead.

"You just couldn't be quiet, could you," I said. "For five minutes."

I had wanted this evening to live up to its billing. I had wanted to be fabulous Uncle Dave. I had wanted Maggie to see us at our best. And all that would have been absolutely possible, if I just could have conked out for a bit.

On top of that, Maggie's clothing was on hangers all over the other room. There seemed to be no room for mine.

I was pissed.

"Shouldn't we be going to dinner?" she said. "It's almost seven."

I didn't answer. The silence buzzed like an asylum.

There was a knock on the door and my nephew looked in. "My mom said I should tell you it's time to eat."

I uncoiled off the bed. "I think I was asleep, George," I said with a cheesy laugh. "I'm at your service."

I walked out of the cabin. George waited a moment outside the door, then followed me.

We didn't see Maggie for a while. We all got seated at a table on the covered porch. The trees were dripping but the wind and rain were gone. I was still feeling edgy and incomplete, cheated of the moment that could have been, but Ed brought me a beer and it tasted like the cure. I faked the jovial uncle.

Then a dark-haired apparition loomed on the front stairs.

"Maggie, we thought we'd lost you," Susan said. She held a chair out and Maggie approached and sat down. She seemed taut as a guy wire, and I felt as if satanic Latin might be the next thing out of her mouth.

For the first time since she and I had gotten together, I had that awful feeling that I don't know this person, she is not of my flesh; the whole thing has been a clever illusion. What were we doing together?

"Hello, Dave," she said. Her voice was deeper than usual.

I ignored her and said to Ed, "This ain't no runny American beer. This is crisp." I looked at the label. "Creemore. New to me. Sure does the trick though."

I could feel Maggie's eyes on me.

"Tough trip?" Ed asked me. "From L.A.?"

"No, the trip was okay. I'm just jet-lagged." I gave them all a pained smile. "All I needed was a quick lie-down in the cabin, but this woman wouldn't let me have it." At last I gave her a smile that said I was ready to be magnanimous.

"You fucking prick," Maggie said.

7

The Maggie File

THERE WAS SILENCE. EVERYONE EXAMINED HIS OR HER DRINK.

I was mortified. I was shamed. You don't say "fucking prick" in front of young children. Maybe they do that down in the US of A, but not up here in Canada, not at my sister's table. These were *middle-class people*.

I had brought this woman here and she had done this. What was even more unpleasant was the implication that I was dislikeable enough to provoke such an outburst.

I said, "Actually, I may have napped a bit."

That didn't seem to prime the pump of banter.

My sister said, "Maggie, would you like a drink? Maybe a Diet Coke?"

"Sure, thanks," Maggie said.

Ed said, "It's been a stormy day. We should all be thankful to be on this dry porch with good food in the offing."

Susan said, "Ed, you can help with the plates."

Somehow the proceedings got going again, but I wasn't able to focus. Susan served a noted family meal that I knew she had chosen for me: pork chops with tomato sauce, garnished with lemon slices. Corn niblets and baked potatoes. That didn't help either. I needed to regain control.

I went upstairs to the bathroom. Leaning on the sink, my first thought was to cut the vacation short, go home tomorrow. Call it off, show Maggie that nobody treats me that way, nobody makes me look bad in front of my family. But that would be weak. I would be wrecking my own agenda. There was still a mystery to be solved here, a Muskoka revelation awaiting. I was here to recapture the key to my life, not to sacrifice it to an uncouth hoodlum.

Then I recalled the adage that revenge is a dish better served cold. I thought, this goes in her file. The Maggie File. I will be my own Muskoka Bureau of Investigation; I will build a case in the calm and systematic manner I am known for. I know how to do pretrial discovery. When we are back in L.A. the trial will take place. Until then, let her behave as she chooses. What she won't know is that her dossier is growing.

I will be her implacable chronicler.

When I got back to the table I grinned at Maggie, just to see what she would do. She was saying something to Ed about her interest in theatre. She caught my look but did not respond.

"I did quite a bit of acting in college," she told Ed, quite able to smile at him. "I was in *Guys and Dolls* and *Dial M for Murder*—actually, I was the lead! My parents have film footage of it."

"You don't want to hide a talent like that," Ed said. "You should definitely pursue it."

"I think you're right, Ed," Maggie said. "Damn the torpedoes!"

"Yes, you should," I said.

"And Dave, what about you?" Ed said. "How's the music business these days?"

He had a right to ask that. After all, it was on the record that I had "gone to L.A. to be a songwriter." But jeez, it wasn't so simple! Ed had a well-defined job: he was a minister; all his moves were laid out for him. But he didn't know the first thing about my situation. It wasn't as if you sat around and wrote songs and if they were any good, bang! the world paid you and you became famous. It wasn't as if I owned a dealership or something, and could report on how midsize songs were doing this month.

So I just said, "I'll let you know if I ever get into it."

Later on, the kids were in bed and Maggie made her excuses and headed for the cabin. I found myself alone with Susan and Ed, which was just what I needed to get back on track.

"So, how has it been, being up here again?" I asked them. They seemed to move apart on the couch.

"Cold," Susan said. Her smile was rueful and she looked as though tiredness was her new escort.

"Wet," Ed said. "It's hardly stopped raining since we got here on Friday—except at night, which must carry some message. We've had lots of games and books, that's been fun." His sad lantern eyes belied that word.

"What about being here—on the island?"

"It's strange. I keep feeling like we've stopped in the wrong place," Ed said. "You can see the old cottage from the dock. Sometimes I've actually caught myself thinking, the weather would be better if we were over there."

"I guess I goofed up big time, putting this little plan together," Susan said.

"No, no! You didn't," Ed said. "This has been fine, and it's going to be more than fine when the weather turns around. Which it inevitably will."

"Well, I'm glad to be here," I said.

Ed brought more beers and some old Canadian cheddar, and in front of the spitting fire I got them to talk about their kids.

"George is a fighter," Ed said. "In hockey and in real life. He isn't the biggest or strongest boy, and he doesn't have the most athletic talent. But let him loose on the ice and you'd better watch out. He's the enforcer on his team! I don't know where he gets it. He won't back down. If he's overmatched, he just takes the blows."

Now they were both leaning forward and their faces were ardent.

"He sticks up for Alicia too," Susan said. "They'll fight at home but no one can even muss her hair in the schoolyard."

"Are they cool with being up here?" I said.

Ed looked at Susan, found no answer. "I think they are," he said. "Certainly Alicia can roll with it."

"She has fun anywhere," Susan said.

"With George, I'm not so sure," Ed said. "He's reaching that age . . . sometimes I have no idea *where* he really wants to be."

After I said goodnight, I found my way down to the shore. The water was having a quiet chat with the dock. The night was still cloudy. I could make out Heron Point at ten o'clock, but not much else except the grey lake that moved like snow on a TV screen. Our old cottage should be straight across the bay, but I couldn't see it.

I stole into the cabin, hoping she'd be asleep. She was.

Hours later there was a glass-shattering scream and I heard mad flailing in the night.

I opened my eyes and I could see her sitting up.

"I don't mean anything by this but I would like to get into your bed," she said. "There's something crawling in mine."

"Go ahead," I said.

She climbed in and we were on our sides facing each other in a very small space. I had to put my hand somewhere so I rested it on her hip. The arc of her panties was under my hand; she didn't seem to have anything else on.

"I'm sorry," she whispered. "I was hot so I took my night-gown off."

"That's okay," I said.

I closed my eyes. But I could smell the lotion she used on

her skin. I tried not to be aware of the curve of her hip. I tried not to be aware of her chest, which was trespassing into the space between us. It was an uphill battle. Pretty soon I was rock-hard.

She put her hand on me. I groaned and she said, "Are you going to apologize?"

"No, I'm not."

"Then you better roll over."

I turned towards the wall, all dressed up with no place to go. *Remember the Maggie File*, I thought.

8

A dock with a view

WHEN I OPENED MY EYES I FOUND THAT MAGGIE WAS
sitting on her bed peering at me.

"Hi, fucking prick," she said.

She looked good in shorts. She also looked frighteningly
alert.

"I didn't wake you up," she said. "I sat here and waited, I
was silent as the dead."

"Thanks," I said sleepily. "You didn't have to be." The
room was bright. Was that sunlight on Maggie's face? No, it was
just daylight.

"David, I have a question. Are we going to have to do everything with them? I go there this morning. They're all eating,
and they want me to join them. It's like they're just waiting to
pounce. I have to explain that I'm going to the bathroom. I was
surprised Ed didn't follow me upstairs. I like them, they're very
nice people. But are we even going to be able to have breakfast
alone?"

"You and I? So we're friends again?"

"Look, we got off to a bad start, but we're here. I think we
should make a new try."

It sounded like she had done a lot of thinking. And her

words were hard to dispute. "Maybe if we give in to them," I said, "they'll get used to us, and then they'll start to leave us alone."

"But what if I don't want to give in to them? What if I believe what you told me in L.A.? I want to have breakfast with you. I want to go for a swim with you."

"We can do that." I rolled onto my back, confused by this whole development.

She said, "So we don't have to have meals when they're having meals."

"No—it's a free country, we can eat when we want to eat."

There was a knock on the door. Maggie's face said *this is what I mean.*

Alicia's voice said hello.

"Come in," I called.

Alicia was wearing a fire-engine-red bathing suit. She crossed the room and took a position by my feet, which were protruding from the covers.

"I'm still in bed," I said.

"I know," she said.

She moved up close and gazed calmly at me. Suddenly every part of my face seemed peculiar. Was it my hair? My nostrils? The wonder of me seemed to have dislodged her mission.

"Have you been sent here to tell us something?" I said.

"Yes."

"Maybe that you're going swimming."

"No," she said. "Mom said to ask you if you want to go with us."

"Swimming."

"Yeah."

"So it's not raining," I said, stalling for time.

The little girl just waited.

"What do you think, Maggie?" I said, sure that she must have been charmed out of her isolationism.

"I thought we were going to have breakfast."

She seemed so legalistic. I couldn't submit. "I think I could

do with a little dip before breakfast," I said. "Why don't you go
ahead, Alicia, I'll catch up with you."

"This is what I mean," Maggie said as I ripped the sales tag
off my swim trunks. "I've waited half the morning to have
breakfast with you."

"I'll be with you before you can pour your juice."

I carried the chamber pot along the wet path.

"You mean you used that thing?" Maggie said.

As we came to the porch, we could see the Stones down on
the dock. I took the chamber pot upstairs to the bathroom.
Coming down I detoured through the kitchen: Maggie was gazing into the fridge.

"Be right back," I said.

I descended the steps and the grey lake and sky were laid out
before me, and the family getting ready to swim. Susan was sitting on the dock looking skinny in a maroon one-piece, examining her toenails through her shades. Ed was crouched on the
shore, organizing the kids. I walked out to the end of the dock.
There were heavy clouds overhead, but the air was clear.

This view must be familiar to someone, I thought. It just
looks strange to me. Like a piece of virtual reality.

There should be a view of open lake on the right. But there
isn't, not from this dock. This cottage is too far into the bay.

What you're really looking at is other cottages on the
island. And one of them, one of them, you don't want to see.
It's the one where you should be standing right now, the one
that was your birthright. You don't want to see it. But you look,
and there it is.

I could just make out the dock, a fleck of white paint across
the bay. It was a sense-datum now, from a philosophy of percep-
tion course twenty years ago—a patch of colour in the distance.

But we were here; this was what Susan had found for us, I
reminded myself. And it was good. I turned to her. The sun-
glasses and visor gave her a look of blank routine.

"Have you tried the water?" I asked.

"Not since Monday. It was swimable. Not warm, though."

"We need some sun," I said. I poked my foot in. A dizzy, cold caress shot up my leg.

"This is ridiculous," I said. "It's only August 30th. It should still be warm."

"It's the 31st."

"What are you saying, that the water got cold last night?"

"No. I'm not sure it ever got warm this year."

"So how do you get in?"

"Well you don't wade in. It drops off fast. I go down the ladder. Ed walks off the dock."

"Uncle Dave!" Alicia yelled. "Hurry up and come in." She was plashing along below me, grinning up from amid her blonde curls. An inflatable ring was wrapped around her, Donald Duck's head cruising right below hers.

"I'm coming in. Believe it," I said.

I went down the ladder with my T-shirt on, reached knee depth and found that nasty cold that makes your bones ache. I glanced up the hill and I could see Maggie, sitting on the porch, her shades reflecting the sky. My original barrel of monkeys, stranded. I had to get this done.

I went down two rungs. The water clutched my balls. "Man," I breathed. I pushed down to shoulder level. The T-shirt was saving me. I've *always* been a wuss about the water, I told myself. This isn't because I'm forty-one. I took a deep breath and shoved off, gasping for air. I dove, and couldn't see anything under there, it was too deep, and when I came up I was in Muskoka, really there.

I rounded the end of the dock. Alicia was ten feet away, looking in towards Ed. I went under, took in a mouthful of water, surfaced behind her and let it fly. She yelped, turned, screamed with delight. I went under and did it again, and she managed to dunk her head and return fire. Then I grabbed her, I couldn't help it, it was really an impulse to hug her, but I wasn't sure about that so I lifted her as far as my arms would reach and dropped her on the lake. This was fine with her and I did it one more time; then I stopped, clutched the dock, and hung there, getting my breath.

The water was still cold, and I still hadn't touched bottom.

George was on the shore with Ed. A contraption just like Alicia's girdled him. The kid was skinny: you could see his ribs below the plastic ducky. He was looking at me.

"I don't want to wear this stupid thing," he said to his father.

"You wore it on Monday," Ed said.

"It was stupid then too."

"Well you don't have to wear it. But you thought the water was too deep, remember?"

"It wasn't too deep," George said. "It was too cold."

"Now that *is* stupid," his father said, "wearing a ring because it's too cold."

"This *place* is stupid," George said.

I was thinking: at our cottage we could walk alongside the dock, it went gradually from shallow to deep. Those who couldn't swim could still wade.

"You know what I do?" I said. "I keep my T-shirt on, and that seems to help."

George and his dad looked at me like I was the referee. "Okay," George said. "I'll get my T-shirt."

I exchanged a parental look with Ed. "This isn't an easy spot," I said. "Compared to you-know-what."

Ed nodded. "You know, if we start talking about it, this whole visit will be about where we aren't, instead of where we are."

"We gotta count our blessings, right, Pastor?"

George came back with a T-shirt on. It had John Lennon's face on it. He gave Ed a sneer and started running along the dock. He launched himself off the end, knees pulled

up to his chest. He went into the drink and came up ten feet
out, Ed and I straining to see, and in a desperate sprint he was
back to the dock and holding on. I was thinking, *he really can't
swim. That took balls.*

"The T-shirt helps," George puffed to me, but the kid
looked cold already.

"You know what else you need to do," I said, feeling a little
bubble of warmth in my diaphragm from the boy's respect.
"You need to keep moving. Work up some heat."

I looked questioningly at Ed, whose assignment apparently
kept him on the shore. "He's good on his back," Ed said. "He
doesn't sink as much that way."

"Okay," I said. "Let's swim out a ways. You go on your
back, I'll go on my stomach."

We did it, there wasn't much chance for chitchat, we came
back in, George grabbed the end of the dock. Now his teeth
were chattering.

"George, I think you should get out," I said.

"I'm okay."

So be it. I executed a duck dive, pulling myself along
underwater, seeing nothing in the murky depths. How deep
was it here, anyway? I came up beside George and said, "If I'm
not back within an hour, send a search party."

I went straight down, feet first, sculling with my hands. Ten
or twelve feet down I hit what passed for bottom on this side of
the bay. It was leafy, gucky, mushy. It might eat my foot. I
yanked it out. I nearly took a breath, then remembered not to.
I sculled back up to the surface.

"I want to get out, Daddy," Alicia said. "It's too cold."

I sputtered and threw my hair back. "Man," I said. "That is
deep. I nearly got snared by the seaweed."

"Can I try it?" George said.

I looked at Ed. "He can hold his breath forever," Ed said,
lifting Alicia by the arms.

We got positioned, face-to-face, took deep breaths, and went for it. The kid went down like a rock; I could hardly keep up with him. He went deeper into the weeds than I did, and so he was able to push off from the bottom, and got up quicker too.

"That was good," I said when I resurfaced. The kid was hanging from the dock. Now he looked blue.

"George, get out of the water," Susan said.

I saw a bar of white soap on the dock, and a container of Ivory shampoo. Where to stand?

Ever the consultant, Ed told me there was a rock under-water that was high enough. I found it, balanced on it, the water was up to my chest. I rubbed the soap on myself anyway, lathered up my head, and took off into the black depths, my hair squeaking through my fingers.

I broke the surface, chilled now.

Then I remembered Maggie.

But Maggie was gone. I guess I don't eat yet, I thought. I walked to the cabin, dreading what I would find.

She was sitting on her bed, looking at a book I had bought her.

"So how was it?" she said.

"It was fine. I like George. How was your breakfast?"

"Fine." She went back to her reading.

"Maggie. Cut me a little slack."

"That's okay." She didn't look up.

"You have to understand—" I said.

Her face cut me off. "*I* have to understand," she said. "I *do* understand." And then she started to cry.

I didn't know what to say. I sat down beside her. She was sobbing now. You're supposed to let people cry. But I shifted closer, put my hand on her back.

"You don't have to feel guilty," she said. "This isn't about you." She cried some more. Her nose was running; I got her

a Kleenex. She laughed once and said, "All you did was go for
a swim."

I gave a tentative laugh of my own. "I just couldn't say no to
them."

"I understand that." She sighed. "That's what I was crying
about."

I looked at her quizzically.

"I don't feel that way about *my* family," she said. "That's why
I was crying."

"Oh." Oh. I started to get it. Why is it always so obvious
once you hear the explanation? She had told me about her
family: they didn't sound too happy. I got an image of women
stranded in the same house, worn down by emotional ambushes.
A girl maybe too clear-eyed for her own good. Wonderful
Italian aunts, just out of reach.

So it wasn't me. Or it wasn't all me. I could hardly accept
this mild verdict. I had an image of a hand zipping up the
Maggie dossier.

She gave me a teary smile. "I'm not letting you off scot-
free," she said. "I want you to go for a swim with me."

"Okay, but I haven't eaten yet."

"And I'm sure they're ready to eat."

"No, no, I'll go with you."

She opened a small suitcase. "I bought two new bathing
suits," she said, her tone instantly brightened by the mention
of shopping. "I think I'll try the white one." She disappeared
behind the wall that separated the two rooms.

I waited on her bed, feeling battle-worn. Maybe I could
somehow negotiate this impasse, stay loyal to both sides.

When she reappeared, she took me into fantasyland. So far
in our relationship there had been a slight modesty to Maggie:
she had allowed me to see her body close-up, in separate
segments, but she had never really paraded at a medium distance, not even in her underwear.

I thought I knew why. Full-figured girls like her were never sure their shape was acceptable, in a world obsessed with bonerack models. I had sometimes knuckled under to the same thing, had been coward enough to conceal my true tastes in women from my male friends.

Anyway, the result of this societal victimization was that I had never been allowed to ogle the whole woman, all at once.

I don't think Maggie realized that this bathing suit was going to change all that. But it did. It wasn't revealing; in fact it had a high neckline, up near the throat. But it was the most racily form-fitting garment I had ever seen, a single, seamless piece of white cloth. The way it sheathed her body, it made her look more naked than naked. I felt like a teenager, a dirty old man, a protective father, and maybe Pablo Picasso. For the first time I could take in the whole sculpture from feet to head. It hit me like a happy poem. The improbable miracle of her curves—the long-legged hourglass just as nature had intended it. I turned a little red. She was Loren all over again. No, she made me forget Loren. And Woolf.

All I had to do now was not make her self-conscious. But it was too late.

"You hate it!" she said.

"I don't. It's good. It's really really good."

She searched my face. "You think I look fat and you don't want to be seen with me."

She had a tiny piece of the truth. I did feel awkward about the Stones beholding her in such graphic detail. She was like wholesome porn.

"Please believe me," I said. "It's the best thing I've ever seen."

She grabbed one of my flannel shirts. "I think I'll wear this over top," she said. "Till I get in the water."

9

The rain people

I SAT ON THE DOCK WITH MY FEET TOUCHING THE water, to signal my participation in Maggie's swim. I peeled an orange and dropped the pieces in a paper bag. Susan had yelled that lunch was on. That was too bad.

My goddess seemed very much at home in the water, for someone who had never been near a lake. She churned along nicely out there, doing a good smooth crawl.

A few raindrops were starting, nothing serious, just enough to remind you that the clouds weren't going anywhere. I was content to be on the dock. It didn't seem to matter whether I went in again. I had already had my token Muskoka swim, complete with a dash of horseplay. It was really kind of odd being here.

Maybe that's what happens as you get older: increasingly you assist at other people's rituals. You go to a cottage and it's all fine, but it's just a cottage. You talk, and you eat, and you hope for a good book; and then you go back to L.A. where your job is, and you're just fine, you couldn't be any finer.

I felt the dock planks shift, and George was standing there in a Tilley hat, holding a fishing rod.

"Did you know it's raining?" he said.

"Yes I noticed that."

"I'm fishing anyway. Or else I'd never fish."

"It's been that bad?" I said.

"Pretty much."

George brought a pail and a green tackle box over, and sat beside me. "Usually I cast," he said, indicating Maggie in the water. He took the lure off his line and opened the tackle box. It was dark green metal, weathered.

"Is that my dad's?" I said.

"Yeah. I got it when they sold the cottage."

George put a hook on his line. He reached into the pail and started tipping up the rocks inside it. "Do you live in Hollywood?" he said.

"Hollywood, no. I live in Pasadena. It's up near the mountains. Maggie lives in Glendale, closer to Hollywood."

"Have you seen any Kings games?"

"Yeah, when Gretzky was in town. I used to buy a scalper's ticket and sit in the VIP seats."

"So now, you'll be all over them."

"Yeah, since the trade. Took him long enough to join me in L.A. You've got some crayfish there."

"I've got one. Alicia and I went down the shore. We turned over a million rocks."

"We used to get good crayfish over by the bridge," I said. Across the bay, near the Moore cottage, there was a creek that ran out from the island interior, with an old wooden bridge across it. The rocks under the bridge were a haven for the crawlers.

"I know. My dad used to take me over there. Only we went to see the turtles."

"Yeah?"

"Yeah. We had to sneak up on them, they were sunning on the rocks. Then we made a noise and they all dove for it."

George pulled out the crayfish. It was small, but alive. The tiny legs were wriggling. Gripping it between his thumb and forefinger, George brought the hook close, ready to pierce the tail. Suddenly his grip closed, and pieces of the creature tumbled on the dock.

"It crumbled," he said.

"You boys coming in?" Maggie said, grinning up at us from five feet out. "This water is gorgeous." Her hair was wet, her grey eyes bright. She looked like she'd been born in the lake.

"We're getting wet enough up here," I said.

The rain people climbed the steps and found Susan on the porch.

"I need a bath," Maggie said. "I'll get some clothes." She started for the cabin. I lingered by the steps.

"Wasn't she just in the water?" Susan said, with the tone of a hall monitor detecting a code violation.

"She's a woman who loves to bathe."

I picked my way along the path in my bare feet, wondering why my sister and I were resisting the idea. Why shouldn't Maggie have a bath? I should be able to find a reason.

In the cabin Maggie said, "Go ahead and eat. I'm over my fixation." She grabbed a big towel and collected some clothes while I changed into something dry.

"Baths are good," I said. "Though we usually wash in the lake."

"Baths are very good," she answered cheerily.

She headed down the path, and I followed like a caddy with no clubs. I didn't seem to be needed. Without any help from me, she had pulled her hair up in a bun, in a way that perfectly showcased the white of her neck and shoulders against the amber woods. I caught a whiff of emotional quicksand: I knew I had a certain talent for demoting myself to glum hungry voyeur. I'd been there before and I wasn't going back. The thing to do was keep speaking.

"You enjoyed your swim?" I said.

"I did. It's different—never hitting the edge of the pool."

"Right. Good point. I'm glad, and surprised."

"You thought I could not like Muskoka?"

Susan sat with me on the porch. Her smile was alarming; it seemed to require a physical effort.

"So what do you think of this place?" she said.

I chewed on my sandwich. "I can't get over it."

"It belongs to the Russells. Cindy Dunlop is the daughter—she works for Calvan Realty too. I didn't know her that well, then one day we just started talking about cottages, and she mentioned they had a place on Bayne Island."

"Unbelievable. It's old Muskoka."

"I have to ask you. What is in that sandwich?"

"Avocado, red onion, refried black beans, tomato."

"Refried black beans? Ick."

Her good humour seemed so thin. It reminded me of *Rosemary's Baby*, the scene where the girlfriends corner Mia Farrow at her party and make her admit she's sick.

"Are you okay?" I said.

"I'm sort of okay. I've had a bit of a fever. Low-grade, but it doesn't seem to go away. I thought I had it licked, and it came back."

"How long have you had it?"

"I'm not really sure. I think I was okay in June."

"In June! That's ridiculous." Now I *was* one of the girl-friends.

"It was gone for a while though. They put me on antibiotics, which seemed to work. I may be just run down."

"So it's good that you came here. This'll fix you up."

"It should. It should. It hasn't been too strenuous, with the rain. We haven't exactly been overexerting."

Alicia appeared. "Mom, I have to go to the bathroom, and Maggie's in there."

"Did she say come in?"

"No."

"Then you'll have to wait."

Susan leaned in confidentially. "The Russells left us a note, you know, instructions," she said. The authority she had taken on in her mother role was daunting. "They mentioned the septic tank. It's been overloading—they had lots of people here. We've been trying to go easy on it, but with the weather, we don't always get in the lake. Ed thought it was smelling yesterday."

I was still thinking about her medical problem and nearly missed the point.

"Oh, you mean Maggie's bath," I said. It seemed like an hour since she had gone up there.

The screen door banged. There she was, resplendent in a celery-coloured summer dress, ready for a garden party.

Susan and Alicia stared at her. "That is beautiful," Susan said.

It was nice. Why *not* a scooped neckline with thin, jaunty shoulder straps—just the ticket to keep this sailor at attention.

"Thank you," Maggie said. "And now, I am ready for a David Moore special. No beans, though. Give me provolone."

"You brought provolone?" Susan said.

"We brought everything."

After she ate, I followed her to the cabin. Not because she had asked me to—she hadn't. Not because I had anything to do out there.

"If it clears up, will you take me for a canoe ride?" she said, settling onto her bed.

"Sure."

She got her book in position. It was *To the Lighthouse*, a used hardcover that I had bought for her in Calvan. She started to read, then looked up at me. "Can I help you?"

"I don't think so." I stood there like some old hound dog that can't get off a scent. I looked at her smooth calves and thought, where exactly did this go wrong? An hour ago she had been on this same bed crying and I had been the one holding the cards. Now it was different. She seemed to have found her rhythm, and I seemed to have lost mine.

I still wanted her from last night, and I wanted her from this morning. I just plain wanted her. But it felt like her midnight refusal was still in force. I didn't know how to revive that negotiation without losing even more ground. I needed to pull myself together. This was the woman I had been ready to ditch when we got home? Now she was my drug of choice. What had I done with her dossier?

I picked up my copy of *The Selfish Gene*, and settled onto my bed. I had read it a decade ago, but this time it was really sinking in. The gene, not the animal that carries it, is the real protagonist of history. We are expendable; the genes just use us and move on. Even our emotions, I was thinking, even our emotions are just conveniences tolerated for their survival value. It was chilling. What Maggie's body was doing to me right then was just window-dressing in the Darwin store.

That didn't make it any less distracting. I tried to focus on the passage, something technical about two populations of birds. I couldn't keep it straight. So I lay back, gave in, let my eyes feast on her.

"Dave, pul-lease." Her brown curls shimmered. "Don't you want to spend some time with your family?"

The man of the house

I WOKE UP TO FIND MY SISTER STANDING THERE. SHE HAD a jolly look on her face, as if she had just received some gift—memory loss maybe.

"Come with me," she said. "I have a surprise."

I followed her to the cottage and found everyone else assembled in the living room, with a slide projector and a screen.

"We went through all the old slides in Mum and Dad's basement," Susan said. "You won't believe them."

I sat beside Maggie, who cocked an eyebrow at me.

Susan cut the lights and Ed got the show rolling. The first slide showed my dad and his dad in the driveway of the house on Vernal Street. They had long dark coats on and weren't smiling. They looked like they were in *The Godfather*.

"The two lawyers," Susan said.

Maggie squeezed my knee, as if to say, *she doesn't even know you're a mere paralegal.*

Then there was my brother in his cowboy duds, at age six or so, looking as cuddly as a puppy. It was impossible to believe that child had grown up to be a computer technician.

"He's cute!" Alicia said.

The Kodachrome pictures continued. They had an uncanny depth of hue: it seemed as if colours had been more intense back then. There was our beagle, Winston, curled up like a cat on my dad's lap. My dad, a dark-haired rake.

There were shots of people on the dock, my mother in a black bathing suit and a petalled bathing cap. There was an amazing slide of the beaver lake, a green expanse with dead trees coming out of it—my brother Greg and I had dragged the canoe in there and eaten sandwiches.

"It looks real," George said.

The next picture was obviously taken from the boat; it showed Winston at the end of the dock, his nose straight up in the air and his ears hanging down.

"He's bugling," Susan said, "because we're leaving him behind. He used to tell the whole lake."

Then a slide of the family in the boat: Joe and all four kids. "That's your aunt Lorraine, and your uncle Greg," Susan said to Alicia. "And that's me, with the short hair. I was what, nine?"

"That isn't you," Alicia said.

"It is! And that's Uncle Dave driving the boat. Isn't he handsome?"

"I like that boat," George said. It was a tawny cedar-strip with an outboard motor.

"Uncle Dave had to go out in the middle of the night and pull it up on the ramp," Susan said. "If it was a stormy night, Mum would hear it crashing and wake him up."

"God, that's true. I would go down in my pyjamas, with the wind going crazy," I said.

"Where was Joseph?" Maggie said.

"He was in Calvan," Susan said. "We were here all summer; he just came up on weekends, and for a couple of weeks of vacation. David was the man of the house."

"What's this one?" Ed said. "I don't remember choosing it."

It showed a blue teapot, sitting on the dock, with the beagle sniffing it.

"Is that the one—the one Dad was supposed to sink?" I said.

"Your grandfather sank the wrong teapot," Susan said to Alicia. "You'll love this story, George."

"I know," George said. "I've heard it twenty times."

The slides jumped through the years. We saw my older sister Lorraine and her husband Boris, their kids showing up, bigger groups on the dock. Ed made it into the show, a young Ed with some hair on top. And the last slide, George. Baby George in his grandfather's arms.

"I guess they switched to prints after that," Susan said.

11

The public beach

THE NEED TO PEE WOKE ME UP.

It was still dark in the cabin. I stepped out onto the path and went ten yards in the opposite direction from the cottage until I found a good pissing tree.

I was somewhat pickled. After the slide show, Susan had let people forage at will, which was very unlike her. I found myself alone on the porch with apple slices, cheddar, and red wine, reading a history of Muskoka steamboats. When everyone else went to bed, I moved my picnic to the living room. At three in the morning the bottle was done so I went back to the cabin.

I was about to do that now when I noticed that the tree trunks by the shore were glowing. I went down a side path and stood on a big rock. The lake looked like blood. The sky was dark, except for a layer of red-hot coals in the east, above the mainland. I could see the bottom of the sun, a ruby just disappearing into the solid grey overhang.

So this is when it comes out, I thought. And then departs.

I went a little farther down the shore and looked up at the cottage. To my surprise there were people on the porch, females who didn't know a naked man was prowling the rocks. I surveiled them from behind a tree. It was Maggie and Alicia, both in nightgowns, at the table. I could see cereal boxes and I could hear spoons clicking. This seemed like a benign if odd development; I decided to get some more sleep.

The sky was still overcast when I mounted the porch around noon. Maggie and Alicia were sitting on the swing, looking at a whale book. Next to Maggie in a deck chair was George, sipping some cola.

"What kind of whale is this?" Maggie said, glancing at me.

"A right whale."

"The tails are horizontal, not like fish."

"They don't breathe underwater," the girl said. "That's why they have to blow."

"Imagine having barnacles all over you," Maggie said. "It's like being an old boat."

"I need a drink too," Alicia said. "George, please help me with the ice cubes?"

As soon as they were gone Maggie stood up and pulled me over to the railing. "I had a chat with your sister," she said in a low voice.

"Oh, yes?"

"She is some piece of work. I tried to apologize for the other night and she said that I was rude."

"Outrageous."

"Well it is! I mean, what about your behaviour? Does she think I wasn't *provoked*? Then she deigns to forgive me, so I decided to be nice and tried to have a conversation. She talked about herself for twenty minutes. Then she asked me how you and I got together and I thought, okay, she's actually interested, but as soon as I started telling the story she checked out."

"She has a lot on her mind. Here comes Alicia."

Unable to explain my sister, I left them on the swing and wandered around the corner of the veranda. At the far end Ed was leaning over a big barbecue.

There was tarry plaque congealed in mid-drip all over the grill, and Ed was attacking it with a wire brush. I had always admired his handyman mettle; the few times I had been at the cottage with him and Susan, he had spent the whole time working while everybody else frolicked.

I sank into a wicker chair to watch him.

"How are you doing, Dave?" he said.

I groaned. "I don't even know." We both laughed.

"I'm confused," I said. "I seem to be caught between two camps."

"Two camps?"

"Well, there's Maggie, and there's you guys . . ."

"You have a spitfire there," he said. "A spirited filly." He smirked and gave my leg a little kick.

"I guess."

"How 'bout you?" I said.

His face fell. "I'm worried about Susan. I can't seem to come through for her."

"You—what do you mean?"

"She put so much into this holiday. It was supposed to be the great return, you know, all the bells would ring."

"I get you. The good old days of Muskoka."

"But I can't seem to get it right. It doesn't gel. The kids aren't really into it; Susan is no better—she's been sick."

"Jeez Ed, I don't think you can blame yourself. You've had nothing but rain, the water is too cold for the kids . . ."

"George hasn't even had his first solo boat ride that he should have had long ago. If we had kept the cottage."

Ed flipped a bunch of gunk onto a piece of newspaper, and turned his hound dog eyes on me. "What were we thinking," he said. "When they put it up for sale?"

That was a really good question. I only knew my side of the story, and it wasn't noble. "I don't know, I was just moping around L.A. I know you guys tried to talk to me about it. I was distracted. I dropped the ball."

"You're not the only one," Ed said. "Alicia was having medical problems, we didn't have a lot of funds . . . we should have talked to your brother and Doreen. Nobody seemed to be paying attention."

"Amen."

"Do you know that prices around here have more than doubled in the last four years? It's completely out of range now."

"I think I never really believed they would sell it," I said. "It was my mother driving the whole thing. Crazy."

"When Susan told me it had sold to some man in Toronto, I don't know, it was like I was hearing it on the news. It didn't register."

"So here we are," I said. "Stuck on a clammy shore, staring at it. Almost worse than not coming." I looked at Ed to see if he would share the dark humour of this, but he looked stricken.

"Susan is at the end of her rope," he said. "I've been praying about it. If this holiday fails I don't know what it's going to do to her."

I almost got the feeling he was worried about being jettisoned from Susan's sinking ship. I hadn't expected so much pain. I nearly said, what do you think is the real cause of her troubles—but just then it occurred to me that it might be him.

So I said, "I haven't been helping. I've been worrying about myself."

"You did help. The kids like you a lot."

I thought things over. "You know what we need?" I said. "We need to go to a beach with a nice sandy bottom and have an old-fashioned Muskoka swim. And I know where there is one."

Susan came around the corner bearing a plate of wieners, split open with surgical precision to expose the inner surfaces. "Now don't burn these," she told Ed.

"Honey," he said, "we may have had a divine inspiration."

"This is more like it," Maggie said. "Travel, adventure, sight-seeing."

"I knew we'd find the formula," I said.

We were drifting out from the dock, the aluminium boat straining to float this much livestock. The engine wasn't going yet because Ed was conducting a seminar with George in the rear. Alicia was on the middle seat between me and Maggie, holding Maggie's hand. The two of them seem to be major pals now.

And the whole group were in my debt, although only Ed knew it. My plan would salvage the week, stave off disaster, and save Susan's ass. Give the kids a chance to experience the kind of user-friendly swimming they used to have by their own dock: shallow water, firm bottom. Public beaches weren't big in Muskoka, because cottagers preferred their pleasures to be private. But there was a fairly decent one on the next island north of Bayne.

Selling the proposal had been Ed's job, since I was letting him take the credit. At first no one had welcomed the concept, probably because of the weather. So Ed had sweetened the pot with a promise of ice cream cones on the way home. Alicia's support had begun to swing the vote, and I had chosen that pivotal moment to weigh in for the yays.

"Now what gear do you want to be in?" came Ed's voice from behind.

"Neutral, obviously," George said.

"That's right, because you're starting it. But check it, because people leave it in reverse sometimes."

George clicked it around and reported that it was in neutral.

"Okay, go for it," Ed said.

George pulled on the cord and nothing happened.

"What do we . . ." Ed said.

"Choke it," George snapped.

Susan sat in the bow facing us all, with a look of infinite patience. I've seen worse than this, her face seemed to say. She seemed as unlikely to be shocked as she was to be delighted by anything further that could transpire. Next to her, the rest of us seemed like excitable rookies.

Finally George got the boat moving and we slogged out of the bay like some amphibious aluminium corral. The landscape slipped by us, with that curiously static look that cottages have sometimes.

I pointed up ahead, where the shoreline went on for miles. "That's all Bayne Island," I said.

"Is that why it all looks the same?" Maggie said.

"I guess," I said.

Really, it was hard to explain why this landscape should be seen as glamorous. It was better to be in a canoe, maybe at twilight; it was better to glance up from your tackle box and see a peach sky—to be taken by surprise. Wasn't that what Virginia Woolf had said in some essay? "Mr. Kipling's Notebook." The dark-eyed, petal-lipped Virginia had actually been talking about how to make a summer evening jump out in a piece of writing. But she would agree that the same point applied to real life. She knew that landscape doesn't shine when you want it to. She knew everything.

God I missed her. The one that got away, haunting me lately.

One winter night twenty years earlier, I was in my carrel deep in the stacks of the University of Toronto library. I opened her book called *The Common Reader*, and she came and pulled up a chair beside me. As I turned the old pages, a secret alliance was made. I was the awkward undergraduate from southern Ontario, and she was the beautiful genius who had committed suicide at the start of World War II. God, I was intimidated by English literature when she took me by the hand. In the world of music I had always loved and hated at will, but in this forbidding domain I thought I had to like whatever they said was "great." Virginia was witty and personal. She treated me like an equal. She even said something bad about "The Waste Land." We hooted in the carrel, her knee touching mine.

I had read her spectacular novel the previous summer, but now I dove in deep, into her diary and her letters, her essays and her other novels. Everything about her made sense to me: her sadness, her fear, her seriousness and her tomfoolery. The only thing I could never figure out was her marriage. I read her nephew's biography of her and five volumes of her husband's autobiography, but I was still perplexed. Leonard, the man who had changed her name from the charming Stephen to the forbidding Woolf. The brilliant, acerbic Jewish man who fell in with a bunch of WASP intellectuals at Cambridge, did a nasty stint in Ceylon, and then returned to court Virginia in 1911. An ugly mother to boot, but strong and faithful. He obviously worshipped her literary abilities and the two of them did amazing work together; their Hogarth Press published everybody from T.S. Eliot to Virginia Woolf. But there was something more there, something wrong with that marriage; on an emotional level, something didn't add up.

Or maybe I was just jealous.

I resolved to find out what her latest biographers had unearthed.

"See that farmhouse-looking place?" Susan said. "That's where the store was. The Guthries that we talked about."

Some kids waved from the old dock.

In the next bay we passed a lavish modern compound with a big boathouse and an airplane. "That's Hardin's place," Ed said.

"Nice," Maggie said. "Where does he land?"

"He bought the whole interior of the island," Ed said.

"He's got his own airstrip, where the farm used to be. There's
a rumour that they're blowing up the beaver dam and putting
condos in there."

"The poor beavers," Maggie said. "All that work for nothing.
A lot of mud and sticks down the drain." She and Alicia looked
sad at this thought, then they burst out laughing. Just like the day
before, Maggie was wearing one of my shirts for cover. It was spor-
tively unbuttoned, giving me tantalizing glimpses of the bathing
suit. My shirt was making more time with her than I was.

"Actually it *would* be sad if they blow up the dam," I said.
"That's a valuable wetland." Alicia and Maggie mustered
solemn expressions.

We heard a low, throaty whistle. Alicia pointed off to the
right. "That's the Segwun," she said.

"Wow, it's pretty," Maggie said.

"It's the last one," Ed told her. "The last of the Muskoka
steamships. There used to be a whole fleet of them, going back
to—when was it, George?"

"1866."

"Right, 1866. The Segwun was rescued from death in 1969. It
was rotting in the water at Gravenhurst, and all the others were
gone. Took them twelve years to rebuild it. It still burns coal, runs
on steam. They serve a fine dinner on the sunset cruise."

"Dress-up," I said.

"Really," Maggie said. "That would be fun."

"It's turning up the river," George said.

Eventually we reached the channel between Bayne Island
and the next one north, Mabel Island. For a moment we could
see straight through to the long stretch that goes all the way to
Port Carling. "If we went through there," I said, "you'd see
quite a dramatic vista."

"Nice to know," Maggie said.

But we had to push on past, and soon we were making a
slow left into a large bay. A long, narrow pier jutted out from

a strip of sand. There were four or five boats docked, and as we got closer we could make out several family groups, and a little throng of guys in their twenties.

"I thought it was a private beach," Maggie whispered to me.

"If it was, we wouldn't be able to use it."

"I mean secluded."

"Do you want me to land?" George said.

"Sure," Ed said. "You can't solo if you can't land."

What George had to do was a little like parallel parking between two boats. It wasn't easy. We were about to ram a large powerboat when Ed said "Reverse it," and we skidded sideways into the slot.

"George, you're good," Maggie said.

We climbed out onto the long dock and everyone seemed to be wondering what to do. Here in this bay, now that we were out of the breeze, it was quite hot. The young guys were in the water, looking at us. Maggie clutched her shirt around her, did up a few buttons.

"Over there?" Susan said, and pointed to a fairly unoccupied part of the beach.

We trundled down the pier, families staring at us from their stations in the water.

"Have you noticed anything?" Maggie said to me. "That kid is out past the dock and it's only up to his knees."

"Don't say that," I whispered. "Get with the program. It's what they wanted—it's shallow."

"We wanted water."

I couldn't believe she was so insensitive to team dynamics. I gave her a stern look which hoped to bear the message: *This is a moment when, for the sake of the children and Susan, everyone must pretend everything is ideal.*

We reached the beach and Ed strode industriously in, like some Olympic walker who had wandered off course. "It's great," he shouted. "Really warm!"

Susan followed for about ten steps, then stood there like a sergeant surveying a minefield.

Then I waded in too, halfway to where Ed was. I actually launched myself into the water, and immediately ricocheted up with a coating of sand on my belly. Hiding my pain, I slid more delicately onto the surface.

By now Ed was eighty feet out, looking like a human crane, the knobbly knees still not immersed, the head oddly unfeathered.

"I don't know," Maggie said. The kids halted on each side of her. They had been on the verge of going into the water.

Susan and I advanced on the beach in a pincer movement.

"Come on," I said. "It's not over your head."

"No shit," Maggie muttered.

Susan and I stood there expectantly. Maggie tentatively undid her buttons. Then she saw him: one of the twentyish dudes had quietly migrated under the pier, to our side. He was standing fifteen feet away holding a can of beer, which I suspected might raise Canadian legal issues. He was about six five, bony, and had steel wool sprouting out of his shoulders. He was watching Maggie in a smug way, as if to say, *this is my line of sight and I'll aim it where I want.*

She had apparently been ready to parade half-nude in front of four families of strangers, but this guy had tipped the balance. She was looking ahead at the acres of shallow water. She was balking.

"It's nice," Susan said.

A little ways along the beach, a toddler started to bawl. "He got sand in his diaper," we heard a mother say.

Maggie looked at me with an incensed expression, as if her own behind might be in peril too. "Sorry," she said. "I'm gonna pass."

"Come on in, Alicia," I said.

"Not. This sucks," the girl said.

"George?"

"No thanks. It's too dumb."

"You go ahead," Maggie said to Susan.

The two Stone children followed their leader onto the dock. Maggie strode past the guy with the beer, not acknowledging him. She walked out to the boat and they sat down, their legs dangling.

And now we waders were in a real quandary: do we fake it for appearance's sake or do we cut our losses? I was the first to give up, marching angrily out of the water. Susan stood looking at Ed, now a few miles out and hardly up to his thighs. At last he turned, and we watched him throw up his hands and start the long trek in.

On the way home the configuration in the boat was slightly different. I was in the front now. Susan sat stolidly on the seat next to Maggie. She had reclaimed Alicia, who was on her lap, clearly let down by the failure of the outing. And Ed was driving the boat, while George crouched in the other back corner. No one was saying anything.

The dock was ahead when Susan said, "Ed."

I came out of my funk and realized what he had done. He was about to land at our old cottage.

We slide past the end of the dock, everyone staring.

"Is that . . . ?" Maggie said.

Susan nodded grimly.

There it is, I was thinking, there it is. Still vexed by Maggie's epic insensitivity, I couldn't seem to understand what I was experiencing. What was it like to look at it, why was it so strange? The green dock, the crooked pumphouse, the trees, the brown cottage on the hill—they were too familiar, too personal. I couldn't get a handle on the feeling.

How clear the water was: I could see rocks on the bottom.

"The Elsinore isn't here," George said. "I saw it at the Marina." It had been our larger boat with the big Evinrude engine and the convertible top.

Ed made a turn and we passed by again, going the other way.

"The flag isn't flying," Alicia said.

"That means they aren't home," Susan told her quietly.

Ed had to be mortified now. He could hardly have twisted the knife any more effectively. This was the place we had never had to rent. Life just went on here, naturally. How could we be banished when we had forgotten more about it than anyone else would ever know?

"Weren't we going to get some ice cream?" Maggie said.

I slunk off to the cabin, frustrated and forlorn. The echo of Maggie's laughter came up from the shore. The more alienated I became from her, the more infuriating I found her beauty, which apparently I wasn't going to partake of anytime soon.

This only intensified my resentment of the failed swim. I couldn't lose the sense of her colossal unawareness—she didn't even see that she had single-handedly scotched the whole deal, much less appreciate what it meant. It irked me that she could just sail past these reefs while the rest of us got scraped and bruised on them. It had been the same with her language at dinner on Tuesday, an offence that flared anew in my mind.

Yet I didn't want to confront her. I was mad enough to do real damage, and then I would be the bad guy. *Just stay away from me*, I prayed.

"I'm not going to bother you," she said. "I just ran a bath, I need my clothes."

I must have drifted off. This time she hadn't even tried not to disturb me.

"That was nice of you to discourage the kids from swimming," I said.

"Don't be ridiculous. No one was swimming."

"They could have. They are shorter."

"But they didn't want to."

"It isn't that simple. We could have got them in, with your help. It was for Susan, you know. So it wouldn't seem so pathetic that we're at the wrong cottage."

She gave me a thoughtful look. "I'm going to play some cards with them after my bath, if you want to join us."

"Looks like you've made a real hit with them."

"You think? But I'm a nobody. They need some uncle time."

"No they don't."

Just let me get back to L.A., I was thinking.

"Well, they need *something*," Maggie said. "Especially that George."

"What do you mean?"

"You haven't noticed? The kid is depressed. He's just going through the motions."

Nothing like this had occurred to me.

"I don't know," I said. Did she have more insight into my own nephew than I did?

"Who wouldn't be depressed, with them for parents?" she said. "I don't think Susan even likes Ed." She was at the door with an armful of clothes.

"By the way," I replied, "you should consider bathing in the lake. You're wrecking the septic tank."

12

Pure shampoo

IT WAS FRIDAY AND TO BE FRANK, I HAD GIVEN UP ON THE week. Maggie would be leaving the next day, and in my own mind I had already broken up with her. Our whole holiday was out of whack, and maybe it was my fault, maybe hers— I didn't really know or care. I was finally in a state of equanimity.

So when she proposed bathing in the lake, I just said sure.

She gathered her equipment and we portaged to the dock. Ed and Susan had gone to town for supplies so it was quiet.

She was standing on the ladder, wearing the now standard-issue shirt over the bathing suit.

"Can you take my shirt?" she said.

"Why do you even have it on? There's nobody here."

"There are people moving on the next dock."

I shrugged.

Just then George came down the steps. Maggie said, "Your uncle is behaving badly. He's cranky today."

"I am not cranky," I said. "I'm in quite a good mood."

"He hides it well," Maggie said.

"George," I said, "I'm gonna go in the water. You take her shirt, if she gets around to it."

"Brute," Maggie called. "George, you are my Lancelot. Arthur there is too old to serve me."

George flushed. Maggie handed her shirt to him and dove sideways off the ladder.

I crouched on the shore that angled into the water. The clouds were beginning to break up. One Foot Island was bright green. Then the whole bay lit up and the far shore was blazing against the granite sky. I looked behind me, that's where the sun must be, above the Russell cottage. But I couldn't see it. I was still in the shade, and most of the dock was, because of the thick evergreens that crowded the shore. This place faces north, that's the problem, I thought. Even when it's out, the sun can't get to us.

I dove into the cold water and swam around the dock, came up the ladder and stood beside George, drying myself.

"Let the meeting come to order," I said. "The swim supervision committee." We watched Maggie move through the silver waves.

"The wind has shifted," I said. "You know what my dad used to say. A change in the wind heralds a change in the weather."

"Red sky in the morning, sailor's warning," George said.

"Did we have a red sky this morning?" I said.

"I don't know."

"You slept in too, huh."

Things got kind of quiet between us. I was fresh out of topics. I watched Maggie plough across the water with her smooth stroke.

"Maybe she could teach you," I said.

"Where did she learn to swim?"

"That is a really good question," I said. "I don't actually know. She certainly didn't learn in any lake. I guess she went to some pool in L.A. Or Columbus."

"Are you a lawyer?"

"No, George. Your grampa is, and his dad was. I'm just a paralegal. We help lawyers. I never wanted to be in law. But I answered an ad in the paper, and there I was."

"So what did you want to be?"

"Oh, that. Bob Dylan. I wanted to be Bob Dylan."

"Will someone show me where this secret rock is?" Maggie said.

George pointed into the water. The rock was too deep for him to use, but he knew where it was.

"And now George, I'm sorry but I really am going to need your uncle's help."

Maggie got balanced on the rock. The water was up to her throat. She stretched one arm out to hold the dock. "I'm on tiptoes," she told me. "I'll need you to hand me things."

This was irritating. I felt like some puny, long-limbed creature with protruding eyes. She would need me to hand her things. I was tired of her tyranny. Every situation was about her body. She got to show it or withhold it as she saw fit. I wouldn't have minded if she had been an exhibitionist, at least that would have been straightforward. But this covertness, all it did was draw the spotlight to her. Which was a power play too. Yesterday at the beach, the duel between her and the guy with the beer—it had determined everything, and I hadn't even been involved. I was just a spectator, like everyone else. And now I was supposed to be her attendant, her eunuch.

She pulled her shoulder straps down, and looked around. George went by, discreetly heading back up to the cottage. Working underwater, she got the suit off. She held it up, wrung it, extended it to me. Her smile was game. "I guess I'm committed now," she said.

I threw the wet garment onto the shore behind me. Now she couldn't get to her suit without my help. People were still coming and going on the next dock. She followed my glance. "Damn," she said.

I had to take some kind of stand. At least I could assert my authority over Cottage Behaviour. "You don't need all this paraphernalia," I said. "You really just need shampoo and soap."

Maggie gave me a beleaguered look. "So you're telling me you don't want me to shave my armpits?"

"No, I'm not saying that." That was a tough one. Maybe not the best place to pitch my anti-cosmetic tent.

"Well then, will you please hand me that jar."

And so, kneeling on the dock, I waited on her. There was a small mole on her right armpit. I waited for the razor to snag on it, but with some perverse chivalry of its own, it didn't.

She loosened her hair, which until now had been up in a bun, and handed me several elastic rings.

"Can you give me that shampoo?"

Okay, this was it. "At least use the Ivory," I said. "That's what we all do."

"Why should I do that?"

"I don't know, it's pure."

"Okay, if it's pure." She picked up the bottle and perused the small print.

"Don't bother," I said. "If you're going to make a big thing out of it."

"Sodium laurel sulphate," Maggie said. "Dimethicone. Tricetylmonium chloride." She looked at me.

I thought it over. Still to come would be conditioner, then soap, then the suit again.

"So you win," I said, and I stood up, and I walked away.

She said one plaintive word, "David." I was on the third step when I heard her sob. I looked back and there she was, crying, not to me, to herself. The picture of honest discouragement.

After all, she had been trying to do something awkward and uncomfortable, and very possibly irrational, because I wanted it. I had told her not to use the bathtub. All she had really

needed was moral support, and I had reacted with a vendetta.
What the fuck did I expect from her?

She had done everything I'd asked. She had bonded with
the kids. She had loved the lake. She had tantalized me with her
beauty—maybe a little too much, but still. Her reward, from
me, had been more adversity. Me trying to make her an out-
sider.

I went back to her. "I'm sorry," I said. "We were doing fine
here."

"I thought we were," she said. "I can't seem to do anything
right with you."

"Yes you can, you always do right." I wanted to go underwater, crouch on the rock, make sure her feet didn't slip.

I slid down the shore, face-to-face with her, and managed
to perch my ass on a ledge below the surface. "What do you
need?" I said.

"I don't need anything." She laughed through her tears. I
seemed to bring on this mixed weather condition. "Just my
shampoo."

The process got accomplished, all of it, and soon I had a
clean woman in front of me, naked in the water, wet hair glis-
tening, blue lake behind her. The line of her cheek was like
marble. I loved her so much it was giving me fits.

"I have to have a picture of you," I said. "From this angle."

I raced up to the cottage. Alicia was on the rug, playing
cards. I didn't see George. My camera was on the bookshelf,
untouched since we had arrived.

"I'm trashing me," Alicia said.

I sprinted down and it was all still in place. The sky was a
deep blue, how had it gotten that way? I perched in the water
again, and carefully lifted the camera off the dock.

She was oddly backlit, not by the sun but by the lake itself.
I should try another lens. This wasn't easy to do, my position
was precarious.

"It's a good thing I only have three lenses," I said. I screwed on the wide angle. It was interesting but it distorted her. Better go back to the thirty-five millimetre.

"David."

"Yes."

"If you keep me here much longer, you're going to have to bring me a book."

"Which one do you want?" I screwed the lens on, my movements cramped by urgency.

"Not Virginia. I wouldn't want to get it wet. Joan. It's an extra copy."

"I'm nearly there," I said. I looked through the camera, trying to keep my balance.

"What's it about, anyway?" I said. "The Joan Didion."

"Playing it as it lays. Freeways. I don't know. Abortion. Despair. Show biz."

I peered at her through the lens. "This is perfect!"

"I must look awful."

"No, you don't."

"I've been crying."

"You look beautiful."

"Well we know your taste can't be trusted."

"How do we know that?"

"By looking at your wardrobe."

"Don't smile. Give me that look. Yeah."

"Should I be holding on to the dock?"

"Yeah. I like the arm out."

"Am I too . . . exposed?"

"No, the water is all reflections. I like this perspective. It's a lake's-eye view."

"Then take it."

"I did."

13

Provolone

I LAY ON MY BED IN THE CABIN. IT WAS LIKE TWILIGHT IN there with the pines all around and light rippling off the lake. I heard her bathing suit hit the floor.

"Move over," she said.

She looked down at me.

"What am I going to do with you, Musk?"

She had a way of descending on me so that her hair formed a sort of cave around my face, that didn't let me move. Then, within that grotto, her mouth came down on mine, and her kisses told me a long and engrossing story. It resembled the one I have just told you, though it seemed to be from a different point of view.

When we got back to the cottage the sky was blue and somehow we had synced up with the family schedule. Ed and Susan were back from town. It was officially lunchtime, and everyone was hungry.

Maggie made George a sandwich with provolone and mortadella, and he seemed to like it, so I asked for one too. Then Ed wanted one.

"What is this bread?" Ed said.

"Just a crusty Italian loaf," Maggie said.

"And you found it where?"

"In Calvan. We found a real Italian deli."

"Is there any more of that?" Susan said.

As we sat munching, Ed announced with a lot of fanfare that he had gassed up the boat and that it was available for George to use. The kid was finally going to get his long-overdue first solo boat ride. He didn't seem very excited about it.

Susan brought out butter tarts, fresh from town. The bakery in Bracebridge made the best anywhere, better than home-made. I bit into one. Dark and rich, the ultimate Canadian art form.

George took one and trudged down to the dock.

"Life preserver," Ed yelled.

"We saw the Guthries at the marina," Susan said.

"Really," I said. "How do they look?"

"Exactly the same. Ralph Guthrie still looks like Paul Newman."

The afternoon had a soundtrack. Birds chirped, a wood-pecker tapped, and the maple leaf flag flapped on the pole. We heard the Johnson motor start and then it was just another Muskoka sound, droning along the lake.

"Who are the Guthries?" Maggie said.

"They're a couple of bays up," I said. "They've been on the island forever. They're real Muskoka people, not dilettantes like us."

"We aren't dilettantes," Susan said. "We're cottagers."

"We were," Ed said. He got up from his chair.

"Ed," Susan said. "Don't go and watch him. Let him land it on his own."

The afternoon was declining, steaks were marinating and I was on the porch with the kids, opening a bottle of Mondavi Cabernet that I had imported myself. No one else was drinking, but to my thinking that just put the onus on me. I settled

onto a straight chair and took a big slug of wine. Maggie came
out of the living room with my guitar and said, "Here, Uncle,
sing for your supper."

I did. I started with "It Doesn't Matter Anymore." Maggie
joined in on the bridge, where it goes minor and renounces all
crying and trying. Her clear soprano drew a surprised look
from George.

Alicia clapped at the end, and George asked if I had written the song.

Oh, to be that young and open. I said no.

"Buddy Holly wrote it," Maggie said.

"No, he sang it," I said. "But in fact it's a Canadian song.
Paul Anka wrote it."

"Was it at the same time as the Beatles?" George said.

"No, Buddy Holly died in 1959," I said. "He was B.B.
Before the Beatles."

George had announced earlier in the week that he was
"tired of Elvis." Apparently he had recently moved on to the
British Invasion, in what I thought of as his re-enactment of
the Journey of Rock. He also liked modern people like
Crowded House, but his new obsession was the Beatles.

"When did John Lennon die?" George said.

"Oh, gee." I looked at Maggie. "Early eighties. Around
Christmas time? It's hard to keep track in L.A."

"December 1980," Maggie said. "That would be A.G. After
George."

I noodled on my guitar.

"Why don't you do one of your songs?" Maggie said.

"Yeah, I could," I said. *But what if they glaze out on me. Kids are so
honest.*

Maggie was looking at one of the pillars that supported the
veranda roof. "There are carvings in this pillar, under the paint.
They're really intricate." She ran her finger over the depressions
in the surface. A hummingbird hovered beside her, dipping into

a flowerpot that hung on the pillar. We all watched it until it whirred away.

I was still wrestling with Maggie's challenge. I didn't want to cop out completely, but I didn't want to submit one of my real songs. So I started a blues groove in E, and sang the first hackneyed words that came into my head: "I was walking down the street . . ." When I got to the word "street" I sang it real high, lending it a false drama, as if a street was a very unusual place to be walking.

Alicia laughed.

I pressed on. "I used to live in Toronto," I sang, or really chanted like a cantor: "on Dundas . . ."

I looked at Alicia. She and I wailed STREEEEET as high as we could.

"And then I would get up in the morning," I sang, "and have some bacon and eggs and if I needed to go downtown I would probably stand outside and wait for a . . ."

"STREEEEEEET—," we hollered.

"—Car and when it came I would ride it all the way to Yonge . . ."

It wasn't complicated. But Alicia loved it. It was like a comedy version of the Primal Scream. The problem was, you needed to be in Olympic shape to do it, which I definitely wasn't. I had felt my temples bulge on the last "street." But the show had to go on.

". . . and I promised myself I would never again live so close to the . . ."

I went silent. The other three delivered the *coup de grâce*. They gasped. It had been a rousing success. Except that my heart had lost its anchor. It drifted off on its own, beating too thin and too fast. Why was I trying so hard, I wondered. What failing mark so terrified me?

I pulled on my wine and called on my heart to return to its berth.

"You WASPs are jolly tonight," Maggie whispered in my ear.

"Do you want to share that with the whole class?" Susan said.

"I was just saying the spuds were sinful," Maggie said.

And she was right on both counts. The potatoes, fried simply in butter with a few onions, had been mouth-wateringly good, and there was a zing to the dinner table. Maybe the two camps had finally coalesced into a new entity. Ed returned from putting coffee on and rubbed Susan's shoulders. How much hotter could this orgy get?

The kids had been excused a while ago, but they couldn't seem to forsake the magic circle. George was back with that book about steamboats; Alicia with a piece of birch bark on which she was writing a letter.

"Tell me, Dave," Ed said. "Who's going to be the next president of the United States?"

"Dukakis," I said.

"It has to be," Maggie said, "because Reagan has been a disaster and Bush is a joke."

"So, Maggie, do you really have to go back tomorrow?" Susan said.

"It must be time to go," Maggie said, "because I can honestly say I don't want to." She explained that she had promised to spend a few days with her parents in Columbus, and would go on to L.A. from there.

"But will I see you again?" I said, floating on the wine.

"I'm not sure," she said. "I have to stay open to all options."

"Such as?"

"Oh, you know. Handsome bus drivers. Rich airline passengers."

"You better be careful," I said, "or we'll put you on the bus to Moose Jaw instead of Toronto."

"Better that than a bus to the Moose," she told me. It was

her nickname for an administrator at the law firm, on whom I had once had an inexplicable crush. I choked out a laugh; the Stones tentatively joined in.

"So you like Muskoka," Susan said smoothly.

"I do. It definitely casts a spell."

Alicia said, "What would Indians use to write on birch bark?"

Gears were turning all around the table, but George was the first to engage. "You don't call them Indians. They're Native Canadians. Second, they didn't have writing. And third, there wasn't any mail then."

"I didn't say it was a letter," Alicia shot back.

"They may not have had writing as we think of it," Ed said, "but they did have symbols, for example on their pottery. And wampum."

Oh, here we go, I thought. Ed will now demonstrate his prodigious memory. His powers of recall were impressive—I had seen that before—but it always seemed to me that his logic was a little weak.

"Did the Indians believe in Greenpeace?" Alicia wanted to know now.

George laughed.

Susan said, "In a way, honey, they started it. They respected nature; they lived in harmony with it. That's what Greenpeace wants to do now."

"Not really," I said. "The Indians were pre-industrial. They didn't have to deal with pollution. Greenpeace is trying to stem a mighty tide of filth."

Ed shook his head seraphically. "The Indians weren't so perfect," he said. "They didn't have sustainable agriculture. They just had lots and lots of land. They used it up and moved on. It has even been argued that their own religion misled them into that approach."

Susan glowered; not, I thought, because she cared to agree

or disagree with what he had said, but because it was inconven-
ient. For my part I found Ed's last comment absurd, and was
waiting for a chance to pounce.

"So how do we know what they were like before we got
here?" Maggie said.

"Well, archaeology mostly," Ed said.

The last thing I could accuse myself of was a good memory
for facts, but I had recently seen a documentary about *The Jesuit
Relations*, and saw an opening. "I'm surprised to hear you say
that, Reverend," I said. "I would have thought you'd give more
credit to the Holy Fathers. Those dedicated Jesuits, who insisted on writing down everything they saw." I savoured a sip of
wine. "It was quite ironic. The very guys whose microbes were
about to kill the natives, functioned as a team of professional
reporters. They wrote it all down in incredible detail—and the
next second, the whole way of life was gone."

Ed looked confused.

Maggie said, "I'm not sure that's true. Have you asked *them*
about their way of life?"

"Who, the Jesuits?"

"No, the Indians."

"No I haven't," I said, and reaching the limit of my temporary knowledge, I changed the subject. "Let me ask you guys
something. Do you know if anyone showed up at the Moore
cottage today?"

There was a long silence after this question. I turned a little red. But then Ed piped up. "I don't think so. Apparently he
bought it mostly as an investment. He hasn't been there for
over a month. Not since early July, apparently."

Susan frowned at Ed. "How do you know that?"

"They mentioned it over at the marina." Ed picked up his
water glass and turned it appraisingly.

George looked at his father.

I looked warningly at Maggie. I had told her today that I

wanted to go there. I was afraid she might let the cat out of the bag, especially since I had just cavalierly ignored the taboo against talking about the old place.

She grinned impishly at me and then said, "How long did you guys have the cottage?" I shot her a look, but George answered. "My grampa's dad built it in 1928," he said. "Originally."

"So, what was it like, you know, growing up here?"

I said, "I think it was a release from, what would I call it . . ."

"No. I want to hear this from them," Maggie said. "How about Alicia?"

"Alicia was four when they sold it," Susan said.

"Okay," Maggie said. "Anyone else?"

"Well, I didn't discover the place until I was courting Susan," Ed said. "But I fell in love with it. Being on an island, seeing that lake every day. What else? I liked that there was no phone, and there was always more painting to do. The windows, the doors, the trim. That wind never quits."

"The windows, the doors, the trim," Alicia said.

"Susan, I need to hear from you," Maggie said. "You're one of the old guard."

"I don't know," Susan said, and her face softened. "It was really different living up here—and we were here all summer, the four kids and Mum . . . I guess what I liked was that I got to do more grown-up stuff. Mum needed my help, cooking, washing the clothes in the lake, going for groceries."

"Again with the work," Maggie said. "What about your social life? Was there any?"

"Oh, sure," Susan said. "There were kids on the island, other cottagers' kids, all around it."

"If I may speak," I said, "it used to be amazing. The Guthries had a store then, where everybody went. Our sister Lorraine worked there one summer. There was a path all around the island, behind the cottages, and kids could walk home if they wanted to, at night. Maybe they still can, but the bridge isn't

there, so no. You'd have to walk through the swamp. Anyway we
hung out, swam, water skied, and had sex. Not. Sorry."

"So, it was just like home, only a different gang?" Maggie said.

Susan and I both said no at the same time. "It wasn't, for
some reason," I said. "We were, I don't know, untouchable. I
mean we could visit people or invite them over if we wanted to.
But most of the time we didn't want to. And that was what was
great. We weren't shoved into the peer group every day."

"You forgot George," Ed said. "I know three things that
George liked."

George flinched in anticipation.

"Boats, boats, and boats," Ed said.

Maggie and I were doing the dishes, with help from Alicia.

"There's a 'Designing Women' special on tonight," Maggie
said. She took a dried plate from Alicia and set it on the shelf.

"Cool," Alicia said.

"That violates cottage protocol," I said, scrubbing a frying
pan.

"There's a TV in our cabin," Maggie said. "I found it
behind a bunch of paint."

"That's where it stays. We don't do TV in Muskoka."

"What do we do?"

"We amuse ourselves."

Ed, who was standing at the kitchen door, picked up this
wavering torch. The traditional cottage games were Password
and Pictionary, but he had a grander vision tonight. As we
assembled in the living room he said, "Let's play charades, but
instead of just one person presenting the charade, the whole
team will act it out together."

"Who does that leave to do the guessing?" I said.

"The other team does the guessing."

"Then who wins?"

"Everyone," Alicia said.

It still made no sense, but there was no stopping it. So it was time to create teams. Maggie and Alicia conscripted Ed, and that left me with my sister.

"George," Ed called. "You're on your mom's team."

George came in from the porch and stowed himself in the backmost chair. "It's windy out there," he said.

It was decided that the Outsiders, as they had christened themselves based on the fact that none of them had ever been named Moore, would go first. Maggie and Alicia dragged Ed into the kitchen and made sibilant noises.

At last they reappeared against the backdrop of the mahogany staircase that led to the second floor. They mimed a door opening. They shambled forward in a group, peering left and right. Then they all put the brakes on. Ed gave a stagey nod of the head, and then they began to shuffle sideways with their knees bent. Susan and I yelled out premature guesses, as if speed would make up for lack of insight.

"Ducks crossing a beaver dam!"

"You're architects inspecting a half-built house!"

"It's a mine field," I offered. "Or a family in a restaurant."

Alicia gave me a wrong-but-you're-close reaction.

"Or it's just lame," George said.

As the three actors struggled sideways, Alicia livened things up by pretending to step on something and then to apologize. They seemed to be lowering themselves into imaginary chairs, and soon a mixed bag of emotions—led by dazzlement and horror—crossed their faces.

Maggie had now broken the third wall and was watching me quizzically. Alicia remembered to mime the eating of something from a source on her lap. Ed followed suit.

"Okay, you can stop now," George said. "You're in a movie theatre."

The performers cheered and subsided onto chairs. "That was an amazing concept!" I said. "You really put it across."

"So, the Outsiders win the Oscar," Ed said.

Maggie and Alicia, in a Pavlovian response to their own make believe, decided to prepare some real popcorn.

I looked at Susan. Her thin smile seemed to say, I told you so. Her conspiracy had scored a point: some cottage silliness had happened.

And then she cocked her head, and her brow furrowed. "Somebody check the boat," she said.

I followed George out the door. There was no peace in the night. The tree branches, even the stars, were agitated. I was halfway down the steps, looking up at the sky, when I heard him yell "Dave." I ran down to the dock and saw what had happened. The tin boat had worked itself out of its slip. In grabbing its rope from the water, George had stretched out too far, and now he was about to go in the lake.

I dove onto his legs and hauled him back to safety. We pulled the boat out of the water.

"Good move," I said. "It almost got away."

He laughed. "So did I."

We stood there a moment, catching our breath. Nothing had calmed down. The night was still in a tizzy.

I was ready to go up. I could see the yellow windows squared off against the darkness, lending a glow to the evergreen canopy. I could hear the women's voices. It was a weird feeling—that sense of a cottage that you get when you're down by the lake at night. Like you're remote from it, and already back inside, at the same time.

"Does it ever bother you—that it's there?" George said.

"What?"

He was looking across the water.

"I know it's there, but I can't see it," he said.

"Yeah."

We stared into the distance. The opposite shore of the bay would have been undetectable if it were not blacker than the sky.

A telltale lack of stars.

The wind outside the cabin almost covered up the trickling sound I was making in the chamber pot.

"Is that you?" Maggie whispered.

"Sorry. I was trying to be quiet."

I could just make out her form, rising in the next room. "Now you've made me want to go," she said.

"Well come on over."

"I am not commingling my pee with yours." She climbed out of bed. She walked over and clutched me as I stood up. Her skin was warm.

"Wait, don't let go," I said. I squeezed her close to me. My cock had swung up to attention. She tried to kiss me but I wouldn't let her.

"Your breath is fine," she said.

"No it isn't."

"Then you're coming to the cottage with me, and we're taking care of this right now."

"Taking care of what?"

"Me, and you."

"Okay, but we're coming as we are."

I steered her from behind as we moved through the woods. Our bare feet found roots, moist spots, depressions. The wind blew on our bodies.

There were no lights on in the main cottage. It was like approaching a haunted house.

With one loud creak of the screen door, we got inside.

I brushed my teeth and then left her in the bathroom.

When she came down the stairs I was waiting at the bottom. I stopped her on the last step, so she was taller. Like a sexual force field, I dared her to lean into me. She did and we got caught in a wild, resilient kiss that tasted of mint.

I backed over to the rug and laid myself on it. She stood

above me, her body angry with shape. She was a mockery of anything incomplete I had ever found in the world.

Her thick hair pressed my skin as she descended. I wanted her to ride me, but she made me wait, turned me ferocious like she was. Then we had to have it and we grasped each other and fit her to me, all our heat concentrated there, ready to rock on the arc of my spine.

She seemed in the grip of some disease and I caught it too; I couldn't be satisfied, I just wanted to load up with more of her. This is probably what teenage sex would have been like, I thought. If I had had any.

"Don't," she said later, blanketing my mouth with her hand. "You can laugh when we get outside."

14

Old cedar

AND THAT SHOULD HAVE BEEN IT. WE HAD REACHED A place of grace; there was no need to take a further risk. So when I awoke before dawn and knew I was going to the old cottage, I tried to steal out of the cabin.

But Maggie detected my plan. "It's my last day here," she said. "You can't not take me with you."

My gut said no, but my brain said: we're just finding our feet again, I have to say yes.

The dock was clammy with dew. We slid the fibreglass canoe onto the lake. The bay was pale yellow. There was no one else on the lake, not a bird or a boat.

As we got near the Moore cottage, its windows shone like fragments of sky. We looked carefully for signs of occupancy, but there was no boat and no flag flying.

I tied the canoe on the lee side of the dock where the Elsinore used to sit. We stood and looked at the lake. A yellow sun started to show over the horizon.

"Are you sure it's okay to be here?" Maggie said.

"We're fine for a while. It's early."

She sat and dangled her legs over the edge, looking through the clear water at the unslimy bottom, flat rock with a little sand on it.

I went to the other end of the dock and sat down with my knees against my chest, facing the hill.

All we needed was a clandestine swim and a quick tour, but I couldn't help looking for more.

I wanted to see the beauty, the myth, but I kept running up against defects. The pumphouse door that didn't close true, the cement vein in the second step. The pine branches that encroached on the path. I knew them so well. But even them I couldn't get a grip on, because of all that distracting motion. So much movement: so many souls up and down the steps. And I was part of it: I could see myself, coming down the hill.

It was preposterous that this place should not be in our lives any more. It would be like saying that my father's face now belonged to someone else.

Twelve years ago, wasn't it, I had come here in the fall. The permanent student had finally gotten his PhD, and then the train had gone off the rails. I wrote more songs and started failing auditions. Fell in love and got my ego broken ... drove a Toronto cab. Meanwhile I turned down a university teaching job—any more school seemed like death. Visited home and my dad would not speak to me.

I was fucked up bad and I came up here. I crashed through the sunny woods and painted in oils and got so hot and sweaty that it was easy to bathe in the cold water of late September. At night I stood on this dock under the stars and it was all right. The cottage forgave me for my sins.

So I'm thinking: if I could still come here, I would not be adrift. I am a minor league bureaucrat; I live in the filth of L.A.; I am a guy who writes songs that no radio plays. But none of that would mean so much, if I could still come here. The Calvan house we grew up in, that was sold long ago; my parents' current abode has no history. This was the last home left.

How could I have been so stupid? What was I thinking that year? For months before it finally sold, there were phone calls with my parents and my siblings, the alarm was sounding. That's when Susan said maybe she and Ed could handle half the price. But where was I? Walking the sidewalk of downtown L.A., trying to find a good tuna salad sandwich, obsessing on the unattainable Maggie. I had no dependents to drain all my money away. I, the childless, wifeless one could have saved the family jewel.

"How could I be so stupid?" I said.

I could have phoned my mother, I could have said *Irene, call it off*. She was only doing it for neurotic reasons anyway. I could have persuaded her not to sell, but I preferred to show how fricking understanding I was. *Of course, Mother, the place is too much worry for you.*

I let it go. I just let it go.

(A shadow passed over me. It was Maggie, moving my way.)

I could have raised the money. I had miles of credit, and I had the stint in San Francisco coming up that would have allowed me to pay it back. I took my eye off the ball.

"How could I be so *stupid*," I said. My voice creaked on the first syllable like a pump that is starting to flow. I sobbed, rocked on my ass on the dock. I wept.

"It's okay."

It was Maggie, crouching beside me.

"Please don't comfort me," I said.

She stood up.

"Can you let me have a moment?" I said.

I ignored her retreat along the dock. But like a pickpocket, she had the victim role in her grasp.

Well, she wasn't the one hurting. I was.

And I wasn't done.

Someone else had been playing the role of me. How long had I waited like an understudy in the wings, while the wrong actor fucked up the part? Who was that goofball, desperate to score high marks in a law firm? Who was that, staying in a desert city because of some "music industry"?

Christ, if I could only have been *this* guy, the one who got it.

Maggie cleared her throat. I pivoted on the old cedar boards and regarded her with sore eyes. She stood by the ladder, majestic in the sun.

"Are we going to swim?" she said. "It's getting late."

I shook my head, trying to hang on to the voice of this place.

"I can't talk," I said.

"Then I'm leaving."

"Why don't you? Take the canoe."

"Fine, stay here and obsess on the past." She picked up a paddle, looking frantic. "I don't know how to steer that fucking thing," she said.

"I'll take her home," a voice said. It was George, appearing from somewhere beyond the pumphouse. So he was here too. Maybe he had been watching us. The penny dropped: I hadn't seen the tin boat on the dock this morning.

"I landed at the Felder's," he said. "I'll show you the way." It was the next cottage over, not visible from across the bay.

Maggie took some of her stuff out of the canoe. "I won't be needing this," she said, and threw something at me. It slid along the dock and dropped into the water next to where I was sitting.

"Oh, sorry," she said.

I looked down into the water. It went under and then floated up on its belly. It was *To the Lighthouse*. I didn't know she had brought it this morning.

She and George disappeared along the shore path. I heard the tin boat head out.

I sat there for a while longer, but it was no use. I had no more tears and no more thoughts.

Thanks to her.

And we were supposed to tour the cottage together. Well, I would tour it alone.

I climbed the steps. Most of them were just natural stones cleverly wedged into the hill, but the big one near the bottom had needed cementing years ago. Ralph Guthrie's work was still holding strong. I remembered my father's solemn tours of the property with the local man, the respectful way they had worked out what needed to be done.

There was a flat place on the hillside nearby. My father had stood above me, shouting at me. The hole in the rubber raft that I was supposed to repair had gotten all torn and messed up when I used the scraper wrong. I was about George's age. Sitting on the hill, losing it. Looking back now, it was amazing to me how angry my dad had been. Just fuming mad. It must have been symbolic; I had failed to be like him.

What happened next? He came back after a while and tried to apologize. He couldn't quite do it, he just told me what my mother had said. "Dave is good at different things than you." Perhaps he was implying that she was correct.

I gained the top of the hill and stood ten feet away from the cottage. Now imagining that I was showing it to Maggie, I saw it as she would: a rather plain structure, really just a rectangle of walls with a shingled roof and a chimney. It wasn't huge, it wasn't charming, not even the color was particularly appealing. Just a stoical dark brown with white trim.

Maybe it was better that she hadn't gotten to judge it.

I turned to face southward.

Through the white pines, a wide expanse of lake stretched into the distance, all the way to Gravenhurst. One Foot Island guarded the bay. The hilltop where I was standing managed to be both peopled with trees and bright with sunlight. There was aspen, poplar, birch, maple and oak, as well as evergreen. The floor of pine needles was dry and firm.

Unlike the Russell cottage, this one had just a simple porch with a bench at one end and no railing. A couple of ragged deck chairs sat upon it.

It had been a cabin first. That's right Maggie, a cabin. Then in the forties they had put up this structure. After the war.

I peered through the front windows.

The old fireplace was still intact. The massive bulwark of rough sienna bricks looked like it was meant to be on its own in the woods—perhaps a free-standing home for raccoons or skunks—not set inside a pleasant habitation with varnish on the floors and glass in the windows.

Homely. But wasn't that a Dave Moore original above the mantle?

Not really a mantle, just a ledge where the chimney began. But nailed to the pitted surface, indeed, was a small water-colour in a birchbark frame from Camp Ganawa, a patented Muskoka image that I had turned out with suspicious regularity. A point of land, a gnarled pine, a far shore, and a couple of clouds. Productions like it had once been considered evidence that I was the next Tom Thomson.

It was still there. *Everything* was still there. The same orange and teak furniture in the living room, the same yellow vinyl kitchen chairs around the dining table, and when I looked closer at the bookshelf, the same old paperbacks.

The Carpetbaggers, on the middle shelf. The formative book of my teen years, the one my friends had all passed around, the one where the half-brother was tortured by his sister's sexuality. The manual of masturbatory boot camp.

I saw my grandfather's simple old oak table, where we ate meals and gathered for games. Why did we only play pig at the cottage, I wondered. It was a crazed card game where you passed cards around and forgot to watch each others' noses—which were touched when matching cards appeared. I thought of a dinner the summer after Grade 12, when Scott Chesley, my best friend, was up for the weekend. Was it my birthday? At the annual regatta he and I had won the adult men's canoe race, though he had never sat in a canoe before. Then that evening he had us all in stitches with his impressions of quirky old relatives of his that we didn't even know.

I went around to the right. I looked up at the side wall that rose to the inverted V of the roofline. I had been up there on a ladder, with paint and a brush, on a sweaty summer day. Wearing my father's huge army shorts that billowed out on the breeze. For some reason I had had no underpants on—I must have run out. I made the mistake of thinking about Liz Coppel, who wasn't even that good looking, but it didn't matter in those days. She was female. She was part of the island gang, she sort of liked me, and I was fourteen. I started imagining what might happen if I had the guts to ask for it. So Joseph came out to see how I was progressing with the paint, and I found myself with a major hard-on and my father was standing right under me, and the shorts billowed out. I tried to hold them, knocked the can of paint and grabbed for it. Now after all this time, my twitching arm was still trying to save Joseph from the splash. Another sonly triumph.

At the rear of the cottage, I looked into the first of the three bedroom windows. This had been the girls' room.

It had been here, one rainy afternoon, that my older sister Lorraine had decided it was time we tried smoking. Lorraine was braver than I, and so she had been the one who ended up vomiting on the floor. I handled the cleanup, and that may have been why I was the one who never touched cigarettes again.

The pink wooden vanity was still against one wall, with its quaint little drawers and twin cupboards flanking a tiltable mirror. There had been yearbooks on that shelf. Where were those yearbooks now?

I walked under pine boughs to the middle bedroom window. I saw two old metal beds, and between them a small table.

I was picturing myself and my brother Greg rising early, getting in the canoe before dawn, slipping through the mist on the lake. Trolling for largemouth bass. One time we were in the canoe and we figured out how you can tell that something

is an island. Because when you follow around the shore, you
end up back at the same place. But then we had a startling
insight. If you travel long enough around the *outside* of a lake,
you will also come back to the same place! So even the mainland was an island.

Why did I know Greg so well? It was because we came here.
We were six years apart. In Calvan, that was huge. That was
insurmountable. Here it meant nothing.

I lay by the wall on a summer night, with Greg asleep in the
other bed, wishing there was a storm or something so that I
wouldn't hear my parents clink their rye glasses in front of the
fire in the living room. And my father saying, "Give him time,"
and then I realized he was talking about me, and surprisingly,
was taking my side. That was after first year college. Then I
heard the hard edge of my mother's voice chipping away at me
in the darkness. She felt that I didn't have enough direction, or
something. No goals. It was the night I should have discovered
that my long-time secret ally was also my secret accuser. But
somehow the insight hadn't stayed. The room was tame now; a
bar of sunlight snoozed on the wall.

I got to the master bedroom, with its deep blue paint job
and its whole wall of graceful varnished shelves that held
canned soup, blankets, swim gear, binoculars, tools, paint
cans. Had my parents left that stuff here too?

I thought about Sapir Bonner on that double bed, after we
smoked a joint with the gang in the living room. Sapir with the
wiccan hands that could make you hard by stroking your wrist.
It was the first time I had my friends up here without my parents being around, the beginning of a new phase for the cottage. It was my M.A. year; six of us had come up from Toronto,
and the cottage was transformed by our reckless disregard of
the rules. We drank, we smoked dope, we sang, we skinny-
dipped, and best of all we didn't eat at the proper times. We
took a canoe ride at 2 A.M. and got splashed in the dark by an

alarmed beaver, thirty feet from the dock. It was the same old stage set, but a new play. The cottage had taken it all in stride.

This tour has to end, I thought. *Just one more thing.*

I stepped through a curtain of cedars onto the old path behind the cottage. The trees were stationed like old men in a club. I walked among them, came even with the outhouse by the fence. I turned, looking for the spot.

There it was, you could see the flat area between the two trees, where the bell tent had stood. It was a used army tent that my dad called Moore's Folly. It was a sort of teepee made of heavy canvas, and had flaps all around it that you could roll up to let the breeze blow through. The image of the table came to me. A flat piece of driftwood with four birch logs as legs. It sat between the beds and held our comics and our flashlight and our bottles of pop. I would turn off the light and regale Greg with dramatic farting announcements.

The leaves stirred on the ground.

I had walked out here to look for my mother. It had been so strange. I was about nineteen. She had left the dinner table, just got up and bolted, because we were all teasing her about some stupid cooking thing. Mocking her divine apple crisp, I think. Pretending the crust wasn't quite crunchy enough. Susan wasn't there—no other women were there that weekend. My dad had delivered the last smart crack that made her bolt. I sat there, waiting for him to go after her. He just kept eating.

I found her in the tent, sobbing violently, saying that she'd never been good enough for Joseph. I had never seen her that way. So despairing, so abandoned. She talked to me like an equal, told me awful, painful stuff about her fears of inadequacy, going way back. I saw for the first time that she was just a person trying to have a relationship. That meant that Joseph was just a guy. She told me that my father "could have had a political career" if the role of hostessing a crowd had not made her so stressed out. (How old had she been then? In her late forties. Not much older than I was now!) I had felt honoured, had hardly known how to console her. But I had tried.

So we *were* allies. Weren't we?

My tour had taken much too long. Fearing my canoe would be discovered, I hurried out of the forest.

I took a cursory look at the kitchen, which had yet more shelves by Joseph. The Moores' motley rank of drinking glasses was still there. The same mishmash of dishes and plates. One of my mom's good bowls—the flowery Royal Doulton china—was sitting on the floor with mouse poison in it. The same pots and pans hung above the stove. The guy had just taken over our stuff.

I tried the hammock near the clothesline. It was frayed, but it held me.

The bright sunlight seemed to quash any thought. There was an oar on the ground, rotting in the grass.

It was time to go.

BOOK TWO

The city

15

The whip kick

GEORGE IS STANDING IN THE SCHOOLYARD. IT IS 8:30 ON Tuesday morning. The sky is too blue not to have a lake underneath it. But the shining expanse in front of him is only grass, still green from all the rain, with hundreds of kids starting to beat it to brown. They're all so excited to be back at school. What is wrong with them? George's classmates seem to think it's a big deal to be starting at a Grade 7 and 8 school. They think they're in high school.

The same old groups have already formed. It's all so predictable. At the top of the heap are the jocks, led by Donny Canning and Adam Riswick. They've already started to torture the nerds. George is treated as an honorary jock because, even though he isn't the most gifted athlete, he is one of the most ferocious. So they allow him—in fact, expect him—to hang with them and joke around some of the time. And they look the other way about him being buds with Tim Cahill, who is a definite nerd. That makes George one of the "cool" people, which is a wider category. You don't have to be a jock to be cool, but it helps. Then there is the newest group, the homies, who are into rap. And the ordinary kids who are not total rejects.

That leaves the dirtbags, the losers who don't fit anywhere.

George can see two of them, Graham Doole and Laine Meyer, over by the tree. Laine is overweight and dresses like a gypsy. George doesn't really mind her, but he has to pretend he does; the jocks caught him liking her last year and he got punished. Graham is another matter. Nobody likes Graham, except Laine. He is fat and ugly, a total geek who is usually attached to a camera, or starting last year, a camcorder. George can see one in his hand now, even though he's trying to hide it. If Laine didn't hang out with Graham, she might have a chance. As it is, George has to steer clear of her.

Tim Cahill comes running up and says, "Dylan Baker just told me that you and Jennifer Bull like each other."

"So?"

"Well, do you?"

"I just got back from Muskoka like ten minutes ago. Jennifer Bull was gone all summer. Give me a break, okay?"

Tim is thirteen and is supposed to be George's best friend. He looks like he's grown about eight inches over the summer by stretching out the same number of pounds he weighed before. His nose looks bigger too, which makes you notice his thin lips. It would be better if Tim would shut up or talk about something else, but he won't let this one go. His doggy brown eyes stare into George's.

"So, how come you know she's been away all summer?"

"You don't need to know," George says. He can't be bothered explaining that Alicia is best friends with Jennifer Bull's sister, and was broken-hearted when the Bulls hauled their kids away to Quebec last June.

"How was camp?" he asks Tim, just to sidetrack him.

"It was weird. I didn't crap for two weeks." Tim starts to talk about the black widow spiders in the outhouse.

Fifty feet away, in a little throng that is her clique, Jennifer is looking at him. She and her friends are the coolest of the girls. Not all of them are very likeable, but they are all good-looking and popular. In George's eyes, Jennifer is the only one worth anything. He and she had something going last year. Never mentioned, just something that happened when they looked at each other.

Which George never did anything about.

Now another year is starting. They get to be in Grade 7, whoopdee do. Any minute now, the teachers will come out and form them all into lines. It will go on and on.

Jennifer is taller. Her hair still looks the colour of honey, but it's cut to curve closely around her smart face. He remembers what she looked like in her bathing suit in the bedroom at the Russell cottage. Too bad she wasn't actually there. She is still looking at him and Cindy Cramer and Brie Cullen are giggling.

George hears himself say to Tim, "Wasn't there a real bathroom anywhere?"

George starts walking.

"Where are you going?" Tim says.

Before Jennifer can say hi, George takes her shoulders in his hands. The word "George" comes out of her mouth but then he is kissing it. Her lips are soft and sweet. She doesn't pull away and it lasts quite a while.

The schoolyard goes quiet, then a chorus of Oooooo's rises up. They finish the kiss. George looks at Jennifer. Her face is a beautiful question. He would answer it, but no words come to mind.

George is sitting on the edge of the swimming pool at the Y. It is Thursday at five. His mom dropped him off half an hour ago. His dad is supposed to be there to pick him up in another half hour. Then there will barely be time for a quick dinner before one of his parents has to ferry him off to his piano lesson. Then he will walk a few doors down to where Bill Nash lives, so Bill's father can drive them to the last baseball practice of the year. He has been up since 5:30 this morning, when he rose to do his paper route. He is exhausted. On both sides of him thirty boys and girls are spaced out along the rim of the water. Noise and fatigue, cold and chlorine. His skin is all goose bumps.

Mr. Bolton is back on the job, pacing the side of the pool and barking orders, making sarcastic comments about stragglers during each exercise. Now he walks over and looks down at George.

Bolton tells George to do a length on his back, with his arms stationary at his sides, demonstrating the whip kick for the whole group. Bolton likes to use George as an example, because although George is skinny and has trouble with some strokes, he is smart enough to at least try to do it right.

George swims over to the shallow end, pushes off on his back, and tries to do the whip. It should be simple enough. Thighs on the surface. Lower legs hang straight down from the knees, then snap them in a wide arc back up to a straight-leg position. George's trouble, aside from his teeth starting to chatter, is that every time the kick propels him forward, his head digs into the water and threatens to drown him. He has to flail with his arms to get to the surface, then has to shake his head, cough out water, and generally lose all cool in front of thirty miserable kids.

"Arms at your side!" Mr. Bolton barks, because George has started to compensate for each kick by sculling his arms under him. George locks his arms to his sides and gives a huge kick. This one propels him down into the deep end, and he sees with inverted open eyes the giant number 01 on the wall of the pool coming at him, and barely puts his arms out in time to prevent a head-on collision. After executing an unscheduled somersault underwater he scrabbles to the surface and hangs himself on the concrete edge while waves of high-pitched laughter break over him. Mr. Bolton blows his whistle and strides around to where George is.

"Okay, now do it right," he says.

In the cavernous silence, with his teeth now audibly clicking, George climbs out of the water and faces Mr. Bolton, who has twenty-five years and a hundred pounds on him. George is shaking from the cold. He picks up a towel from the stack folded on the bench and pulls it around him like a cloak. To the amazement of Bolton and the kids, he says, "Why don't you?"

He steps towards the entrance to the showers, where hot water awaits.

Mr. Bolton is on him before he can get through the doorway. He grips him by the right bicep, digging in.

"Don't you ever talk to me like that," he tells everyone in the place. In seconds he has dragged George twenty feet back to the edge of the deep end.

"Now get back in there and show me a whip kick."

"You can't make me do anything."

"Stone, so help me if you don't get in the pool right now I'm throwing you in."

"So do it."

Mr. Bolton shoves him roughly by the shoulder. George knifes into the water sideways. Down at the bottom, his right hand finds a recess where a metal grate sits in the wall. It is easy to grip the edge of this, allowing him to crouch on the bottom like a crab. A warm current comes through the grate and jiggles against him, bringing comfort to his freezing body.

It is good to be down here. He can see the kids lined up along the edge, their legs dangling towards him. Cut off from the upper world, he hears only pale echoes of shouting—high-pitched voices and a low one. No one has to do the whip kick now. After a while his arm gets tired from holding himself down here, so he lets some air out of his lungs and a huge bubble floats up and disappears. Now it is easier to stay put.

The pool looks interesting, seen from the inside. It is like a puckered turquoise tent billowing above him. He looks straight up and can see Mr. Bolton leaning over the tent, his hands on his hips.

Fascinatingly, the water isn't as turquoise now, it is more like pale blue, and the surface is getting farther away. Mr. Bolton is still there but he's smaller. There is no noise anymore, and George sees his father, in a jacket and tie, talking to Mr. Bolton. Bolton is in major doodoo now. Paint from somewhere is turning the water white, George can't see through it. Suddenly a big hole opens and his father is coming, he's taking a swim with his clothes on. He grabs George in his arms. Like a huge frog, he pushes off from the bottom and before you know it they're in the air again and George is coughing up water onto the cold cement.

16

The festive board

I WOKE UP IN THE LITTLE GUEST ROOM ON THE HALF-interred lower floor of my parents' house in Calvan.

For a moment I was perplexed by the fact that there was this universe to return to. That was the only downside of naps: they often left me confused like that. It seemed unbelievable that instead of nothing, this detailed world should exist, the one that bred blue curtains, raspberry bushes, and myself. I was afraid the whole pageant would wither, that it was not real.

Life is a willing suspension of disbelief, I told myself as I crossed the hall to the bathroom. Then the shadow came back, that I was living under. I had failed in Muskoka. My maiden voyage with my true love had stumbled and fallen. It should have been a bright report I could give myself and my parents, but instead it felt like an accusation, an embarrassment. Mercifully, they hadn't asked me much about it, other than a few questions about the weather and the kids. The whole trip made little sense to them and no doubt they were wary of its meaning.

In the small bathroom I was distracted by an epiphany: I suddenly comprehended the clues to a dark secret of my parents' lifestyle in this house. It wasn't a house I was overly familiar with: a smallish split-level on the northern outskirts of the city, to which they had moved in the mid-seventies, just before I set out for the United States. In order to have less to manage, they had abandoned the larger house, built in 1955 and close to the city core, where their children had grown up. And thus they had joined my sister Susan and my brother Greg in suburbs on the rim of the city, where nobody could walk to anything unless they really liked walking.

And in its lower bathroom I now saw a tiny black comb with a few white hairs in it, a beige shaving cup and brush, and a can of denture powder. It could not be a coincidence that my father's morning accessories were close to the "guest" bedroom, not to the master bedroom upstairs. How odd to think that on the few occasions I had stayed here, I had been inconveniencing my parents by forcing them to sleep together. I had a piss, tried to comb my hair into the uncombed look I liked, cleaned my mouth with some Macleans, and stepped out into the hall.

I could hear the low rumble of Joe's voice now; maybe that's what had awakened me from my nap. Joe must be home from his Friday at work; they'd be having a little chat in the kitchen. The dinner I was about to go up to would be the fourth one of this visit. I felt that I could almost slip back into the pace of their routines, could be the son again. If I couldn't make it with Maggie, maybe they were the answer. If they just didn't ask what I did with my time all day, if they left a little cash lying around for me to pocket, I could show up at mealtime and prowl at night, could fade into this city and find someone to touch down some stony street.

This reverie was interrupted by the sight of my father, who was halfway down the stairs from the front hall, looking dapper in a short-sleeved dress shirt with an olive tie. He had his office gleam: there was a spruce look to the smooth old face, a distinction to the trim white moustache. True to custom, he was wrapping the warmth of his smile in words of exaggerated formality.

"I've been asked to summon you to the festive board," he said, not commenting on how long he had watched his son stare into space in a dark hallway.

"I was just on my way up," I answered. As my father strode into the kitchen, I went around the other way and planted myself in my place on the side of the long dining table. I wished my parents were still in their wine period—a short-lived era around 1973 during which a bottle of dry red, usually Spanish, had been a proud fixture at their evening meal, so that my desire for alcohol at dinner could be satisfied without having to announce itself.

I decided to have a beer and manoeuvred behind my parents, who were crouched in front of the oven examining a roast of pork tenderloin. "You'd better take it out, honey," my mother said, and my father obediently lifted the aluminum pan onto the stove. On closer inspection my mother doubted that the meat was cooked, though it looked to me like it had been a while since it passed Crispness going the other way.

I poured my beer into a glass as my father said, "We can put it back in for a few minutes."

"No! You'd better carve it now!" sputtered Irene.

She had only needed to hear her own idea seconded in order to reject it. I returned to the table and sat down for the second time. My father carried the pork in, and standing at the head of the table, started to slice it. My mother brought in serving dishes with boiled potatoes and green beans, and to my horror, a bowl containing one of her salads.

"Is that the festive board?" I asked my father, indicating the piece of wood on which the tenderloin rested. My father, taken aback at this probing of such a well-worn idiom, had to collect his semantic powers before replying.

"No, I believe *this* is the festive board," he said, tapping the teakwood surface of the dining table.

"Well, let's get festive," I offered, and knocked my glass

over as I tried to receive my mother's plate, now bearing meat, from my father. Fortunately the glass was empty, and I was able to catch it before it rolled off the table. The passing and filling of plates was soon completed and I sprang again from my chair, this time realizing that there was no salt or pepper on the table. I brought these controversial items back, along with a fresh beer I had nervously grabbed from the fridge.

It was very quiet here. My parents didn't play any music while they ate, and there was no street noise at all, let alone the steady destruction that passed for silence in L.A. I could hear every clink of cutlery, every incision of teeth. Mercifully my father started to talk.

"I ran into Red Borden at the club today," he told Irene.

"How did he look?"

"Well, he looked a lot better, in fact he claims that he's back to jogging. But he said Audrey is sick again. I don't know if she's getting out these days at all."

"Poor Audrey."

"But he spent most of his time bending my ear about Ron, his eldest grandson, who is now on 'Much Music', whatever that is. I guess he's on the hit parade, and Red says the girls are wild about him. Red said he made it just in time, he was almost over the hill."

"How old is he?" I asked as casually as I could.

"Oh, I don't know, twenty-two I think. Oh, and Red said the duplicate bridge game has folded completely."

I was sinking into something similar to the non-existence I had been worried about earlier. Could my father really not be aware of the implied comparison between my own musical career and that of Red Borden's grandson? Did they even know that I had devoted the last decade and a half, the prime years of my life, to songwriting? Or did they just take my failure so much for granted that it disappeared from the landscape?

I tried to stop my embarrassment from showing. After a

while I realized that my parents weren't going to notice unless I had a raving breakdown at the table. So I decided to turn the other cheek by asking my father about his job. I got a surprisingly informative answer: they were thinking of moving the firm because the old building on Bearer Street was too small now. Joe was genuinely exercised about the decision. Bearer Street was a legal stretch in the heart of Calvan's downtown, an area I loved because of its pre-war houses and fine old limestone buildings dating back to the nineteenth century.

"The younger partners look to me for guidance," Joseph said. "And they're right; we have far too many people for that space now. The proposal is a former factory way out on Twining Road. It would have to be completely remodelled inside."

I had a sudden sense of panic. They couldn't let this happen. My father's professional life was among the most precious things in the world to me, and this would disturb it—maybe deform it.

"Dad, is there a possibility that you could keep the core of the firm, maybe the barrister part, in the old building and just create a satellite office for the rest? Do you really want to give up having the Registry Office and the Court House right down the street?"

"I don't know. I don't know whether that's been considered. I suspect that Robertson and Sanders have already made up their minds to move."

I couldn't restrain myself from subjecting Joe to a stream of reasons why the firm must retain its longstanding base. But I was tiring my parents, and after a while I realized it. A strange protectiveness towards my father could get me in its grip. Strange when you consider that I had always been afraid of him. Strange when you consider that he had not forgiven me for walking away from an academic career, and it was my deep suspicion that for most of my life, he had detected in me some corrupt strain that he sensed was going to lead me off the

straight and narrow. Yet during all those years when I didn't
know how to please him, I had been looking out for him.

Like one night when I was a teenager. We watched a new
boxer named Cassius Clay fight the ageing, crafty veteran
Archie Moore, and my dad kept making sage predictions to the
effect that Moore would take him. My dad cheered when his
namesake connected at all; but to me the old boxer, shuffling
around with a hunched-over posture, looked pathetic. I was
instinctively allied with Clay, but if there was any way I could
have stopped his elegant destruction of Moore, I would have.
After the fourth-round knockout, I went down to my bedroom
and cried uncontrollably at the picture of my father gamely
backing a man on the wrong side of time.

And now Irene was on my case to take some salad. I spooned
some into my bowl, noting the unerring accuracy with which my
mother had hit her culinary target. There was nothing leafy
about it: knife-chopped chunks of head lettuce, red-rimmed
coins of radish, sharp-edged crescents of tomato, and sucking
them under, a puddle officially referred to as French dressing.
As I began to chip away at this offering with my fork, another
silence fell over the table and I smiled nervously at my mother.

"You're making fun of my salad," she said in a defeated
tone.

"No, I'm not! It's good. I just don't have much room left."

She shook her head.

She and I had had a rough week, had never managed to
find the wavelength that we used to share. Usually there would
have been some moment—it might be when she was telling me
about her interactions with her grandchildren—when her soul
would shine through and I would see the fineness of her per-
ceptions, the depth of her heart, and I would be glad that she
was still in there. But this time there had been nothing. Except
for me snapping at her when she thought I was driving too fast.
And a strange moment when we were talking about how my dad

would never retire; we were laughing about it and suddenly she ran into the kitchen. I found her huddled against the fridge, and she would have been crying except that her eyes had this new condition that didn't allow them to produce tears. I asked her what was wrong and she said, "I just don't know what I'm going to do when he . . ." She couldn't say it, but I knew she meant his death, and somehow I knew it was the lack of warning that was unnerving her, the fact that it could just happen. Then I remembered what Susan had told me about the cottage: that my mother had started having panic attacks anytime my dad would leave her alone on the island, even just to go for gas.

I settled down on the twin bed with *The Adventures of Tom Sawyer*. I had found the old book on my parents' bookshelf, and had been losing myself in it for two days. It was like a land I had once passed, long before I had made any wrong turns.

Later I heard my parents' voices next door in the family room. My father's bedside clock said 10:45; they must be getting ready for the late news. I decided I could use a dose of it too.

They seemed glad to see me. Or rather, Joe seemed glad to see me; Irene was sitting erect on her throne with her eyes closed and her feet on a hassock.

"Do you guys need anything?" I asked, deciding that I couldn't sit down with them unarmed. They didn't. Their glasses of rye and water were in a plum state of replenishment. And would be until Joe announced that it was time for bed, in an hour or so. I found no beer in the fridge and had to descend to the fruit cellar where a few Molsons remained. Then it was back to the kitchen to load the old breadboard with crackers and some three-year-old cheddar I had bought this week in the deli down on Montreal Street.

They both wanted a cheesie; I was busy supplying them when the news started. A typical Canadian woman was reading it, not like the anchors in L.A. who had to be blonde. This one had dark hair in the short Canadian style, brown eyes, and full lips, with just a hint of parental gauntness in the face. Her accent had the crisp consonants so rare below the border. The video cut to footage of federal M.P.'s hurling crudities at some cabinet member who replied, "Perhaps the Honourable Members should check their own behinds," to a tumult of raucous laughter from his allies.

Suddenly the TV shut off with a loud bleat like a lightbulb burning out. My mother, brandishing the remote control, had killed the set as she did every time a commercial came on. She would now gauge the interval, then turn it on again as the last ad was ending. Not for her the effete solace of the mute button. Joe, utterly comfortable with the dead air this created, was looking jolly and wanted to say something to his son.

"Dave, is that a Molson you've got there? I've seen you in the ad for Molson's, the one where you're sitting on a dock. I saw it on wrestling."

I had no idea where to start, in reacting to this amazing utterance. The vistas of my father's ignorance of me were breathtaking.

"Oh, that ad. The one where I'm on a dock. What are you talking about?"

My father laughed with good grace. "It's a handsome dark-haired type sitting in a deck chair with a fishing pole. I saw it, and it had to be you—didn't it honey?"

"Oh Hon, I didn't see it." Her eyes were closed now as if to back up her point.

I wanted to bark at him. This was just the latest instalment of my lifelong inability to convey the real nature of my life to my father. But what came out of me was lamely factual.

"Dad, I don't do acting. I'm not an actor. I've never been in a commercial. Believe me, I would have told you if I'd gotten onto a major ad for a Canadian company."

My father's momentum was barely dented. "You've got to see it. If it comes on tomorrow, I'll alert you."

The TV snapped to life again. Scene switch to the high seas: a reporter whose eyes had far too much soul to allow him to become an anchorperson was talking from a Canadian naval vessel. It was us against the Spanish Armada, apparently. I was lost in strange insight. Apparently Joe didn't have me typecast as a failure, otherwise he couldn't have "seen" me in the commercial. He just thought I was up to something down there in the land of images, and the presumption, so far from being negative, was that such activities could land me on the TV. All I had needed to say was nothing. I was already a success and didn't know it.

"Look at this," my mother said. Her eyes were open, watching gays and lesbians parading in Toronto, protesting a fund-raising appearance by the provincial Minister of Health. A naked woman held a sign with a caricature of the minister, and the message: HE NEVER MET A VIRUS HE DIDN'T LIKE. The TV pinged off again, though no commercial was starting.

"So, this Maggie," my father said. "Is she the one?"

"Oh Mojo," my mother said. "Why would she be the one?"

"I don't know," I said. "I thought she was."

"Trouble at the lake?"

"I don't know." Here he was, asking me the right questions. Was this the best I could do?

"She seemed to be a merry sprite," Joseph said.

"I think she is meant to be," I said. "I don't know if she is, with me. I don't know if we are really a team."

"She's also a paralegal, is that right?" Joseph said. The sound of this, coming from him so politely, made me cringe. I knew how the few paralegals in his firm were regarded: it certainly wasn't what he had imagined for me.

"She is, but she doesn't really pursue it," I said. "She could be a superstar, but she mocks it and resists."

"Does she. Well, she may have her reasons."

My mother snapped the TV on again.

17

Runner at third

SATURDAY. I WAS SITTING ON A FOLDING CHAIR AT Calvan Park, next to Susan. Feral parents were screaming along the sidelines of George's championship baseball game, and my sister screamed with them. Dappled green sunlight failed to allay the adults' tension as they urged on their boys, who stood glumly out in the stark glare of the diamond.

It was a moment of stillness for the young players, two out in the bottom of the ninth with the Royal Smokes in front by one run. The potential tying runner for the Bruter Box team (the BBs) was on second. The would-be winning run for the BBs, a chunky thirteen-year-old with dirty blond hair tailing out behind his hat, was in no hurry to make his way to the plate. First he used three bats to loosen up his shoulders, and then he took his sweet time selecting the one he wanted to swing.

"Either this kid is really nervous or he's really confident," Susan said to Ed, who was sitting in a deck chair beside her with his arm around Alicia. We could see George, who was catcher for the Smokes, motor-mouthing to the kid. I was glad to see him talking. He'd been silent for most of the game, seemingly not into it.

"What is George saying?" I asked. Somehow I knew my colleagues would have the answer.

"Probably something along the lines of 'I've got your sister's shorts here, do you want them?'" Ed said. "And 'better back off, this guy pitches way inside.'"

Finally the batter finished digging a bunker with his cleats and went into his stance. He'd already hit one out of the park in the sixth, and he was a threat to do it again now. The momentum was with the BBs anyway; they'd fought back from a five-nothing deficit to make it five-four.

The first pitch missed inside, then the Smokes pitcher settled in and threw two quick strikes. The parents were screaming again. The batter's father, standing right beside Susan, barked out, "Eye on the ball, Melvin!" at exactly the same time Susan yelled, "Easy out!" and they turned to glare at each other.

The next pitch floated in and Melvin's bat ate it alive: a line drive that took a chip out of the shortstop's glove and headed into deep left, where a tall kid chased it.

"Go Tim!" Susan yelled. "That's Tim Cahill," she shared with me.

The third base coach waved the runner past, the Tim kid was just getting to the ball, fifty parents were howling at once, Susan was on her feet and almost on the diamond.

George planted himself with his right foot on home plate, blocking the line from third base. The runner was coming fast, the throw wasn't even in the air yet. George lifted his glove up, acting like the ball was almost to him. The runner, a tall kid who was not skinny, hesitated for a moment and then barrelled forward. Silence had fallen on the park. A serious collision was about to happen and it was either heroic or illegal or both, because only now was the throw launched into the air.

The kid came on. George wasn't even looking at the ball, he was looking at the kid. George waited there like a man with nothing left to lose. He lowered his head and shoulders and raised his forearms like he was in a different game. There was a loud crack as George's head sank into the other boy's ribcage, and the two of them went down like rotten trees. Eons later the ball fell harmlessly into the dirt, fifteen feet up the first base line.

A collective gasp, then more parental screams:

"Get the ball!"

"Interference!"

"He's out!"

Both teams were mesmerized, nobody knew if the game was over. George lay on his back, not moving, while the other kid writhed on the ground, with his teammate Melvin, who had missed third, crouching beside him.

Susan was running across the diamond with Ed and me close behind her. I was thinking, who is this kid? Why didn't I get to know him better at the cottage, maybe understand what he's going through in his life?

People were starting to gather around the fallen pair; Susan broke through them and got to George. "Honey, honey," she said, and took his face in her hands. His green eyes opened.

"Is it over?" he asked.

"Yes dear, it's over," she said, not seeming sure what she was referring to.

His eyes closed.

18

The wrong note

SUSAN LOOKED SURPRISED WHEN I FOUND HER IN THE coatroom at the back of Aran Street United Church. I wasn't known for my church going, but it was a sad Sunday morning and it seemed like the right place to be. I was even dressed sort of respectably, in a light brown shirt with a faint blue stripe, pleated woollen pants, and a thin retro tie.

"Where's Dad?" she said.

"In Arthur. He got a call this morning from a client, some widow on a farm. He headed right out there."

God she looks whipped, I thought, wondering for the nth time why women don't realize that make-up only emphasizes infirmities. My sister was wearing an absurdly glamorous outfit, all black and pale gold, and I wanted to hug her jacketed body, but I was afraid it would snap like balsa wood.

"How is George?" I whispered, and was amazed as her features forced themselves into a stance of optimism.

"He isn't conscious yet," she said. "But the doctors say it's not a deep coma, his readings are good, he's vocalizing a little, and it's day-to-day when he will come out of it." She seemed like she was ready for a press conference.

"Yesterday I think he was responding to me," I told her.

Irene and I had visited George in the hospital, and I had tried
to talk to him. "I told him the Argos were trying to draft him
and he seemed to shake his head—like it was a bad joke."

Susan's bright red mouth was trying to lift at the corners,
but I wished I hadn't conjured the moment so well, because I
could see terror and despair looming behind her paper skin.

"We'd better get in there," she said. "It's after eleven."

"I can't go in yet. My party is still one person short."

"No. Mother came?"

"Yup, she's here. Down in the bathroom."

I was left standing in the shadows with a long row of empty
hangers. The choir had started singing. There was a loud
wooden bang from the basement, and a few minutes later my
mother appeared in her sapphire-blue sweater and skirt, looking quite chipper.

"We're going to have to run the whole gauntlet now," I
told her.

"I'm not sitting up at the front, it's too loud," she said, and
we stepped into the aisle. There was, after all, very little gauntlet to run. I was shocked to see that the place was mostly empty,
and those who were there had gathered to the front pews, so
that Irene and I had our choice of most of the church. She
tried to turn into a pew near the back, but I grabbed her in my
best James Garner manner and steered her forward, whispering,
"Mother, we don't want to look like a splinter group."

"Don't be silly," she complained, but she allowed herself to
be propelled to a more suitable pew. We ended up six rows
behind Susan and Alicia. The first hymn was in full throttle and
the massive organ notes shook the cavern. There couldn't be
more than thirty people there, and it was a fine September day
with everybody back in town. I could remember as a child barely
being able to squeeze into my family's portion of our designated
pew, because the place was so packed. I would sit and wait for my
father to slip me a peppermint Life Saver, smelling the mothball

odour of the big man in front of us, while the Reverend F. Wesley Teal, the United Church's answer to Orson Welles, steered sternly towards the island of compassion.

Now it was the Reverend Edward Stone at the helm of the Lord's ship, and the scripture lesson was about to begin. "I am going to read today," Ed began in his warm tenor, "from the thirty-third Psalm, verses thirteen to twenty-two."

"The Lord looks down from heaven," he read, "he sees all the sons of men."

Ed looked out at us and his gaze seemed to rest on Susan. I wondered if I was supposed to take the word "sons" literally. The Lord was looking down on George.

Ed continued. "From where he sits enthroned he looks forth on all the inhabitants of the earth, and observes all their deeds."

Okay, I thought, George *did* something. It didn't just happen to him, he did it.

"A king is not saved by his great army; a warrior is not delivered by his great strength."

This was bad news, no way around it. George had great strength, that was right; George was a warrior, we had seen that; and now Ed seemed to be trumpeting from his pulpit the information that these qualities were not going to do George one bit of good. I wondered if Ed should be leading a service today.

"Behold, the eye of the Lord is on those who fear him, that he may deliver their soul from death ..."

I doubted there was a chance in hell that George "feared" the Lord, or had any other attitude to him; and my sister's presence in the church had never been anything more than social. Yet Ed seemed to be saying that for these non-believers there could be no deliverance. I hoped my sister wasn't paying attention.

Ed looked at his page and seemed to skip ahead. "Let thy steadfast love, O Lord, be upon us, even as we hope in thee."

That was a little better.

A white-haired woman rose and delivered a melody almost wholly concealed in vibrato. Then as we all got up to sing "Mothers of Salem," I looked at a stained-glass window on the north wall that I had always admired, showing Christ with little children on his lap.

I had decided to assume that nothing really bad had befallen George, that he would come out of his coma soon, in one piece. This was the only way I could sit here and submit to this quaint diversion. At the same time I was struck by the way Ed carried the role of minister, by the way his ordinary guy vibe was ennobled by the mantle he bore.

Meanwhile I was trying to cope with the delicate challenge of sharing a Hymnary with my mother. As we stood side by side and sang, I glimpsed the fact that she had once been a young person, as I still was in my own eyes. She had once been a teenage girl; she probably stood and held one side of a hymnbook while one of her older sisters held the other. I had had this intuition before. At a big family dinner in a German restaurant I had asked her to dance, and as we walked hand in hand towards the dance floor, I had felt what my father must once have felt: the touch of a woman—not a parent—a woman who didn't know what was coming or much about the guy she was walking with, but was ready to give the music a try.

The room was warm and the sun was bright; I was finding it hard to concentrate. When I tuned in on Ed again he was in mid-sermon. I caught him saying, "I'm referring to the account of creation that appears first in Genesis, not the later one in which Eve is made from Adam's rib, which rightly angers feminist thinkers."

That was interesting to a chronic non-attender like me. Were feminists now featured on the normal church menu?

Ed said, "In verse thirty-one, we read: 'And God saw everything that he had made, and behold, it was very good.' Now you may be wondering why I'm making a big deal out of the creation story, something most of us don't take too literally anymore. Well, I'm trying to make a point, that it's not enough for good things and good people to exist, they need to be witnessed."

I had seen Ed preach a few times, but today—of all days—the man was on a roll. If only the turnout had been bigger. It was downright embarrassing. Looking at the effort he had put into this sermon, you would have thought it was going out to thousands, not this ragtag crew.

Just when he had me, though, he seemed to go astray into an endless discussion of the word "witness." Did it mean to see something, or did it mean to tell people about it? I didn't really care.

As my mother fidgeted and looked at her watch, Ed got further sidetracked into respect for other religions, a dangerous topic in my view because it invited the idea that all religions were equal and therefore all merely literature.

And then suddenly Ed was back on the topic of witnessing, only now it meant being a martyr. "A martyr is someone who will die for what he has seen," Ed said, "die rather than dishonour a truth he has witnessed."

That really seemed to sound the wrong note. I thought of George, lying yesterday on a hospital bed, breathing sightlessly, wires stemming from his head and his arms to monitors that graphed in green and blue. And the unforgettable sight of George at home plate.

Was my nephew trying to die? Was that what Ed was saying? He had stopped talking. He stood there, looking in the direction of Susan six rows ahead of us. The congregation stirred uncomfortably. This sermon had obviously been composed during happier times and it was badly misfiring now.

Ed's eyes fought their way back to his text.

"There is a reason why, even in today's two-earner families, you will find a mother racing from work to see her son give a four-minute speech, or you'll see a father fighting traffic to make it to his daughter's dance recital. It's very simple, somebody has to be there."

Ed paused again, seeming to doubt his own track record.

Then he read some more words that could obviously not have been planned for this occasion. "We are God's representatives in each other's lives," he said. "Our loved ones need our gaze to flourish."

Ed pulled up lame. Below him I could see Susan, trying not to be conspicuous, her shoulders hunched up and shaking.

Ed had unconsciously wandered towards her. He was off his leash, standing on the steps, still holding his sermon in his hand. He looked down at his paper and read, "Our finest moments are not when we force our loved ones to do things, or urge them, or prevent them. They are . . ."

His paper dropped like a leaf, and he went down and sat beside his wife.

The choir started singing.

19

The lee side

I JUST WANT SOME LEMONADE. THE KIND WHERE THE BOX has a waxy coating, and a straw that punctures the foil. Hospitals have that. I used to get some when my mom and I were visiting Alicia in here. This time, I haven't seen any. Whatever they're giving me, it isn't lemonade.

My problem is that somebody found my off-switch. My body is lying on the bed, with wires coming out of it, but it isn't awake.

But I am awake. I'm looking down at myself as the nurse comes in. She has grey hair but a young face. She says, "Hello George, how are we today?" but my body just lies there. She finds my blue hospital robe all scrunched up and two of my wires pulled off, but my IV is still in. It's my leash that keeps me from wandering.

She rolls my body over, puts a plastic sheet under me, and starts to give me a sponge bath.

Much as I'm enjoying this, I'm going to leave her and me in the room and go down the hall, see if I can find some of that lemonade.

There's a room with visitors sitting in it, and a big silver fridge. A lady opens the fridge and I see lemonade boxes in there, but they don't do me any good.

So I go out the window and float above the hospital. I can see the shiny black roof and the woods across the street.

I go higher and I can see all of Calvan, out to Fake Lake.

I think about that Friday at Lake Muskoka, when I got up real early and took the boat to the cottage.

I got up real early and took the boat.

There I am now, walking up the hill from the Felder's dock, sneaking up to the cottage. He—me, that is—looks in the bedroom window and he doesn't see anyone.

Meanwhile I'm on the roof. The old chimney's bricks are loose, but it's still standing. It has a piece of wire mesh over the top of it, held down by four bricks, to stop birds or bats or leaves from coming in, but the screen is totally gummed up and needs cleaning. My dad used to climb up here on the ladder and take care of it.

I float behind the cottage. The woodshed is falling down, and there isn't much firewood left, which is getting rotten anyway. I watch as the real me walks around to the front. He notices the place doesn't look quite level. It sags in the middle. The white trim on the windows is peeling.

He goes up on the porch and I'm hoping he'll go in, but of course he won't, because I know what happened that day. We both hear a noise down on the dock and his heart jumps in my chest because maybe the real owners are here.

But it isn't them; it's Dave and Maggie. I hide behind a tree and then I go down the hill and I end up behind the pump-house, watching and listening. I am inside him now; it's all happening like it did.

Dave starts to have the meltdown and then Maggie gets mad and I step out and say I'll take her home.

I lead her to the Felder's dock and we putt-putt away from shore. If I am going to have Maggie in my boat, I wish it was a better boat. She is opposite me in the stern, her eyes clouded over.

"I guess I wasn't very nice to him," she says. "I could have cut him some slack. I do feel bad for him."

"I don't," I say.

Uncle Dave looked sad, but I just feel mad. Mad at all of them. They all lost the cottage. My parents lost it and Dave lost it, the whole family did, except Maggie of course.

"So, did you take a look around?" she says.

"Yeah."

"And?"

"Not so good."

"I'm sorry," Maggie says, but then her eyes brighten. "George, don't go back yet. I'm sick of this island. Take me for a ride."

I rev the engine all the way up, but a Johnson Twelve isn't going to scare anybody. I steer towards One Foot Island, looking over at the Russells' side of the bay to see if anything is going on. Is that my dad on the dock?

We pass behind One Foot. Waves gleam in the channel, not big ones yet.

"This is cool," Maggie says. She is amazing looking. Her hair shines in the wind, her long legs point right at me.

I know what is about to happen but I can't do anything to change it.

As we go around the corner of the island, Maggie says, "Oh, gosh."

Coming straight at us is a big launch with about eight people on it, because I wasn't looking where I was going. I make a desperate right and we thread the needle between the launch and the south shore of Bayne, where it's shallow and dangerous but I don't hear the engine hit anything.

The people on the launch are all waving as we go by about fifteen feet away. Maggie stands up to wave at them and I yell "Don't stand up" and her shirt billows out and she loses it and the people on the boat yell and hold up their drinks.

Maggie grabs the gunwale and sits down again. We look at
her shirt flying onto the rocks.

"We can't get it," I say.

"That's okay, it's one of Dave's."

Then we're free and it's time to pay attention to the giant
waves that are coming at us. It's a west wind, strong, blowing all
the way from Bala with nothing to cut it. The water glints, grey
and blue.

"What is this?" Maggie says. "I thought it was a calm day."

"We were on the lee side of the island," I say.

"This is amazing!"

We scoot along, cutting through the waves crossways, and
it feels as if we're going real fast. It will be hard to turn around
because when you hit this kind of wave broadside, it can
swamp you.

We come to a small island next to Bayne, and I decide to
use it for cover and make a U.

In the lee of the island things are calm. As we glide through
the green shade, Maggie hits me with an awesome smile. I give
her one back.

"I'm really glad I met you, George," she says.

"Me too," I say.

"I'm sorry this week has been so topsy-turvy."

"Not your fault."

It's quiet for a moment.

Then Maggie says, "George. Look at that. Can we go in there?"

"Don't know why not," I say.

It's a neat little beach, in its own cove. I steer the tin boat
in and run the bow up on the sand.

We get out and Maggie says, "Let's run into the water."

"I don't have my bathing suit."

"Shorts will do." She takes my hand and we boot it off the
sand, kick-stepping into the waves; Maggie laughs loud as we
both get splashed.

"This is beautiful," Maggie says. "Our own lagoon."

We swim for a while and Maggie asks me about the island. I tell her that a lot of these smaller islands have just one cottage on them. It's probably on the other side, the people may even be home.

"So we shouldn't overstay our welcome," Maggie says.

On the ride back she wraps herself in a big towel and I let the wind dry me. It's harder going this way because our direction is with the waves, and we keep being lifted up and dropped. Sometimes when I get the timing right, we surf on a crest, and Maggie grabs my knee.

Coming around the corner of Bayne Island past Whispering Walt's Point, I suddenly remember what kind of reception is most likely waiting for me.

I can see my dad standing on the dock. Looking like a storm cloud.

Too late I realize we don't even have our life preservers on. Oh well.

With my dad watching, I come straight at the dock. But I turn too soon and bash the back of the boat against it, which almost knocks Maggie off her seat.

She gets out of the boat and says, "George, great ride. Very exciting."

"I'm sorry to hear that," my dad says.

"I'm gonna get dressed. Gotta pack," Maggie says, but she doesn't leave.

I tie the boat in its slip and my dad stands there.

I put my foot on the first step.

"Stay right there," my dad says. He sighs and shakes his head. "Do you have any idea how many rules you just broke?"

"Not really," I say. *Twenty-three? Fifty-one?*

"Let's start with don't take the boat without permission. Then we'll get to don't go out of sight of this cottage. Then we'll think about what the heck you were doing with no life preservers on."

I don't say anything. This is all bullshit but I don't know how to prove it. I am thirteen, I took a boat out. Big deal.

"I hope you enjoyed yourself, because that may just be your last ride," my dad says.

Maggie is watching and I wish she weren't.

"It's not even the rules," my dad says. "It's that you weren't honest. We are going to have to go into this."

My mom comes down the steps, and just now Uncle Dave approaches in the canoe and he's listening too.

"What is going on?" my mom says. "Where did you go on your ride?"

"No place special."

"I think he went to the old cottage," my dad says. "That is *trespassing*."

"Is that right?" my mom says.

I glance at Maggie and our eyes meet. Then I say to my dad, "If you hadn't lost it I would've already been there."

"George," my mom says.

"George."

Only I'm in the hospital bed and I'm awake and it's the nurse saying my name.

20

The streetcars

GEORGE IS SITTING ON THE CARPETED STEPS THAT LEAD
to the front hall. Any minute now, Tim Cahill should be here
with his mother. They'll drive back to Tim's house and the
whole family will get organized and hit the road. They're going
to visit Cahill relatives on a farm near London for the weekend. It has cows and horses and they can shoot Tim's uncle's
rifle.

It's a place where you have fun. George knows that. He
went once before, over a year ago. He remembers joking
around with Tim while sitting on huge brown horses that were
climbing a steep hill. He used to joke around with Tim.

George has been home for two weeks and his mother says
he's doing much better. She's glad to see him cheering up, and
doing a little schoolwork. Tim brought him the Grade 7 math
book and he figured out some problems. His mom has missed
some work because of George being home, but she has seemed
a little happier with him there. She's catering to his every need,
even brings him Diet Coke while he watches TV. George knows
she's trying hard and doesn't let on about the way he is.

They've gone. Mom, Dad, and Alicia left an hour ago for
Toronto. His dad has some meetings. His mom is going to have

some tests at a hospital. Alicia will get to tag along with her, and of course they'll go shopping.

His parents both hugged him when they were leaving. They don't really know where he is these days. He doesn't really know where he is either. When he woke up in the hospital he felt okay. He saw the nurse's grey hair, then she turned out to be young and looked a bit like Maggie. She was nice. She and the other nurses joked with him. But then his mother's face came to the door and he felt himself sink again.

Now other people walk around him and think he's in the room, but really he's still somewhere else.

It's Saturday today, Saturday morning. At breakfast his mother said he should eat up. She said it was the third day of autumn, September twenty-fourth. It didn't matter what day it was, George couldn't eat anything.

It's 10:58. George hears footsteps on the front walk, and the sound of the screen door opening. As the knock comes, he realizes that he can't go with them. He can't spend a weekend being not there with the Cahills. There's a louder knock on the door.

The house needs to be noisier. George runs to the stereo and turns on a cassette of his mother's, something by Phil Collins. He turns on the washing machine. It isn't that loud so he turns on the dryer too, and leaves the door open. Then he runs to the front door. His suitcase is sitting there. He stuffs it deep in the closet. Opens the door.

"Where were you?" Tim says. "We're in a hurry. Let's go."

"I'm helping my mom. She decided not to go to Toronto this weekend. I have to stay with her. Sorry, man—I tried to call but your line was busy."

"What do you mean, you can't go? Great, I don't even want to go now. It's just gonna be my cousin."

"Grant, huh?"

"Yeah, Grant the turd-mover. Shit, why can't you go, just because she's staying?"

"I guess she wants me around here. I'll catch you next time. Say hi to Grant for me."

"Yeah, right. Later." Tim takes a look at him. "Are you okay? When are you coming back—you're missing everything."

"I don't know for sure. Maybe next week."

"I'll see ya, George."

Tim goes back to his mother's car, signalling to her that it's a no go. She waves to George with a concerned look, and he closes the door.

He turns off Phil Collins' whining. Turns off the laundry machines. Goes to the window. Mrs. Cahill has backed out of the driveway but she's still sitting there, jawing and looking at the house. She is dangerous. She may be wondering if she can talk Susan into letting George go. George pulls back behind the curtain—did she see him? But then her Volvo disappears down the street.

George has no plan, only to get away from the house.

He walks out to Waller Road. A city bus is coming his way, on the other side of the street. Maybe he'll go downtown and look around. He runs across and climbs on. An old lady with blue hair smiles at him.

In his dream he is lying on the dirt. Next to him is a thick stone wall, which he can barely see. Above him, so close it's almost touching him, is a blue canopy, stretched out in all directions, rippling. He lies there for a while and then turns onto his side, trying to realize where he is. With a horrid surge of familiarity, he recognizes that he's underground, way underground. He raises his arm and pushes on the silk canopy. There is stone behind it. It's just a membrane below a mountain of stone. Panic swamps him and he tries to get up, banging his head against the limestone vault.

The blow to his head brings him awake. He gasps for air and fights to contain the bounding of his heart. The bus is crawling up a steep hill—through the window he sees James

Hodgert High School go by. They've already left the downtown behind!

He pulls the bell cord and gets off at the corner. As the bus groans out of his view he heads along Buckingham. He would like to see his grandfather. Maybe he's home right now.

When he reaches his grandparents' driveway, both cars are there.

His grampa is in the backyard. He's standing at the propane barbecue in a short-sleeved beige shirt and loose brown shorts that go to his knees, nearly meeting the sturdy beige socks that climb up from his moccasins. He's got a metal spatula in his hand and he's tapping it on the closed lid of the barbecue, in time to his own singing. His deep, warm voice misses the tune by a few feet. The words are something about "I love you" underlined in red.

The last couple of lines are sung directly to George.

His grandfather shows no surprise at seeing him; just beams at him in a happy way. He says, "Well, you're here, old friend, and lunch is in the final stages of preparation. Although I'm not sure Grandma has set a place for you. We'd better check on that."

His grandmother appears in the doorway. Behind the screen she looks porous, like a design on cloth. She has on a purple skirt and a blouse with bright purple flowers.

"Honey," she says, "we have to remember to put the buns on in time. I don't want the patties burnt." She doesn't see George, who is standing by the wall.

"The buns," his grandfather says. "Three buns to be exact. Unless we're going to consign our grandson to a bare patty."

"What in the world are you talking about?" she says, pushing the screen door open.

"Hi, Grandma," George says.

"George!" she cries in a tone of fright. "What on earth are you doing here? Aren't you going to London this weekend with the Cahills? Oh, no. I wasn't told anything about a visit from you today."

"Grandma, I'm sorry. It wasn't a plan. I just came over. I don't need any lunch."

"And we're very glad that you did," his grandfather says. "It is an unexpected pleasure. A very great one. Now why don't you sit down in that chair and we'll get you something to drink."

"And of course you'll have to eat something," Irene says. "I haven't set a place for you. And I've taken out the wrong number of buns. Oh dear."

"I'm having a glass of beer," Joseph remarks easily, "which I don't think you want. Let me see if we've got any pop."

His grampa disappears into the house. George settles down into the wooden lawn chair. It's peaceful in the enclosed little yard, there's shade from the ivy on the wooden lattice, and he can hear birds twittering in the oak tree.

He doesn't mind listening to them fussing about the situation. Maybe because no one else planned his visit, this feels like the first time he's ever sat here.

Grampa is back with a glass of diet ginger ale. "I think your uncle left this behind when he departed for L.A. It should do the job."

George watches his grandfather at the grill. It's a familiar sight. At the cottage it was real charcoal doing the cooking, brickets that would flame up when the grease fell on them. Sometimes the man he called "boat-grampa" would let him hold the old Sunlight Liquid bottle and spray the water. This created huge clouds of smoke and on one loose-lidded occasion, a lake of soggy charcoal. His grampa was shirtless in those days, sunning his old torso as if it were Schwarzenegger's. George would hold his gin and tonic for him if the barbecuing got complicated. When the meal was served, anything good about it would be credited to George.

His grandfather turns to him now and says, "How is your mother?"

George is about to utter a normal reply when he looks into Joseph's eyes and realizes that this man is ready to listen to what he actually thinks. There's nothing stopping him from telling the truth.

"I don't know. She likes having me at home but now I see her more of the time, and she's . . ." He pauses to think. "Talking didn't use to make her tired. And she's sad. I heard her cry in her room."

His grandfather listens to him, and then seems to reflect on what he has said. His steady gaze is like oxygen to George.

"And what about you?" the old man asks him.

"I'm fine," George says in kind of a hurry, uncomfortable with turning away so soon from the path of truth. "I'm not weak. But I sleep a lot. I'm not sad. I'm fine, compared to my mom."

"But what about not compared to your mom?"

George looks him in the eye and again draws courage. "Grampa, I'm sort of . . . sunk."

His grandfather walks over to him and puts his hand on his shoulder. He crouches down and pats George's knee. "Now I'm glad you told me that."

The grace of this gesture makes George remember what he wanted to ask him. He says, "Grampa, why did you sell the cottage?"

Joseph's blue eyes go blank for a moment, and then they stray to the sky. He gathers himself and looks back at George.

"You know, we didn't know what else to do with it."

"We couldn't give it to all four children. Too messy—ownership split among four parties. We couldn't give it to just one—that wouldn't be fair to the other three." He frowns thoughtfully. "So we put it up for sale. Even offered a lower price if one of the children came forward to buy it. But none of the four did."

"Maybe nobody had the money," George says.

"That may be, unfortunately."

There's a pause. George says, "Grampa, why couldn't you just not do anything? Just keep it."

Joseph nods slowly. "What was the urgency. That's what you're asking. I've sometimes asked myself that same question."

Irene is at the door again. "Honey, you haven't asked me for the buns."

Joseph raises the barbecue lid. "I do want the buns, you're right on time. George, can you get the buns from your grandmother and bring them out here? I'm just going to move these patties off the heat."

In a few minutes they're seated at the dining room table. His grandma serves piping hot fried potatoes and raw carrot sticks. Both look perfect, but George has no desire to bite into them.

They all open their burgers to add condiments. Irene stares at hers. "This patty is black!" she shrieks. "You've left them on too long—while you were yakking. I knew it." Her shoulders sag. "How can he eat that," she says.

"They may indeed be well-done," his grandfather says.

"They're okay," George says. "I'm not that hungry anyway, Grandma."

The two old people munch glumly on their burgers, and George tries to chew on a carrot stick. It forms a fibrous mass in his mouth that he can't seem to swallow. *They don't even know why they sold it*, he is thinking.

After a while he hears his grandmother's voice. "George, how did you get here? You didn't walk all this way."

"I took a bus. The Cahills aren't coming to pick me up till four o'clock. I got bored."

"And you came all the way across town to see us. I'm amazed. I just didn't expect it."

He feels like saying, "I didn't either," but he keeps quiet. Short stories work better than long ones, when they aren't true.

"Well honey, you'll have to drive George home," she says.

"He can't be trying to catch a bus out there on Mossbank again."

They look at his grandfather and something odd happens. He turns to the empty side of the table and says, "He can catch a streetcar, can't he? I would go with him, but I've lost my schedule." Still facing an empty chair, he says, "The best laid plans, eh?"

"That isn't funny," Grandma says. "There aren't streetcars in Calvan. You'll drive George home."

His grandfather looks at him for a long time, seems to come back from somewhere else. Then he says, "I will be happy in the service."

George walks out to the garage with him. It seems even colder, and the air is even clearer. George doesn't know what to say.

"Grampa, I can walk. I'll catch a bus later."

His grandfather has opened the car door; he stands there and leans on it. "You want to walk, and I need to drive. I don't see any great problem here. This may be a very propitious day for both." At this point he gives George a graceful army salute, and without another word, climbs in behind the wheel and starts the car.

He isn't making sense. Where is he going to drive? George gets into the car.

"You're coming with me?" Grampa says.

"I think I should."

They back out of the driveway and head down the street. *Are we going to the Cahills?* George wonders. His grampa doesn't even know where they live. No point in going there anyway, they've already left.

It's his call, George decides. The old man makes a left onto Mossbank Road. His hands are mottled. But they are a young shape and they still look perfectly usable. Soon the car reaches the top of the big hill and the downtown is in view. They pass the huge old red brick houses that line the descent to the river.

Across the bridge, waiting at the light, his grandfather points ahead.

"We're joining the streetcar track now," he says. "It sweeps across from Trafalgar, and on down Twining."

Meaning it used to, George thinks.

"Now, we'll find some in the square," the old man says. "They have a staggered schedule." He pronounces this last word in a weird old-fashioned way that sounds funny to George.

"I don't know the sheh-joo-will," George says.

His grandfather peers over at him. His eyebrows look like a garden run wild. "Why would you?" he says. "You pronounce that very well, by the way. You must not be watching enough TV."

They proceed down Trafalgar with its old stone buildings to St. George's Square, another red light.

"The streetcars wait here," his grampa says. "That's the one you want, over there. It'll take you all the way to Fergus. Then Aunt Bertha will come and get you."

The light has been green for a while. A couple of cars honk.

"But then you'll think, I've come a long way just to husk corn," Grampa says. "We'd better get a move on, we won't be catching any streetcars today."

George is relieved at this statement. Maybe the old man was just thinking back. George has never had this kind of worry about him before. "I hate husking corn," he says. "It's impossible. You can't get all the thready things."

His grampa pulls into a parking space. "I don't think we're supposed to stop here, George. Our orders don't involve any loitering around." He opens his door. "Mein Feurer can't know about this."

George isn't sure what he said. But he thinks it meant Grandma. They get out and walk back towards the square.

"What can we get you?" his grampa says. "You didn't eat your lunch. We'll get whatever you want. You can't recuperate if you don't eat."

This is a welcome statement. Grampa must be all right if he knows what happened to George. And to his own surprise, George is hungry. And knows exactly what he wants. There's a hot dog vendor right here by the Royal Bank. Grampa buys him a Polish sausage with the works, lots of sauerkraut. They sit on a bench in the sun. The hot dog is excellent. They both have lemonade. Good lemonade.

"So, we don't always take orders, Herr Stone," the old man says. He pats George's shoulder.

"This is real tasty, Grampa. You should have one."

"I will sometime. George, sometimes you have to do what someone wants you to do. Sometimes you don't get to do much of anything else."

"Okay."

"It hasn't been easy. With her."

"With—Grandma?"

"Yes. She's had a very hard time. You know, she is afraid and that means I'm not doing my job. But you asked me a good question and you deserve an answer. You deserve an answer."

"What is she afraid of, Grampa?" George says.

"Now that is a good question too. She may be afraid of being alone."

"Alone, huh."

While they've been sitting here George has seen at least three people from school, going into or coming out of the Eaton Centre across the street. One of them was Laine Meyer, the unpopular brunette. Before his accident the kids were starting to talk about "the square" like it was the new hangout this year. It's close to their new school, you can walk it in twenty minutes or there's a direct bus. Interesting what's been going on while he's been away.

The old man gets to his feet and adjusts his golf hat. "There's no time like the present," he says. "We'd better get you where you're going."

"I can catch a bus from here, Grampa."

"Are you sure? I'm at your disposal."

"I'll be cool," George says.

"Well, I see some buses coming in now. I will leave you to it." The old man starts to walk away, and then turns back again.

"George, your grandma was anxious on the island. I couldn't even go to the marina without her. She is anxious all the time. Even when we were in Calvan, it seemed to prey on her, the cottage. She just couldn't let it be."

"She worried about it?"

"She did, and not for any good reason. You were taking very good care of the place. With help from your mom and dad."

"Not like now," George says. He took a good look around before Uncle Dave and Maggie showed up. The place was awful.

His grandfather shakes his head, waving off that signal. Then he says, "And you never stopped shining that boat. I always thought it would just go to you, if we waited long enough."

"The boat?"

The old man smiles. "That too. That too."

"I saw the Elsinore," George says.

It was at the marina, way down at the end. It still had the big Evinrude engine. The convertible top was filthy and the woodwork was cracking. George had always kept it up for his grampa.

Who now leans over and kisses the top of George's head. And says, "Well, well."

21

The shallow end

GEORGE STAYS PUT ON THE BENCH. BUSES FILL THE square and throb. He sits there until his grandfather's wake is gone. A bus driver gestures to him and he shakes his head.

Finally air brakes hiss and engines grind and the buses move out. It gets quiet again. College kids walk by, laughing. An old woman with a tiny dog sits down across the street. *I'm not waiting for anything*, George thinks. *I'm not on anybody's "sheh-joo-will." Nobody told me to be here, and there's no place I have to go next.*

He doesn't feel happy, but he's not depressed either, for the first time since he can remember.

Two girls come out of the Eaton Centre and unlock bicycles from a rack. As if because he didn't ask for it, one of them now proves to be Jennifer Bull. *I don't care if she comes this way*, George thinks; *so that means she will.*

And she does. The two girls are carefully walking their bikes across Trafalgar Street. Both are wearing jeans and pale T-shirts, with flashy jean jackets. Jennifer's friend is Brie Cullen, the other perfect blonde from school, who is known to be high maintenance, and who tends to be snobby to everyone except Jennifer.

Halfway across the street George can tell that Jennifer sees him. She breaks into a sort of scolding smile and heads straight for him, ignoring the lines of the crosswalk. Brie follows reluctantly.

"Hi Jennifer," George says.

"Oh, just hi?" Jennifer says. "Like this is normal? What are you doing here, George?"

"Not too much."

"Are you waiting for a bus?" She looks around like she isn't convinced. Then words rush out of her. "We thought you were sick. Maybe still in the hospital. I didn't know if you were dead. And now you're just sitting here."

"I do other things too," George says. "Let's see, I had a hot dog."

Jennifer laughs. Her blue eyes won't loosen their grip on him. Brie is acting squirrelly because she wants to get going, but George and Jennifer don't pay any attention.

George is thinking, *I'm really on Jennifer's radar screen. This girl that I fantasized about, that I dive-bombed with a kiss, worries about me when I'm not there.* It gives him a weird, adult feeling about her. He feels like he should have called her or something. He says, "I've been home for two weeks. I didn't die or anything."

Jennifer sags in relief, letting her bike hold her up. "I just didn't know what to think," she says.

"I didn't either."

"So, like where are you going now? We're heading over to Brie's."

"I don't know," George says. "Maybe for a walk." It isn't much to offer; he wishes he had a limo or something.

"A walk? Where?" Jennifer looks stricken at the news of a plan that she wasn't in on.

"Nowhere. The river." George has a sudden inspiration. "I want to show you a place I found down there."

"You do? And you knew you'd be seeing me right now."

"I know you're here," George says, stretching his back.

"Jennifer," Brie says.

"George, it's nice if you give some advance notice," Jennifer says. "How can I go with you?"

George can't even believe she's *considering* it. Isn't she worried that he'll grab her and kiss her again? Because that's exactly what he's picturing, on the riverbank by the footbridge.

"Your call," he says mercilessly.

Brie drags on Jennifer's jacket and they start to move away like a contraption with four wheels.

"Are you going to be at school?" Jennifer calls.

"Monday," George tells her. And they disappear down Montreal Street.

And now it's quiet again, and the world is different again. George had no idea the square was so entertaining. He almost doesn't mind that he was named after it—if his dad wasn't joking.

Leaves skid along the curb. He's done with this bench. He heads across on the WALK sign.

As soon as he hits Bearer Street he sees Laine Meyer up ahead. She must have come out of the mall while he was talking to Jennifer. She is arm and arm with a shorter kid who has to be Graham Doole. Who else would wear an oversize trench coat and a hat like a detective in an old movie? George is overtaking them because they keep laughing so hard that they have to stop. They seem to be telling each other a killer story, maybe reliving something that just happened.

It seems weird to George that two people who are considered losers should be having so much fun. He's not sure they have that right, Graham especially. The kid moved to Calvan last year. He has big lips. He is fat. And he is a total geek. Laine is not as bad, but is still outside the circle of acceptability.

Last year George got caught "liking" her—Adam Riswick started the rumour and it got out of control and he was declared "Out of It" by his friends. It all started when George and Adam were assigned to work along with Laine on a reading

enrichment project, on *The Secret World of Og*. Of course Adam
tried to trash her. It was understood that she was different in
all the wrong ways. She was overweight, she had bad hair, and
she did her homework in rough and then recopied it in good.
But George thought her ideas were good and he didn't *not* like
her. So he resisted, and that's when the jocks' hammer fell.
The worst punishment they stuck him with was when they
ordered him to say "Madame Fatso, I mean Madame Fossell" in
the middle of French class. He did well and he made it back
into their circle. And stopped acting like he liked Laine.

Meanwhile she has spotted him. She points a camcorder at
him as he makes his way along the narrow street, walled in by
dark houses with law firm names in the windows, on a straight
course for St. George's church and the river.

"Heads up Stone, you're on Meyer-cam," Laine says. She
is pretty entertaining to look at. A big gypsy kerchief around
her head, neon red lipstick. An oversize brown T-shirt, black
jeans, Doc Martens.

"Make sure you get that window too," George says, indicating
the big pane beside them with the name 'MOORE
ROBERTSON' on it.

"Oh, should I?" she says, turning the camera. "Is it
important?"

"Um, yeah. That's who will defend you morons when you
go over the line."

"You're the one who went over the line," the size-chal-
lenged detective says.

"Hi Graham," George says. He has never spoken to this kid
before.

"Hi George."

"So! You showed up again," Laine says. "We wondered
when the big star would make his comeback."

"You did?"

"We had to watch you on reruns," Graham says. He and

Laine laugh as they cross Twining. Again George has the sense that these two have something going that no one even guessed at. He stays with them, wanting to hear what they'll say next.

As they take the footbridge across the river, Graham drops a step behind and Laine puts her hand on George's arm. She has gotten taller since last year, taller than George. It's hard to judge because of her loose clothes, but over the summer she also seems to have lost weight. Her face is different, and not just because of the lipstick. She has cheekbones. Her fingers feel good on his bicep.

"I have footage you know." Graham's voice from behind. "Of you and your girlfriend. 'Hard Copy' footage, hand-held."

"Time out," George says, "I don't have a girlfriend."

"Yeah right, you and Prince Charles," the kid says.

"Whatever," George says.

"Come off it," Laine says, "if you kiss somebody in front of thousands of people ..."

"And we catch it on Video-8," Graham says, holding up the camcorder.

"And that isn't all, not anymore," Laine says. "Are we gonna show him?"

"It isn't ready, I have to edit."

"The voiceovers are already there," Laine says.

"What are you dirtbags talking about?" George says.

"Oh, let's just say it has something to do with Jennifer Bull and her gay sister," Graham says.

"Her sister is gay?"

"Not that sister, her 'sister.' Brie Cullen." Graham and Laine's laughter echoes over the river. George stares at them, wondering how long this has been going on.

"Let's hurry up," Laine says. "I need to tinkle."

They cross Arthur and make a left onto Empress Street, a long incline on the side of a hill, with big mansions above it and cheaper houses cramped along its downhill side. At one of these they stop, go through a gate and down some steps to a basement door.

Into the gloom and onto a flabby couch. George leans back and a TV comes on. It's an interview with Tom Cruise. "Yuk," Graham says and stabs a button on the set. The oversize screen turns a solid blue and the word VIDEO shows for a while and then disappears. Still in his trench coat, the weird kid applies himself to a tangle of plugs, jacks, and connecting cords. His thick lower lip folds and unfolds in profile against the screen.

Except for the light from the TV, the room is dark, but George can make out an old easy chair, a big aquarium with something moving in it, and a jungle of electronic components that spill from a workbench.

Laine comes back from the bathroom and sits beside George. She twists the top off a bottle and starts drinking. Then she pushes it into his hand. It's cold. George takes a swig and coughs. More from the flavour than the texture. It's fizzy like pop, but bitter.

"Do you like it?" she says.

"Sure." He takes another swig, looks at the bottle. It's too dark to read the label.

"It's Labatt's Blue," she says. "Graham. Turn up Frankie."

"Not necessary," the Doole kid answers. "Nous sommes prêts."

"Okay, prêts. Cool." She takes the beer back from George. Graham joins them on the couch. He's holding two remotes in his hand, one big and one tiny.

"What are we watching?" Laine says, and passes the beer back to George. She is sitting with her knees under her, and doesn't seem to care that her leg is touching his. Every time she hands him the beer she rests her hand on his shoulder. She smells good.

"I can't decide," Graham says. "Both are ready to roll."

"Today's stuff," she says.

"We haven't even seen it. I don't usually show unedited stuff."

"What do you mean, we always watch it as soon as we get here!" Laine laughs.

"Not with non-members," Graham says.

"Oh, right. I forgot. Well, what do you say, Stone? You want to see some old stuff?"

George is feeling increasingly blissful. Life seems to have released him from the dull headlock it had him in.

"I'll watch anything," he says, and snakes his arm around behind Laine. She doesn't flinch; in fact she shifts a little closer. Under her loose T-shirt he feels an unexpectedly small waist.

"He'll watch anything," Laine says, and it feels to George as if he and she are in a giddy conspiracy.

"I'm going with the skin collection," Graham says.

"Wait! Who needs a beer?" Laine says.

George and Graham both say, "I do."

When Laine gets back she settles right into the curve of George's arm and they start on another beer. George is afraid he is going to say something like "This is awesome," so he says nothing.

The TV screen goes grainy and they hear an old song with the kind of beat you can snap your fingers to. "It had to be you," the guy sings. "Had to be you."

"I hate modern rock," Graham says. "The good stuff was back in the forties and fifties. Sinatra was it."

The video snow turns into a scene with cars, a motorcade. Then there's a man being shot.

"Cool," Graham says. "Jack Ruby does it live."

The scene dissolves into daytime colour, not grainy anymore, a yard with trees in the distance. Then it pulls in and the view is blocked by a blonde head, seen from behind, with a halo of sunlight. The shot widens to show two kids standing a ways away. George Stone and Tim Cahill, to be exact. Other kids are scattered around. Then George starts to walk towards the camera.

"You got this?" George says.

"If it isn't shot, it isn't caught," Graham says. "We were on her long before this."

"What are you, the FBI?"

Sinatra is singing, "Some others I've seen, might never be mean; might never be cross, or try to be boss, but they wouldn't do . . . "

They see George step right up to the blonde and look at her. His hands take her shoulders. The image shakes as the camera moves around them and they kiss. A loud "oooh" rises from the crowd.

The camera stays on Jennifer. On the couch George forgets to breathe: he never saw this part. Jennifer has a dreamy look on her face. Then it turns sad. Then two other girls close in on her and they are talking and laughing. But Jennifer is somewhere else, by herself, and the screen grabs her and stays on her. Graham is a genius.

"I think he liked that one," Laine says.

"Graham!" comes a voice from upstairs.

"*Shit.* Yeah, Dad." He hits pause and the image of Jennifer pulsates on the screen. It looks unreal.

"Are you in on dinner?" the voice yells.

"Say no," Laine whispers. "I need to go home. We can watch movies."

"I'm going to Laine's," Graham yells. "We're cool."

What is this lifestyle? George is wondering. *No supervision. They tell their parents where they're going. Where does Laine live? How are they getting there?*

"Can we bring the video?" Laine says.

"Sure, it's VHS."

"We have to watch the last part. Stone won't believe it." She turns to George. "He got your baseball game!"

George likes how she calls him Stone. This field trip isn't even close to over.

"We don't usually take a taxi," Laine says, as they cruise along the riverside south of downtown.

"We usually go with Carl, that's her driver," Graham says.

"Oh right, her driver," George says. He is sandwiched between them in the backseat.

"Laine is, what do you call it, oh I think it's called filthy rich," Graham says.

"I'm not," Laine says. "I'm totally clean."

"So, like where's your driver?" George says.

"He had to go fishing with his girlfriend," Laine says. "She's sixty-five years old."

"She looks younger than him," Graham says.

"Well, she isn't. I think he's only fifty. Of course, he used to be in a rock band."

They are flying along a two-lane road south of Calvan. There are open fields, stands of cedar, big houses up on hills. You can see the moon in the sky and it isn't even dark yet.

After a roller-coaster stretch they go left on a side road that turns out to be a long driveway leading up to a big house, a gold roof held up by white pillars. They pile out and Laine leads them in through a carved doorway.

They troop by a swimming pool in a room with walls and ceiling of ribbed glass. Then up some stairs to a kitchen area.

"Where's Marla, I wonder," Laine says. "I'm hungry all of a sudden."

Marla is found on the terrace, watering flowers. She turns out to be a small, pretty Jamaican lady. While she is making dinner, Laine suggests a swim.

For some reason I can do this, George thinks. *I've got borrowed trunks on and I'm on my back in the deep end and I'm not sinking, I'm just breathing slow, in and out, looking through the ceiling at the clouds. I barely have to move.*

Graham is in the shallow end, sitting on steps in the water. Laine stands beside him for a while and they talk and laugh.

George drifts their way.

"We'll do some later," he hears Laine say. "I don't like it when I swim." She stands up and walks to the side of the pool. In her two-piece she is built like a *Sports Illustrated* swimsuit model. What happened to the fat girl? Her legs are not ignorable. And she seems completely cool with being seen.

She dives in to the deep end, not making a splash. Starts doing lengths.

George floats over to where Graham is sitting. "Man, if I had a pool like this at home I could probably be a decent swimmer," George says.

"I couldn't," Graham says. "I don't like the water. I quit Bolton's class, told my mom I had to."

"You have a mom?"

"Duh, yeah. I live with her during the week, and some weekends. She isn't like my dad."

"I guess not."

"She wanted me to keep going to that rat bastard's class. After you did your thing, I said no." Graham is covered in a dark T-shirt, though the room and the water aren't cold.

George flashes back to an incident last summer in Mr. Bolton's class. Graham was supposed to demonstrate the flutter kick, while hanging on to the side of the pool. He didn't do it fast enough and Mr. Bolton made him get out of the pool. That wasn't the worst thing. Besides being fat, Graham has a weird chest with protruding nipples. Mr. Bolton told him, "you have such nice tits you better go sit with the girls." The pool rang with laughter and George remembers thinking, *if I were Graham I would shoot myself.*

"And now we're stuck with him at school, too," George says.

Graham grimaces. "He just had to be at William Bell. That's okay, I'm gonna get him."

George decides to steer to a better topic. "Man," he says, "you've got it going on with Laine."

Graham shakes his head. "I'm like, her girlfriend," he says. His sad eyes are the colour of the water Laine is swimming in.

"Naw," George says.

Again Graham fixes him with those big eyes. "George, you don't even know what it's like to be you."

"Huh?"

"I mean, to be me. I could never do that. I couldn't believe the way you stood up to him."

"Oh, Mr. Bolton?"

"Yeah, 'Mr.' Bolton. If your dad didn't show up I was going to have to dive in for you."

"Man, I didn't even know what I was doing. I was just pissed off."

"Right," Graham says. "And you basically told him to fuck off. Shit, I need *that* on video."

"That's what I mean. I'm like everybody else. You're a fucking genius, you dickwad. Look at the shit you're into."

Graham smiles reluctantly. "It's just video," he says. "I'm like, your paparazzi."

Laine is on the diving board. She calls out, "Hey Stone, are you just going to hang out in the shallow end?"

"Go for it," Graham mutters. "She's into you."

After the swim they go in the sauna. George watches water droplets slide down Laine's black hair and bead on her chest. She asks him if he likes Jerk Chicken. "It's spicy," she says.

"I know I like pizza with jalapeños," George says.

22

Marco Polo

THERE WASN'T MUCH LEFT OF MY DESSERT. THE MOCHA ice cream was reduced to a small puddle. The petals of white chocolate that had garlanded the cake were now in fragments, bogged down in a lake of raspberry purée that I couldn't eat.

I had been back in L.A. for two weeks and all hell had broken loose. My boss, a senior partner named Murry Barr, had hit me with an impossible project. So I had come into work on a Saturday to get it under control. After a scattered afternoon I had broken for dinner at a pasta restaurant up on Bunker Hill.

It was getting cooler by my table. The outdoor heating unit seemed to be directed at the yuppie couple seated directly in front of me, the only other souls foolish enough to be sitting outside. She was clearly an attorney; he had a slightly dissolute air that might mark him as a member of a more creative profession. Maybe he had something to do with the art museum. She was facing me, and was not even slightly attractive. She had a skinny, rodent face fringed by the permed, mustard-coloured portion of her hair. The top of her hair was darker and straight. Because it was Saturday she wore Khaki shorts, Reeboks, and a Lakers T-shirt; but the unexpected coolness of this evening had induced her to throw around her shoulders the all-purpose jacket she

probably had hanging behind her office door—one of those horrid navy blue blazers that help professional legal females mark
themselves out from non-professional legal females, by emulat-
ing the drab uniformity of professional legal males. Her body,
from what I could see of it, was without shape.

This didn't surprise me. I was resigned to the general rule
that when I was out on my own, no one would be worth looking at—not the waitress, not women sitting alone at tables or
bars, not women with other men, not even the men. If Maggie
had been here, the bratty Generation-X waiter who had been
neglecting me this evening would have been a cerebral redhead
with a subtle warmth. And the group on the other side of the
glass wall to my left would have been zany college girls, not two
pairs of middle-aged Chinese tourists. And one of the college
girls would have been hard to ignore, and I would have spent
the whole meal trying to find a crack in Maggie's vigilance.

It would have been fun. Or at least challenging. But this
meal had only been bloating and expensive. Rubbery seafood
in a cheese-clogged tomato sauce. Why had I finished it, every
barfy bite? It sat heavy in my stomach, unmoved by my attempt
to use a twelve hundred calorie dessert as an antidote. My second
cabernet was empty.

It was lonely here on the moon, or whatever asteroid they
had built these office towers on. Eight o'clock, and my food
break had lasted way too long.

I left two twenties, stepped over a wall of shrubbery, and
walked down the hill to Sarronick & Beatty.

The cute display of antique clocks in the lobby didn't comfort
me as I re-entered the building. Inside the elevator, I saw
Richard Ocher coming across the lobby. My least favourite
attorney. I jabbed twenty-seven and stabbed my card key into
the slot, then found the elusive CLOSE button and mercifully,
the big doors lurched shut.

On twenty-seven I used my card key again and the double doors crashed behind me as I headed onto the floor. I ducked into the kitchenette; Lucy the nighttime word-processor was sitting at one of the tables staring into a portable TV with "Hard Copy" blaring on it. I poured some coffee into a styrofoam cup and added phoney cream and phoney sugar.

Back in my office I closed the door, even though my glorified closet had gotten stuffy because the air had turned itself off in this sector. I sat down on my red secretarial chair and surveyed the mess of binders, printouts, and loose notes in front of me.

It seemed much clearer now than it had before dinner that I was in serious trouble. If done properly, Murry Barr's project would probably consume most of three months. Barr wanted it in two weeks. He absolutely *had* to have it in *three* weeks, for a major meeting with the client on October 14th at which Sarronick & Beatty was finally going to demonstrate that it had got this bull of a case by the horns.

SOB was not presently in our client's best books. The client, Connate Insurance, was a major conglomerate with a nasty habit of denying the claims of its giant corporate customers. Then the customers sued for coverage and Connate had to hire firms like SOB to defend them. Connate had been in the habit of throwing legal defence money around the way they did claim denials; but now they had a new CEO and he expected value from his counsel. On this case, what they'd been getting from SOB was a faintly comedic series of lost documents, defeated motions, and inflated bills.

It was my job to put a stop to all this. I only had a few problems. One was that I was just a paralegal, and half the people on my team were lawyers, junior associates who knew less about insurance than they could afford to betray to a member of a lower caste. But at least they knew law and they were smart. The remaining members of my team were paralegal assistants, who didn't understand law *or* insurance.

That left my biggest problem: myself. This project played into my own Achilles' heel.

I could analyze anything, especially if it had nothing to do with the real world. An insurance policy, I had learned, had two parts: a short one and a long one. The short part said, "If you have a problem, we'll pay." The long part said, "Oh, by the way, under certain circumstances we won't pay after all." And then it went on to list those exceptions—for days. A thousand excuses were expressed in language that formed a convoluted maze. Like some verbal sleuth, I could follow this language down every twisted hallway, through every alcove, into every dusty niche. And then I could chart it all so tightly that no one in the firm could challenge my work. It wasn't a job I had ever dreamed of, but over the years I had grasped it like a pit bull. It was what I was good at.

What I wasn't strong on was *factual* research. The truth is I was lousy at it. I had always found facts difficult to absorb and even harder to retain. This had first dawned on me in Grade 5, when I stared at Miss Noak's history test and realized I couldn't remember anything about Marco Polo's trip to China except the name Marco Polo and the name China. But at least I knew what to do. When I received my failing mark, I lifted the hinged top of my desk, put my head inside, and cried.

A lifetime of clever evasion had got me this far. But today I felt like Bonnie and Clyde, innocently stopped on a country road in the sun, turning to see that the bushes are full of guns.

For this project bristled with facts. This time around, Connate Insurance was being sued by the dreaded, monolithic Plandor Corporation. For almost a century, Plandor had dumped toxic waste all over America, in unthinkable amounts at hundreds of sites. Not by accident, either: this was their normal M.O., and now it all had to be cleaned up, or at least contained. Plandor was fine with this, as long as their insurance companies—including our client—paid the bill. But our client, true to its mission in life, had said no. And oddly enough, this time it might be right. Insurance was for accidents, not for messes you intentionally made.

So the battle was on, and it all came down to what I feared most: the specific facts of all those pollution sites. My team was supposed to soak up all those facts, and then use my famous policy charts to estimate the payouts. And Murry Barr had promised the client that vast amounts of new research, none of which had actually taken place, would be factored into our report.

Earlier today I had tried one pollution site. The Pasly site. It had taken me all afternoon just to read the *old* memo, when I finally found it. Pasly was a fucking horror show. It was a big tract of land near Lake Erie. It seemed to break down into at least thirteen different sectors, each with its own complicated history.

I had read it. And the sad truth was, I didn't remember a word of it. I didn't *care* which subcontractor hauled the benzene to the ninth level of hell. This is why I hadn't gone to law school: because I couldn't *do* this.

It was 9:32. Somehow another hour and a half had gone by. The coffee had gone way beyond compensating for the wine. My mouth, even my lungs, felt dry. My neck and shoulders were tight.

I stood and something cracked in my lower back. This project was going to fail. Because nobody on the team could fit the pieces together. And even if someone could, there wasn't time. I would at last be found out and fired. I felt as if an ooze of L.A. rancidity was closing in. When I left my office I would find the building eaten away.

I opened the door. The mahogany-trimmed secretarial stations were still there, reflecting green from the fluorescents overhead. Beyond them, in the outer circle of attorneys' offices, a door was open, and I could see a window in the unlit room, through which the cells of the next building were glowing.

Sometimes on weekends I stole in there, locked the door, and
napped on the attorney's leather couch in the half-light. I
couldn't nap in my own office because it didn't lock. Tonight a
rest would do me no good. I decided to have a piss and then go.

I padded along the hallway, past Maggie's office. Big mistake, I should have gone the other way. On my right a door
sprang open and before I could make the washroom, I heard
Richard Ocher's nasal tenor.

"David. Have you got a minute?"

Reluctantly I faced the associate, now a senior nuisance,
for whom I had worked five years earlier. At that time he had
been a rookie, which made it easier for me to deal with the
sweaty, intrusive, annoyingly shrewd young nerd. Now he was
nearing partner.

"I didn't know you were here," Ocher said in a furtive way, his
magpie eyes darting away from direct contact, even as his physical
person moved about a foot closer to me than anyone other than a
lover should stand. "I can't find the Pending Motions binder in
the Goodall case. It's supposed to be in 2748."

I wasn't even on that case anymore, but I had once been
responsible for the relevant collection, and Ocher knew that I
knew where things wandered to when they weren't filed correctly.

"I need you to just take a quick look with me," Ocher said.
I followed him silently down the long hall, around another
corner and into a large storage room filled with shelves. In a
few minutes I found the binder; it was on an "active" shelf right
beside the clerical table, one of the obvious places to look.

Ocher flipped through the black, vinyl-clad volume, his
attitude somehow implying that I shouldn't leave yet. His thick
hair was dishwater brown and looked like a rug, even though it
wasn't. "This has never been indexed correctly," he told me,
for all the world as if it were a new thought. Too bad his fear of
the frugal sensibilities of his superior, Tolton, had stopped
him from ever authorizing the time necessary to redo the

collection. I waited in impotent silence, knowing any reply would only entangle me more deeply.

"I need copies of tabs 38 and 41," Ocher said, his face exhibiting a combination of embarrassment and sadistic delight clearly unintended by nature.

So do it yourself.

Tell somebody who cares.

I'm not on this fucking case anymore.

While I fought off those tempting replies, I glanced around the room, as if looking for an unmarked exit. But I was trapped. Every inch of this building was dangerous: take a step and you might be snared. Someone might appropriate another chunk of your life, detain you just a little longer in the corporate pen.

"I was on my way to the bathroom," I heard myself say to Ocher. The pudgy associate nodded vaguely, his mind back on his work now that it was clear his will was not going to be challenged.

"I'll be in my office," he said, and for an instant, his consciousness drifted back to me, and he fixed me with a direct look. I realized how lucky I was that this hadn't happened more often. It was like peering into the eyes of a hyena with a piece of lion in its jaws.

Ocher ambled out. I stood in the storage room, looking down at the binder. I knew this was a precarious moment for my already-teetering psyche.

Copying had its own delicate politics at SOB. Everyone did a fair amount of it, in the course of completing other tasks—even attorneys routinely lined up at the machines. But no one liked to be given someone else's copying to do; that was why there was a Duplicating Department. Even the lowliest clerks, whose job descriptions included this activity, sent most of their copying there. I was at the top paralegal rank, even higher than a Coordinator, and it was a gross insult for Ocher to hand me this task.

And it was an insult that Ocher *believed* in. I had it on good authority that he was one of the lawyers who called paralegals "paraplegics" behind their backs. Ocher really took for granted the Absolute Superiority of Attorneys. To obey him now, therefore, was tantamount to acquiescing in that belief. What made the moment worse was that Ocher had done this to me, in various forms, countless times before, and I had resolved that it would never happen again. When I had ceased to be assigned to any of his cases, I had thought my vow was safe.

Just do it and leave, I told myself. But I was shaking, from the coffee and the stress of my own project. I yanked the documents out of the binder and steamed down the hall. The local machine was on auto shut-off; it would take ten or fifteen minutes to warm up again. I hiked to the other end of the floor and found the main machine in the same state.

I took the stairs down to twenty-six: the first machine I came to, a big Canon housed in a tiny room, was up and running. I put my card key in the slot and typed in the endless codes needed to make the client pay for the smallest job. The first document was ninety pages long. I placed about half of it into the upper bin. It started to feed itself through, and cloned pages dropped onto the output tray. With a groan I saw that the print quality was too light. But the gauge was already set to darkest so there was nothing I could do; only qualified professionals were allowed to add toner.

Why do you keep telling me about your needs? That's what I should have said to him. My mind travelled to a nightmarish week I had once spent at a warehouse in Atlanta, crowned by a Sunday night when Ocher had left me to struggle for four hours with a defective microfilm reader while he and Tolton chuckled over their takeout espressos.

I looked down at the machine. It had stopped in mid-document. The display flashed green diagrams, indicating which doors I should look behind, in a computerized treasure hunt that might eventually lead to a jammed sheet of paper.

"Shit!" I screamed, and slammed my fist down on the plastic shoulder of the machine. A section of the top pulled loose and the display changed; now it read: JOB ABORTED. CONTACT SERVICE.

"No," I said. "I can't do this." I left the room, my neck pulsing. *Fuck it*, I thought; *fuck you, Ocher.*

I climbed the stairs to twenty-seven. In my office I gathered my stuff, then got on the phone. The message light was flashing, but I ignored it. I accessed Ocher's voicemail directly. In a monotone I addressed the silence: "Your job is on twenty-six. In the copying room. I have to go." Then I hit the stairs and went down three flights, then over to the elevators. The bell rang. The doors opened. Would it be Ocher or the Max Von Sydow of *Three Days of the Condor*? There was someone on the elevator—but it was just a tired maintenance person.

Waiting faithfully by the curb, its delicate face still reminding me of a fawn, was my VW Squareback. The air was cool and I had gotten away.

23

A perverse conception

THE PASADENA FREEWAY SUCKED ME INTO ITS STREAM
and I was almost too wired to perform a high-speed merge. But
I found a gap in the headlights, and we all hit the tunnel.

It was decision time. Straight ahead and go home, or veer
left onto the Golden State Freeway and go to Maggie's.

Things had been frosty between me and her since I had
gotten back to town two weeks earlier. But pretty soon the time
in Canada had begun to seem like a dream. I couldn't retain
the gist of it. And life in L.A. didn't make sense if we weren't a
couple. A hint of scorn rimmed her attitude but I just kept acting pleasant, like a doofus who didn't know any better. Work
didn't allow us much time together but we went for lunch one
day and things thawed. We'd gotten friendlier but we hadn't
gotten together.

And we still hadn't talked about what had happened in
Muskoka. The visit had become like a gap in our history, a sort
of missing week.

The left lane was jammed. At the last moment I lunged in
and made it onto the Golden State.

When I exited at Colorado, a big fat red moon sat over
Glendale. I picked my way through the glittering intersections

at Central and Brand, wondering how much harm I had just done with Ocher. Could I be fired for insubordination? I navigated onward through slightly rundown neighbourhoods to Maggie's block. Her apartment was half of a side-by-side duplex; it was stylish in a Spanish stucco way, with a dome above the doorway that looked vaguely Islamic to me.

I paused on the doorstep. There was light coming through the strawberry curtains. I knocked, and Maggie opened the door.

She stepped outside. "I didn't know you were coming," she said. "Judith's here and we're not doing too well."

Judith was a friend whom she had mentioned, but never told me much about.

"I'm sorry, I should have called you," I said. "I was afraid to stay in the office another minute."

"No, I'm glad you're here," she said. "Come in and just be you. It'll distract her." She looked me over. "Are you alright? What happened?"

"I'm in free fall at work. Plus I got into it with Ocher and may have really screwed up."

She looked at me, assessing the damage. "Ocher is an asshole," she said. "Come in and have a beer."

I went into her front room and claimed the far end of the couch. She went to the kitchen. When she came back her friend was with her.

Judith was tall and willowy, in black pants and a silk shirt. Her dark blonde hair was tied back; her eyes were penetrating behind wire-rimmed glasses. In a bygone way, she was quite stunning. I seemed to remember that she was a high school teacher.

She sat down at the other end of the couch as Maggie handed me a beer and performed the introductions.

"You look more primitive than I imagined," Judith said.

"I'm sorry, I'm a mess," I said.

"Well, your shirt does have a stain on it." When she smiled her face had sweetness.

"That's true but my real problem is internal," I said.

"Explain, please."

"I'm feeling beaten up by my job. I went in to work today, though it's Saturday; I was getting nowhere so I stayed and got nowhere for five more hours." I related how the Plandor case was playing into my area of greatest weakness: facts. She laughed and said that sounded awful. Then I told them the story of my encounter with Ocher. I managed to slow down and snag the details: Ocher's repulsiveness came through and so did the ignominy of being outranked. Both women laughed and I started to relax.

"You were an academic, weren't you?" Judith said. "What are you doing in a clerical job?"

"It's a long story," I said.

I sipped my beer, feeling some kind of immunity steal over me. I could recall a life in which SOB didn't matter, when offices were for jerks and I had only snobbish feelings towards attorneys, with the possible exception of my father. A time before I was felled by the songwriting virus, when my ego breathed much more exalted air than it had lately. When I was the brilliant grad student confident in my own cerebral prowess. I should be that way again. I could be. The room was full of candles; the antique lamp added a rosy hue. Maggie was snug in the overstuffed chair, watching us like a play.

"Now do I have this correct?" Judith said. "It was your book that Maggie threw into the lake?"

"Not exactly," I said. "It slid in."

"And it was Virginia Woolf? Which one?"

"*To the Lighthouse*."

"Oh, well, at least she chose a good one to dunk," Judith said. Her eyes glinted like swords.

"Why do you say that?"

"Woolf overreached herself with that book. It was a noble failure."

"I liked it. I wrote a thesis about it."

"Did you. Doctoral?"

"No, undergrad. I thought it was the book where she hit her mark."

"Of course," Judith said. "That used to be the received wisdom. But I think it's clear now, the woman was the Woody Allen of her time. A natural humorist, able to skewer the pretentious and the phoney. But when she tried for the mystical, she got too serious, couldn't pull it off."

"By what authority do you say that?" I said.

Maggie watched avidly.

"Do I need an authority?" Judith set her hands on her knees and her blue eyes probed me. "Would a PhD in Women's Studies help at all?"

"Apparently in this case it didn't," I said.

"Judith teaches at USC," Maggie said. "You may be out-ranked again."

"Touché," I said. I took a big slug of the beer. "Do you teach Woolf?"

"She is one of the feminist writers that I discuss. Again, she is great in *Orlando*, and in her satirical essays—that's the real Virginia. She really only hit her stride when she was skewering the male establishment. I think she basically hated men."

"What about Leonard?" I said.

"Oh, he was the exception that proved the rule. Look what she chose in a husband. A man she was unable to have sex with— and he accepted that. A man who would be the first reader of all her books—and he loved them. A man who would run a printing press with her—so she could always get published. A caretaker, a companion. No wonder she loved him."

"She didn't seem to hate Mr. Ramsay," Maggie said.

I was surprised. She had that exactly right. Mr. and Mrs. Ramsay were the central characters of *To the Lighthouse*; they were known to be modelled on Woolf's own parents;

and, if anything, the novel was an elegy to the magic of their marriage.

"She vilified him," Judith said. "The beak of brass, the fatal sterility of the male plunging into the female fountain."

"That's not how it read to me," Maggie said. "She was mocking the male, you're right about that, but it was *gentle* mockery. She seemed to back Mrs. Ramsay in what she felt about her husband."

"Which was?"

"She adored him. She worshipped him. She totally saw through him but it made no difference."

"That is sentimental," Judith said.

"No it isn't," I said. "Sentimental is when you cook the books in favour of the emotion you want."

Judith sank back, shaking her head. Although she had seemed arrogant a moment before, she now just looked absent-minded and at sea. I liked her academic backbone, her feistiness; and I liked her lock of hair that had come loose. She was very cute. I wondered if she was gay.

I decided to throw her a crumb. "You were right about Woody Allen," I said.

"Well of course that's the cliché. *Interiors*—a disaster. *Annie Hall*—a triumph," Judith said. "But the real test is *Hannah and her Sisters*."

"Slow down, what are you saying about *Hannah and her Sisters*?" Maggie said.

"A mediocre hodgepodge," Judith said. "Bland as milk. Commits the ultimate sin: it bores us."

I wanted to laugh, but I didn't. Maggie and I had once talked about the film and I had given a similar opinion and had upset her.

"I think it was a warm, complex movie," I said. "And the best parts were the serious parts. The only thing that weakened it was his attempt to import the old Woody Allen character." I glanced at Maggie and her smile took my breath away.

"That is a perverse conception," Judith said.

"I apologize."

"And does Woody Allen hate men, too?" Maggie said.

"Not so far-fetched," Judith said. "We should take a hard look at that. Another time. I have to go."

Maggie sat next to me on the couch. "Sometimes Judith drives me crazy," she said. "We had a fight before you got here."

"What about?"

"She said you weren't good enough for me."

We both laughed.

"She hadn't even met me," I said.

"I made the mistake of telling her about our trip. She's smart. But she's twisted."

"I liked her though. She reminded me of Alice in Wonderland."

"I was afraid you would like her. That's why I kept you away from her."

She leaned against me and I put my arm around her.

"You seemed to know a lot about *To the Lighthouse*," I said.

"You know, I had a passage I wanted to read to you. That's why I brought it in the canoe."

I thought that over. "What did I do up there?" I said.

"It's funny, I couldn't figure it out until I was telling my parents about it. Then I sort of did."

"Tell me. Everything. I need a story."

She laughed. "Where do I start? They live in a new suburb, outside of town. Pretty sterile."

"This is outside Columbus."

"Right. My favourite aunts live in the city, my mother's sisters."

I might be bad at facts, but I knew this stuff. When Maggie was nine, her mother Adriana had caught her father cheating, and a divorce ensued. The father went out of the picture.

Adriana's parents were from Italy, and her sisters were the wonderful aunts. Maggie loved the whole clan. But her mom got remarried to Darrell, a doubtful sort of guy, and the family moved to Burbank in 1967. Then a year ago her parents had moved back to Ohio.

"Anyway, my Aunt Sally and Uncle Frank came over to visit. She's my favourite."

"Did she have Bijou with her?"

"Yes! Only this Bijou was black. The one that used to steal my panties was white. He died."

"But they've all been poodles?"

"Correct. All three of them. Anyway, Adriana tried to make me change into a dress before they came. I had on designer jeans and a beautiful blouse! Then when Sally and Frank got there, they're making a big fuss about me and Adriana immediately tries to apologize for my being too fat."

"Jeez . . ."

"She weighs, like, one hundred and ten. Eats as much as she wants. Aunt Sally said Adriana was nuts, that I was Ava Gardner. She said she wanted to eat me."

"Smart woman."

"Anyway, we had a good visit and Sally wanted to hear about L.A., but my stepdad told her she should be asking about this lawyer from Toronto whose family I had been visiting."

"What?"

"Darrell likes to exaggerate. Both of them basically want something to boast about—that's my function."

"So, did you go along?"

"Of course not. I told Sally you were just a paralegal, and then I told them about the cottage. Sally asked if your family had adored me and I said no, they didn't even like me, I was too American, I used swear words."

I laughed.

She went on. "I told them about the terrible cabin, the

spiders and the chamber pot. I got big laughs, we had fun. After they left, Adriana actually tried to give me grief for revealing that you and I were sleeping together. She is amazing.

"But then comes the weird part. They were asking me about you. About our intentions. When were we going to get married, and so on. I'm usually flippant with them when they grill me, but I got sincere. I told them I didn't know how promising things had been. I said you were moody and volatile."

"Oh no."

"It's okay; Adriana said, 'I see, he's smart, creative, and emotional. So he's perfect for you.'"

"Good for her!"

"Then I started talking about what really happened in Muskoka."

"Okay," I said.

"I said I seemed to keep raining on your parade. Darrell asked me why. I actually liked him at that moment. I said you went there with an agenda, and I wasn't very kind to it. I said you were looking for your past. But I was just being in a place."

"I don't know what I was trying to do," I said. "It was like, 'Let's go back to our favourite spot and not have access to it!'"

"But you did, you got there. No thanks to me."

"I don't know where I got," I said.

We had turned to face each other and her eyes were without guard or cover. I kissed her. It was the first time since we'd been in Canada.

"You know, Musk," she said, "that week, if you didn't compare it to anything else . . ."

We began to unbutton each other's clothes.

24

Hollandaise

"IT'S TV TIME." LAINE'S VOICE.

George comes to on the couch. The clock says 2:41 a.m. Laine goes to put a videotape in and Graham stops her because there's a movie already in progress.

"This is Frank. I don't even own it," Graham says.

Some soldiers are on a train.

"He's a German in this one," Laine says.

"No, he's *pretending* to be German," Graham says. "He's actually an American colonel. They have to get the train to Switzerland. This is *très* cool."

Sinatra and his buddies look at a map and light cigarettes.

"That's what we need," Laine says. She opens a cake tin full of paraphernalia, from which she takes a joint and a lighter and hands them to Graham.

He tokes, then he talks while inhaling. "It's homegrown," he says. "Mellow stuff." He hands it to Laine, who takes a long drag.

"Have you done this ever?" Laine asks George.

George saw Adam Riswick's brother do it once, but didn't have any. "A few times," he says.

Laine gives it to him and he breathes through it and coughs.

"I can tell," she says.

She turns George's face towards her and props the joint between his lips. "Rookie method," she says. "Open your lips but still hold the J." She has hold of his ears like handles. "Now breathe through it and around it at the same time." George tries and the joint falls on the couch between his legs.

Laine picks it up and gives a low-pitched laugh. "Maybe you should hold it in your fingers."

He tries again and he gets some. It's hot on the back of his mouth, not too hot. "Hold it in," she says.

He does this a couple more times and they pass it back and forth. There's no real effect, other than a dingy taste in his mouth and a slight tickle in his eyeballs.

"Lose the lamp, Graham," Laine says.

They swig on cold beers. The movie becomes more and more gripping. There's a scene where the train is stopped in a Nazi station. An SS officer comes on board, wanting to buy Frank's watch. He's talking German to him and Frank can't reply because he doesn't speak German. The Nazi offers Frank some cigarettes as payment. Frank just stares at him. The suspense is unbearable. Laine is yelling, "Sell it, sell it!" She clutches George's arm. George's brain can see each of Laine's fingers, long fingers with nice red nails, wrapped around his bicep that feels like oak.

"He's *playing* the guy," Graham says from his recliner. "If he doesn't give in too fast, the guy doesn't know he's scared." Sure enough, Frank waits till the German officer ups the ante with nylon stockings. Then he lets him have the watch.

Laine curls up like a cat against George, with one leg over his and an arm tucked in behind him. Her body moulds to his, while her head turns sideways to watch the movie. George feels as if no rules apply to him. At the same time he feels like he should throw a bone to Graham. This isn't totally fair.

"Hey Doole, how many times have you seen this?"

"Once," Graham says.

"Are you gonna tell everything before it happens?"

"If you want me to."

George laughs, and the sound of his laugh strikes him as funny. He laughs once more and that is even funnier. Laine smiles at him in the TV light.

"I wasn't *that* humorous," Graham says.

"I want you to tell me everything *after* it happens," George says. "You can be John Madden."

"Okay, the train just stopped and everybody got out. I think it's because they know we're sick of the inside. Now shut up, I'm busy over here."

George has another fit of laughter and then settles against Laine. He has one arm around her shoulders. His other hand is awesomely free. Sometimes he holds her hand, sometimes he just rests his hand on her legs, which are still the legs he saw in the bathing suit. Only now they're under a long T-shirt, only it rode up above where George's hand is. The whole time he can feel her chest pressing against his ribs.

"I think I'm high," George says to Laine. He tries to adjust his jeans, which are having an overcrowding problem. She reaches down to undo the button.

"Is that better?" she says.

"Oh man," George says.

"We're going down to the river. We have to see the sunrise." It's Laine's voice.

"Cool." George tries to realize where he is. The TV is off. The windows are starting to get lighter. He has a quilt over him, and can vaguely remember lying under it with Laine. He stands and pulls up his jeans, feeling sticky in there.

They go outside on the terrace. It's chilly. The lawn slopes down into mist.

They carry blankets down the wet grass to the woods. A path

leads them through to the riverbank. There's a floating dock and they sit down on it.

"When is dawn?" George says.

"Oh gee, I forgot to consult the schedule," Graham says.

They pass a beer around. "Is anybody else still stoned?" Laine says. "This isn't the mellow stuff. Carl is full of shit."

You can see a very faint pink glow across the river, above a bare hill.

"I think we're too early," Laine says. "You guys, keep me warm."

The three of them lie on a blanket and pull another one over them. This time Graham gets to share Laine.

You can hear some bird saying "luckily" over and over again. You can feel the river underneath you, on its way to Lake Erie.

"You guys," George says. He wants to make a speech, say how different this has been. "If I had went to Tim's I don't hear any," George says.

One of the most fun things you can do is to lie on the bottom of a canoe. I did it once in the daytime. I had my life preserver on, and my mom was in the canoe. It's way more dangerous at night, like this. It's like having no sense of balance. The stars don't tell you when you're tipping and when you're not, so you feel like you're tipping all the time.

Meanwhile something is going by.

I see yellow light. Maybe the moon dropped into the lake. Correction: last time I checked, the moon didn't have a piano player.

I pull myself up on the seat. The night is crazed, big waves everywhere. Maybe ten feet away from me, lit up like a cake, is a steamship. As it slides past, I can see coal-oil lamps on the promenade deck and through the windows. Sparks spray from the smokestack. The boat has a huge paddle wheel with the name WENONAH on it.

Now the rear deck is passing me. There are a few people up there. An old man with a captain's hat on, a woman holding a baby, a man beside her in a dark jacket.

The big boat lurches against something, and the woman drops the baby. It falls into the churning wake.

Before I can react, the old man hops over the rail and swan dives. His hat flies off as he hits the water. I don't believe it, he came up with the kid in his arms. So far he's able to hold it above the surface. His white moustache moves in the waves.

On the boat they all scream and shout. A bell rings and a voice yells "FULL REVERSE!" But the steamer is still going away. The man on the deck stares down at the water, like he's wondering whether to dive in. Finally the ship begins to creep back this way. The old man in the water seems to sputter, and then he disappears. The baby is a fighter though; it's on the surface wiggling its arms. But then it's gone too.

The man in the dark jacket waits at the railing, until he's right over the place where they sank. Then he does jump into the water and flails around. More shouting from the boat: "FULL FORWARD!" they're saying. Too late, the big steamship goes right over the guy. I grab a paddle because now *I'm* in its path. I dig like crazy and get out of the shiny froth and into the dark.

When I look back I can't see the steamer anymore.

Only whitecaps like exploding stars. Water comes over my gunwales. The wind is on me. If I don't keep the bow aimed at the waves, I'll be swamped.

An arm comes out of the water and grabs the canoe. Instantly I have to lean out the other way to keep it level. Now the swimmer comes up and hoists himself over the gunwale. He has a seaweed hat and a huge grin. His mouth forms words but no sound comes out. The words are, "Hi, George."

It is Uncle Dave.

For a moment we're suspended. His weight on one side, and mine stretched out on the other.

Then he lets go.

George springs up on the blanket with his heart flapping in his chest and Uncle Dave's face beating like a strobe.

I just yelled, he says to himself, *I yelled and that broke me out of it.* Where is he now? What day is it?

The river lopes by, a cloudy sky hangs overhead. Then he gets some images. Laine's bare legs, his hand on them in the TV light. The feel of her against him. He has got himself into a new game. Fairly sure it's Sunday and wondering what time it is, he struggles to his feet. His head feels like a broken bell.

What, were they just going to leave me here all day? He picks up the blankets and trudges through the evergreens. Coming towards him down the lawn, wearing tennis whites, is Laine.

"Here, Stone." She hands him a tall glass of orange juice. "It's brunch time. You look like you got some sun."

"I don't know," George says, examining the woolly sky.

On the terrace there's a round table set for four. George downs the delicious juice and a glass of ice water. In the driveway Graham is helping a lanky blond guy carry bags from a vintage Oldsmobile to an apartment above the garage.

Then they come to the table. The blond guy is unbelievably skinny and has long hair, hollow cheeks, and a horsy mouth. He looks like a first try at Tom Petty. They left the forehead too high, didn't cut the nose down to scale. He has a deep raspy voice when he says, "Laine, I brought this back for you." He reaches into a wooden bucket and pulls out a fat blue fish with whiskers.

"I hate catfish!" Laine screams and she jumps up to get away from the dude. Over by the railing she yells, "Keep it away from me!"

"Okay, okay," the guy says. "We'll find another victim." He

puts the fish back in the bucket. "How 'bout you, kid, do you like catfish?"

"They're okay," George says. "They fight about as much as an old boot."

The guy laughs appreciatively. "You sound like a cottage man," he says.

"I am."

"Where's your place?"

"It was on Lake Muskoka. It's history now."

"No shit."

Laine returns to the table and says, "Carl, go and wash your hands. You're not passing Chelsea buns to me with catfish goop on them."

"What if it isn't catfish," Carl says.

"Wash. You just touched a fish!"

"Okay. I have something else for you anyway."

They sip drinks. Graham is hunched over a cup of coffee, looking like he's still asleep.

Carl comes back with a brown paper bag and Laine opens it. It's a necklace, made from leather and beads and blue stones. "That is awesome," Laine breathes. She kisses Carl's forehead.

"It's Indian. A local guy makes them. Traditional . . . or not. I don't know. He's an artist."

"Where were you?" George says.

"By the way, this is George. He's a video hero," Laine says.

"I'm honoured," Carl says. His grizzled voice makes it sound sarcastic and friendly at the same time. He looks like a wino, but his deep-set eyes are smart.

"I was up by Bala," Carl says. "My buddy has a boat on the Moon."

"That's too bad," Graham says. "Must be tough to get to." Apparently he's awake after all.

Carl laughs. Marla comes out with a big tray and unloads fancy egg things.

"Thank god," Laine says. "Real Hollandaise. We had some in Toronto and it was like yellow glue."

The eggs are fabulous, on crispy English muffins with back bacon. The sauce tastes like lemon.

"Marla, a Sleeman, por favor," Carl says. "What's Jamaican for por favor?"

"Jamaican is get your own Sleeman," Marla says.

"She doesn't mean that." Carl's smile makes you think you have your fly down and only he knows about it. "What was I saying, the Moon River, kid. You're a Muskoka type. I am going to give you a fish from the Moon River. You know what to do. Keep it alive till you're ready to cook it."

He seems to be away for a moment. Then he takes a swig of the beer Laine brought him. "You're okay, considering you're a friend of Laine's. I want you to eat it with, you know, your loved ones. Do you have loved ones?"

George thinks about that.

"Yeah, I do," he says.

25

Butterflies

I WAS IN THE SOB PARKING LOT. I HAD COME TO GET MY card key, which I'd forgotten. The lot was not well lit and worse than that, all the vehicles in it were pink. Limos, pickups, compacts, Jags; all were different shades of pink. Was that my VW Squareback? It was pink too. The backseat was a mess; there were beer cans and old newspapers on the floor, like mine. The stereo was torn out of the dash, so it *was* my car. On the front passenger seat I saw my key card. Okay, we can proceed.

I needed to go back up to my office where the big project was waiting; I was losing time. I paced through the parking lot. Weren't there elevators anywhere? Wasn't there a ramp where cars ascend to the street? I tried a door; the stairs led *down*. Nothing went up.

This was bad news. I decided to take the stairs anyway; maybe they went *somewhere*. The door swung shut behind me, making total darkness. I tried it: it was locked. No, I whispered. No, I've got to get back to work.

The stairs went down but there were no doors. There was water at my feet. Something scrabbled past me along the wall. I could hear claws scratching. Now I couldn't even get back to my car.

What was that rat doing? Why was it scratching there? You can't scratch through cement. I felt tears of discouragement on my face; then discouragement turned to anger at the infernal scratching.

"Don't bother," I yelled, and I sat up and I was in bed in Pasadena. The neighbours' neurotic dog was scratching at the fence again, next to my window. It was 10:30 on Sunday morning.

I had left Maggie's at two A.M. because I couldn't sleep. I wanted to be in good shape for today.

Eight hours at SOB would arm me for the week ahead. So there was plenty of time. I showered, got dressed, and ate some so-called Canadian bacon with a fried egg. The *L.A. Times* had a study of presidential candidate George Bush's involvement in Iran-Contra. Selling arms to a terrorist nation, then not remembering that you had, that was a good trick. The calendar section featured the ever-resurgent Neil Young. This had to bode well for my own music, since I was younger than Neil. Slightly younger.

When the food was gone I set out on an energizing walk.

It was a crisp, sunny day, the kind the rest of the world identified with Pasadena. My steps carried me quickly across to Hill, then down to Colorado. It had car dealerships, small offices, industrial buildings. And a few forgotten hotels.

If I didn't have to go to SOB, I thought, *I would stay home and work on "Seaweed Mind."* I had listened to it before going to Canada. Maggie's presence had done the trick. The vocal lived; that was why I had given a copy of it to George. I was finally getting somewhere. I wanted to add a synth part on my Juno 106. In my head I was hearing a possible counter-melody that might work as a cello line.

A horn beeped and beeped again. I turned and there was a big black car, making a U to reach my side of the street. It was Maggie's battle-scarred Chevrolet; she was gesturing to me.

"Get in," she said.

I did.

"Dave," she said, and seemed to consider several alternatives. "Dave, he isn't dead. He's had a stroke but he's still alive and it was serious but they don't know how serious yet. Your dad." She squeezed one of her hands in the other. "I'm sorry," she said. "I'm so sorry."

"Ah, jeez," I said.

It had to happen sometime. Irene had been fearing it for years. And now it came. Not a heart attack, though; a stroke. People came through strokes. Joseph was still in his seventies.

I looked at Maggie. "You're funny," I said. "He's not dead, Dave." A few tears wandered onto my cheeks.

"Didn't you call me?" I said.

"I did. It just kept ringing. Susan couldn't reach you either. So she got my number from information."

"Fuck, I turned my ringer off last night."

"You bozo."

"What did Susan say?" I asked her. We were sitting in the driveway of a video repair shop. She shut her motor off.

"Just that he had the stroke, last night I guess. Susan and Ed were in Toronto so your brother went over to help. Susan didn't even know until this morning. He's in the hospital, in intensive care. It sounds pretty bad. She said they'll know more tomorrow."

"I'll have to go back." I felt butterflies in my stomach: Calvan, airports, planes. Also a strange relief; something other than Murry Barr's project to deal with. A bell was tolling for Joseph. People broke down; they could be had. More tears ambled down my face.

Maggie scrutinized me. "Do you want to go back to your place?"

"Okay," I said. "I better call her."

Susan had pieced the facts together. It had happened last night, in the middle of the night. Irene woke up and found Joseph on the floor; he'd been there a while, trying to get up without waking her. He couldn't move his left arm or leg. He had tried to get out of bed and had just crumpled. Irene had called my brother Greg. He and Doreen went over and they ended up at the hospital all night. Susan and Ed had been in Toronto; this morning Greg got their info and called them home.

"How is Mother?" I said.

"Not good. She can't seem to handle visiting him."

"What is he like?"

"He's drugged. Very drugged. They've got him heavily sedated so he won't hurt himself. He kept trying to get up and walk out. Got mad at the nurses. Now he's too groggy for us to tell anything."

"What are the doctors saying?"

"They say it was not a minor stroke. They say they don't know if the bleeding has stopped."

"The bleeding? I don't even know what a stroke really is."

"Some blood vessels broke in his brain. And the blood spreads, and that's what causes the damage. But if the bleeding stops, that's good. If not it can keep spreading. They say they're going to do a CAT scan tomorrow, then they'll know more." She paused; I heard the line hum.

"One good thing," she said. "The stroke was on the right side, so his verbal side is still okay. He'll be able to talk."

Look what suddenly passed for good news. *He would be able to talk.* I pictured the insidious spread of the blood, the vessel walls breached, the blight extending itself even now. I wanted to be there, to lobby for Joe. Why weren't they doing the CAT scan today? Why couldn't they stop the flow before it destroyed him? I was mighty with useless adrenaline.

"How are the kids?" I said.

"Alicia is okay. She asked a few questions, but she seemed satisfied when she got the answers. George doesn't even know."

"He doesn't know?"

"He's away for the weekend. Poor kid, he was just coming around a bit. This is all he needs. He'll be back today."

"So, should I come?"

"God," Susan said, "I don't know what to tell you. They say he may improve, and be out of danger. Then it could be a long haul. We might need you more then. Or he could get worse; then you'd want to be here. We'll know more tomorrow."

"It's okay," I told her. I was planted in a kitchen chair, and Maggie was standing against the counter, watching intently. I was visited by an odd sense of health and competence—we the younger had this "living" thing down cold. "Keep me posted. I'll decide tomorrow."

Susan was saying goodbye and I tried to send over the line the emotion I felt for her. At this moment it would have been much better if we were a family who said "I love you" out loud, like on TV. But we weren't.

I said, "I'll talk to you soon."

I got up and went to the kitchen window. My Squareback sat in the driveway beside the verdant bougainvillea. I pulled Maggie over to me. We looked into each other's eyes.

"My . . . daddy's . . . dead," I sang. I was adapting an old John Lennon song, from the first, stripped-down solo album.

It was the same tune as "Three Blind Mice."

"No . . . he's . . . not," she sang.

We held on for a minute or two.

"I've got to go to work today," I said, "especially if I'm going to Calvan."

"No! You can't!"

"Hon, I have to. I've got to at least make a plan. Or the whole project could go down the toilet."

"Let it," she said, then saw the look in my eye. "Okay, I'm driving you. And you're coming to my place for dinner."

We were about to go out the door.

"And turn that fucking phone on," she said.

BOOK THREE

The Resistance

26

A yearbook photo

LARRY SHRIFT, A PARALEGAL "COORDINATOR", WAS IN my office on Monday morning.

I had put my father's plight out of my mind on Sunday to grapple with the Plandor project and thought I had found a way to structure it. It was slightly complicated but it might actually work. Now the first setback in my plan had appeared: my boss, Murry Barr, was out of town and wouldn't return until sometime tomorrow. I, of course, might not even be here tomorrow. I was ready to leave at the first signal from Susan, but was still hoping to put the ship on course first.

I had yet to talk to Barr in person about the project. It had come to me by voicemail in his vague style: land the troops and then we'll see what we want to do next. I had a plan now, but I also had questions, and I really needed a session with Barr to get him to focus on both.

As a precautionary measure, though, I was trying to explain my thoughts to Larry Shrift, who might have to carry the ball. Litigation Coordinator was the second highest rank we underlings could achieve (I was a Case Manager, the highest), and I could not figure out how Shrift had attained it. He was already off to a good start at annoying me. His most delightful habit

was to lean back with a rakish, "yeah, I'm all over it" attitude
before you'd finished expressing your thought.

In spite of his self-image, the guy's exterior was anything
but rakish. Rotund was more like it, a short rotund body sup-
porting a large shiny head, across the top of which thin black
hairs were combed. A face that fell a few fateful inches short of
attractiveness. The meagrely lashed eyes with just a hint of
bulginess, the horsy teeth that complemented a gently receding
chin, lots of cheek structure unsupported by any noticeable
bone; and in the middle, wasted on this scrubby plot of flesh,
a perfectly formed, nobly jutting nose.

Shrift was doing his number now, bonding erotically with
the acoustic tiles above my head. "I get it," he said. "Pollution
has to be in a policy year. Like the Moffel site. Plandor stopped
dumping in 1932. But the policies didn't start till the 40s so
there's no need to look at that site. Even though it is worth one
hundred million. I like it."

I desperately needed to take a shit. "That's not exactly what
I'm saying," I said. "Just because the dumping ended doesn't
mean the pollution ended." I wanted to build on this point,
but first I wanted to know that Shrift had absorbed it. So I
stopped dead. This eventually had the effect of pulling him
back to reality, or at least back to me.

"Dumping isn't pollution," Shrift said, trying to para-
phrase words that had never had a chance against his own interior monologue. Then, realizing the absurdity of what he had
just said, he added, "Why isn't it?"

"Larry. Of course dumping is pollution. I'm saying that
when the dumping ends, the pollution may just be getting
started. It may be spreading. The *damage* may be later."

"Okay, let's not beat this one to death," Shrift said.

I was longing to add another ingredient to the mix, but it
was almost impossible to get Shrift to focus on any thought that
was not bubbling up from his own well. I wanted to tell him

that Plandor hadn't bought insurance for their *own* property, so you had to ask if they owned the site, or just supplied it. There were really three questions, and if I could have injected them somehow into Shrift's brain, I would have. Whose property was being cleaned up; when did the chemicals reach that property; and which policies were around then?

I needed to raise these topics with Murry Barr too, because it was becoming increasingly clear to me that these were not easy questions to answer. There were tricky cases, and Barr would need to make executive decisions about how to treat them. Talking to Shrift was a good rehearsal for talking to Barr. Barr, unlike Shrift, got your initial point, but he wouldn't let you add to it because of his compulsion to resolve things right away. So the result was about the same.

"I've gotta go," Shrift said. "The Jauniss site is a mess. I need to go through some new material and try to nail down the perps."

I knew this meant Potentially Responsible Parties, and that's about all I knew about EPA studies. It didn't matter anyway, because if my team couldn't ask the right questions, all their facts would be useless. My optimism was gone.

Shrift exited and I followed him along the wall, and then cut in to the bathroom. Unfortunately Roger Lloyd was a step behind me. The sober, imposing partner, who had been my boss during my halcyon years, established himself in the palatial, suitable-for-handicapped middle booth, while I took the one on the right.

Why anyone would *prefer* to have a crap with other men sitting on each side of him was beyond me, but it was a reliable rule with Lloyd, as was his uncanny ability to arrive in the can exactly when I did. I could hear him ruffling his newspaper, getting it folded exactly right; then came the satisfied sounds of a successful bombing mission. I was unable not to attend to these diversions. And I was equally unable to make any such sounds while Lloyd was in the next booth.

If it had been Shrift, I probably could have; but Lloyd out-ranked me.

Finally he concluded his operations and marched out of the booth, seemingly still unaware of the silent vigil taking place beside him. This was the most puzzling part: wasn't he at all curious as to what had happened to the person who got there at the same time he did? Would a death in the next toilet have attracted his notice?

Back in my office, I found a message from my sister.

"He had a very bad night," she told me when I called her back. "He basically had screaming fits and fell out of bed twice. He doesn't seem to understand that he can't walk. They've had him strapped down but he's so determined that he breaks loose. I guess they had reduced the tranquillizers to see how he'd do, but they've cancelled that. And we've got the CAT scan results."

She went silent. Through the long distance murmur I heard a faint sound of forcible inhalation, and realized that she was crying. I couldn't think of anything to say.

"He's still bleeding," she said after a while. "It hasn't stopped." There was more silence, and the good heart that beat under my sister's unstinting will was speaking to me loud and clear. The sense of a losing battle, of the tide turned against Joseph, was unmistakable.

"They don't know how much longer he's going to last," she sobbed, and I was seeing the little sister whose photo, cut out from a yearbook montage, I had carried in my wallet for years: the bonny, life-embracing smile of the beautiful fifteen-year-old looking back over her shoulder in the high school hallway with the white blouse and the plaid skirt and the textbooks pressed to her chest.

"And he's screaming?" was all I could say, as if this were the highlight of her tale.

"Yeah. He seems to think everybody's against him. The doctors, the nurses, even us—we've all ganged up on him."

I was feeling a kind of "this isn't over yet" determination. I couldn't really fathom my father's screaming; I took it as a brain malfunction, sort of like an epileptic fit. What I saw clearly was the leaking blood. It could still slow down; it could still stop. What did the doctors know? They were trained to see the worst.

"Where are you?" I said.

"I'm at Mother's."

That sounded strange: did she think my dad was never returning? "I'm going to get on the red-eye tonight and be there by morning," I said.

"I think you should," she said wearily. "Tell me when and I'll meet you at the airport."

"No, I'll take the Cal Van."

Maggie walked into my office and stood by my desk. I told her what Susan had said. Again, I seemed to highlight the wrong point. "He's misbehaving, acting up very badly," I said.

Maggie got a fierce look in her eyes and they filled with tears. "He's fighting it!" she said. "He still wants to live. That's why he's kicking and screaming." She subsided into a chair.

She had grasped my father's struggle better than I had. "You're right," I said softly. "He won't go gently into that good night."

"He's scared," she said. "That's why he has to put up a lot of bluster." She wiped her eyes. "He's afraid of it because it isn't a good night."

27

The thirsty man

EVEN ON A RED-EYE I LOVED FLYING, BECAUSE IT WAS AN intermission from reality. You found yourself a paperback in the airport shop—most of them seemed to be about serial killers—and you hunkered down with your Bloody Mary and your beer nuts and by the time you got to your destination you were thinking like a psychopath.

This time it was a biography of Ted Bundy, whose unbearable rage against a certain kind of oval-faced brunette was well documented by the author, a woman who apparently had been his close friend while they both worked at an all-night suicide line. I was utterly sucked in by the book, impaled on the fact that apparent normality was the first clue to the sociopath. An *imitation* of normality—so easy to do. I was chilled by the idea that I, too, might be one of those clever learners, men who duplicate the emotions they see around them, without really catching on to the moral underpinnings.

I raised the plastic shade and saw a thin line of yellow along the rim of the land. I put the book down, feeling the vodka, and slumped against the wall of the jet.

Announcements awakened me and I found that we were already in final approach to Toronto. I had the usual sense of privilege as I passed through Canadian Immigration. They couldn't stop me and they didn't want to stop me, for I had the credentials of birth, the insider status. I felt as if my link to the Moores of Calvan showed in the set of my shoulders, the cast of my eyes. It didn't matter where I had been or what I had done.

I walked down the long hallway at Terminal Two and found the intercity transportation.

"Are you looking for the Cal Van?" a male voice said.

"I am," I said, and turned to find a man with thinning grey hair, clear skin, and eyes as intelligent as I had ever known. We shook hands. A sense of refreshment flooded over me at the sight of my brother's smile, as if some genetic tonic was being IV'd into me. His goodwill was an account that all of my carelessness still hadn't depleted.

"Doreen is about to emerge from the women's can," Greg said.

"Holmes, how can you know these things?"

Greg giggled like a nine-year-old in an old army tent. "The question is not, how can I know them," he said.

"It is, how can you pass them off as hypotheses," I said.

Suddenly Doreen materialized beside us. "What are you two talking about?" she said.

She had the same healthy look as Greg. In spite of their demanding jobs in computer support, he still played hockey and she did yoga.

I hugged her. "I wasn't expecting this," I said.

"You're going to get a lot of surprises," Doreen said, and her face turned sad. The three of us formed a huddle, hands on one another's shoulders.

"God," I said. "This wasn't supposed to happen yet."

"It did though," Doreen said. "You'd better get ready. I don't know which is harder, him or her."

We collected the car and found our way out of the airport maze. Highway 401 rolled by, then Greg turned off and took a clever back route down country roads.

"So, how bad was it?" I asked from the back seat. "Saturday night."

"Bad," Doreen said. "The worst thing was, she hadn't been able to get him off the floor. She was beside herself. She brought us in and pointed to him like it was a crime scene."

"It's so ironic. Or the opposite of irony," I said. "This is exactly what she's been fearing, for what—five years now? I always thought that stopped bad things from happening."

"Ignorance is bliss," Doreen said. "Her only problem was that she knew."

"And it was all about her," Greg said. He glanced back at me, and it was as if a keel moved into place under my soul.

It was seven A.M. Along the road, chilly fall colours broke from the mist. The van passed woods and streams and lots of cornfields, like the ones Joe had walked in as a boy.

My sister opened the door of 15 Gamrie Drive, wearing a ragged old bathrobe. She rubbed her hand across her eyes. "How long have you been out here?" she said.

"I was trying to see if anyone was awake."

"I was," she said.

Irene appeared in the hall behind her, also in a bathrobe, looking better than Susan. "Oh dear, you must be exhausted," she said.

"Well, come in," Susan said.

Irene grabbed me as I lugged my suitcase in. She wrapped her arms around me and buried her face in my chest. "Oh Davy, I can't believe it has come to this." In her voice I heard a faint echo of her parents' family: the Scottish huddling together against the cold and damp.

"I can't either, Mum," I murmured to her, my nose caught in the stale, sweet scent of her hair.

We sipped orange juice in the kitchen. "Do you want to rest?" Susan said. "We were going to visit the hospital after lunch." I got the sense that getting Irene there was no easy task.

"No, I want to see him now."

Susan's eyes flashed a look of approval. "I have to make a quick stop at home," she said, "then I will meet you at the hospital."

"You're not going to go and visit him right now," Irene said. "I can't be ready. I have to have my bath." She started to weep. There were no tears. It made her look like a bad actress.

"Mother," I said. "You can go later, I'll take you."

She shrank into the stairway that led up to her bedroom, her eyes still clinging to me. Suddenly I got the feeling that she wanted to prevent my witnessing my father's state, because that would further stamp it as real. Maybe that's what her own visits did, too.

"I can't go now," she told us again, though no one was arguing. She went up the stairs and I looked at Susan. She shook her head.

"Have something to eat," she said. "Get yourself settled in. I'll meet you there. He's on the second floor. Room 235."

I made a piece of toast and sat at the dining-room table.

I took my suitcase down to the little guest room, opened it on the bed under the window, took out some shirts and hung them up.

I walked into the bathroom. Joseph's shaving kit was sitting by the sink. Like a faithful valet it awaited his return.

I stepped out of the elevator on the second floor of the General Hospital and headed down the hall. I slowed down by the door of 235, took a deep breath, and walked in.

There was an old man swaying in a big straight-backed chair in front of the window. He was wearing a hospital gown; his badly discoloured right arm was wobbling on the metal armrest; his head lolled forward and I could see the dishevelled

strands of his white hair across his scalp. I crouched down on
the floor and looked into his face.

The eyelids were at half-mast, as if in mourning for lost mus-
cle control. Whatever soul still lived within didn't seem to want
much light. The cheeks were stubbly, sallow, sunken. The mouth
was caved in; the chin was wet with drool. I was free to inspect him;
he had no idea that someone was with him in the room.

"Hi, Dad," I said.

The old man shifted dimly in his chair. His right eye
opened a little bit. His mouth emitted a sound.

"It's Dave," I said. And then, "I've come from California
to see you." I couldn't believe the inane jet-setting chirpiness
of my statement.

Joseph's whole torso was quivering with the effort of rais-
ing his head. Big cloth straps crossed his stomach, keeping him
in the chair. His arms looked as if someone had held a hot iron
to them. The back of his hand was a charred homestead.

"Alfona," the old man murmured. "Ou a a fie."

I couldn't believe that this ruin used to be my father. I
heard the formless sounds, but I wasn't really open to the idea
that they meant anything.

Joseph repeated the speech. I got it.

"That's right," I said. "There was a fire. In California. And
you called me to see if we were alright." It had happened in
May: a downtown high-rise had gone up in flames; it was on
the news everywhere. It had been one of my father's rare calls
to me. Not Irene, but Joseph, had dialled the phone, initiated
the conversation, asked if that was near where I worked. We had
strayed into small talk about the Dodgers which was pure fab-
rication on my side, but it had been a cheery exchange.

Looking at him now, I was not at all sure Joseph knew who
he was talking to, though he clearly associated California with
the fire.

"I'm so glad to see you," I told the old man. "You're doing

well—doing better." Joseph tried to respond. His right arm lifted off the chair and pointed to his left arm.

At this moment Susan suddenly emerged from the bathroom on my left. "LOOK WHO'S HERE, DAD. IT'S DAVE! HE'S COME TO SEE YOU, FROM LOS ANGELES. ISN'T THAT NICE?" I realized that by comparison my own tone had been a triumph of camaraderie.

"I'm trying to get his teeth in," she told me. "The nurse can't do it and I'm having trouble too: I don't know how moist to make the cement.

"DAD, I'M GOING TO TRY TO PUT YOUR TEETH IN," she yelled. His shaking formed into a nod and he lifted his head. He tried to open his mouth; the left side ignored his will. Susan managed to work the upper denture in, and tried to press it up against the gums. It held for a precious second and then dropped down onto his tongue.

"Damn, this is what happens," she told me. "I don't think this is the right cement." Then to Joseph: "WE'LL TRY IT AGAIN LATER, DAD. IT'S NOT WORKING RIGHT NOW." She combed his hair and she chattered to him.

"Eny," he said with his eyes as close to open as they'd been so far. "A nay I ca eye wie."

"That's right," Susan said, and she smiled at me. "Rennie is what you call your wife."

"And she'll be coming over today," I said.

Joseph looked in turn at each of us, and seemed to shake his head; I caught a note of commiseration in it. Then he said something else, and raised his mutilated right hand to his mouth.

"You're thirsty, that's right," Susan said. "Dave will get you a drink. I have to go, but I'll be back soon." She squeezed my arm and then she left, and I felt my night of travel hitting me.

"Where is the cup," I said. "Oh here it is, on the windowsill." Looking across the street at the simple stone house where we had lived when I was starting school, I said, "Now let's get you a drink." I brought it back from the bathroom.

Joseph tried to grip the styrofoam cup in his right hand and raise it towards his mouth, but the shake was too much and even with my steadying hand, he was unable to get it to the right spot. "Let me try," I said. I took the glass and tipped it over my father's lower lip; it was right there but the old man couldn't get it, couldn't take it. I put the cup down.

It was too clear that this wasn't Joseph any more. This man didn't know that his children knew the nickname of their mother; maybe he didn't know that we *were* his children.

But on the other side lay one priceless point. He had tried to explain "Rennie" to us. He had tried to tell us what we needed to know. He was still in the game.

I began to babble about anything at all. It was like a parody of the reports I had given my father all my life. They had all been somewhat false, slanted towards innocence, prosperity, and orthodoxy. This one needed to be the best yet.

"I've been working hard," I said. "Working at Sarronick, got a big project. We have a tight deadline. But we'll make it. We always do."

The old man mumbled something. I leaned over to hear. "What's that?" I said.

"I doan know why you tay in L.A.," the old man said.

That was on the money. I took a deep breath. "I don't either," I said.

At this point a young, fiercely alive, very good-looking nurse came into the room. "Hi Mr. Moore," she said. "How are you doing? Are you tired of sitting up in your chair?" To me she added, "We're sorry about the straps—even with them he managed to pull the chair over on himself."

Joseph said no to her question, and then added something of his own.

"You need a drink," the nurse said. She found his cup of

water, tipped it up to his mouth, and fearlessly poured some in. He swallowed violently and got it down, then had a little more.

"That's good," she said. "I'll be back in a bit to get you into your bed."

He said something to me. Something about his left arm; it felt like something.

I frowned, trying to guess. The old man kept trying. I heard water; then it seemed as if he said "like rain."

"Your arm feels like rain," I said.

Then he astonished me by trying to spell a word; the last four letters sound like "I-G-L-Y".

"That is bad," I said.

I took his right hand in mine.

"I'm so glad to see you," I told him again. The old man was rhythmically squeezing my hand. It was like a playful dance of affection. A wave of feeling seemed to be passing over him. It was almost flirtatious, a love fest held in a ruin. Gradually it came to an end.

The nurse came back and gave me a very gracious "you need to go" smile.

I went.

28

The shadow on the roof

ON WEDNESDAY MORNING I TRIED TO PERSUADE IRENE to go with me to the hospital. (She hadn't made it since I'd arrived.) She was still in her pink bathrobe, though the breakfast hour was well past. She had sipped her orange juice, stared at her All-Bran, and never even buttered her toast, which still sat in the metal slot. I hadn't been able to get her to talk, and she had turned off her beloved CBC Radio news when it was barely started.

Now she sat at the dining room table with her untouched cup of coffee. "Mum," I said, "when I saw him yesterday he really wasn't that bad. I could understand him."

"You could understand him." She turned her face to the table.

"Well, he didn't have his teeth in. But he was making sense. He even referred to you."

"He did?" she said.

"He said—it was to Sue and me—out of the blue he said, 'Rennie is my name for my wife.' We couldn't believe it."

Her big brown eyes stared at me, searching for the good news in that story. Her head dropped onto the blue placemat.

"I can't go today," she said.

I left her, feeling like a torturer who had finished his work.

On the hospital elevator I realized that I was scared too—scared of Joseph's dilapidation. That was what had kept me from returning the day before. I stood on the second floor until a nurse walked by and looked at me. That made me start moving down the hall.

Almost immediately I encountered an old guy in a wheelchair, whose posture had the seal of permanence on it. The toothless mouth was hanging open, the head was sticking out at a grotesque angle, and the eyes were staring upward as if there was news on the ceiling. It was not Joseph, just one of his brethren.

My momentum carried me past the old guy, past the nurses' station, past a gurney on which another open mouth was being wheeled to some helpful destination, and then, suddenly, I was face-to-face with yet another old man, out in the hall not twenty feet away, sitting on a wheelchair in a smart-looking navy bathrobe with hair combed, bifocals on, and an alert expression. I barely had time to take in the fact that it was my dad before I was targeted.

"I'm glad you and Susan are here," he said, "because now maybe we can get something done in this place." My sister came out of his room carrying his lower teeth, which she and Joseph proceeded to pop right in—no problem. The upper teeth were already in place; we now had the luxury of knowing every word he was saying. "Have you just come from being with Rennie?" he asked me.

"Yes, I'm staying with her. She'll be along later."

"Do you want to go back in your room?" Susan asked him.

"No," he said, in a way that acknowledged our good wishes. "I'm fine here in the hall." Then in a half-joking tone: "The room is somewhat of a prison."

Susan crouched in front of him, trying to get his left foot back on the footrest. I glanced down at what she was doing, and was shocked at what I saw.

"Wait a minute," I said. "You just moved your left leg."

Susan didn't seem surprised at all. "Oh yes, he can move his leg and wiggle his toes." She switched on her nurse voice: "DAD, CAN YOU WIGGLE YOUR TOES?"

And Joseph did just that. His magnificent toes proceeded to bend like little puppets. The comical nature of this accomplishment was utterly lost on father and daughter, and that seemed just fine to me, who wanted to dance down the hall.

"So, have these hospital people been giving you trouble?" I said.

My father smiled. "My wishes don't seem to carry a lot of weight around here," he said.

I went into the room and dialled my mother's number.

I told her, "I just wanted you to know that you're going to have your husband back."

"What do you mean?" she said, and I described the astonishing return to form.

"Tell Joe I'll be up this afternoon," she said. "Thank you, dear."

Out in the hall I found my older sister, Lorraine, and her husband, Boris, fresh from eastern Ontario, in the act of greeting Joseph. Lorraine made small talk with my father, and everyone tittered after each mundane exchange, like passengers in a plane that has just successfully crash-landed.

"I see you've got your navy dressing gown on," Lorraine said with her usual hint of theatricality. "It looks dashing."

"Well thank you," Joseph replied. "And you have a nice coat on."

"It is, isn't it," she laughed. "I don't know why I'm wearing it though." A short seminar was held on this topic, and everyone agreed that Lori's brushed microfiber trenchcoat was a fine garment, and that she should take it off in this hot hallway.

I was waiting for my doctor brother-in-law to take me aside and say something confidential; Boris could be counted on to do this within five minutes of getting together, and the style of it was unvarying. He had been a general practitioner in Cornwall for several decades now, and his distinctive soft-voiced, rapid-fire way of seeming to share a personal experience while imparting reassuring information had had time to mature like a fine wine. He captured me now in the shelter of one arm and drew me aside. The shrewd eyes behind the wire-rimmed glasses twinkled as the ruddy, unlined face fired out words that were almost inaudible. "I spoke to Dr. Cassler yesterday long-distance. He wasn't giving out any grounds for optimism. They can't in these cases. I really thought your father was not a good bet. I told Lori not to expect much. So this is a surprise."

"I saw him yesterday and I'm amazed," I said. My brother-in-law's collegial manner made me feel as if I was on the inside of the medical profession, looking out.

Boris' quiet torrent of words only escalated. "This is what happens though. I had a patient who stroked; looked so bad I told the family not to leave the hospital. The next day he was talking again; two months later he was walking. Or it can go the other way. But your father is bearing up. If he is stabilized now—and there's no way they can tell that he isn't until they watch him for a while—he could actually get home again."

"He's got his mind," I said.

"The motion on the left side—he may not get that back, not all of it," Boris said.

We returned to the others. Susan and Lorraine were plying Joseph with water and conversation. Everyone agreed that this would be a good moment to adjourn to the private room: all this socializing in the hall felt a bit flamboyant.

I had the honour of pushing the wheelchair. As we entered the doorway I said, "Dad, you've got a great view of the Narwood Bush." I was referring to a small forest across the street from the hospital, where a world-class mental sanatorium

had lurked for many decades, where Bing Crosby was rumoured
to have stayed, and where our neighbourhood tribe used to play.

"Some view," Joseph answered. "They'll probably incarcerate me in there."

We got him into a chair facing the window. Across the
street, two doors from the woods, was a stone house with yellow
shutters.

"Do you see, Dad," Lori said. "That's our old house,
number 206."

"I do see it," he said presently. "Now that black triangle on
the roof. Is that a shadow?"

We all looked. The roof was light grey, and the right side of
it did form a dark, triangular shadow.

"That's exactly right," I told him.

Lorraine asked Joseph how his breakfast was.

"It's hard to tell what breakfast is around here," he
answered, and everyone laughed.

Joseph then launched into a serious explanation of a problem that he was having with his chair. By now I was fighting a
tendency to float up towards the ceiling. It became an art of
great delicacy just to attend to my father's words and give
normal-sounding responses. It was like trying to water a flower
while high on dope—a tough job, but somebody had to do it.

"So the other chair had arms," Lori said.

"And you could hike yourself up," I said.

"And I could relieve this pain," Joseph said, and I looked
at Lori, because the old man's voice had just slipped down a
notch in energy and clarity, and she had noticed it too. He was
flagging.

"Now where was the pain?" I said. Joseph had tried to talk
about this yesterday, tried very hard.

"My arm, and my rear end," came the answer, in a weaker
voice. "They feel like cold water. A tingly pain."

"*Tingly*," I repeated. "That's what you told me yesterday."

"Need to take the weight off it," Joseph murmured. His arms were trying to get a purchase on the edge of the chair-seat. He was stuck.

Two nurses had just come in the door.

"Can you help him?" Lorraine said.

29

A piece of fish

IT'S TIME TO DO SOMETHING WITH THE FISH. WEDNESDAY afternoon and it's been living in a tub for three days.

Things have been kind of dicey since George got back from The Weekend. Fortunately for him, his parents weren't there when Carl dropped him off. So he waited on the doorstep, with the wooden bucket with the fish in it. When they got home he found out they had come from the hospital, and his grandfather had had a stroke. That's all anyone talked about, so his mom didn't notice anything weird about him. Not until she was unpacking his suitcase and found his clothes still clean and folded. He told her Mrs. Cahill had washed his stuff before they left the farm, but his mom looked like she didn't totally buy that. She just didn't have enough of her mind free to find him out.

Monday, his first day back at school since the accident, tanked when he fell asleep in math and was taken to the nurse. She examined him and said he was suffering from exposure and sent him home. George thinks it was more dope than exposure. Good thing he had slept outside and that made his face look that way. His mom kind of bought that he'd over-done it at the Cahill's farm, but again she seemed to sense something else was up.

Yesterday he got through the day, but today was the first *good* day. The weather burn on his cheeks was gone and his eyes looked normal. He had some energy for class, though he didn't manage to talk to Laine and Graham.

Meanwhile there's the fish. When his mom first saw it on Sunday, she said, "Marge Cahill sent you home with a live fish?" His dad looked at it and said it was a catfish. Alicia said it was gross and they started laughing. Then they dumped it into a big metal basin and ran cold water in. It seemed to like its new home.

Now, as he and his dad carry it out of the garage, his mom pulls into the driveway.

"We're wondering if we're really going to eat this monster," his dad tells her as she walks up to them, toting her red leather briefcase, her purse, and a grocery bag. They all look down into the basin. It's slowly circling. Long and sleek. Bluish. Huge eyes sticking out. And those monster whiskers, like antennae.

"Well, I told you we either eat it tonight or we get rid of it," his mom says.

"We're supposed to eat it," George says.

"What do you mean we're *supposed* to?" his dad says. "Who issued this order to us?"

George doesn't answer and Alicia says, "We can't eat it unless we kill it."

"The Cahills gave it to us to eat, is that right?" his mom says to George.

He nods.

"Then we're back to the original problem," his dad says. "The one who caught it is the one who should prepare it for cooking." His dad often says things like this; George thinks they must come from the Bible.

"That's not possible," George says. "I didn't catch it." He aims a steady gaze at his father. "Could you kill it, Dad," he says, "and then show me how to clean it. And then Mom can cook it."

His dad looks at his mom, gives a goofy smile and shrugs. "Okay, let's carry it around back so the whole street won't have to watch."

George and his dad carry the big tub around to the backyard, sloshing the water. His dad gets his hand around the fish, right behind the gills, and picks it up. It wiggles like crazy and its whiskers fall off.

Alicia screams and then runs into the kitchen to tell their mom, who comes out holding a cob of corn. George's dad stands there looking like he did something bad. The fish flaps at his feet, white belly on the green grass.

"I took hold of the darn thing," his dad says. "The whiskers fell right off. They were tied on—they weren't real."

"It's not a catfish," Alicia says.

"It was *disguised* as a catfish," his dad says. "I don't know what it is. It's not a bass. It has a spiky fin on the back. I got pricked."

George walks over to his father and looks down at the fish. "Well if we're going to kill it, let's kill it," he says. "Let's not torture it."

He leans over, picks it up in his left hand, grips its head with his right, and twists until a clean snap is heard.

His dad looks at him in a shocked way. "That's how to do it," he says. "I'll get your tackle box out of the garage and we'll scale it." He tilts his head thoughtfully. "Catfish don't have scales. It looks more like some kind of perch."

His dad takes over and does the work. When the fish is clean his mom shakes it in a paper bag with flour, salt, and pepper, and fries it. She doesn't seem too convinced by the whole thing. George sees her take a big hunk of leftover meat loaf out of the fridge.

After George and his dad clean up the backyard, they all sit down to eat.

"It unnerved me," his dad says, spreading butter on his cob of corn. "The whiskers coming off. I looked at it and I just let go."

"I would have been unnerved before that," his mom says.

"What was it?" his dad says, looking at George. "Somebody's idea of a joke, I guess."

"I wouldn't know," George says.

"You don't seem to know much about this fish," his dad says. "You haven't told us who caught it, why we're supposed to eat it, or why it was disguised as Groucho Marx."

"And I'm not going to," George says. He gets busy on his corn.

"Maybe if we eat it we could stop talking about it," his mom says.

"I don't want to eat it after I saw it flap," Alicia says. George and his dad don't make a move either.

All three look at his mom. She reaches over and moves a piece of it onto her fork. She lifts it into her mouth.

"It's good," she whispers. "It's *really* good. I've never *tasted* any fish this good."

"Oh sure," his dad says.

"You can't fool me," Alicia says.

"I may eat it all," she tells them.

But this doesn't happen. They all get into it, even Alicia. George and his dad have a competition to see who can eat it the most slowly, because it's so good.

The meat loaf hardly gets touched; the rice and corn are contenders, but the fish is the definite winner.

"I did two crisis interventions and a funeral today," his dad says.

"I guess you're, like, batting five hundred," George says. His mom laughs.

"Did you see Joe this afternoon?" his dad asks his mom.

"Yes, he was asleep. He didn't look any better than this morning."

His dad looks sad.

"I did have one small piece of news," his mom says. "About a house."

"No. You sold it? The Arthur Street house?"

"I don't think they can turn back now," his mom says, and she gives his dad a killer smile.

"Honey," his dad says. "That is great."

"I made it through another day of school," George says.

"So did I, except for choir," Alicia says. "Oh, by the way, Dad ..."

"Yes?"

"You forgot to say grace."

"I did," his dad says, and at this moment they hear the front door open and Uncle Dave rushes in. His face is flushed and his eyes are bloodshot.

"Hi guys," he says. "Sorry to invade your meal, but Irene wants her slippers that she left here, and I already forgot to pick them up twice."

"I know exactly where they are," his mom says.

"Can you sit down for a while?" his dad says. "There's plenty of food."

There is still one piece of fish left on the serving plate. His mom says, "We just ate the most wonderful fish. George brought it from his weekend. You should have a taste. We've all been raving about it."

"It's a very weird fish," Alicia says.

"Maybe I should taste it," Uncle Dave says. "I can't stay though. I'm already late." He reaches over and picks up the serving fork.

"No!" George says. "Wait." He lunges at the plate and pulls it to safety against his chest. "I have to save this—I'm saving it."

"George!" his mother says. "Uncle Dave can have a bite."

"He won't want just a bite," George says.

"Who on earth are you saving it for?" his dad says. He gives Dave an embarrassed smile. "*I* almost ate that piece."

Still holding the plate against his heart, George looks at all of them.

"It should go to Grampa," he finally says, and he sets it down on the table again, now rendered untouchable.

"But if you want a taste you can have one," he tells Uncle Dave.

"Listen, it's not an issue," Dave says. "I didn't come here to steal fish from you. I'm sure it's very good, but you know what? I've already had dinner and I was just trying to be polite."

"It's good that somebody was," George's mom comments.

"Now if I can just have those slippers," Dave says, "I'll be out of here."

"George," his mom says. "Go up to our bedroom and on the chair by my dresser you'll see Grandma's slippers. Bring them down here please."

George rises from the table, unable to look at anyone, and retreats up the stairs. He finds the worn pink slippers with the white fuzzy lining.

He brings them down and hands them to Dave.

"You're not saving *these* for anyone, are you?" Dave says.

"No, you can have them," George says.

Dave says "See you tomorrow morning" and goes out the door. His dad begins to scoop out some Sealtest butterscotch ripple.

"I guess it wouldn't be appropriate," his dad says, "to thank the Lord for this ice cream."

30

The prisoner of Zenda

AT NINE A.M. I HEARD THE DOORBELL. I GOT OUT OF BED
and wrapped a towel around me. When I opened the door
Lorraine and Boris were standing there. They had already
been to see Joseph and were about to leave town. They had
news: Dr. Cassler had been in to see the patient. He said we
were in for a long haul; that it would be months, maybe a year,
before Joe could go home again. Physiotherapy wouldn't even
start until he was moved to St. Vincent's Hospital, which
wouldn't be for some time.

"How was he this morning?" I asked, thinking things would
never get back to normal.

"Oh, he was pretty good," Lori said. "He sneezed and I
said that means you'll kiss a fool, and he laughed."

After Lori and Boris left, Irene agreed to go to the hospital with me. But in the early afternoon we were both overcome
by drowsiness. I headed for the lower bedroom as my mother
settled down on the living room couch. I managed a few more
pages of Mark Twain, my Gamrie Drive refuge; as Tom Sawyer
stole in to his own funeral I drifted off.

I was awakened in the dimness by Irene, hovering over me
and saying she was ready to go. The open book was lying on the

pillow beside me; I had drooled on its ancient cover; my jeans were bulging with an erection that I somehow connected with the image of Michelle Pfeiffer; my features were mashed by sleep and my breath was awful. But Irene was standing there, coat and purse in hand.

The usual dread seized me in the hospital corridor, this time augmented by the fear that Joseph would not live up to the spin job I had treated my mother to.

We walked into the room and my dad was in a chair, with straps around his torso and an agitated look. Two nurses were changing his bed; they explained that they had put him in the chair just for the moment but that he needed to rest as soon as the bed was ready.

But Irene advanced to him, apparently not intimidated by the situation. "Honey," she said, "have they got you all strapped in?"

He gave her an immediate answer, but neither of us could make it out and I realized with a sinking heart that for some reason Joseph's teeth weren't in. Irene bent over him and he said it again, and somehow she was able to understand him.

"Like the prisoner of Zenda," she repeated. "Oh, poor Mojoe, I don't know why they have to treat you like this."

"It's for his own safety," one of the nurses said.

"We understand," I said.

"We'll have him back in the bed in a minute," the other nurse said.

Joseph was again saying something to Irene, and again I didn't have a clue what it was.

"I'm doing fine," she answered him. "I'm just lonely for my guy."

He burbled, and his head moved up and down.

"Poor Mojoe," she said, and she took his head and pressed it to her bosom, stroking his errant white hairs with her red-tipped fingers. "Poor guy—it's been pretty hard on you, hasn't it?"

I was heartened by how my mother was contending with the situation; she had marched bravely into the breach. But I didn't like the way my dad was coming off. He was stronger than everyone thought; he just *looked* weaker because he couldn't communicate properly.

It was weird how the whole situation seemed to turn on the teeth. Until this week I had never seen my father without them, and I was amazed at how their absence made him look like an old derelict. Worse than that, it made people think his mind was impaired. The difference between the Tuesday Joseph and the Wednesday Joseph had been mostly about the teeth!

I went over to the good-looking nurse, and drew her aside. "Sandy, I was just wondering..." I said. "I was wondering why— or what is the reason, that my father's teeth haven't been put in. He seems to do a whole lot better if they are."

Her eyes were wearily amused.

I tried again. "You know, he can still communicate. The stroke didn't take that away."

She took a deep breath and put her hand on my arm, as if to still my spinning wheels. "Mr. Moore removed his teeth. We put them back in at your sister's request, and he took them out again."

"*He* took them out?" I said. "I'm sorry."

"That's okay," she said. "You're trying to watch out for him. So are we."

I backed out into the hall and hovered in the light that was like the light from a perpetually cloudy sky.

31

Cold water

As recess begins on Thursday morning, George is determined not to be caught by the jocks again. They are over by the school wall, trading wisecracks and half-heartedly bouncing a basketball. For two days he has had to hang with them, which means he still hasn't caught up with Laine and Graham.

The jocks had been waiting too long to peel a strip off him, since his bizarre new achievements. So they pounced. They made a show of teasing him, but he could tell that his imitation of a brick wall at home plate was admired, and his public kiss was secretly respected. They didn't seem to know whether to dump him or crown him king. One thing they couldn't do was declare him "Out of It" like they did last year. He had already done too many of the weird-type things that they sentence you to do.

Two of them, Donny Canning and Adam Riswick, are watching him now, but George walks on. He has a feeling they need him more than he needs them. They are so hung up on all their rules about how you can act. What the fuck are they afraid of? He stops in the middle of the schoolyard, not far from the Cool Girls. Jennifer Bull smiles at him without stopping whatever she is saying that's making the other girls *ooh* and *ah*. George gives her a little wave and looks back at the jocks. Even the way they stand is like a rule: trying to look cool with their T-shirts hanging out and their backwards baseball caps. George can do it too: it isn't very hard.

What *has* been hard, all week, is hooking up with Graham and Laine. Other than worrying about his grandfather, whom he plans to visit today, the only thing on George's mind has been Laine and their awesome weekend. All he wants is to be with her again. But he hasn't even come close. In class she has been low-profile. She sent no signals, so he took the cue and played it cool too. That was a fun game for about a day but then it got old. He started wondering if the weekend had ever happened.

Outside of class, George has been hijacked by the jocks. Who, to make matters worse, are still including Laine on their "uncool" list. Their reasons for dissing her never looked that good to George, but now they look like crap. He watches them as they humiliate Terrence Swanson by throwing his knapsack around, not letting him rejoin his scabbie friends, who would include Tim Cahill if he weren't sick today.

George spots Laine now; she's over by the fence in the dirtbag group. Except Laine doesn't even slightly belong with them anymore; the jocks are just too ignorant to know it. They don't see how she has changed, and they have *no idea at all* who she really is.

She's in a huddle with Graham, the all-time poster boy for dirtbagness. Which only proves to George that the whole thing is stupid.

Screw the jocks, they are the real dirtbags.

He approaches Laine and Graham. "Hey guys," he says.

"Hey Stone," Laine says. "How's your fish doing? Carl wants to know."

"Oh, the fish. It's history, except for one piece. We ate it yesterday. It was awesome. It wasn't a catfish though."

"I know. Carl told me about the whiskers. He just put them on to scare me."

George laughs. "I still don't have a clue what kind it was. Not a bass. My dad said it could be a walleye, except it was blue."

"So George," Graham says. "I have two words for you: video day. It has to be next Saturday. Not *this* weekend, I've got a mom weekend. Next weekend. I've already looked at it. It blows "Hard Copy" away."

"Which video is this?" George says.

"It's called The Lingerie Sisters," Graham says. "Your girlfriend is going to knock your shorts off."

"I told you, she isn't my girlfriend."

"Yeah, he told you," Laine says. She presses her chest into his arm. "Why do you keep saying that, Stone?" A bolt of relief and anticipation strikes his heart.

"Why do I," George says, smiling at her.

"'Cause you're in denial," Graham says.

Across the schoolyard, George can see that the jocks are restless. They have forgotten to act cool, having been demoted to spectators of the George-Laine-Graham show. They are trying to hide their interest, probably making smart remarks, but they sense something.

He looks over at Jennifer, and she too seems to be checking out their new alliance. What is this—suddenly *he* feels like he's on "Hard Copy." The recess bell rings, and George says, "I'll get back to you on that weekend thing."

In French class, he notices Jennifer Bull looking at him again; or rather, he keeps turning and catching her looking away.

"George," Madame Crothers says in a loud, sweet voice. "Peux-tu répondre?"

"Oui, je peux," he answers.

"Lèves-toi."

George stands up.

"Réponds," she tells him.

"Je ne sais pas la question," George says.

"Tu ne sais pas quelle est la question," she corrects. After a righteous pause, she tells him to sit down, and calls on a more worthy candidate, Dale Hufton.

George seats himself, looks over at Jennifer and she's blushing. *What is it with her*, he wonders, and then he clues in. Her friends have probably teased her about The Kiss until she can't stand it, saying he's a threat to do it again. And she does want attention from him, just not another kiss maybe. When they talked in the square, it was like they made a date to get together at school, and he has totally dropped the ball. In fact, after that crazy weekend, he lost the ball. He catches her eye again, gives her an apologetic shrug.

And then school is over and it's time to carry out his plan. Alicia is going to Alison's for dinner so he doesn't have to worry about her. He runs all the way home. In the fridge he finds the leftover fish in plastic wrap and puts it in his knapsack. After catching a bus downtown, he walks from St. George's Square up to the hospital.

He is twenty feet into the hallway on the second floor when he sees Uncle Dave and Grandma coming towards him. She has her coat on, her purse in her hand. Dave has an arm around her.

"Oh, George, you're here," she says. "Well, you won't be able to stay long—he needs to rest."

Uncle Dave takes a few steps with George and says, "He's in bed now. You're fine, just sit with him and talk a bit. He'll be glad to see you."

"Thanks," George says. *Why was I so down on him last night*, George thinks. An image of a wild tippy canoe goes through his mind, making him feel queasy about his uncle. Then it's gone.

George sits down in the chair next to his grandfather, pushing the mobile tray out of the way. His grampa's head is half buried in the pillow. His eyes are almost closed. His cheek is yellow, with spots of purple on it; his arm is like that too. His face doesn't look like his.

It's very quiet in the room. Voices echo from far away. Air whistles in and out of his grandfather's nose. Cards sit on the table. Their flowery covers seem out of place. A white cup sits beside them—the old man's supply of water.

George sits patiently; he is glad to be here, glad he made it in time. His mind drifts to the bench on the square where he sat with Grampa before all this happened. He feels as if they are both resting on it now. He doesn't feel weird being here in the hospital room, any more than he did on that bench.

His hand is sitting on the cold metal rail that runs along the bed. Then he feels a hand on his. He looks over and the old man is gazing at George from under his heavy lids.

"Grampa. How are you feeling?"

Joseph shakes his head and his eyes roll, as if to say, "You don't want to know."

"I brought you something." George reaches into his backpack and takes out the china plate with the canopy of plastic wrap over it. "All the way from Muskoka."

The old man looks at the fish and shakes his head again, this time with a humorous, incredulous hunching of the brows, and he snorts.

His voice says something. The words are all blurred but George cradles them like a football pass, until he has a grip: "What do I need that for?"

George smiles at him and says, "To make you strong."

His grandfather starts shaking and a tear comes out of his right eye: he's laughing again. "Then I better eat it," he says.

George takes the plastic off and looks around. There's no fork, and anyway his grandfather doesn't have his teeth in.

"Leave it here," Joseph tells him.

"We're going to put your teeth in, Mr. Moore." A very

pretty nurse has come in. She goes into the bathroom and George hears water running. She comes out with the teeth, each artificial gum coated with white paste. "Here we go," she says, "let's sit you up." She pops in the dentures, and fits the old man's bifocals over his nose and ears. Then she pushes the table up against his stomach, and brings a tray from the hall. She stops because George's plate is occupying the surface.

"It looks like your dinner is already here," she says in a nice way.

"This is an hors d'oeuvre, Sandy," Joseph says. "And I have been told that it's not optional."

"Well," she smiles. "Your grandson is laying down the law. I hope he has better luck than I do when I give you orders."

"But if I obeyed your orders," Joseph tells her, "you wouldn't spend as much time in here."

"No, I would be helping other patients," she scolds him, lifting a forkful of fish into his mouth, "who need me much more than you do."

He chews it and swallows. He smiles at the nurse. "Well, now you're making me feel guilty," he says.

"And that's just what I mean to do." Her fine eyes and her red, smiling mouth turn on George in a way that starts his crotch humming. The fish is consumed, and George gets up to go.

"You're not going to see your grampa through his dinner?" she asks him.

"I have to go home."

"Do you. Well that was very thoughtful of you to bring that snack for Mr. Moore, wasn't it counsellor?"

"It was," he says, but she's already steering his own hand, laden now with a forkful of mashed potato, towards his mouth.

"Bye, Grampa."

As he goes out of the room he hears Sandy say, "Now dear, these beans are not here for decoration."

32

Making it up

I HAD STAYED TOO LONG AT THE PUB. IN THE TWINING Arms, a fine Calvan pub in a burly brick house downtown, I'd gotten caught up in a study of Virginia Woolf's madness that I had found at the Word Shop, Calvan's best bookstore.

When I was an undergraduate I had accepted Virginia's periodic breakdowns as just another of her charms, possibly related to the painful detachment that stood out in her writing. It never occurred to me that both of these things might have sprung from ordinary abuse. But such, according to this book, were the facts. Documents from her own hand clearly recorded that from age six to twenty-two, she had been sexually molested by first one and then the other of her older half-brothers, the Duckworths. Now faced with the missing piece, I felt guilty for not having noticed that there was a puzzle. The icing on the cake was that the insufferably conceited Leonard, who was in a better position to penetrate his wife's problem, never seemed to pay much attention to the *content* of her illnesses, to the (shame-ridden) things she actually said when she was "mad." Instead he subjected her to that era's treatments for "neurasthenia," which included force feeding and being forbidden to work. And eventually it overtook her; in 1941 she felt it coming on again, and with impressive efficiency she drowned herself.

Meanwhile it was Saturday at 4:30, and I was running late. I was supposed to be at Irene's right now, to take her to the supermarket. But I hadn't even seen my father yet, because of that damned tasty book.

I drained my glass and rushed out of the pub. The day was bright and I put my shades on. When I reached Bombay Street I was forced to park two blocks away from the hospital. Halfway around the curved driveway, two men in business suits passed me going the other way. One was about my age, a handsome guy who looked red-eyed. The other was twenty years older, grey and sombre looking, carrying a briefcase. They didn't notice me, but after they'd gone by I realized they were Sanders and Robertson from my dad's firm. They must have been visiting Joseph.

I sprinted in to the elevator and caught it open. I ran down the hall, into the room, and it was empty. There was no one in the neatly made bed. My gut turned cold. Was this my first look at the abyss we'd all been fearing? Was I seeing the moment after my father had died? Was that why Sanders had looked so ravaged?

I scanned the room: my father's navy dressing gown was still slung over the big chair; there were still greeting cards on the bedside table. They hadn't even had time to clean up.

I went out to the nurses' station in the hall. There was no one there. Oh god, this was exactly what it would be like if an unexpected death had just happened.

I headed down the hall, heart sinking. The older nurse was coming my way. "Do you know where my father is?"

"Oh, they've taken him for some tests. He had some visitors and then they wheeled him out not long ago."

"Is he okay?"

"He's fine. His friends, they had him signing documents."

The next day Irene and I walked into Joseph's room. There was a warm breeze coming in the open window and sunlight on the wall. He was in his chair; he looked good.

"How are you, Dad?"

"Fine, Dave, except I'm having a little trouble remembering some things." He said this with such serenity that I thought he might be joking.

"Like what?"

"Well, for instance, I'm not sure what visitors I've had today."

"You're not? Well, I think we're the first ones here from the family."

"That may be, but Paul Curtis was in here a while ago and I told him you'd already been in to see me this morning."

"You did! Well I wasn't—not today."

I explained that I had been in yesterday afternoon, but hadn't gotten to visit. Joseph was pretty sure that the nurse had told him that. Irene and Joe chatted about Paul Curtis, a long-standing client of Joe's who owned half the strip malls in town. Greg and Doreen arrived; they had been visiting Joseph most evenings. They were closely followed by Susan and Ed. It was Sunday and the congregation had gathered.

Joseph wanted to be hiked up in his chair and I asked Greg to help me do the job. We were pulling the chair out from the window when Susan cried out, "Greg! Don't move!" She crouched down at his feet and came up holding Joseph's lower teeth in her hand like a prize. Everyone started to laugh.

"This is ridiculous," Susan said. "They could have been crushed."

Susan went into the bathroom, cleaned and prepped the teeth, and brought them to Joseph. He at first tried to put them in on top, where there wasn't a vacancy, then got it right.

I sat on a stool beside his throne, while the other five arrayed themselves like an audience in front of us, on and around the bed.

"I looked across the hall this morning," Joseph told me, "and they seemed like they were in church!"

I looked across. There was a group of dressed-up people. "They do look like they're in church. And it is Sunday."

"I waved to one guy," Joe continued. "He came over and talked to me for a while. I asked him if they were in church and he said no."

"Did he know you were joking?" I asked.

"I wasn't!" This got a big laugh from the bed crew, who were amazed to see Joseph poking fun at himself, in quite his old deadpan manner.

"I introduced myself and so did he," said Joseph. "His name was Alf Willman, his wife Mary was there with him and they were visiting her mother, Gertrude. Alf is in carpets. He has a big store in Cambridge."

"I thought you couldn't remember anything," I said.

"I can't," Joseph said. "I'm making it up!"

More big laughs; Greg was ecstatic on the bed.

"Well, you're pretty convincing," I said, feeling that the crowd didn't want this dippy dialogue to end just yet. "I hope I have it together half as much as you when I'm eighty."

"I hope you do sooner than that," Joseph said.

33

To escape scrutiny

MONDAY WAS MY LAST DAY IN CALVAN. I WAS BOOKED ON a seven P.M. flight.

I walked in to find my father fast asleep on the bed. I settled down on a chair beside him. After a while he surfaced. He was a little dishevelled and quite stubbly; his neck looked thin.

"You know what I've been thinking about?" he said. "Driving. And what it represents to me."

I steadied myself. This was the kind of moment we'd never had.

"Freedom?" I suggested.

"Yes."

"Normality?"

"Yeah, normality too. Now, Irene and I were supposed to be going up to Huntsville to inspect a lodge for our bridge group. And that trip keeps coming into my mind. But it's out of reach."

"I know what you mean," I said.

"I am obsessed with our 'rekky' plan. To have that taken away from me—just an ordinary junket, you know. I can't seem to accept it." Joseph paused. "*That's* what driving means to me."

I sat quietly for a moment, enjoying my dad's use of quaint

British lingo from World War II. "Rekky" was such a fine nick-name for reconnoitre: it made me see khaki shorts and berets and Jack Hawkins.

"I also find myself thinking about the merits of moving," my father said.

I nodded, wondering what he meant—moving his body? Changing rooms? Transferring to St. Vincent's?

"Your mother and I have gently discussed it. The upkeep at Gamrie is too hard for us now. Maybe we should be renting somewhere where those matters are taken care of."

"That makes sense," I said carefully. It struck me that maybe this decision had already been made for him. But it was great that he seemed to be seeing the stroke as a signpost on the path forward, rather than a step backward.

Joseph lifted up his plastic cup and took a long drink. Then he continued the steady unfolding of his thoughts, that I couldn't believe was happening. "I have also noticed that I don't seem to be able to remember exactly when this hap-pened," he said.

"Well, it was Saturday night—nine days ago, at Gamrie Drive. I think it was three in the morning or something."

"Now it doesn't seem to me that I've been here over a week. It's Monday today," Joseph said. "But how did I get here?"

"Greg and Dory came over and they called an ambulance. Of course, I don't remember this stuff very well either." I smiled at him.

"You were still in L.A., that much I know." He gave me a look of scientific wonder. "Imagine that, all that chunk of time just gone."

"You were in shock, you didn't know what was happening. That's not a sign of serious memory loss."

"It may not be. And I'm told that I should be greatly rejoic-ing that it came on the right side. The nurses explained that."

"I don't know about rejoicing, but yeah," I said.

"I tried to read this paper earlier," the old man said solemnly, "and I wasn't doing very well. I'm not sure if the problem was comprehension or eyesight."

I nodded. I wondered how many other heroic little struggles had faded into obscurity.

"Why don't we try to figure it out," I said.

I folded the *Globe and Mail* front page on the mobile table directly in my father's line of vision. We adjusted his bifocals.

"Read me some of it," I suggested, and the old man proceeded to do just that. The words came out steadily and correctly. It was a story about a cover-up by the provincial government of a ministerial gaffe.

Joseph was doing fine until he came to the phrase, "to escape scrutiny."

"Can you help me with that?" he asked.

"Well, it means to avoid being found out," I said, but my father was still staring at the page. I expanded: "They tried really hard to avoid being found out. They lied."

"But to escape," he said. "Doesn't that mean to get away?"

"Wait a minute," I said. "Look at me, Dad. Don't look at the words. Now what if I said, 'If that nurse Sandy thinks she can come in here waving her ass around and still escape our scrutiny, she's badly mistaken'?"

"I would think you'd be right," my father said.

"So would she escape scrutiny?"

"Not by a long shot," he said.

"So you still know the words. You're just having trouble translating from print."

Joseph looked sceptical.

"Right now," I said, "your brain is rewiring itself. If it has lost one area it'll rebuild in another location." How I knew this I wasn't sure, but I felt pretty confident about it.

The conversation continued. My diaphragm humming with pleasure, I watched as he just kept getting things right. We had never had a chat so leisurely, so steady, so intimate. It was as if we had climbed a mountain in a freezing rain, to find at the top a sunny meadow.

BOOK FOUR

Thanksgiving

34

A left hook

I DID NO READING ON THE FLIGHT TO L.A.; JUST SAT AND basked in the Joseph saga.

He was going to recover. I'd given the ship's wheel the right spin, steering the precious man back to shore. Uncharacteristically, I turned down beer and wine on the plane. When my meal came, I ate only the wild rice and vegetables, letting the chicken go. A beatific peace sat upon me. The flight attendants smiled. The Japanese man on my right struck up a lively conversation. I napped for a while. An announcement woke me up: we were on final approach.

I saw Maggie's face in the throng by the gate, and her smile that always had a touch of irony. How much irony I would soon learn.

We had spoken once while I was in Calvan, but that was before I knew where things were going with my father. As her black monster flew along the Santa Monica Freeway, I covered the ground in detail. It wasn't an opinion I was presenting, not a belief about the old man's prognosis; rather it was a revelation of the triumph that had already taken place. "Even if he dies of it in the end," I told her, "he's still beaten it."

"But he's not going to die, is he?"

"No, of course not." I leaned back in the tattered seat and tasted the strange, dry California breeze coming in the window.

"This Willie Horton ad," she said after a while. "Have you seen it?"

"No."

"It's evil. It shows Dukakis letting a murderer out of prison, who then rapes a woman. It's going to sink the campaign."

We went to my place. It wasn't long before we left words behind. In my dark bedroom in the little house, I caught fire from her. And it was like it had been in Muskoka, revved up, blooming, heady.

And we lay like two spoons, my hands interlocked with hers on her smooth, flat stomach.

"I have to tell you something," she said. "I found out yesterday." She waited.

"Okay," I murmured into the nape of her neck.

"I took a test, the home test. It was positive. Judith saw it too."

I sucked in some air and expelled it. A narrow chasm opened between my belly and her back.

"What made you take it?" I said.

"My breasts were feeling weird."

"But you've been on the pill," I said, as if that trumped any other information.

"I never stopped taking it. I still am. Which I probably shouldn't."

"So how could you be pregnant?"

There was a long silence. She rolled like a log in a harbour and lodged against me. "Davey," she said. "I *am* pregnant."

She rested her cheek upon my chest. She said, "I missed the pill, the day I flew here from Columbus. I was distracted. I didn't think it would matter, because I was just starting my week of taking blanks anyway."

"Makes sense," I said.

"But Judith said an extra day with no pill could have allowed me to ovulate, the next time my body wanted to. Which maybe was the week before last."

"That's when we got together again."

"Right."

"But how could the test already show it?"

"I don't know. I guess my hormones react fast. Judith says you can't trust a negative this early, but a positive is a positive."

"So what does Judith think we should do?"

She laughed. "I didn't ask her."

"How about you?" I said.

She drew a deep breath. I felt her relax against me. "Well of course I know we didn't plan it, and it would probably be a disaster," she said, and she shifted against me and her legs were warm.

"Probably," I said.

"You think?"

"Well, it's a little sudden."

"Come on, we've been seeing each other for a year!"

"That's true. But don't we have plans?"

"Do we?"

"I don't know, I thought I was supposed to finish my demos, and try to get something going with them. And you're supposed to finally try your acting ..."

"Actually that's not my plan anymore," she said. "Judith and I are working on a screenplay."

"That's great."

"Yeah, it's got a really neat premise. It *looks* like a ghost story but it turns out to be something else, which I can't tell you until you read it. So I'm not going to do acting."

"Well, you know what? I've decided to give up on music! So this is perfect."

She laughed, and then we were quiet for a while.

"So what do we do?" she said.

"I don't know. I think we have to decide together. Figure out what we both want."

She rolled onto her back. Our arms were still touching.

"Are you saying I don't have the kid if you don't want to?" she said.

"No, no. I don't think I said that."

She waited.

I said, "Maybe what I'm trying to say is, we don't do something as momentous as having a kid without agreeing on it as a couple."

"Well excuse me," she said, getting up from the bed, "help me out here if you would." Her tone was sweet reason. "What if you vote against it: then I would still have to decide what *I* want to do, wouldn't I? I mean it *is* my body."

"Don't do this to me," I said.

I heard her running a glass of water in the kitchen. She gave me a good dose of isolation; her speech still hung in the air. Then the bedroom wall stirred with her shadow.

"You can't mean," I said, "that you would go off on your own, raise a kid, and I'm supposed to not be involved?"

"That would be your choice, Dave."

"I don't think so."

She was standing in my bedroom doorway, nude as they come, her convexities catching the yellow light from outside. The body I loved had proven to be a Trojan horse: it had had eggs concealed inside it.

"I didn't *know* this would happen," she said.

In a few short moments during which I sat like a stump on the bed, she gathered up her clothes and disappeared into the kitchen.

"Don't go," I said.

"I need some space," she said.

As her car chugged away, I realized that life had nailed me. I felt like an ageing champion who has finally been caught, not by some cleverly disguised uppercut, but by the plain old left hook that he has successfully eluded so many times before. It was a drab, ignominious moment. It made all the elaborate, evasive dance of my past life seem like a bad joke. I had been tagged.

Her line about making her own decision if I opted out was the stopper. I couldn't get around that. If she had the strength to face her situation without me, I was done.

It wasn't even worth any more sweat. My hand glided out in an automatic way and found the on-switch of the clock radio. Dr. Merle Boone, most perverse of the radio evangelists, was sounding forth in his infuriatingly slow Western drawl, his voice like a cracked mountain. He was explaining why we have to conclude that Jesus made it to England during his "lost years." I listened for a while, grinning in the dark at Boone's amazing silences. The man expected the world to wait while he played with himself. And I did wait, wanting to be assured once and for all that the King of the Jews really belonged to the Anglo-American tradition. Then lofted on a frail breeze of humour, I crossed the bars of streetlight on the kitchen floor, pulled a beer out of the fridge, and drank it on my bed.

After a while I turned Dr. Boone off, unable to sustain my wake-like levity. The original mood of defeat returned and began to branch into two separate streams, one of anger, the other of guilt.

The anger was that my exotic Maggie should suddenly turn out to be that most bourgeois of clichés, the mother wannabe. That all along, beneath her veneer of irony and unconvention-ality, she was just waiting to have a kid.

The guilt was less articulate, but at bottom it arose from the very same point: that she had this talent, this gift of mother-hood, that I had never acknowledged. And might be the one to sabotage.

But again and again, as my mind trotted out the reasons why the pregnancy couldn't continue, I was impaled on the point that it didn't matter what I thought; I wasn't in control. For she could answer: those are just reasons why you don't have to be part of this, and I'll grant them if I must, but they still don't mean I don't want to do it. And even though the discussion hadn't even taken place yet, I was convinced that I wouldn't be able to make her understand my answer, which was: you can't have the kid alone, because I wouldn't be able to leave you in that predicament!

For hours the battle raged, like a rehearsal that had been mistaken for the play. I consumed three beers. The voices subsided only when I settled into guilt; but the discomfort of that only stoked my resentment again. Pacing around the living room I realized that I absolutely must report for work in the morning. My clock said 5:21.

35

The dreaded chart

THERE WERE ELEVEN MESSAGES ON MY VOICEMAIL. TWO of them were from associates who needed me to spoon-feed them the rudiments of insurance theory; seven of them were extremely urgent calls from Larry Shrift, none of which bothered to share their subject in any way.

The last two messages were the most worrisome. They were from my boss. In the first, Murry Barr urgently requested input from me so that he could respond to some problems the client had with my Chart of Insurance Policies. (Barr shouldn't have sent that chart to the client: it wasn't final.) The second message, sent at eight this morning, was even more disturbing: it implied that the first message was sent *yesterday*, not today. Apparently Barr had thought I was returning to work on Monday. Apparently he had already responded to the client, and now would like to see me in his office ASAP. He must have found his answers somewhere else—I didn't want to think about where, since literally no one besides me had really mastered the policies.

Ever since I had sat down at my desk I had been on edge, afraid that everyone who passed my door would be Maggie. I was scared that if I saw her, I would crack. At ten I got up

and gingerly approached her office door: it was open and the
office was dark, except for a glint from the pine lamp I had
made, painted metallic pink by her. She must not be coming in
today. That made my heart sink, but it bought me time to cope
with Barr.

Armed only with a yellow pad and a pen, I climbed to twenty-
eight and peered into Barr's office. The brisk soldier voice
bade me enter, using my first name. I advanced to a shiny,
lime-green armchair as Barr turned his uncomplicated face
back to some documents he was discussing on the phone. For
ten minutes I sat there like the perfect adjutant, making subtle
adjustments in posture that implied I was deep in thought.
Never did my eyes press on Barr; that would suggest that my
time was as valuable as his. Finally the call ended. In his gruff
voice, Barr unfurled his caring nature. "Dave, welcome back.
How was your trip? How is your father?"

"He's excellent. Or better than he was." This didn't seem ade-
quate at all, but before I could improve it, Barr went for closure.

"That's good news. These situations can be difficult."

Unnecessarily dragging out the discussion, I said, "I'm
sorry I couldn't get back sooner."

"Not a problem. Your family is much more important than
anything we're doing here."

Even though the big partner turned his attention back
to some jottings on his desk, I got the uncanny feeling that
he actually meant what he had said. *So what am I doing here in
L.A.*, I thought to myself: *I'm betraying a principle that even Murry
Barr subscribes to.*

"This is what I faxed to the client yesterday," Barr said. He
handed me a sheet of paper. One glance at it revealed a problem: it missed a crucial clause in one of the policies. That
oversight could potentially expose unlimited funds of the
client's.

"Where did you get this information?" I asked grimly.

"In your absence I called on Shrift, who accessed your back-up materials for me. I believe he had help from Maggie Taylor."

Oh no, I groaned to myself. *How could she have let Shrift figure anything out?* It irked me that even though Maggie and I didn't work on any of the same cases, people assumed she knew whatever I knew, as if couples share a hard drive.

"I have a problem with this," I said. "I don't believe this policy lacks a pollution exclusion. It just has an unusual one."

"Well, we can't afford to slip up on a point like that," Barr returned sternly. "Dave, I've mentioned this before. You can't be the only one with access to the answers."

A retort sprang to mind: I'm not the only one with access; I'm just the only one who takes the time to use it.

"Right," I muttered.

"If we're going to amend this, we'd better do it fast," Barr said. "I want you back here with your changes by 10:30. I have a conference call with the client in two different cities at that time. Meanwhile we have other things to worry about."

He proceeded to inform me that the deadline for the big project had been extended till the last week of October, but that the *scope* of the project had been broadened: the client had issued a twenty-page, detailed template, to which every site report must now conform. Thirty sites in Canada had also been added. Updated reports were expected on all sites.

"Can you ask Marilyn to step in here on your way out," Barr said. There seemed to be no opening for me to tell him that the deadline was two months too soon.

In my office, with ten minutes left before Barr's conference call, I frantically searched for the notes on which my draft chart was based. They weren't there. I called Shrift and found out that he had given the document to Maggie. I raced to her office, turned the light on. I couldn't find my work. In despair, I dialled her number. She answered.

"Hi," I said.

"Where are you?" she asked.

"At SOB. Look, I'm sorry but I have to ask you a work-related question."

There was silence, or the murmur of many coaxial cables.

"Are you okay?" I said.

There was another pause, and then I heard her say "Not really," and I heard a sob, and then a click.

I was standing there, out of ideas, when Shrift crashed in and said "Sorry. I had it after all."

When I came into Barr's office at 10:35, the big partner was on the speakerphone, faking affability in a loud voice. He waved me to a chair, maintaining his warm vocal performance without a hint of feeling on his face, and extended a paw to receive the page with my changes.

"I've got it here now," he told the blower. "The Exclusions column should read as follows."

I suffered through Barr's recitation, in which no paralegal work was credited. I then made motions of leaving, since there was no more danger of my findings being garbled. But to my surprise, Barr indicated with a raised hand that I should stay. I soon found out why.

"You want the finalized chart ASAP," Barr repeated, ignoring my attempt to get his attention. "You will have it, Timothy, on your desk tomorrow morning."

"And it'll include the pre-1950 policies?" came the dulcet voice of the head in-house lawyer at the client's home office in New York.

"Absolutely," Barr pronounced. "No good without them."

I wanted to show my appreciation for this reckless promise by collapsing into a writhing mass on the carpet.

Now Barr shamelessly engaged in fifteen minutes of "old boy" personal banter, something neither he nor Tim Niven was really any good at. I didn't even try to leave. At last the attempt at male bonding was concluded, and Barr shut off the phone and started jotting on his yellow pad, not obviously aware that I was still there.

I decided to launch some information in his direction. "I've never looked at the pre-1950 policies," I said. "I was holding off until we could try to find better copies in the plaintiff's new production."

Barr looked up from his writing; his blank gaze rested on me. The visual contact was becoming unbearable, and I blurted out, "Why do they want the policy chart so badly, anyway?"

Barr finally seemed to surface in the same sensory pond where I was treading water. He put down his pencil and looked at his ageing paralegal in a sincere, nurturing way, which gave me a warm, boyish glow in spite of myself. "They have their own project going," he said. "They want to run numbers on what all the policies are worth, taken together."

"But that's impossible," I said without hesitation. "Because we don't know how many occurrences we're dealing with. And the policy dollars are per occurrence."

Occurrence was another name for accident. No one knew how to count pollution occurrences. Was every drop an occurrence? Every dumping? Every chemical? Every site? And this was really just the smallest thorn on a ferocious thicket of complexities, as I had tried to point out many times to Barr.

"They *need numbers*," Barr said. "We're talking possible settlement. Now I assume you don't have a lot of spare time to be sitting here."

Isn't this how it always goes, I thought. During several years of pretrial discovery, the attorneys for both sides milk their clients for literally millions of dollars in fees; then when the harsh realities of trial are finally approaching, the lawyers suddenly awaken to the wisdom of settlement, and the always-foreseen loser is advised to pay the always-foreseen winner the same amount that could have been paid at the start.

I was too incensed to reply. "Can I have that back," I said.
With my sheet in hand, I started away from him.

"Oh, Dave. There has been an odd complaint about you.
From Richard Ocher. It came up because I have asked him to
come in on the Plandor case, to help us ram it home."

"That wasn't . . ."

"I have no wish to address the merits of this little duplicat-
ing scuffle, but I'll expect you to smooth it over with him, and
I'll expect there to be no more incidents of this kind.
Understood?"

"Understood."

"One other thing. The client will be sending you a box of
policies on a new case. An analgesic with painful side effects.
They'll need your astute analysis."

He punched his phone and started speaking to his secretary.

In a fit of irreverence, I considered taking an early lunch. I
could climb the hill to the Wells Fargo Court where I would
undoubtedly find a music magazine with a suitable feature arti-
cle, and a well-lit seat at the upscale Cal-Mex restaurant with
the good corn-bean soup. That might well stave off reality for
as much as two hours. But I didn't have two hours.

So I worked. Fairly quickly, I was able to piece together the
best available version of each pre-1950 policy. But by two-thirty,
interruptions and fatigue were slowing me down. And by four
o'clock, various setbacks had weakened me, throwing serious
doubt on my chance of meeting the deadline. With tragic clarity I saw that I *could* make it, but that, in my emotional state and
given the amount of competent help available to me, I wasn't
going to.

I couldn't concentrate on policy language because the
sound of Maggie in pain was muting everything else. I kept
rereading the same lengthy clause, one I had understood in the
past. The Filipino clerk who would normally have handled the

physical jobs of rerunning, copying, packaging, and transmit-
ting the chart, turned out to have left for the day at noon.
Blood was pounding in my head instead of my lungs.

At this hopeless moment I thought of my dad on the first
day at the hospital, the sunken mouth and sparse white hair all
dishevelled; and, sitting there in my secretarial chair, I started
to cry on the latest printout of the dreaded chart. I moved my
head to spare my precious document, and then the door of my
office opened.

Maggie looked at me, and her expression slowly went from
cold to something else. She walked over and put her hand on
my shoulder. I tried to stop the tears but her hand didn't help.
I looked up at her with puffy eyes and said, "He was trying to
figure the world out."

"That's okay," she said, patting my back.

I wiped my eyes with a Kleenex and said, "I'm in deep shit
here."

Maggie, who was capable of any level of paralegal work that
she set her mind to, perched on my desk and glanced down at
the really quite respectable-looking document that was sitting
there.

"What kind of shit exactly?" she said.

Once the two of us had melded into a team, I lost my sense of
incapacity. I was able to do my part now that an ally needed my
output to do hers.

Only a few times during our well-tooled operation did she
make me pay for my words of the night before. I had just
reminded her that a page of the chart needed to be reprinted
before being copied. She said, "Is that part of our plan as a couple?"

"I hope so," I said.

Against all odds, we made the midnight courier deadline.
As I walked her to the parking lot, there was an unspoken truce
between us. We wouldn't talk about Personal Topic Number

One. When we reached her car I stopped her with a hand on
her arm, and said, "Thanks for saving my ass."

"You owe me," she said.

I went home alone, grateful to be in one piece, grateful
to be still not beyond the pale of her forgiveness. Having
made Tuesday's impossible deadline, I decided to sleep in;
and when I woke up at eleven, with the unfamiliar feeling of
being completely rested, I knew SOB wasn't going to get me
today. I left a message on Barr's voicemail, then a hello for
Maggie too.

I cleaned the bathroom, which had last felt Ajax in July,
and then I started to scrub the kitchen. As I was attacking the
linoleum floor with a sponge mop, I felt a whole new approach
to the Maggie situation taking form. All I really wanted was a
real talk, where we would look at both sides of the question. If
we could do that, we could reach the right decision and I would
have no problem with it.

If she would just let me express all my concerns, including
the rational, practical ones, who knows, I would probably end
up voting for the kid. She would charm me into wanting it as
much as she did—assuming that she did. She had never really
said that; just that she would have to make her own decision if
I wasn't onboard. If she *was* on the yes side, she would probably
make me see it as a wild and crazy excursion that I couldn't bear
to miss. Maggie had a knack for getting her own way: sometimes the light of anticipation in her eyes was too hard to resist,
you couldn't dampen it. I just wanted the true costs to be
acknowledged—from that base I could go anywhere. In my
mind I had a vague sense of fiscal and other consequences that
should be looked at, and some of these, I had to admit, might
lead even Maggie to the conclusion that we shouldn't go ahead.
But a secret, sunny corner of my heart was open today. And in
it sprang a green shoot that would have surprised her.

At two o'clock I called her office.

"What are you doing there?" she said. "I've already had to dig up three things for Murry Barr."

"I'm lazing around."

"Are you. I'm happy for you."

"What'd he ask you for?"

"Never mind. What are you doing?"

"Well, I was analyzing the debris in my bathtub drain and your name came up. Actually, I'm wondering if I could take you out for dinner. To a nice place out on the coast."

"Chez Ray."

"Yeah, Chez Ray. Not good enough for you?"

She paused. "Does this mean we're all chummy again?"

I laughed. "Look, I just want to talk it through, openly. But I want you to know I have feelings on both sides."

"You do?" Instantly she sounded moved.

"And I want you to know I'm for you, not against you. I'm not stupid enough to think I'm the only one with something to lose."

"You're not?"

"I don't want to be Mister Con all the time. I'm sick of that role. I want both of us to say everything we feel."

"But that's all I want too."

"Well then why don't I pick you up at five?"

36

The status quo

IT WAS ONE OF THOSE CLEAR FALL DAYS WHEN L.A. LOOKS like a wide-screen, Technicolor advertisement for itself. Solid white clouds skated across the blue; burnished skyscrapers gleamed; pretty vehicles buzzed along the Santa Monica freeway; a strip of silver ocean shone ahead. Maggie turned the radio on and it was playing an early Beatles tune, John at his most soaring.

We walked hand in hand into the restaurant. It was on Ocean Boulevard, on the cliff that overlooks the Santa Monica pier and the beach. A laid-back place with a tropical ambience, it had peanut shells on the floor and a surprisingly elegant steak and seafood menu. A lime sunset put a glow on the table where we settled; the bartender, who looked like a retired surfer, came over, lit our red candle, and took our order for a Mai Tai and a lemonade.

I had on a fancy shirt in beige linen that Maggie could never get me to wear; I felt sleek as a cougar.

"I'm sorry I didn't get to change," Maggie said.

"I'm not." I took her hand. She was wearing a mauve dress, long-sleeved, high necked and finely tailored.

"I always expect to look up and find Jim Rockford sitting at the bar," I said. "I did see Kurt Russell in here once."

"No you didn't," she said.

The drinks arrived and I took a hit of the tart, rummy liquid and smiled at her.

"You know what's going to happen," she said. "We're gonna have a great time, and not get around to the talk."

"That would be just like us."

"Irresponsible." She gave me a smile that looked anything but irresponsible.

"Right. So, let's order and then get very serious."

We looked at our menus and I found that as long as there would be a buttery baked potato on my plate, I didn't really care what else was there. I ordered a small sirloin. She went for the fresh perch, and our blond host took the menus.

I looked into my Mai Tai.

"You said you had feelings on both sides," Maggie said.

"I did. I do."

"I'm listening." She propped her chin on her hand, turned her calm grey eyes on me.

The door was open. All I had to do was walk through.

"I'm afraid," I said. "I'm afraid if I say anything good about the kid you'll clamp onto it and that'll be that."

"I might *agree* with you, true. Would that be so bad?"

"It would be if I end up not agreeing with me."

"Okay, I'm gonna be very considerate here. I won't say anything until you're done. Then I shall speak."

But I still couldn't do it.

I had a vision of the conversation that should be. A fair, wide-ranging discussion. We would look tenderly at the pluses, which were: we would enjoy being parents; we might even be good at it; we might have a great kid. Then we would survey the problems: the financial burdens, the life sentence to miserable jobs at SOB, the derailing of our creative dreams. At last, with a sweet, sad grasp of each other's hands, we would reluctantly conclude that a child just wasn't in the cards. Not yet.

That was how it should go; but what if it didn't? I was still haunted by her willingness to slog on without me. That took me out of the game. "Look," I said, "I just think we should agree off the bat that we're in this together. That we both do this, or else it doesn't happen."

She took a long look at me. She lifted her lemonade towards her lips, then put it back down. "You're trying to say that if we decide what we really want is to have the kid, you can still get cold feet and back out, and I have to go along with you."

"That's not what I'm saying." I took a pull on the Mai Tai, searching for better words.

"I can't say that, Dave. Sure, I'd rather work this out together. But if not, that'll be a different situation. I'll be on my own. I don't know what I'll do. I won't let you force me into some promise now."

I felt some hatchway of stubbornness close over me. "Then I can't talk about it," I said.

She looked appalled. "You're trying to threaten me."

"No I'm not."

"You're saying if I won't give you veto power, you'll walk out on the discussion."

"You are the one who's trying to threaten me," I said. "You're saying if I don't agree to the baby, you'll just exclude me from the process."

"No I'm not. I'm saying if we can't agree, I don't know what I'll decide to do." She hushed the last words because the waiter was coming.

The salads shone like postcards from a better time.

"It works both ways," she said when the waiter was gone. "If you can veto a baby, I should be able to veto an abortion."

"Those are two different things." I fended off the perky stare of a tomato slice.

"To have a kid is a major step," I said. "It changes everything. You don't do it if one person is uncomfortable with it. But having an abortion just leaves us with the status quo."

She pushed back her chair, staring hotly at me. I had a sickening feeling that she was going to walk out. "The status quo is that I'm *pregnant*," she growled, and rose to a standing position.

"No, wait," I said, and grabbed her wrist, terrified that the verdict might come down without my even making my case. "Don't go. I'm sorry. This isn't what I wanted. Let's talk about it. Forget vetoes."

Reluctantly Maggie seated herself again.

"You think I necessarily want this?" she said. "Losing control of my body, the weight gain, the pain? The responsibility?"

"I'm sorry," I said.

"I just want to look at it, play with it for a while in the sun. Not expose it to a decision yet. Then maybe I'll be grateful if we talk ourselves out of it. But can you just stop pressing my Stubborn button?"

"I'm sorry," I said.

"So tell me your positive emotions."

I speared some romaine with my fork. I studied the blue cheese dressing. I put the fork down. "Can I just tell you what I'm feeling?"

She smiled a little. "Okay."

I pulled on my drink again. It was half empty. "What I'm feeling is . . . I'm supposed to be a songwriter. That's my big claim to fame." I gave her my best self-deprecating look. "And I'm running out of time. No, let's be real. I ran out a while ago. But I still don't feel like I've taken my shot."

"Okay, that's honest."

"My plan was to pay off my debts." I was beginning to pick up steam. But she looked detached.

"I'm deep in debt. I haven't told you how much. It's embarrassing. It's maybe fifteen thousand. I'm afraid to add it up."

"I'm in debt too, Dave. Everyone is."

"But I have to get free of SOB before I can do music. I need some time off. And I have to pay off my debts, and save some money, before I can leave." I gave her a trapped look. "Maggie, I'm forty-one."

She dug into her salad. "Tell me one thing," she said. "The last time you took time off to do music—when was it?"

"It was 1982. I took ten months off."

"What did you *do* during that time?"

I looked at my drink.

"Let me guess," she said. "You bought a lot of equipment, and you did a lot of recording."

I shifted in my chair.

"Did you go out and sing? Or send tapes out?" She went back to her salad.

My jaw tensed. "If you're saying I don't care about my music, you're full of it. I've killed myself over my fucking demos."

"And?"

"They aren't good enough."

"Why not?"

"I don't know." My glass was empty. I tapped it nervously against the table, looking for the waiter.

"It's the vocals," I said. "You nailed it: when I'm recording, they never seem to come out right."

She nodded patiently. "You were better live." She ate a piece of tomato. "But you don't go out and do it."

"I don't know how," I said. "I've always had a problem with auditions. I go dead."

The waiter was passing. I waved my glass, in vain.

"You did okay," Maggie said, "when you sang that song for me with the tape rolling."

"It seemed that way. I gave George a copy."

At this moment the food arrived, and our beach-boy host seemed distressed by my untouched salad. He set down our steaming entrees apologetically.

"You could have somebody else do your vocals," Maggie said. She put a finger over her mouth, as if she'd gone too far.

"I've thought about that. But singer-songwriters have to do their own stuff."

She rolled her eyes and sighed.

"I wasn't always a loser, you know," I said. "I was *good* at philosophy. I had a job offer before I even finished my PhD. I could have been an academic."

"And you could have had a cottage," she said.

"Yeah, I probably could."

"And that's what your life is about."

"No, I walked away from those things, for music."

"That sounds like you," she said. "Always walking away. So you never give your heart and soul to anything. With one exception."

"Namely?"

"Your stupid job." She took a bite of her perch.

I fiddled with a glazed carrot and laughed. "Well at least I'm finding out what you think," I said. "It's great to know my music is a joke."

"You could still do your music, if you wanted to," she said. "I could work."

"Maggie, at least be realistic," I said. "We would have to move in together, get a house, probably get married. You'd have to take time off. I'd be at SOB for the rest of my life."

"Wait a minute, time-out!" she said. "Where did all this come from? Suddenly we're Jack and Jill Middle Class?"

"Maybe so," I said, cracking my baked potato, which was grey inside. "Children are difficult, they're expensive. They have to be brought up properly. Everything changes. You start worrying about what street you live on, where the good schools are. You suddenly need tons of baby clothes. And a washer-dryer."

"But I love baby clothes," she said, laughing.

"I know you do. I *know* you do." I had to laugh too.

"Look," she said. "Try this scenario. I leave town, you don't even know where I am. I have the baby or I don't. If I have her, I raise her myself. You never even know the outcome. You are blissfully unaware. You can go on making demo tapes until you're seventy."

The room seemed to list to port. "That's naïve," I said. "And by the way, why did you say 'her'?"

"I don't know. Judith thinks it's a girl. So what am I naïve about?"

"Me. You're naïve about me. Once I was faced with a kid, I couldn't just merrily go on with my life."

"Let me see if I've got this straight. Because you're so responsible about children, I can't have one?"

I gave her a miserable look.

She stood up. "This is really good fish, but I don't feel like eating it."

37

The lingerie sisters

IT'S SATURDAY AFTERNOON, AND TIME IS RUNNING OUT. George is sitting in his mom's Corolla while she runs into the realty office. The clock on the dash says 4:12. He is already regretting that he accepted her offer to drive him downtown. His real plan is to go to Graham's house and he is supposed to be there at 4:30. But that isn't what he told his mom.

He was ready to leave home on his bicycle at 3:45, and would have easily made it to Graham's on time. But after his mom interrogated him about his outing and he told her his cover story, she insisted on helping.

She comes back now with a sheaf of papers that she's shuffling through.

"I need to make one quick stop," she tells him.

"Mom . . ."

"It won't take two seconds. I think I know the house but I've got to be sure."

They take Kitchener Avenue all the way around to the bridge, cross the river and head up Empress Street. Halfway up the hill there's a prominent For Sale sign.

"This is the old Bader mansion, your grampa's partner Hank Robertson used to own it," his mom says.

She is looking to the right, up a long lawn, while George is looking to the left at Graham Doole's house. There doesn't seem to be any activity there.

"George, up *there*. The one with the big white porch."

"Oh, right."

"We have to drive up behind it, see if it's number 143. And I want the handout on it." His mom makes a right up a very steep street and then another right into a back alley that goes behind the big houses.

"I wondered how they got into these places," George says. "It seemed like a long hike from the street." The clock shows 4:31 but he's so close that he isn't too worried.

They ride down the alley and reach the rear of number 143. You can tell it's a three storey red brick house, and it's real big, but you can't tell much else. "Yup, this is it," his mom says. "It doesn't look like anything from this side, does it? But I know this place. I've been to parties here, when Hank had it. You wouldn't believe it, bay windows, chandeliers, a grand piano, everybody dressed to the nines. That's how they used to do it. It's a classic Calvan mansion. Not quite a mansion. Bart is going to love it."

She drifts forward so they can see the wraparound porch on the side.

"Who's Bart?" George says.

His mother's face colours. "Lee Barton. He is . . . new. I better go find the literature."

"I can get it," George says quickly. If she gets out of the car, she'll be forever.

"Okay, I don't see it here. Try around on the porch, by the front door."

George walks under huge oak trees, up the steps onto the wide porch and around to the front, which looks down on the river and beyond it, the whole downtown. Standing by the front door is a lady in business clothes holding some colourful papers.

"Is that the literature?" George says.

"It is, and who are you, young man?"

"I'm George Stone. My mom asked me to pick up some."

"Well, I'll give you one for good luck, but I have to tell you the house just sold. Literally an hour ago." She hands George a brochure with bright pictures on it. "Stone—not Susan Stone's son?"

George nods.

"I'm Meg Noughton, I've worked with your mom. Is she here now?"

Sensing doom, George says, "She's in the car, but we're running late."

"Well, say hello to her for me. And I'm sorry this place sold too soon for her. Will you tell her that?"

George has just spotted, way down on Empress Street below them, Carl's vintage Oldsmobile pulling over to the curb. He can see the unmistakable Laine heading down the alley beside Graham's house.

"You will tell her?" the lady says.

"I will," George says, and sprints back to the Toyota.

"It sold, Mom," he says. "We better go."

"No! It sold? Rats. Now I *know* it was the right place for Bart." She takes the brochure from George and, to his consternation, decides to majorly study it. "Look at this. Pretty fancy. The photograph is so . . . wide. I need to know how they do this. Where did they take it from, a helicopter?"

"Mom . . ."

"*What*, George? Oh, okay, I know. Darn, I can't believe this. It sold. The sign didn't say that. Who told you it sold?"

"Some lady. Meg something."

"Meg Noughton is around there? She gets all the good ones. Maybe she knows another place like this." His mom opens her door.

"Mom, please. I'm late already. We gotta go."

"George, what *is* it? You'll *be* there! What if you are a little late, the kids will be in the mall, and McDonald's isn't going anywhere. So hold on to your jockeys." His mom giggles like a girl and they peel along the back alley in reverse. Then she steers back down to Empress Street, hardly able to stop on the steep incline.

"Go left," George yells as she turns right.

"I can't, you ninny, it's one way. What is it with you?"

"Let me out here," George begs her.

His mom laughs. "You said you're meeting Tim and the others at the Eaton Centre. I've made you late and I'm going to get you there. I'm sorry, George. I'm a little distracted. This could be very big."

As they turn onto Mossbank Road, George wants to kill her but he forces himself to ask, "Who did you say he is?"

"Nobody important," his mom says.

Finally they get to the mall and she lets him loose, after making him promise twice to get a bus home by eight P.M. George's hope is that he may be out long after that, but she doesn't need to know.

It must be close to five o'clock when he runs down to Graham's side door. He knocks on it and nothing happens. Then he sees the plastic bag hanging on the knob.

Inside there's a note and a video. The video is *The Sound of Music*. The note says,

where were you, stone? waited for ever.
have to go for food in kitchener
best burgers and frosty freez.
then whatever—a movie ?
later,
Laine and Gr.

Then in different printing it says,

George, dig the Lingeray Sisters.

— your paparazi.

Back in the mall George stares at a Crowded House CD for ten minutes. He likes their song "Better Be Home Soon" but can't decide to buy it. He walks through the fluorescent blare, glumly imagining what it would be like to be riding in Carl's car with Laine beside him, on the way to some awesome burger joint. Then her house, or some movie. He could have been back, all the way back. Why did he get into his mom's frickin' car when he saw Carl's Olds? Why didn't he just refuse her original offer of a ride? He wants to put his fist through a store window.

He takes a bus home and finds the house empty, according to plan. His parents are both out and Alicia is at Alison Bull's house, Jennifer's sister who is her friend.

So it's just him and *The Sound of Music*. In the fridge he finds a Molson beer. He sits down in the basement room which houses the ping-pong table, his dad's desk, and the TV, and opens the *Sound of Music* box. The video inside is labelled with Graham's bad spelling, "The Lingeray Sisters." He puts it in.

First he sees a shot of aisles in a department store. It may be Eaton's. He swigs on the beer. It tastes cleaner than the ones he had with Laine. He hits pause, gets up, turns the light off. It's quiet in the house, he's going to enjoy this or die trying. Back in the chair, feeling his frustration ease from the beer, he hits play.

The camera is moving through aisles of clothing, around glass display cases where jewels glitter, along a wall of jeans. Because of the cameraman's small stature, it's like seeing things from the point of view of a tall dog. The footage is bright and a little grainy, and it shakes sometimes, just like on "Hard Copy." So far there have only been the sounds of a store, but now a whispered play-by-play starts.

"We're moving towards the underwear department, where our star has been sighted," the voice says. "You go first!"

Now Laine can be seen, looking monumentally tall as her silhouette blocks the scenery into which she is leading us. She makes a right into an open archway and we follow. There are several doors ahead on the left. She keeps going, into the last one. We do too; the camera shifts out of kilter and now we're looking at Graham's Oxfords. A lot of rustling and jostling; then we see Laine on a bench.

"We're in the women's dressing room area," the whisper continues. "Do we see our target?"

Graham snickers and Laine holds a finger over her lips. Her grainy features turn away for a moment and then swing back to us. Her large mouth forms the words, "Our target is talking to her sister."

Now the camera tilts to the left and we see out the door to the hallway in front of the dressing rooms. Jennifer Bull is standing there talking to Brie Cullen, Perfect Blonde Number Two. They are standing surprisingly close to our vantage point, but not looking this way, and Brie can be heard for a moment saying, "Just try it! I want to see it *on* you."

We hear the two girls going into the next cubicle, talking and occasionally screeching with laughter. Laine still occupies the right half of the picture. She has a look of concentration on her face. The left half of the screen shows the hallway. Into it comes Brie, preening herself in front of a full-length mirror and exchanging comments with Jennifer. There's an unclear speech from Jennifer, and then Brie says, "Let me see it anyway!"

Graham's voice-over whispers "Switching to hi-speed," and the action slows down, drastically, to a dream-like tempo that is grainier and darker and affects George like a drug. Brie floats like a goldfish in the purple darkness, her movements so slow it could shred his brain. Laine's face is clearer, but it too shifts like an underwater plant, the sparkle leaking from her eyes and teeth. The sight of this makes George's crotch begin to throb, and he takes another swig of the beer.

Jennifer emerges in a spaghetti-strapped nightgown that barely reaches below her panties. Like dye spreading across coarse canvas, her image bleeds over the screen, pale blue and white. But it is not her image, it is Laine's, that puts a flame to George. Red lips parted, black hair a crescent rocking by her ear.

And it is the feel of Laine's hand that George remembers. The fact of what she actually did, makes it so easy to imagine it now. It's not a fantasy; it's a reality he can conjure at will. On the screen the two blonde angels float, and the eyes of Laine feast on George, seeming to know what he is up to. The image of Jennifer disappears for a moment, then it is there again, this time with a long robe swirling around her. The warm hand tugs on his prick. He feels like he's ten feet long.

George is in love with the Laine on the screen. Behind the scenes, able to outsmart the world. Her eyes seem to know so much, more than children know, more than adults who are all the same. Looking at her face on the screen, everything is pulled together for him. There is room for all of it, the warmth at the bottom of the pool, the steamboat in the night, the old man in the hospital. They all belong now. If any of them were changed, this Laine moment wouldn't be right.

The screen dies into blackness and so does the room. He could come now; he has done it a few times since that weekend. But he doesn't. This isn't about him whacking off alone. This is about him being with Laine.

38

Three kinds of death

LAINE IS IN CHURCH ON SUNDAY. RIGHT ACROSS THE
aisle from George, with two people who must be her parents.
The father is old, but still has a dangerous look to him, like Clint
Eastwood. The mother looks to be George's mom's age, sandy
haired with features like a bird. He has seen them in church
before, but not often. Laine he has hardly ever seen in church.

Laine is famous now. She doesn't look exactly like the girl in
the video, yet she must be that girl. George has noticed that
every time she sits down, her black dress rides up above her
knees. The dress is not sexy: it has short sleeves, a large floppy
white collar, and white buttons. But it fits her. Her knees, in the
pantyhose with the white shine, are perfect. Even with them
showing, she looks like Sunday School. How is that possible?

George feels something tugging on him. It's Alicia, pulling
him down onto the pew. "The song's over," she whispers. His
face turns red and he looks at his father, at the pulpit. It's time
to listen to today's scripture.

"Then Noah built an altar to the Lord . . ." his father says.

And took of every clean animal and of every clean
bird, and offered burnt offerings on the altar. And

when the Lord smelled the pleasing odour, the Lord
said in his heart, "I will never again curse the ground
because of man."

His dad looks up, right at George. He thinks, *was that about
me?* But his father turns back to his book.

"Neither will I ever again destroy every living creature as
I have done. While the earth remains, seedtime and harvest, cold and heat, summer and winter, shall not cease."

The words clatter onto the floor of George's mind like
coins in an empty drawer.

He checks on Laine. She is looking straight ahead. Her
mother is looking over at George, with enough attention to
make him look away. Not before he catches a smile on Laine's
mouth.

Everyone is saying the Lord's Prayer. George joins in,
"Forgive us our trespasses . . ."

He looks again. Mrs. Meyer is flipping through a hymnbook. For a second, Laine looks at him. No facial expression.
Just that look, like on the TV screen. Oh god, she is good. He
can smell her perfume, the same as that weekend. He feels her
fingers on his thigh. Not hers, Alicia's.

"George!" his mother says, indicating that he should stand
up for the second hymn. She also looks good today; she must
have caught it from Laine.

They sing "This Is My Father's House." George sits down
with everybody else. The sermon is starting.

"What is Thanksgiving to you?" his father says.

Laine, George answers.

"To me it means the feeling of being safe for another year,"
his father says. "Safe from hunger. Safe from disaster. Safe
from death. And that's what I want to talk about today: death,

three kinds of death actually, and what they can teach us about
Thanksgiving."

George tries to think about death. And Thanksgiving.
Thanksgiving is when the left side of your body is glowing from
her rays.

"The first kind of death lies just ahead of all of us who sit
here today," his father says. "If we hadn't been through it
before, no doubt we would greet it as a total calamity. But we
have gone through it, and made it out the other side. The
other side is called spring. The first death is winter."

His father smiles out at the congregation. "The Pilgrims,"
he says. "They barely made it through the winter of 1620. And
when the next fall came, and they had a harvest, they gave
thanks to God. They should also have thanked Squanto, the
Native American who gave them seed corn. And God — and
God, of course."

George is thinking about tomorrow. Getting with Laine at
recess, maybe. He *can* be with her again; it's a slam dunk. But
he wants to be with her alone. Not at Graham's, at her place.
What would it be like to kiss her? He can't believe he didn't.

"The second kind of death cannot be dodged," his dad
says. "For most of us it is not coming soon, but to all of us it
will come."

George slips his hand into his pocket, trying to free himself. His mother is looking at him. His face is red. He doesn't
just have a rock-hard dick. He also has a pulsating bladder. Try
to listen to Dad.

"We all die. Yes it's scary, yes it's sad—but it doesn't end
life. Our children follow us. The new tree grows out of the
decay of the old."

George can't take it any longer. He leans behind Alicia and
whispers to his mom. "Okay, go now," she nods.

He starts down the aisle. Laine's mouth smiles again. He
hears his father's voice. "The third kind. Death of the group.

Noah without the ark ..." George goes through the door at the back, into the gloom of the coatroom.

Down in the basement he works his way along a cluttered hall, finds the men's room, uses it.

When he comes out, Laine is standing there.

"I couldn't hack it with the church thing," she says. "What is that, like, about? Is that guy really your father?"

"Is that guy *your* father?" George says.

Laine laughs. "I know, he is kind of old. He's cool though. If he didn't drag me to church. I don't know where they got that smart idea. Probably guilt-tripping."

"I've seen them here a few times," George says. "I didn't know they were yours."

"Some people think Carl is my dad; he's around a lot more than they are."

"Where do they hang?"

"All over. My dad has houses. Florida, England, stuff like that. They have to check in with all of them."

"England. Cool."

"So, where were you yesterday?" Laine says.

"Watching you."

"Oh, really. Did you like me?"

"Yeah ... I liked you," George says. "But you could have waited for me."

"I wanted to, but Graham was hungry. He ate two burgers. And then a giant popcorn at the movie."

"Don't tell me about it."

"The movie sucked," Laine says. "So, Stone, what do we do now?"

It makes George laugh, her talking her "Stone" talk in that girly dress.

"I know a fun spot," he says, and he takes her hand. She lets him lead her up the wooden stairs into the gloom of the cloak-room, then up the carpeted stairs to the balcony.

"This is where the angels sit," George whispers.

"That's why there's no one here," Laine says.

George takes her down to the front pew and they sit close together, looking over the smooth wooden rail at the captive congregation. George puts his arm around her as her user-friendly dress rides up above her knees again.

"This is cool," Laine whispers. "It's like a date!" This thought elicits a laugh from her, that would have caught the giant echo chamber of the church if she hadn't cut it off in time. As it is, a sound like a very loud squeak does make it into the public space. Below them a couple of heads turn.

At his pulpit, George's father is reading.

Behold, that cruel day comes,
with wrath and fierce anger,
to make the earth a desolation . . .

Laine says into George's ear, "Your father needs to lighten up."

George sees a lifetime of Sunday services in a new, hilarious light. The musty people, the stern words, the weird songs, are too funny. He starts to laugh silently and Laine puts her hand over his mouth, her eyes begging him not to infect her with his humour. But he's overheating from not making any noise. Sweat breaks on his forehead, tears come out of his eyes, and they both lose it and the bottled-up laughter peals out of them.

Down below, people start to look and George pulls Laine onto the floor between the pews, where the two of them pant like fallen wrestlers.

"Do you think they saw us?" Laine whispers.

"I think they heard us," George says.

Laine's face takes on an easy look as she continues to lie in his embrace, like they're camping and it's time to go to sleep.

"Kiss me," George says.

"I will," Laine says. She tilts her head, seeming to check the air for any signs of danger, but there is only the sound of the congregation singing "Praise God From Whom All Blessings Flow."

Laine touches her soft mouth to George's, and he kisses her, not quite finding the right way to move, but loving the way she lets him try.

Then they hear steps on the stairs, and George knows with horrible certainty that he is about to see his mom.

"Hey," George says. "Do you want to go to the Hallowe'en dance with me?"

"That would be awesome," she says. "Can Graham come?"

39

Switching roles

IT WASN'T MAGGIE'S FAULT THAT I GOT NO SITE RESEARCH done in the days after the Chez Ray incident. She stayed away from me. She didn't come to work on Thursday, and she never came near my office on Friday.

It was my fault: I kept stewing over our situation, replaying our dialog in my head. And it was Murry Barr's fault: he bombarded me with trivial tasks. And finally, it was the fault of that oldest law of Law Firms: if it ain't due this week it doesn't exist. I did manage to get Barr to agree to a meeting on Monday, where we would face up to the client's new demands and hand out final assignments.

Then on Sunday afternoon I emerged from a weekend mélange of beer, old cheddar, and bad TV movies, to find I had a severe Maggie deficit. She might have our baby, or she might not. But I couldn't go on not being able to call her.

"Oh, it's you," she said when she picked up the phone.

"I was just wondering, are we ever going to talk?"

"Not today. Sandra and Bill are coming over."

"Well tomorrow then. At work. We'll sneak off somewhere and we'll figure this out."

"What's to figure out?"

"I don't know." I considered. "I don't know. But we can't be like this." I paused again, worn down by our estrangement. "We still haven't really communicated."

"Whose fault is that?"

"Mine. I'm chicken."

"And you think you're the only one."

"Yeah, I guess."

"I'll see you tomorrow."

The Glendale Freeway was fast on Monday morning; I made it to SOB by 8:30. I got right to work on briefing materials for the three o'clock meeting. I was rolling nicely when the phone rang.

It was Susan. "I just wanted to say hello and give you an update on Dad. And wish you a happy Canadian Thanksgiving," she said.

"Oh, right. So, how is he?"

"He's good. He was wide awake when I went in at about eleven this morning. He's in a little hot water, though. Sandy told me they took him to a group exercise session down the hall today and they ejected him."

"What do you mean—did he get out of step?"

My door opened and Maggie looked in. She seemed bright, charged up. I waved to her apologetically, while Susan answered.

"No, kicked out for being disruptive. He was yelling and objecting to everything. I guess he didn't like being ordered around."

I thought back to the original reports she had given about Joseph, right after the stroke. This sounded like the same thing. The rage, the confusion. Which I had seen none of when I was there.

"That sounds bad," I said. "We want him doing exercises. We want him understanding what's going on."

"Oh, he's okay. They're starting to work his arm and his leg in his own room. Anyway, we're having quite a crowd here for dinner." She already sounded as if her purpose in calling me was completed.

"But wait," I said. "What did *he* say about the group session?"

"I didn't really call him on it. It wasn't that easy to understand him, anyway."

"What do you mean?"

"Well, with the teeth not in, you know what it's like."

"But the teeth have got to be in. Every day."

"I think they were trying, last week. But the nurses say they don't fit anymore."

"Susan, this is ridiculous. I just saw him a week ago and they were fitting fine."

"You're right. I don't know, they said he's not comfortable with them. Sandy said there may be some tissue loss."

I could hear in her voice that she needed to be off the phone. Somebody, probably Alicia, was grousing to her in the background. I wasn't on duty with her in Calvan; it was not my place to press her on this. We said goodbye.

I knew I should go and talk to Maggie; I didn't want to get off on the wrong foot with her today. But I couldn't let go of what I had just heard. No one was on the denture case. They were being lazy, being careless, making up excuses. His gums had shrunk—what a crock! They were turning him into a loser. They were isolating him, this brilliant man who had been able to analyze his own reading problem, who had actually asked himself whether the cause was faulty eyesight or faulty comprehension. They were letting him slide.

I was in a fine stew over the laughable, unconscionable triviality of the mistake that was being made. The nurses, and even my sister, didn't see that talk was like oxygen for him. Words were the stuff out of which his soul was made. If they robbed him of words, they would rob him of life. They *couldn't* do this! If the gums really had shrunk, they should fit him for fucking replacement teeth. If dentists had to be summoned, fine. The man had money. I was so steamed up my glasses were clouding.

I called my brother's work number. Greg answered and I told him my vision of what was happening and why it must be stopped. As always it was easy because there was nothing I could transmit that my brother would have trouble receiving. By the time I finished, I was laughing with relief. Greg clearly got the point. In his solemn, warm way, he promised to address this matter, to try to restore full communication to our father.

I was still in a froth after we said goodbye. I walked around to Maggie's office and filled her in. "But now I'm really up against it," I told her. "I have a meeting with Barr and the gang at three."

She looked at me with the eyes of one who has no illusions. "I'm not going to get on your case," she said. "You were the one who said you wanted to talk today."

"Just give me till one o'clock," I said. "We'll go for lunch."

"I have to be back by two. We're having an Acid Rain meeting."

At 1:10 I turned from my desk to find her standing pointedly in my doorway.

"I know, I know," I said.

She stepped towards me. She was wearing a forest-green sweater with fine gold trim. Her chest took up a position on a level with my famous desk lamp.

"I don't want to get you upset," she said. "I know you're facing a deadline. So I'm just going to tell you I have to go to Judith's tonight. And if you don't talk to me today, I'm not going to take it very well."

A chill passed across my gut. I turned away from my work and folded my hands in my lap, trying to drag my mind away from the insight I had just had into the client's fifth topic-heading.

"Okay. Let's talk."

She closed my door and stood alertly in front of it. There

was a subtle yet irrepressible gleam in her eyes: the high spirits
of a warrior at last released into combat.

"Now I have a brilliant idea," she said. "We are going to
switch roles. I am going to tell you the many excellent reasons
why you think we shouldn't have this baby. But first, you are
going to tell me why we should."

I started to answer, but she held a hand up. "Let me clarify,"
she said. "Not *your* reasons for having it. My reasons. You're
going to play me. It's a negotiating technique. Begin when
you're ready."

"Don't you want to get some lunch?"

"I don't have time."

"Okay," I said, feeling winded. "Okay, let's see. Well, we
should have this baby because you're thirty-two and . . ."

"Thirty-three."

"Thirty-three, right. And it is the right time and we don't
know how many more chances we'll get."

She waited at the door.

"And we should have it," I continued, "because . . . because
whatever we could do without a child, we can also do *with* a
child, or if we can't, that's just too bad, because . . ."

Her look was like a caution light. In spite of it, my mood
had turned—I was sick of this farcical exercise. My meeting
deadline hovered in the background like an impatient cab
driver. This was extortion. My phone started ringing; the
voicemail light started flashing.

"I can't talk now," I said. She stared unrelentingly at me.

Suddenly, out of my confusion one fact loomed up and
demanded recognition: this pregnancy was never the plan.

"Okay," I said, "this must be your point. Even if we lose
our options, it is just too bad, because we knew when you went
on the pill that it might not work; after all it's only 99.9%
effective. And why would somebody go on the pill if she didn't
want to get pregnant?"

Her face was dark as smoke.

"I can't do your point of view," I said. "It doesn't make sense to me. I don't even know if I can do my own."

"You just can't deal with a new situation," she hissed. "It might force you to wake up."

"Maggie," I said.

She turned back to me on her way out. "I'm on my own," she declared. "That's what you've told me."

40

A slippery slope

I SURPRISED MYSELF: ANGER WON OUT OVER FEAR, prudence, empathy, or any other reaction. Grimly, I threw myself into my own agenda.

I took a lunch break, revelling in the lustrous variety of the corporate women who paraded up and down Sixth Street. I strode into the meeting for which I was not prepared, thinking, *none of you has bothered to do any special homework; why should I?* And I exposed the absurdity of some of the lawyers' comments, pointing out that they didn't know the policy provisions to which they so glibly alluded.

No effective planning took place: Barr wasted half the meeting with a stern lecture on how important the deadline was, instead of telling us how we might go about meeting it. I spent the rest of the week on other things. I was only responsible for two sites anyway—I could do them next week; and if the rest of the team was pissing in the wind, it wasn't my problem.

Not until Saturday did my not caring begin to wear thin. On that day I woke up early, and in my sunny living room, happened on an old episode of "The Fugitive" in which Richard Kimble befriends a young girl who has been neglected by her parents. I got thoroughly sucked into the story, and was moved when Kimble's road-weary honesty saved the girl from a spiteful accuser.

I went for a long walk in a canyon north of Pasadena, sat on a cactus-festooned promontory above the city, and tried to hear the voice of my conscience. When I got home there was a pale rose twilight everywhere. My tan rental house was glowing on the green lawn; the eucalyptus trunks were peeling away my ego.

I need ethical counselling, I announced to myself: I'm going to call Gayle. She was my academic friend, a forbiddingly bright philosophy PhD student whom I had hired at SOB during a break from her graduate work. Not only was she a close friend who had often played free shrink for me (and for whom I had done the same), but she was also a bona fide specialist in ethics.

That she was also a woman who had once made a move on me seemed less relevant today than her unfailing loyalty and her credentials as a moral philosopher. Although I thought of myself as pro-choice, I had been bothered during today's sojourn in the hills by a tiny, nagging uncertainty about the morality of ending a pregnancy.

Gayle would know the latest moves in that conceptual game; from her logical control tower she would talk me down onto the feminist tarmac.

She was home, and surprised to hear from me. After some small talk I said, "So, can I come to the point?"

"You mean there is a point to this babble?"

I told her the bare bones of the situation.

"So, I take it you two have disagreed about the correct course of action," she said in a consolidating way.

"Not exactly, that's what's weird. We haven't had a *chance* to disagree, because we keep arguing about the terms of the negotiation. It's really dumb, and it's my fault."

"Go on."

"Well, this is going to sound sleazy, but I've been saying

that we can't discuss the pros and cons unless we agree in advance that we don't have the kid if one of us doesn't want it."

I heard Gayle laugh. "That sounds like a very safe position for Mr. Moore to take."

"It does. But I'm actually serious about it. Gayle, I don't think Maggie and I are the sort of couple who are going to have a kid and both of us not be fully involved in the future of that kid."

"Clearly."

"So I think it's only fair that we don't have it unless we both want to."

"Okay . . . but tell me something. Have you guys been taking precautions, as they say?"

"Precautions! She's on the fucking pill. She has been for six months. Before that we sensed ovulations and lived in fear."

"Is this the same pill the rest of the country is on?"

"Yeah. She missed it, for one day. Apparently with our fertility that's all it took."

"Okay, so this is an unwanted pregnancy. A scrupulously avoided one. So what do you want to do?"

"Well, she doesn't seem at all sure that she might not want to have the kid. I'm not even sure what she's feeling, because . . ." I looked for a graceful way to explain how I had muzzled the discussion.

"Don't tell me how she feels," Gayle said in a calm tone. "Tell me how you feel. Do you want a baby in your life?"

I fidgeted in my chair. My hands were sweating. "Is that even the question?" I said. "If it is, I guess the answer is no, it would screw all my plans. I'm too old, I don't even know that we're right for each other . . . but I'm not sure that is the question. Look, I don't even know if abortion is right. There's a human being inside her, I don't know if it's okay to kill it."

"It has got human DNA, but it is not a person," Gayle said with massive authority. "It's a fetus. Aborting a fetus is not murdering a human being."

"Have you heard of that film," I said in a voice like someone whispering in a cold crypt.

"*The Silent Scream.*"

"Yeah. I keep thinking about it."

"You've seen *The Silent Scream*?"

"No, I haven't seen it. I've heard about it."

"It's a piece of patriarchal, fundamentalist propaganda. It proves nothing."

"I know it doesn't *prove* anything," I said, feeling shaky but oddly resolute. "I think we each have to confront it with our own intuitions."

"Confront what? It's a sonar-generated image of a non-verbal organism: you can't argue from that to consciousness or pain or anything with moral consequences."

"Isn't that a little pat? A cat is a nonverbal entity, but if I watched enough film of your cat I'd probably impute consciousness to it, and if I saw you holding a match to its little nose I'd probably impute pain."

"That's not the same thing." Gayle's command of her topic sounded a little less absolute.

"Look," I said, "I'm just saying I'm not sure *theory* is how we get to other people's minds. I think nature gave us intuitions. I don't know what a fetus looks like after a couple of weeks. Maybe if I did, I would have an instinctive take on it—that's not a person."

"You don't want to start down that slippery slope," Gayle said smoothly. She seemed to have recovered her professorial aplomb. "Just stick with the main question. Do you believe a woman has a right to decide what to produce with her own body?"

"Of course," I said impatiently. "Of course I'm pro-choice. So is Maggie. What do you think, we're Republicans? But given that, I'm trying to see how a person would go about *making* that choice."

"Well, I can't walk with you down that path," Gayle told me.
"Why don't we assume there's no objection in principle to terminating a pregnancy. Then we get down to you and Maggie.
That's easier, isn't it? You *should* terminate because as a couple
this would not be a rational move for you. It's not a responsibility that you were ready to take on, or that you have any
obligation to take on."

"That's what I've tried to tell her. The financial burden,
the impossibility of pursuing music, the perpetual nine-to-five closing around you—it's ludicrous."

"Ye-ess." She welcomed her wanderer back to the corral.

"So that's it." I took a deep breath, then was quiet for a
moment. "But the odd thing is—and I haven't even told her
this, because I'm such a creep—I sometimes get this image of
her with a child, of all the gifts she would bring to that situation. Of the sheer fun she would have with it." I struggled for
control over my voice. "And then I think it would be a crime to
stop that from happening."

"That's sentimental. You don't embark on a twenty-year
enterprise with that kind of rationale. Given the doubts
you've expressed to me, you don't embark at all. It would be
irresponsible."

There was a long silence; I heaved a big sigh. "Gayle, you
are a breath."

"I won't ask of what. And now I'm going to have to let you
go, unless you're still troubled."

"I'm not troubled. I've just inspected myself and I seem
remarkably free of trouble."

"Take care, Dave."

"Thanks," I said, and I sat in the burgundy chair, watching
the motes dance in the last pink rays coming over the windowsill.

So I was okay. It might be time for a beer. But I didn't
stir. I was thinking about Maggie, how she had been with
Alicia. Maggie, who had never quite honoured herself with

the credentials of adulthood. Who couldn't give in and play the political game at work. Who only got a firm grasp on her self-esteem when she was under attack, then lost it if she won. I was thinking how easily, how smoothly the world could reason Maggie out of her baby, how remorselessly Gayle's logic was able to give me the authorization I needed.

I couldn't help it; I was seeing Maggie as the threatened creature, the vulnerable one, the soul who could be had. Maggie, who was afraid to dress her own yearnings in any but the most casual, flimsy, playful fabrics. Maggie, who at bottom might be almost as much of a coward as her traitorous boyfriend.

Who the fuck was I to forbid her? What great riches did I bring in compensation?

My legs carried me to the telephone. I was sitting, staring at the phone, when it rang.

It was Maggie.

"I don't want to have it," she said. "I'll get too fat."

"You will?"

"I'm kidding. I don't want to have it, for the same reasons you don't. I've been thinking and thinking about it. It would be a giant chore, like you said. We don't need it. What we need is us, that's more important to me. I've been lying here imagining how you felt helpless and betrayed, and I decided it was ridiculous. Are you there?"

"I'm here."

"Good," she said.

I was in the grip of a suffocating moral dilemma. Should I accept the surrender or should I say what I had been about to say? I found a compromise, known as the past tense.

"I was just gonna call you," I said. "I was going to say we could have it, that I didn't have the right to deny it."

"So it's O'Henry time."

There was a long pause. I could hear her breathing. It was

as if we were holding hands. I couldn't say anything, not one word that might affect the outcome. The silence was sacred.

"I never really thought it was real," she said. "I had fun playing with it, but it wasn't real. You know?"

I was choked up. "I don't know," I said.

I was thinking in my heart, maybe it would be the most beautiful thing we could do. And then I realized I had said it out loud.

"I thank you for saying that," she said, sounding more in possession of herself than I was. "If the time comes, we'll do it. We didn't plan it for now, you're right about that."

I still couldn't talk, and she said, "Let's stop worrying about it."

41

The reign of Maggie

Sunday morning was blindingly bright on Walnut Street in Pasadena as Maggie and I emerged from the Appletree Inn, having partaken of its sumptuous buffet. I had stayed mostly with the stir-fry concept, Maggie in the omelette area, and then we had converged on the berry crêpes.

Before we had gone to sleep in her bed the night before, I had pretty much spilled my thoughts about the kid, while managing to keep them in the "I was going to say" mode. I also admitted that I had been unfair: I shouldn't have asked for promises about what she would or wouldn't do on her own. I even told her about my desire to see what a fetus looked like, just to get a gut reaction. She, having apparently decided on the abortion, wasn't very desirous of any such skirmish with reality; but this morning over her omelette she had surprised me by suggesting that we visit Vroman's and see if they had any books on the subject.

Nevertheless, she still seemed good with our decision, and she was in a light-hearted mood that had no fangs in it. It's true, she was adopting a kind of facetiously regal attitude, as if I was a courtier who must now be in service to her; as if her renouncing her wish to bear the child had conferred new obligations on me its beneficiary.

"Can you go and get the car sweetheart," she said on the blazing sidewalk. "I'm too full to walk to it."

"But of course," I told her.

As I walked through a green churchyard to the side street where my Squareback was parked, I added to myself, "And then we'll go to the bookstore and hope our boat isn't capsized." This was a new age, I realized: the era of "what Maggie wants, Maggie gets." She had already decreed that all logistics, and any expenses, of the abortion were to be handled by me, and this had seemed much too small a price for me to pay for her sacrifice—the motives for which were so unclear that I was afraid to inquire into them.

I drove into the hotel's circular driveway and retrieved her from the shadows in which she was protecting her skin. She set herself on the seat beside me, adjusting the skirt of the Brazilian festival dress she was busting out of today. She was a caricature of blooming health, from her rich brown curls, sneaking loose from a scarf, to her feet wrapped in leather sandals. She was fanning herself with the Sunday *Times* magazine, wrinkling the portrait of Warren Beatty that adorned it.

"Careful of my friend," I said. "He did put me in some pretty good company when he rejected my song for *Heaven Can Wait*."

"Yes, I know—you've told me. You knew his cousin, blah blah, you almost broke into the big time without unpacking your suitcase—I've heard it all before."

"I might have had Dusty Springfield singing 'As If You Knew.'"

"Right. Get me to the air conditioning."

We pulled up beside Vroman's and miraculously, there was an empty space right by the door. "Will this do?" I asked.

In the store we slipped into normal roles. I disappeared into the fiction section, trying to remember what review I had seen recently that piqued my interest in killer viruses. Maggie went into the art section. After a while I gave up on remembering the title I wanted. A sign caught my eye: maternity books, second floor. I went up there and soon fastened on a picture book that contained actual photographs of the unborn in the womb. The first one I hit was a huge colour shot of what looked like an alien from a Spielberg movie: it had long, skinny arms, little hands with clearly separated fingers, a purple darkness inside the torso that must be the heart, and on the side of the huge, translucent orange head, dark orbs, almost like bruises, that would some day turn out to be eyes.

Seized with trepidation, I made myself look at the text. It said nine weeks after conception. Where were we now? Six? Could the creature really be that big? I checked the text and the length was stated as 2.4 inches. The photograph was blown up to triple size.

I descended the stairs, thinking, maybe if you saw it actual size . . . A hand grabbed me. It was Maggie, steering me to the science section where she'd found a tome on our subject. She pointed to a sort of diagram, maybe it was a photograph, in black and white, that showed a brain. Except the brain had no detail yet, no articulated subparts.

"It says the brain wiring isn't in place until about five months," Maggie told me. I read along with her, smelling her sweet breath and basking in the reflected light of her attention like a toad on a bright lily pad. The cerebral cortex had to form; there had to be neurons, axons, synapses. All that didn't happen until twenty to twenty-four weeks.

She flipped to another picture, much like the one that had spooked me. An alien with its giant head bent forward.

"It's cute," she said. "But look at this one."

She turned back a few pages. I saw what looked like a worm with a blowout at one end and a pointed tail at the other. A quarter inch long, it said. It was shorter than my little fingernail.

"This is four weeks," she said. "It's still called an embryo up until eight weeks, and then it's a fetus."

"And we're at six weeks," I said.

"No we aren't! We're just starting week four, dummy."

Could that be correct? Then I realized I had been counting from when she was in Columbus. She was right, of course.

And I was like a guitar string wound too tight.

"I think you need some air," she said. "Let's get going."

We passed through the store and I spotted the book on viruses: *Deadly Replica* was the title. This time, the review had said, it *was* lethal to humans and it was loose in Phoenix before they found it.

I didn't even think about detouring. We marched out to the street and encased ourselves in the hot car.

Maggie said, "I'm so thirsty."

Normally I would have put her off until we got home.

"Why don't we stop at the Shell Station on Fair Oaks," I said.

42

An unlined ditch

I WAS PINNED, WITH THE PASLY SITE ON TOP OF ME. IT was the first Plandor site I'd ever looked at, that day when I ran afoul of Ocher; and it wasn't treating me any better now than it had then. Unfortunately it was one of the two pollution sites that I had to personally report on.

The bottom line was, I needed to figure out the bottom line. How much was Plandor's share of the cleanup? The SOB team had collected a mountain of EPA studies, court documents, and newspaper clippings. I had spent Monday scrabbling through these materials like a mouse in a dumpster. All they had done was make me want some cheese. Now it was Tuesday and I was no farther ahead.

The big meeting at which Barr would critique the final reports was set for the 28th of October—a week from Friday—which didn't seem to be close enough to shock my brain into gear.

Meanwhile I had to work up the Ranner site too; and the new box of pain killer policies sat in the corner, awaiting my attention.

I wasn't doing any better with the abortion arrangements. We'd made our decision on Saturday and I hadn't even called a clinic yet. The time element could still overtake me; the sand of week four was running through the hourglass; the picture book pages were turning.

Well at least I can do that, I told myself, disgustedly putting aside the Pasly stack. I got a Yellow Pages from the main SOB switchboard room. I found a section called Family Planning and dialled a clinic number.

A female voice answered, mousy, young sounding.

"I'm inquiring on behalf of a friend who is pregnant," I said, groping for a way to say what I was inquiring *about*.

"Can you have your friend call us directly?" the voice answered.

"She's asked me to handle this for her."

"Well, we could make an appointment, and she could come in and see us, for counselling."

This didn't sound exactly right. "I'm not sure counselling is what we're looking for," I said, feeling like I was walking on eggshells.

"We like to make clients aware of all the options. There are many possible options that not all girls are aware of, and we want to be sure she is making an informed choice, doing what she truly thinks best, before we go ahead."

This sounded worse and worse. I was gonna have to go for it. "Well, my friend is not a girl, she's a thirty-three-year-old woman, and she already knows what she wants, which is to terminate the pregnancy."

"Is she aware of the dangers of abortion for someone that old? There are physiological dangers. Has she ever had an abortion before?"

I thought hard and drew a blank. "I don't know."

"Well, we would want to discuss all this with her. If she has, the physical dangers are much amplified." The speaker didn't sound so young anymore; my gut felt cold. The soft, insistent voice plodded on. "Infection, bleeding, endometriosis. There is a serious danger that the patient will not be able to bear a child in future. She needs to consider that. Not to mention the emotional scars. There are other options. We can provide guidance and help, so the baby can end up in a good, loving home. Would you like to make an appointment for her to come in and talk with us?"

"Let me consult with her," I said. I hung up, sweating.

Why hadn't it occurred to me that there were procedures, that you had to *qualify*? This wasn't like getting a tooth pulled. The thought of real medical consequences, of losing the option of having children in future, was more than sobering. If it was really true it made our decision for us.

Part of my psyche was ready to concede the whole point, if only to stop the reeling sensation. Then it dawned on me. *That wasn't an abortion clinic that I was talking to: that was a pro-life agency.* Suddenly it was so obvious it was laughable. An abortion clinic wouldn't talk like that. The Falwell troops had infiltrated their enemies' section of the *Yellow Pages*.

The phone rang and it was Susan.

"I've been to see Dad," she said. "I wanted to give you an update."

"Well the first thing I want to know is, were his teeth in?"

"No they weren't." Her voice sounded blunt.

"Susan, I spoke to Greg about it. If they don't fit, we get new ones. But we *keep them in.*"

There was a long pause. This wasn't like Susan; her agenda was usually clear and forthcoming.

"I'm not sure you have the picture," she finally said. "I'm not sure we're talking comeback."

"What do you mean? I just saw him a week ago. He was incredible."

"It was *two* weeks ago," she said. "I—I just saw him yesterday. He's not the same."

"I'm sorry."

"I remember on Thanksgiving, he still seemed pretty good. Since then he's gone downhill. They moved him to a different room. It's supposed to be a ward. He's on Three now. But he's all alone in there, a big empty room with just his bed in it. He's kind of out of the action. We're not sure he's getting the same care."

"You're kidding. Jeez."

"That's not even the main problem. He's a mess. He's lost a lot of weight. His skin is terrible; it's yellow."

"But what about *him*, was he still there?"

"He is still smiling when he sees us. I don't know if he knows who we are. His left side is gone, even the face." I could hear her fighting for control. "I hate to be telling you this. I think he's losing. The damage must have spread some more. It's beating him."

"I can't believe this," I said.

"I don't think there's anything we can do. He's not eating. Lori thinks he may have *decided* to die."

"He may know it's hopeless."

"So I'm not sure teeth are the issue anymore."

"Maybe not."

"Though I wish he had them in, because he still says things to us, when he can focus. He seems to come and go. He's been telling people it's snowing in his room. I think that's what he's saying."

"Snowing. He said that before. Oh no, it was rain. His arm felt like rain was on it. So now it's snowing?"

"I guess. I just wanted you to know what was happening." She paused again. "I only hope he doesn't hit a plateau and then linger forever. No one could take that, least of all Mother."

"How is she?"

"Bad. She goes to him, but I don't know who it's worse for, him or her. I think she's in permanent shock."

"Sounds like I may be coming back there sooner than I thought."

"I'm almost hoping so. How are you, anyway?"

I didn't even try to tell her. I just said, "Work is heavy, Maggie is good." *Work is good, Maggie is heavy*, I should have said.

We hung up and I stared at the deposition of some dick-weed who had dumped ninety thousand tons of petrochemical waste into an unlined ditch by the Great Lakes.

43

There are no dragons

IT'S BEEN A LONG TIME SINCE GEORGE HAS HAD A chance to talk to Laine. All last week he was shut out. Monday was Thanksgiving, then Laine was gone for three days, and then on Friday during both recesses he had to help Mr. Bolton organize gym equipment. (Maybe because of the swimming incident, Bolton has been trying to befriend him.)

Laine didn't show in church on Sunday. Finally, yesterday, George was outside during recess and she was at school; but he couldn't get rid of Tim Cahill. So he's been reduced to observing her in class, trying to get a feel for her attitude. And it's been mostly the big tease: she doesn't look at him. Recess is coming up fast, at 10:35.

Everyone is supposed to be writing a paragraph about something that happened to them on some past Halloween. Mrs. Tindale has put three words on the board: COSTUME, PLACE, and REACTION. George finished his paragraph five minutes ago. It tells about the time he was dressed as a pirate and they came to the Beasleys' house and Mrs. Beasley was holding a giant bag of candy and George stabbed it with a wooden sword.

Mrs. Tindale is helping Kevin Brown over in row one, and Jamie Dermott is wandering the aisles in a state of mental emergency. Mrs. Tindale looks around and says, "What do we do, Jamie, when we have a question? Two things."

"Stay in our seat and put up our hand," Jamie says.

"Correct," she tells him. "Why don't you do that, and as soon as I have time I will get to you."

Jamie ambles back to his desk, but soon the room is full of rustling and fidgeting, and two more people are on the loose. Mrs. Tindale looks around again and mumbles something to Kevin, and then she says, "I guess we're all pretty much finished with our compositions. I am going to walk around and collect them, and each person is going to put his or her head on his or her desk and stay very quiet."

She does this and pretty soon the whole room is silent. George steals a look at Laine and catches her taking a note from Graham Doole who sits right in front of her. She has on her usual loose sweatshirt: it says Asthma Angels on the back. She reads Graham's note in her lap. Her fingers crumple the note and let it drop on the floor. Her hair falls across her cheek like a black fan.

"Now," Mrs. Tindale says, "are we ready to pay attention for another twenty minutes? Kyle Lawrence, it makes it tough for me when you're talking while I'm trying to talk. Jenny Bull has been waiting since last week to tell us about her assignment. We've been looking at legends and heroes of the British Isles— what we call mythology. Now Jenny is going to tell us about three heroes she found in her reading."

Jennifer steps up to the front of the room. She's wearing a Mickey Mouse T-shirt and jeans, which on her look like something from a fashion magazine. She has a purple pin in her hair. Her cheeks are a little flushed from being in front of the class.

"It can be a girl, too, can't it?" she asks Mrs. Tindale.

"Yes, of course, it can be a hero or a heroine," Mrs. Tindale says.

"I found three people. All in the same book," Jennifer

says. She's holding a book and looks like she wants to open it and read what it says, but she's not supposed to. "Robin Hood, Little John, and Maid Marian. They lived in England, in Sherwood Forest. They had their own TV series once."

Some kids laugh and Jennifer does too.

"How many of you saw that, maybe on video?" Mrs. Tindale says. A few hands go up. "It was a book long before it was on TV," she goes on. "Can you tell us a little about the story?"

Jennifer talks for a while, and really gets going on a part about Maid Marian sneaking out of the Sheriff's castle to warn Robin Hood of a plot. George knows the story—his mother used to read it to him—but he doesn't remember this part.

"Thank you, Jenny, that is excellent," Mrs. Tindale says. "You can see how a story like that could last. Now, we have talked about mythology. Would you say this story is mythology?"

Jennifer thinks for a moment, then says, "I would say no because it's true."

"You mean, there really was a Robin Hood and he did those things. That's a good answer."

Kyle Lawrence says loudly, "There was no Robin Hood. He's like Santa Claus." This gets a huge laugh from the room and the fat redheaded kid, who sits at the front of row two, turns and scopes out his exploit with a grin.

"I'm not sure that's true," Mrs. Tindale says. "Have you researched this, Kyle?"

He nods his head with his mouth gaping open and gets another laugh.

Tim Cahill has his hand up. She says his name and he says, "There was a Robin Hood. I saw a book that proved he actually existed. We watched an old Sean Connery movie and my brother looked it up." Everyone is ooh-ing sarcastically and Mrs. Tindale tells them to show some respect.

Jennifer Bull is still standing up there and suddenly she comes to life. "I know a hero that isn't true," she says. "I saw his book too. St. George." She looks right at George with a smile that says, *I'm showing you up.* "He killed a dragon and there are no dragons. I looked in the Encyclopaedia at the Public Library and he wasn't even in England."

She smirks at George as if he started the story. He wonders why she had to go to all that trouble to look it up.

"Now that could be a good example of mythology, Jenny," Mrs. Tindale says. "What I remember is that St. George is the Patron Saint of England. So if he was never in England, that would surprise us." She seems unsure, and it's almost 10:35.

"I had hoped to get back to Halloween this morning," she says. "I wanted to hear from our Halloween team on the origins of that festival. It comes from what we call Celtic mythology, and Rebecca and Diego know all about that."

The beep goes and everyone is starting to move. "I want you all in your seats," Mrs. Tindale says. "I will dismiss each of you *by name* and then you can get up *quietly* and leave."

She chooses Laine second, Graham soon after, and George second last. "Saint George Stone," she says. "I'm going to have to check on that, see if you really existed." Then she finally stops talking to him.

Out in the schoolyard Tim Cahill pounces on him. "Hey Saint, what'd she say?"

"Nothing."

"I think she likes you, bro."

Laine is under the tree over by the fence, talking secretively with Doole. "Wait here, can you," George says to Tim. "I need to tell you something."

"Oh, sure," Tim says.

"I'll be right back." He walks over to Laine and Graham. Laine gives him a very open look, and it makes the back of his neck tingle. Again her face looks famous. He sees the eyes that made her a TV star. They are even bigger and darker in person.

Sometimes he feels too young with her. But most of the time he hangs on to the other moments: when he felt like a sixteen-year-old.

Right now he can't read her.

"Hey guys," George says. "What are you hatching?"

"Nothing too big," Graham says. "A little Halloween fun."

"The dance is Friday, right?" George says, worrying that Graham is encroaching on his plans.

"Right," Graham says. "Are you free that night?"

"Not really. Am I, Laine?"

Again he can't read her: was that a smile or was that a *smile*?

"I'm serious, man," Graham says as the bell rings. "We might need you that night."

"What for?" George says, wishing he could somehow get rid of Graham.

"I can't give out the details. It has to do with Mr. Bolton."

As they enter the school, Jennifer Bull is standing down the hallway with Mrs. Tindale. Just as George sees a chance to get Laine alone, Mrs. Tindale calls out to him.

"George Stone, are you good with machines?"

"Depends on the machine," he says.

"Well, Jenny here has a problem. She is in charge of advertising for next week's dance, and it's supposed to go up today. Or actually yesterday. Our new colour copier is refusing to run, and I told her she'd have to do black and white, which is too bad if you look at this."

Jennifer holds up her poster like evidence in a trial. It's a cartoon she drew of two orange pumpkins dancing in front of a band made up of multicoloured candies. It's really good, but he already knew Jennifer could draw.

"The repair guy won't be here until Friday," Jennifer says. "That's only a week before the dance."

George isn't sure why Jennifer thinks he can fix a colour

copy machine. And he is ticked off that Laine slipped out of his grasp. But he can't just ignore these two females.

They find the machine in an alcove off the library. "It just keeps flashing E7," Jennifer says.

"What is E7?"

Jennifer shows him a card that is attached to the machine. It says "E7, empty paper supply."

"It's not broken," George says. "It just needs paper."

"No, we put paper in it," Jennifer says. She pulls out a tray and shows him the stack.

"That's dumb," George says.

"So what do we do?" Jennifer looks at him beseechingly.

This poster job must be very important to her. Her usually perfect blonde bangs are twisted and her blue eyes are troubled. George has an impulse to reach out and fix her hair.

"Chill a little," George says. "I don't think it's broken, I think it's more like, mixed up."

"How do we unmix it?" Jennifer says with a laugh.

"We have to make it think about something else," George says. "It's just a stupid computer inside the thing."

Jennifer is shuffling through the tabbed cards. "Maybe we should give it a different problem!"

George likes where her mind is heading. "Perfect," he says. "Make something else wrong that we can fix."

"A paper jam!" Jennifer says. She gives him a high five and her face breaks into a smile so bright and healthy that George almost has to red flag her for looking so good. Strangely, he seems for a moment to see the adult she will someday become. Their two smiles sync together and George feels as if their being kids is just a temporary ruse. He also feels like he's high on grass.

"Are you two accomplishing anything?" Mrs. Tindale appears in the doorway. "I'll give you ten more minutes, then it's back to study group."

"We have a plan," Jennifer says. "George is really smart."

"It's her idea," George says.

"Maybe you shouldn't give credit until you see the result," Mrs. Tindale says.

Using a complicated diagram on one of the help cards, they figure out how to open the front of the machine and pull out part of the main mechanism.

"Crumple up some paper," George says, "and I'll shove it in."

Jennifer leans over to watch him insert the paper and again he has to laugh—such a perfect profile studying the guts of a copy machine.

"So, I never heard about your summer," Jennifer says. "My sister said you went to the cottage."

"We went to one. Not ours."

"How come?"

"My grandparents sold it four years ago. *I* went to it though."

"You went—to your old cottage? Even though you guys don't own it anymore?"

"Yeah. There was nobody staying in it."

"Was that weird?"

"The place was pathetic. It isn't even level anymore. The woodshed is falling down."

"We should buy it back," Jennifer says. "Fix it up!"

George laughs. "We should."

He has the crumpled paper in a good place. He presses the mechanism home.

"I like your poster, you know," George says.

"I'm in charge of advertising and I don't even have a date," Jennifer says. "Adam Riswick asked me but I said no."

George slams the last door shut and they look at the error display. It goes blank for a moment and then flashes E4.

"We did it, we created a new problem," George says. "Now let's make it go away."

Jennifer says, "How about you?" as he opens the machine up again.

George is crouched down with his head in the copier. "Excuse me?" he says, removing the paper.

"About the dance."

"Oh, yeah. I think I do." George closes everything up, and gets to his feet. The machine now says RESET and he presses that button.

Without any warning, the display changes to READY. It's amazing, they actually did it. George is elated but Jennifer seems less overjoyed than before.

She says, "I better get my copies made before it screws up again."

"We got it, didn't we?" George says, unable to give up on the high they were sharing before.

"Yeah, we did," she says, and produces a smile that isn't up to the Jennifer standard.

It stays in George's mind as he walks down the hall with the unaccountable feeling that his rescue mission failed after all.

44

A Degas print

A STRANGE THING HAD BEEN HAPPENING TO ME DURING the recent Reign of Maggie. I was getting a whole new look at my own soul.

We were watching TV at Maggie's place—or rather, I was channel surfing—after dining at a restaurant she loved called Osteria. Maggie came out of the bathroom and sat down beside me on the couch, that quaint-looking, overhanging dotted green couch that I had always said supported the upper back instead of the lower. I was clicking through the channels, in that rhythm where you show each one just long enough to reject it, sometimes just for a millisecond. Maggie yelled out "Wait! Go back."

I had just hit an episode of "China Beach" on which a wonderful looking hooker was reminiscing about a dangerous john, but because of Maggie's Reign, I couldn't stay on that anyway. So I went back a channel, to what turned out to be *The Philadelphia Story*. Now this was a "classic" that I didn't like (I thought it paled beside the charming *High Society*), and normally I would have resisted watching it. But I couldn't, not during her reign. So I moved to the easy chair to let her get comfortable on the couch, where I knew lying down under an afghan would soon cause her to drop off. This too I would usually have protested: only conscious people should get to choose the channel. But even though it was a Friday night after a week of SOB futility, I held my tongue, sat in the easy chair, and watched the movie quietly.

And she did drop off, and every time she woke up, her beloved costumes were there to greet her, and pointed dialogue was being served up. So she had a relaxed, pleasurable, and cozy evening. The tired pregnant woman, having escaped from her place of clerical captivity, got to do what she wanted, with her man for company.

And I sat there and the movie wasn't a masterpiece, but I felt protective towards her, found myself thinking Cary Grant really wasn't bad in it, and then got goose bumps during the ending with Maggie gently snoring beside me. When I turned the TV off to avoid being bombarded by some fresh subject, this startled her. I said, "It's okay, the movie's just over," and had a brief flash of what it might be like to be a really nice guy.

Then later in bed she asked me to rub her back, not heavy rubbing but a very light kind that I specialized in, where you touch so delicately that the skin surface has to guess whether it is being touched. I did this, with devotion and skill, for at least fifteen minutes, while she lay on her side, turned away from me, absolutely silent. The silence said, if I wanted you to stop I'd be saying so. And I honoured it.

Now this might have happened even on a normal night, but not with such patience as on this first Friday of the Reign, and certainly not with so little expectation of reward. Usually such an extended period of concentration on Maggie's nude back would have left me more than primed for more, and able to communicate this fact to her without saying a word. But this night I controlled the response. I let it rise off me like steam and dissipate into the night. I let her sink, with a grateful murmur, into sleep.

Then it was morning and she was nervous about what we had to do today, so she made greater demands on me.

"Really scrub it," she said as I leaned over the edge of the
tub, applying a soapy washcloth to her still-not-adequately-
served back. She had her hair up in a turbaned towel. The
whole bathroom was suffused in some wonderful petally odour,
and over her shoulder I could see her breasts curve out of sight
like twin ski slopes. We hadn't had any form of sex for a week
and her reign had given her a strange new freedom from modesty. I dropped the washcloth and started rubbing with my bare
hand, wanting to slide it over her shoulder. I felt like a spider
on a Degas print.

"I know what you're thinking," she said, "but is it okay if I
don't want to?"

"Sure, it's okay," I said.

"Can we have bacon and eggs?" she said.

"Certainly."

"I want two eggs, not in the same pan with yours."

"Not with mine?"

"No, then the whites run together too much, like it's all
one egg with three yolks."

"I'll use two pans," I said.

Somehow finding the street and parking the car occupied us
enough that we didn't really notice the gathering until we were
about to wade through it. Men and women in suits and ties.
Clean-cut, young. Signs. Pictures on the signs, colours like an
accident in the meat section at Ralph's. Maggie and I were past
them when three of them rushed over and formed a cul de sac.
"Do you mind if we speak to you?" their leader said.

"Yes we do," I told him, and we barged through, and
gained the sidewalk by the building, a modern one with dark
windows like any office.

"We're only going for a test," Maggie said over her shoulder.

Inside we had to sign in, then take a seat. There were four
other women gathered around the room; I was the only man.

This was it, I was thinking. If we get through this, the day of the procedure might even be easier. We had decided to have it the next Saturday, October 29th.

I didn't even want to look at Maggie. So far she seemed to be seeing this as just an appointed task to be taken care of. I needed some innocuous thing to say, just any harmless talk. But nothing would come.

At last she spoke. "When we get out of here," she said, "I want to go to the fabric store."

"Not a problem," I said.

BOOK FIVE

Our Trespasses

45

No Graham

GEORGE'S FATHER IS SICK ON SUNDAY SO THEY DON'T GO to church. George calls Tim Cahill and asks him if he wants to go for a bike ride. Tim says he'll be right over and George waits in the living room.

Then Alicia runs in clutching her neck. George knows what is wrong and races to the bathroom to get her kit, and injects her with the adrenaline. She starts breathing better right away. His mom comes in from the backyard and takes Alicia in her arms.

His dad comes down for a glass of water and finds all of them in the kitchen.

"What else can happen?" his mom mutters. "I brought these stupid cookies from work. Beryl Nixon made them. No nuts in them. How am I supposed to know? I guess she must have used peanut oil or something; people think it's healthy."

"Are you okay?" his dad says to Alicia.

She nods.

"It's scary," his mom says. "But you knew what to do, didn't you. You got help, but you could have done it yourself if you needed to. George was right there, took care of you. That was very good, excellent."

His dad goes to the sink and runs cold water. The phone rings. His mom picks it up.

She says, "Hello to you too." Something in her voice makes George pay attention, but all he can hear is her half of the conversation.

"You did.

"You do.

"Well that's funny. I wasn't aware that was happening."

His mom's face gets a little red.

"You know, not everyone is just some new prospect you can manipulate," she says, and George's dad looks up from the newspaper he's reading.

His mom looks positively tense.

"I am sort of in the middle of something here," she says. "Which has been known to happen when I am in my home. This is not really a time to discuss business. And I am not sure we have any left to discuss." She hangs up.

"Who on earth was that?" George's dad says.

"Just a very annoying client."

It had to be Bart, George is thinking.

"Somebody I know?" his dad says.

"Just a new one. A new client. He claims to be interested in the old Bader place on Empress Street."

"Didn't that Meg lady say it was already sold?" George says.

His dad looks from him to his mom.

"That deal fell through; it's for sale again," she says. She goes to the window and smoothes her hair.

"That's a huge place!" his dad says.

At this moment Tim Cahill shows up and it's time for their bike ride.

"Don't go past the expressway," his mom says.

Without answering, George shoves Tim out the open door. They cross the expressway on Rivervale and ride northward single file until they cross the river ten minutes later. Then George turns right on Bombay and traffic is lighter and they ride side by side. Blue sky, warm air. Narrow tires crunching through fallen leaves.

"So, Saint, what is it with you lately?" Tim wants to know.

"Don't call me that."

"Okay, what is with you?"

"What the fuck are you talking about?"

"Okay, S.G., if you want to play dumb. But people notice things, you know."

George just keeps pedalling.

"If we aren't friends anymore, just say so," Tim says, and he looks over at George.

"Why wouldn't we be friends?" George says.

"Well, let's see." They're hitting an uphill grade, but Tim stays right with him, and still has enough breath left to talk. "Because you spend all your time either staring at nothing or staring at Laine Meyer? And even when you're with me you're not? And you say you have to tell me things when you don't?"

George gives him a furtive smile. "Okay."

"So what's going on?"

"Nothing." George considers. "A lot of stuff has happened," he tells Tim. "I've been a bit wacko."

"I'll say," Tim says, sounding big-time relieved.

"I'll tell you about it someday," George says.

"So it's all over?" Tim says, like a needy eleven-year-old. "Even with Laine?"

"Maybe not with her. But I'm not nuts anymore."

"Are you sure?"

They reach the hospital and George hangs a left into the driveway.

"I don't know if you want to go in," he says to his friend.

"Sure I do. I like your grandfather."

"He's different."

"I know he's different. My gramps had a stroke too."
"Okay."

They walk into the room. George is embarrassed by the size of
it, with his grampa like a lone player in a huge gym. "They
moved him here," he whispers. "I don't know why."

They go over and it's awful to see. The old guy is all different colours, mainly yellow and purple. You can see all his
veins, muscles, and bones. His mouth is wide open and pointed
at the ceiling. He doesn't smell good.

Tim isn't saying anything; he looks shocked and stands back
from the bed. George gets close and takes his grandfather's
hand, holds it in both of his, and pats it steadily.

Tim steals up and whispers, "Is he in a coma?"

"No—he's cool, he's asleep." George no longer believes his
grampa is cool, but he doesn't want to say that in front of him.

They stand there for quite a while. George puts his grampa's
hand down and sits in the chair. Tim looks out the window.

"What is that woods?" Tim says.

"The Narwood Bush."

"They're building something in there."

George gets up and looks. You can see a structure through
the trees, right where the forest was, where his mother and
Dave and all of them grew up.

A deep voice booms behind them and they both jump. The
old man just said something. He says it again. He's looking at
George. The old man's arm is shaking. George goes over and
catches his hand and pats it. "What did you say, Grampa?"

He says it again. It seems to start with "ori" and ends with
"ation." Sorry? Modation?

"That's okay, Grampa."

The old man looks at him. His good eye is red under a
half-closed lid. A tear comes out of it and George sees a crust
on the lower eyelid. He takes a Kleenex out of the box and dips

it in the water cup. He tries to wipe the eye; some of the crud comes off.

He feels Joseph's arm snake around him and clutch him. "Good boy," he seems to say. He presses George closer, his head wobbling on his thin neck.

"I love you too, Grampa."

The old man smiles at him. Even without the teeth, it's a smile. George smiles back at him, and makes small talk for a while, telling him about the good weather and their ride over. After a while George can't handle it anymore, the misery the old man is in. He suspects that Grampa is trying to hide it for their sake.

"We better go," George says.

Out in the hall Tim says, "He's not too bad, huh?"

"He's done," George says.

They ride backstreets to the downtown. On Trafalgar, George sees a familiar white Oldsmobile parked in front of Moody's Blues. He doesn't want to do this to Tim but he thinks he's going to go crazy if he doesn't get together with Laine.

"Man, I have to do something. I'll be right back."

"Oh *sure*, George. Like I'm gonna wait around."

The bar is almost empty. It stinks of smoke. It's dark except for a couple of tables near the front that are sliced by sunlight. At one of them Carl is sitting.

"Hey, kid. What's going on?"

"Hi Carl."

"Jimmy, bring this kid a ginger ale. What brings you to this corner of town?"

"I was riding around," George says. "I saw your car."

"I'm not very good at incognito. I guess when they come for me, they're gonna get me." He smiles at George in an easy way and drinks his beer.

"Are you off today?" George says.

"Not really, I like to drop by here, see if the chairs still work. I have to head back to the palace any time now."

"Can I get a ride?"

"Out there? I'm not gonna say no to you, but have you thought this one through?"

"Yeah."

"You want to pay the girl a visit, huh. I'll take you, but I don't know if you're going to like it."

"Is Graham there?"

"No, I don't think he's there . . ."

"Then I'll like it."

"You better take it from here, sport," Carl says as they get out of the car. He heads for the garage and George walks up to the massive side door of Laine's house. It doesn't feel right to knock on it and be just someone wanting to come in. So George takes a deep breath and pushes it open.

He doesn't see anyone till he reaches the pool area. Then he sees the right someone, coming up the ladder from the water in a black one-piece bathing suit with very high thighs. She pushes her wet hair off her face and stands there for a while before she sees him.

"George! George Stone!" Laine says. It sounds odd coming from her, seeing as she only ever uses his last name.

"We were just taking a swim," she says. "You can too, if you want."

"That's okay," George says, looking around and not seeing anyone else. "I just wanted to talk."

"To talk?" She sounds a bit alarmed. "How did you get here?"

"Carl," George says.

"That's weird," Laine says.

"I ran into him. Go ahead and swim. I'll be here."

"I need to do my lengths," Laine says. She gives George a

kind of over-the-shoulder glance that makes him feel as if he is not on today's schedule. Then she plunges back in and is soon passing back and forth like a well-oiled machine.

George sits on a plastic chair and watches the afternoon light start to drain from the ribbed windows. Laine gets out of the pool at the shallow end and calls to him. "I'm going in the sauna, come and talk."

That doesn't make sense, George thinks, I'm not dressed right for that. But he seems to have no choice, other than to sit by the pool alone. He follows her to the sauna, pulls his Reeboks and socks off at the door and goes in.

"I'm sorry, it's hot," Laine says, and then laughs. "It's supposed to be, though. You can take off your stuff."

"I'm okay. It was getting cold out there."

And it's getting hot in here. Laine steps over to the corner, facing away from George, and pulls her bathing suit off. He feels awkward and looks away even though he's behind her. She comes back wearing a white towel and sits on the wooden bench. She doesn't seem at all conscious of his gaze; she just seems like an athlete doing her routine.

"I'm getting fat again," Laine says, looking down at her chest that curves into the towel. "That can't happen. We're going to France in ten days."

George is thinking, I should put my arm around her or something. But her body is gleaming from the heat, he is starting to sweat in his T-shirt, and nothing feels right.

"You should take your clothes off," Laine says.

"I should." Reluctantly George pulls off his jeans and T-shirt, and sets them on the bench. Now he is sitting beside her wearing underpants. It isn't cool.

Laine runs her hands through her hair and says, "So, like, you have to talk to me?"

"I don't have to. I want to," George says. "I want to talk without Graham around." *And that's how the dance should be.*

"He was here yesterday. He got some great video. But today we've got no Graham."

"Yeah. I like that, like in the balcony."

"The balcony?"

"At church."

"Oh, right. Hey, I think my water bottle might be on the diving board. I'm dying of thirst. Can you?"

George goes out to the pool. The cooler air makes his body clammy as he walks along the side. There's nothing on the diving board, but there is a water bottle in the hands of a guy standing on the ladder.

"Looking for this, old man?" he says. "I nicked it when I came back from the WC. Thought it was Laine's actually."

At first George thought he was an adult, but on closer inspection he seems to be a well-developed teenager, around five-ten, sandy-haired, and buff. He could be fifteen or older. He's wearing a bulging red Speedo and has light blue eyes.

"It *is* hers," George says. "I'm supposed to get it." As soon as he says this it sounds as lame as a ten-year-old—but it's too late.

"Well, I think she can spare some water. I'm Simon, I'm the second cousin from across the pond."

"I'm George."

"George?" He pronounces it 'Joj.' "That's a good English name."

The guy is looking at George's crotch and suddenly he remembers he's in his underwear. "I wasn't swimming," George says, and that sounds really lame too.

"No need to apologize," the boy says, and gives George a bright, jocky laugh. "Where is the little princess?"

"In the sauna."

"Oh, brilliant. I hate the bloody things. Let's go give her a dose." He dips the bottle in the pool.

In the sauna they find Laine lying on her back, with her eyes closed and her towel half open. Simon tiptoes up to her and empties the water bottle onto her head. Laine leaps up, screaming, and beats him on the chest with one fist, clutching the towel around herself.

"You bastard," she yells. She wraps an arm around him and rests her wet cheek against his chest.

"This bird is oily," Simon tells George, while kissing the top of Laine's head. "No wonder I hate saunas."

George picks up his clothes and heads out. By the pool he pulls them on and stands there, hearing more laughter and shouting coming from next door. It has gotten quite dark and he doesn't care to find the light switch. It seems like a good time to blow this pop stand. He is close to the door when he hears her yell.

"Hey, Stone, we're gonna have dinner in a minute."

She runs up to him, still in the towel. "Are you going to stay?"

"I don't know," George says. To his shame his eyes are wet.

"You have to stay, Simon is just here for two more days, he's cool, you have to get a load of him."

"I think I did," George says. He tries to smile and he can't, a ton of sadness is on him.

Laine seems to notice him for the first time. "Are you okay?" she says, but she looks around, apparently trying to track where Simon has gone.

"Today was weird," George says. "I saw my grandfather." He can't think of any other way to deflect the real reason for what he's feeling.

"Your grandfather. Cool." Laine's teeth are chattering a little.

The English kid appears at the other end of the pool and she yells. "SIMON! Are you done with that shower? Stone, I have to get warm or I'm, like, gonna be sick. Stay for dinner."

"Okay, I guess I can."

Laine and Simon disappear.

A misshapen moon swims in the pool. George goes for the door.

Outside it's clammy and foggy. George climbs the steps to Carl's apartment above the garage. He knocks and after a while the door opens.

"Come in, kid," Carl says.

"I don't really . . ."

"Just come in for a minute. You need a ride home, I figure."

George goes in and stands near the door, while Carl goes into a small bathroom. Except for that, the apartment is one big room. There's a worn green couch, two electric guitars that look as old as Carl, and a Gibson amplifier. Piles of books lie on the floor and a poster on the wall shows a rock band named Consternation that has a guy in it who must be a younger Carl.

George nearly leaves, not wanting to have to talk or even be seen.

Carl reappears, looks George over. "Kid, I'm sorry," he says. "I shouldn't have brought you out here."

"It's okay."

"No, it isn't. Let's get in the car and get you home."

On the road, there is just the noise of the engine and the cool air coming in the window. George can feel Carl look at him now and then.

After a while, Carl says, "I've been wondering about that place you told me about. Did you say Bayne Island? Across from the mouth of the river?"

"It's on Bayne, farther down," George says. "Do you know Heron Bay?"

"Okay," Carl says. "I think I might know your place. Pretty old, always has flower boxes on the dock."

"No," George says.

46

The wet boys

AS THEY CROSS THE FOOTBRIDGE, LAINE TAKES HIS ARM
again, playful and mysterious. It's cooler today, but still clear.
On her wrists are big silver bracelets; he can feel them jangle
against his arm. Apparently he's number one again.

She didn't show at school for three days. George was half
expecting never to see her again. Maybe she had moved to
France or England. He was back in the depths, only this time
there was no anger, just emptiness. He felt that he'd been beaten
by a better man, beaten without a fight. He dragged himself
through his life. Then on Thursday she showed up, and right
away it seemed like she was back in George's corner, even giving
him soulful looks in class. George started to feel like he'd been
a fool, overreacting to nothing; Sunday had just been a glitch.
He should have kept his cool and known she would come back.

Now it's Friday, October 28th. The dance is tonight,
Simon is history, and the girl is his.

Behind them, Graham is lighting up a cigarette. "So,"
Graham says, "you brought the video, right?"

"Shit. I didn't," George says.

"I need it for tonight. You're gonna have to go home and
get it."

"Whatever."

"I'm serious, man. This is the night. You have my only edited copy."

"Why is this the night?" George says.

"Didn't you watch the thing?" Graham says.

"Yeah, the lingerie sisters."

"Not that part. Further on. The Bolton Files?"

"What Bolton Files?" George says, wanting to get off this topic.

"He has a wicked plot," Laine says. "He wants everybody at the dance to see Mr. Bolton on the big screen. But I don't."

"Mr. Bolton and the wet boys," Graham says.

"I say that plan sucks," Laine says. "I want you shooting, not showing anything."

"I don't know about you, Doole," George says.

"You will tonight," Graham says.

"So you're going to the dance," George says.

Her eyes appeal to George. "He's not going with us," she says. "We'll just see him there."

"I guess so," George says.

They come to the long grade up Empress Street and they split into single file. Nobody says any more and George is glad of that. The contact with Laine has put him where he doesn't care one way or the other about Graham's stupid videos. He just wants to be on a couch with Laine in the dark.

Near Graham's house George gets the feeling he's being watched. He looks up at the big red house where he and his mom went, number 143, and way up in the attic he thinks he sees a woman in a bra, standing at the window.

But they've arrived at Graham's. They go in the door and down the steps. It's just like before. The wires and equipment. The light from the aquarium. He didn't notice last time, but it's a triggerfish on patrol.

He sits on the couch and Graham hands him a beer. He

swigs on it and then Laine reaches for it. She isn't sitting next to George, but she's still showing signs of big excitement. Graham lights a joint, and they pass it around. As usual, Frank is singing, something about the summer wind.

Graham crouches by the TV, rummaging around. "I'm gonna show you the Bolton stuff," he says. "Some if it, but you'll have to imagine the editing, since you didn't bring it." He pulls out a bunch of his video-8 cassettes and shines a flashlight on the labels, his lower lip flexing like a worm.

George decides that he doesn't matter. The grass is easing his mind, the beer tastes crisp, and Laine is looking good, showing off a skimpy top that was under her cape. They'll watch some twisted thing that Graham has cooked up and she'll invade his space and it'll be cool.

Sinatra sings about a piper man.

George reaches for Laine's hand and instead of attracting her, his touch seems to set her mouth running.

"Stone, it's so brilliant. He came back from Montreal today. He isn't going home to England, he's going to France with us next week!"

"Who?"

"Simon! He's coming tonight, we'll pick you up at eight and you won't even recognize us!"

"I won't?" George says.

"We're going to look totally old. We're going as the Queen and Prince Philip! Carl's doing our makeup."

She actually believes I want to hear this, George thinks. *I'm supposed to clap for her. She doesn't even know who I am.*

"I've found a piece of it," Graham says.

The TV screen lights up, showing a big stocky actor with wolfy eyes and teeth, carrying a teenage boy into a room. "He's John Wayne Gacy," Graham says.

The boy is thin and has stringy blond hair. Gacy ties him up and takes his shirt off. Then there's static, and then a shot of boys in the shower; it's kids George knows, jocks in the gym shower at school. The shot goes on for a long time. "This is combined with Bolton stuff, in the edit you have," Graham says. "It looks like Bolton is watching them."

Laine pushes the beer towards him and he shoves it away. "This is sick," George says. "You can't do that. I mean, he's a bastard, but there's no way. You guys are nuts."

The door crashes open upstairs. A voice yells, "Hello?" It's George's mother. She is coming down the stairs, saying his name. Then he sees her, staring into the semi-darkness.

"George?" she says.

"Yeah, I'm here." He gets up to go.

Graham says, "I need that tape. If you don't bring it I'm coming to get it."

George tells him, "Screw your video."

His mom doesn't say a word to him all the way home. Just white knuckles on the wheel and her lips compressed until they're white too. No seat belt, barely slowing for stop signs. He tries not to look at her but when he does, she's silently crying.

In the driveway she cuts the engine and sits like a statue, staring straight ahead. Then she bursts out: "We're going to sit down and we're going to talk about this. And you're going to tell me about that weekend. Is that where you were?"

George just has time to say "No" and she opens the car door. He follows her into the house.

The phone is ringing. She picks it up and he hears her say, "Stan, I can't, I really can't." She's quiet for a while and then she says, "Why can't Cindy show it?" George feels a reprieve coming. She says, "Okay, okay, I'm on my way."

She turns to George and looks at her watch. "You know what? It's only 1:35. I'm taking you back to school."

"Mom," he says in a draggy tone.

"Get upstairs and change your clothes, you stink of that stuff. We'll talk on the way."

"Mom," he moans again, but she's like a marine.

In his room he throws on different clothes and then looks on his dresser for Graham's tape. It's not there. He hears her calling and heads down the stairs. She's holding his jacket out to him impatiently. He looks at it and tells her, "I better not wear that either."

She sniffs it. "You're right. Take this." She hands him an old one that he hates, a black polar fleece.

In the car she says, "We don't have much time so I want you to give me straight answers. Who were those kids?"

"Graham and Laine."

"Graham and Laine who?"

It sounds like a knock-knock joke. He can't think of a punch line. "Graham Doole and Laine Meyer."

"Whose place was that?"

"Graham's father's. He stays there on weekends."

"Why wasn't his father there?"

"I don't know. He gets home later."

"You don't know." She is getting really pissed again. "I'm not going to ask you what you were doing there, because I could see what you were doing there. George, I want the straight goods here. You've been funny now for two months. You weren't at the Cahills' farm that weekend. Is this what you've been doing?"

"No," he tells her, making it sound like that's all there is to say.

"Then where were you when you were supposed to be with the Cahills?" she asks him.

"Nowhere. I went out of town." It sounds lame.

"You went out of town. On business. Where out of town?"

"I went to the cottage." *At least, I dreamed about it. Maybe I should have done it.*

"Oh, you went to the cottage. And how did you get there, walk?" She pulls up across the road from the school. She's blocking traffic.

"No, I flew," he says, remembering another dream.

"George, don't play head games with me! This isn't funny." She looks like she might do anything—maybe turn around and drive home again.

"I hitchhiked," he improvises. "I tried to go to Bracebridge." The more he talks, the better this plan sounds. "I didn't get too far," he says.

She looks shocked, then relieved, then her face softens and turns concerned. "Why would you do that, poor boy?" Now she's really thinking about it. "Where did you sleep?"

"I slept by a river," he says, picking up the truth right where he'd dropped it. "I was okay, Mom."

"Jesus, George. You are full of surprises." Someone is honking behind them. "Look, this is not acceptable," she says. "Not at all. We're going to talk about it tonight. Now listen to me. Your sister is going to be home at four o'clock, after her dance practice. I want you waiting there for her. I'll be home by five. Is that understood?"

"Yeah, Mom."

"Now get going." But she reaches over and grabs him, and hauls him across the seat. She hugs him hard, her cheek on top of his head.

He opens the door. Then he thinks of it. "I'll need a note," he says.

"Tell her you'll have one on Monday. You were sick. Be home by four!"

Say hi to Bart, he thinks.

He walks in to the middle of a two-hour class with Mrs. Tindale. He's only about half an hour late. He goes straight to his seat before she can say anything.

But she stops and stares at him. "And where have you been? Did you get lost in the halls?" Titters break out around the room.

He tells her what his mom told him to.

"Oh. Well, you should have a note now, but I guess we can

live with that. You're not exactly living up to your name, Saint George."

"Don't call me that!" he screams.

She walks over to him. "I'm sorry, George. I hope you're feeling better. It's just that I was going to tell you, I looked up your namesake. I finally got around to it. And it seems there really was a Saint George, though he probably never saw a dragon. And he wasn't English. Actually, they think he was a martyr in Palestine. But very little is known about him. And that's all I wanted to tell you."

George looks up at her, thinking, *and why the fuck are you telling all this to me?* But he holds it in and gives her a phoney smile.

"Now, class, we were talking about Halloween. We've talked about past Halloweens, with your compositions. Which were very entertaining. The festival of Samhain, the bonfires on the hill, the food for the ghosts who may be roaming. We've talked about the history of Halloween. What does that leave?"

"The future of Halloween?" Tim Cahill says.

"That's right, and it's not too distant a future, is it? I believe there is a dance tonight?"

She's still standing right beside George's desk, as if he's her partner. *Don't do it,* he's thinking, *don't ask me.*

"George Stone," she says brightly, "what are you going to dress up as tonight?"

"I'll give you a hint," he says. "You're going as my dragon." The class is silent for a moment, then they giggle.

She stares at him. "I just might," she says evenly. "Jenny Bull, what about you?"

47

Stone's eye

BY THE TIME GEORGE GETS HOME HE'S DECIDED WHERE
he *is* going. He might not be able to get away tomorrow; he has
his chance right now if his parents don't show up too soon.

It's 3:50. He looks again for Graham's videotape. He
means to deal with it before he goes. Maybe burn it and leave it
at Graham's. It's not in his room; he turns over all the clothes
and other junk to make sure.

Maybe Alicia took it. No one else would move it. He checks
her room: as usual it's a total mess. After five minutes he gives
up searching among the stuffed animals and nature books.

He's waiting on the inside steps when she comes in at 4:05.
"Uh, Alicia. Little problem. I'm missing my videotape, *The
Sound of Music*."

She takes off her jacket. She's got yellow tights on her skinny
legs. She's out of breath.

"No you're not," she puffs. "It's in my room."

"Where in your room? I *need it*," he growls.

"Keep your shorts on, I'll find it," she says. "I need a glass
of water."

"Get it later. Show me the tape." He blocks her way into the
kitchen.

"Okay, dummy. If you're too blind to see it." They troop upstairs and she looks around. "You took it."

"If I took it why am I looking for it?"

She stares at the floor, kneels down and moves some animals around. She looks up at George. She gasps and turns red. "It's at Alison's."

"What do you mean it's at Alison's?"

"We took it over there to play, with some other ones. We took the tape out and she was like, 'What is this? The lingering sisters?'"

Time stops for George. The tape is in Jennifer's house. "Did you watch it?"

"No, who wanted to?"

"Well, you're going over there with me now and we're getting it."

"No I'm not. Mom told me to have a cookie and a shower. And you have to stay here 'cause she's not home." He watches her trying to act sure of herself. She's right but this time she's wrong.

"Go have your cookie," he says. "Mom'll be home soon, or Dad'll be home by six."

"You can't go!" she squeals.

"Alicia," he says, "are you my friend?"

"No."

"Yes you are. So do me a big favour. Tell them I just went out for a walk. Okay?"

"No," she says, but she sounds unsure.

"I'll see you . . . when I see you," he tells her.

She's staring at him, looking upset.

He crouches down, takes her shoulders in his hands. "You'll be fine. So will I. I just have to get out of here." He gives her a peck on the head.

He grabs his backpack. He looks around: what else does he need? His water bottle. That's it, he's out of here.

"Alicia," he says, "don't tell them I went to the Bulls'. If they get worried, tell them I'll be back tomorrow. Or Sunday."

"Where are you going?" she whines.

"To the Bulls'. Get your cookie."

He gets off his bike in the Bulls' driveway five minutes later. He knocks on the front door. It opens: Jennifer is standing there. She's wearing a white T-shirt, not much else. Her hair is wet.

"Are you going to the dance?" he says.

"Yeah, I'm going with Tim."

"He didn't tell me."

"Come in," she says.

He stands in their living room, suddenly not sure what to say. He hasn't really talked to her since they fixed the copy machine.

"I wasn't expecting a visit from Laine's boyfriend," she says. She is friendly in an unfriendly way. He turns red. But he's got to get this done.

"My sister left a videotape here. I need it." It comes out sounding like some obnoxious jock.

She looks offended. "Alison's not here. You'll have to come back later."

He can't believe he's going to blow it. He's never seen Jennifer look so forceful—maybe this is how she is at home. She has no makeup on, her face is scrubbed clean. She doesn't look like an angel. She just looks good. Too good for a guy who hangs out with Graham and Laine.

George sags against the doorjamb. He's out of ammo; in the wrong. Jennifer sets her hands on her hips. Her T-shirt barely covers them. She has long legs. *Don't stare at them, Geek.* "Look," he says, "I really need it now. Can you help me find it?"

"You want me to crawl around my sister's room with you?"

He meets her eyes. It comes back to him, what happens sometimes when they look at each other. It's been like that for years, whether they talked or not. Guess he blew it, big time. He doesn't want her to see that tape, ever. She'll think he's a sleaze. But he figures he's not going to get it tonight. He starts for the door, his eyes burning.

"George, what is wrong?"

Frustration wells up in him, taking him by surprise. "Just show me where her room is," he says.

"Okay, okay. Let's go look."

She leads him down a hall and into a room. It looks like a copy of Alicia's room, only with different stuffed animals. Jennifer starts rummaging around. "What kind of tape is it?" she says.

"Just a tape. A video."

"What is it?"

"*The Sound of Music.*"

"You came here to get *The Sound of Music?*" She starts laughing. "Do you need *Mary Poppins* too?"

Why did Graham have to choose that box? "It's not even mine," George says.

Jennifer looks up from the floor. "It isn't yours?"

"No—it doesn't matter. We're not gonna find it anyway."

"Sure we are, but you're not *helping*. You gotta get down with me, bro." She grins at him, looking like a sitcom star.

They both go crawling around the floor. They start looking everywhere. They peer under the bed, under the little desk. They move every book, every toy, every animal. Jennifer holds things upside down and shakes them. Coins come out of a kangaroo's pouch.

George finally sees some videos on a shelf, behind some fairy tale books. "Look there," he says.

"Bull's eye!" she yells. Then she hears what she said and says, "Or Stone's eye." They're both on their hands and knees, like they're playing horsey.

"George," she says, laughing. "I hope you really need this tape." He looks at her and forgets to breathe, she is so perfect.

For a moment he can't even remember why he wants the fucking thing. They are suspended there, on their hands and knees, their faces inches apart, her lips ready, and he wants to go for kiss number two. But he waits too long.

She squats on the floor. She's on a mission, whistling, sorting through the tapes methodically, one by one.

"Wait, there's one more on top of these books—YES! *The Sound of Music.*" She hands it to him. "Now you can have your Julie Andrews thrill," she says.

He opens it. True to his luck, the movie inside is *Mary Poppins*.

"Great," George says.

"How did I know that?" Jennifer says. "I'm sorry." They stand up and go back to the living room. They look in the TV cabinet, in the VCR; it isn't there. She's still thinking. "There's nowhere else to look," she says. "That's the only place she hangs out with Alicia."

"Thanks," he says, but he's brutally bummed. Not just about the video.

They stand at the door. She hooks an arm over his shoulder, resting some weight on him. "You'll find it," she says. Again they are so close. If he weren't so down this would be an awesome moment. It's like Laine never existed.

"You're not gonna tell me why you need it?" she says.

"It isn't *The Sound of Music*, it was just in that box. It's a video Graham Doole gave me. It's sort of . . . embarrassing."

"Embarrassing? Darn, I wish we could find it!" Her eyes drift off to the side. Then she screams, a scream of joy. And picks a tape off the shelf by the door. It's not his. It's *E.T.*

"Don't you see?" she sings. "We saw the box for this in Alison's room." She goes racing down the hall, he hears her yell "Yes!" from inside the room, and she comes bounding back, waving Graham's video at him. Then she reads the label.

"The Lingeray Sisters. Linger-ay. Lingerie?" She squeals. "George, what is this, is this porno? This is an all-new you!"

He reaches for it and she holds it away from him. She bounds over to the television and he comes after her, but she pops it in and has the remote going. "Let's give this a look-see," she says, still full of play.

The image comes on, right where he doesn't want it to be, Graham's voice whispering, "We're in the women's dressing room area. Do we see our target?"

Jennifer subsides onto a chair arm. This has her full attention. Now the screen shows Brie Cullen coaxing Jennifer to try on the nightie.

"I didn't make this tape," George says, but it only makes him sound guiltier.

"I remember this," Jennifer says. "This was ... in September. This was the day I saw you in the square. We went to Eaton's." She furrows her brow. "This was before you even came back to school."

They've reached the slo-mo image of her in all her finery, with Laine's face in close-up on the other half of the screen.

"Your girlfriend," Jennifer says. "What else is on here?"

George is thinking, don't let her rewind and see the kiss, she'll think that was set up for Graham. Don't let her fast forward to the Bolton stuff either.

"This is what you do?" Jennifer says. "While I'm ... never mind."

George opens the door. Everything has turned to shit.

"Get out of here," she says. She pulls the video out of the machine. "Take this with you." It hits him in the chest and cracks open, tape spills out.

He picks it up and backs away from the house.

Mission accomplished. He stands his bike up and throws the video in the basket. It's getting darker now. The loose ribbon of tape shudders in the breeze.

She is in the doorway. Tears on her face.

She is beautiful, wonderful, the best. She rules.

48

Roy with the horse

WHEN HE GETS TO THE NORTH END OF TOWN HE LOOKS back at Calvan. Over the city, clouds are glowing like peaches in a creamy sky. Jennifer is there. But all he can do is ride away.

Frogs gripe in a swamp nearby. Beyond the swamp a white moon rises, a few nights past full.

A truck goes by. Then a car, then another. He isn't ready to hitch, so he crunches along on the gravel shoulder of the highway.

He passes an auto repair place with trash burning in a barrel. Tosses Graham's video in. Rides on.

Soon Fake Lake will be coming up on his left. It seems like a good time to ditch his bike and try to get a ride. He leaves it against a tree.

Sticks his thumb out, walks on. Past Fake Lake, into the farmland darkness. There's hardly any traffic; nobody even slows for him.

Up around a curve, he sees something white. It's a horse, a big white horse, rippling in the darkness. He stands behind a tree at the edge of the woods. A man is leading the horse to an old truck that's pulled over by the highway. He's talking to it. He takes it up a ramp into the truck, closes it, walks around to the driver's door. George circles around to the right. It's an enclosed van hauled by a cab. On the side of the van it says LAKES' VIEW STABLES, Huntsville, Ontario. There's a door on the side of the van. It's not fully shut. The engine is revving, there isn't much time.

George steps in and pulls the door closed, hoping the horse doesn't immediately bite him. But it's okay, he's in a separate compartment in front of the horse. Stinky though. And hardly room to stand. The smell is coming from straw, big bales of it, piled up beside him. He climbs up on them. There's room up here, and there's air: a small vent is open, you can see the high-way. He lies on his stomach. The truck is moving now, gaining speed, rocking a bit side to side. There's a big hole over by his feet, open to the rear compartment where the horse is. Well, the horse seems pretty quiet. Maybe he's asleep.

George comes out of a dream. He was flying again. He sits up, remembering where he is, and finds that he's not alone.

The horse has stuck his big white head into George's com-partment, and one large eye is studying him. George looks back at him. He seems like he's waiting for George to say something. "What woke me up?" George says. The horse's ears prick up and he gives a small shake of the head. The truck's not moving, that's what it was. He goes to look at his watch and it isn't there. The door opens behind him.

"Well now, we have a stowaway," says a male voice. The man is short; his face is ugly and likeable. There's a truck stop behind him.

"Has our penthouse been treating you all right, my young man?" he says. "Sometimes we get complaints about a jiggly ride." He has a British accent.

"The horse has been staring at me," George says.

"Has he. Well, he's a friendly old Holsteiner. Used to be a very fine jumper. The pity is, he may have been observing you, but not with his eyes. They are bright, but they don't see much.

It's the brain—it doesn't take the message. And the Calvan Veterinary professors can't do a thing about it. They say it's the result of a virus."

George looks back at the horse. Still staring at him, but now the image is sadder.

"I'm afraid we're not going any farther tonight," the man says. "But you're welcome to stay." He climbs up in the van, giving George a more careful inspection. "Are you coming from, or going to?"

"Both, I guess," George says. "Aren't you going to Huntsville tonight?"

"No, I'll be going there first thing in the morning. But I've got a friend here, you see. I don't get to be with her that often. She'll give you a nice dinner, with pie."

"No thanks."

The man reaches up and grabs George under the arms, pulls him right out of his slot, and sets him down on the pavement. Then he dusts him off.

"You're not more than fourteen," he says.

"No."

"I don't think we want you hitchhiking out on that highway." He glances out at the dark ribbon with the lights whizzing past.

"I'll walk."

"It'll take you a while to walk to Huntsville, even if you're faster than I used to be."

"I only want to go to Bracebridge."

"Oh, we're past that. It's ten kilometres back."

"Then I'll say thank you," George says, imitating his accent. And starts down the road, to the south where the oval moon waits.

"I should talk to herself about this," he hears the guy say. "Or maybe I shouldn't." He stands there talking as George gets farther away. Then at last George hears a faint "Good luck."

At first the highway seems unnaturally dark. He's not used to seeing it without headlights shining on it. But soon he realizes it's not as dark as he thought. There are three islands of white cloud overhead, with channels of sky between them. They're like fluorescent bulbs. The air is cool. It feels good to walk. Ten kilometres isn't tough, if you don't think about it all at once.

But there's only so much to learn about barking dogs, loud trucks, and dust. And dark woods that crowd the shoulder.

It seems like a couple of hours have passed. He must have gone ten kilometres by now. There's a sign on the other side, where another highway crosses. He gets closer, hoping it'll say Bracebridge. It doesn't. It says Utterson. Great. Where the hell is Utterson?

Why didn't he put some water in his bottle? Pure water. That's what he needs.

Out of patience, he starts to run, gets winded, and slows down. He looks around just in time to see a lit-up car backing along the shoulder, the passenger door open. It must have just passed him. Somebody is trying to pick him up. He starts running again; finally whoever it is drives away.

There's been a strange buzzing noise in the distance for a while now. Wait, it isn't in the distance. It's in his pack. He opens it up and finds his Walkman playing. He puts on the earphones: it's too loud. He turns it down, gets his pack on again, and continues down the road.

His new favourite song is in progress. He discovered it last Sunday after Carl drove him home from Laine's. He was so bummed he could find nothing better to do than put on Uncle Dave's cassette. He could take or leave it until he found this song.

The harmonica wails over a crazed guitar. Then the voice starts again:

I'm a stranger to you
And you are to me

It's not a thing
That I'm glad to see
There's no room left
Where we used to be . . .

The night is like his own music video, with the dark road
and the moon and the big islands of cloud.

Then he hears honking and pulls the earphones off. People
are shouting at him from across the highway. A car has pulled
over. He starts to run again.

"It's Mandy," a voice says. "Mandy and Roy!"

Who the fuck are Mandy and Roy, he wonders. Serial
killers, probably. He picks up the pace, boots it along the
shoulder of the road, and looks ahead for any side road he
can take.

They're in the car now and keeping parallel to him, honking and yelling. The driver screams, "We're trying to help you!
It's Mandy, from the restaurant!"

What restaurant? Oh.

"Roy, with the horse," she hollers.

Okay, okay. He makes an arm gesture to say all right, you
win. He checks the road and crosses over.

In the backseat, George is thinking fast as the woman tells
him about her irresponsible boyfriend with the jockey-sized
brain, who had to get other things out of the way before he even
told her about the boy on the highway.

"It turned out not to be ten kilometres," Roy says. "More
like twenty."

"Now, where are you going?" she says. "Roy said
Bracebridge."

"No, I'm going to the falls."

"What does he mean, Roy? The falls are in Bracebridge."
Her fuse seems awful short.

"Maybe he means the other falls, not in town, under the

highway. The South Falls, you know, Muskoka Falls! Is that where you're going, boy?"

"Yeah," George says gratefully, "Muskoka Falls. My grandmother lives there."

"And what is her name?" the woman says.

"Irene. Irene Moore. She lives alone."

There is no response from the front seat. After a while Roy says, "Jesus, Mandy, he's just visiting his grandmother." But this does no good. She seems to be reloading: soon she'll have to fire at somebody.

George says, "You can let me off here."

"No we can not." She exits at the next ramp, crosses the overpass, and turns onto a side road.

"Now, George, this is where you direct me to your grandmother's house."

I should make it complicated, he's thinking. So it'll look real. They pull into the little village that he went through once with his dad. It's not big enough to allow much complication. George directs them to make a left, then a right, then a left. They are about to rejoin the same side road again. On his right George can see shining water. The south branch of the Muskoka River, only twenty feet away.

"This is it," he says.

"What do you mean, this is it?" the woman answers, looking at a rundown hotel-restaurant with a faded sign on the window that says COLD BEER. "Roy, look at this place."

"Hey, lady." George taps her on the shoulder. She turns to look at him. "This is where you stop helping me," he says.

Her mouth goes slack.

He opens the door and steps out. He can hear her say, "Does that beat all?"

He slams the door.

Roy says, "Good luck kid."

George walks calmly to the end of the street. Two roads pass right over the falls: the little side road they came in on, and up above it, Highway 11. A paved lane leads down the hill beside the falls. He takes it. There's a gate near the top, blocking the way for cars. It's padlocked. George goes around it and continues down, with the falls thundering on his right.

Beside him there's a pipeline that looks like it's made of giant wooden barrels. It carries the water down the slope to the power station below. Then the river gathers itself in a pool and heads west. If he had a boat, it would carry him all the way to Lake Muskoka.

But that is more than he can handle right now. All he wants is a place to rest.

49

Vacuuming day

THE PICKUP GAINS SPEED, AND GEORGE SITS IN THE BACK watching the grey river unspool next to the road. It's already Saturday afternoon; he finally got a ride with some local dudes and their dog. The houses along the shore are all decked out for Halloween. The 31st is Monday, but a lot of people are celebrating it tonight.

Last night he crashed near the falls. He woke up at midday, dragged himself along the road to a diner, and ate a burger.

The truck slows down. The guys inside bang on the window, grinning at him and indicating, "Do you want to get off here?" He guesses he does: they are nearing the smaller marina by Portal Lake. It won't be as busy there and he has a better chance of putting a plan together.

He climbs down and the pickup kicks up some dust and takes off.

I need a boat, George thinks. The marina consists of a barn-like structure containing boats in slips, a launch area, and a dock with an office. Some kids are hanging around over by the dock, smoking and talking. Nobody seems to be doing any work and no adults are in sight. There's a heavy cloud cover over most of the sky.

Next to the boat barn is a rack with canoes for sale. George
ambles over to it, acting like he's just killing time until somebody
comes to pick him up. The canoes are of all types, mostly used, a
few new. There are fibreglass ones, metal ones, and a couple of
older cedar-strip specimens, somewhat the worse for wear. One
of these near the bottom of the rack catches his eye and he steps
closer. It is dirty and scraped up but the pearl colour still shows.
It has his grampa's printing on the hull, JMM. For a moment
George's universe reels, and he can't seem to see straight. How
can the canoe be here? Didn't he leave it on the lake? Slowly he
pushes the vision aside and thinks his way back to last September.
He looked around the cottage; the canoe was gone. Right.

He slowly pulls the canoe out of its slot and drags it across
the scrubby ground to the shore. There's a paddle tied into it—
Uncle Dave's paddle, decorated at summer camp. One edge of
the blade is cracked off but it's still plenty wide.

There's also an iron anchor in the canoe, blistered with
rust. It still has a coil of rope tied to it. He'll take that too.

Sliding smoothly onto the lake, he paddles around the boat
barn and into the teenagers' view. He hopes none of them
knows the canoes too well. He heads on across the water, keeping as far out as he can, heading for the Cut that takes you
through to the mouth of the river.

It seems like he's gotten away without a murmur when one
of the kids yells, "Hey bozo, is that your canoe?" He can hear
them guffawing and arguing, deciding whether to bother with
him or not.

"We're onto you, loser," comes across the water.

"Trick or treat," a girl yells.

He is getting close to the Cut now, pretty worried but within a few yards of escape. Taking a last look behind him, he sees
that a car is pulling up by the office. Someone gets out of it and
the kids seem to be distracted by that. Before anything else can
happen, George powers through the cut and turns the corner.

As he passes through the mouth of the river, Lake Muskoka is up ahead, glinting black and yellow. A heron is perched on a log. He comes too close and it beats its wings and sails off into the trees. It looks like a pterodactyl, old and sea-coloured.

A cabin cruiser comes up behind and nearly swamps him. A woman in a baseball hat waves to him; a man lifts a beer glass his way, and their wake rocks the pearl canoe. Then there is nothing. Just an empty lake to cross. Low furrows, the wind behind him. Most people probably closed up their places on Thanksgiving.

It's a long paddle, hard work. With every stroke he can see Jennifer, down on her hands and knees, grinning at him.

He comes into the bay and the sky is grey except for a yellow swatch above the horizon. He passes the Moore cottage; no boats at the dock, the flag isn't flying.

He knifes through into the beaver creek. At the first narrowing he looks ahead and there is no more creek, only a puny trickle. What he just entered is now an inlet of the lake. He climbs onto the bank and walks on through the loggy bush. Suddenly it opens up in front of him. A plain of dried mud, big cracks all over where the surface has split open, tree corpses rising out of it. This used to be a pond; the dead trees were in the water. He looks to both sides and finds that he's standing in the long arc of the beaver dam. It's been blown apart and he's in the breach, where the pond all spilled out.

On the flat you can see where the beaver lodge used to be. It's been torched, with everybody in it, apparently. He walks up closer and finds a nice trophy. A beaver skeleton, stripped and dried on the dirt. He kneels down to examine it. Something gleams through the eyeholes. He tips it up and out falls a bullet, the tip flattened with the impact.

Okay, they're all toast. That's what he wanted to know.

He paddles to the cottage and ties up. The wind is from the south now. Walks up the steps—darkness is closing in—and stands on the porch. The key is likely over the door, where it always was. So what? He lifts up his foot and shoves it into the door. It was never much of a lock. He does it again, and it crashes open.

So, here it is. Turn on the lights, let's look around. Everything the same, only dirtier. Same yellow walls. Same furniture. Same match-holder on the mantle, made of popsicle sticks. He bats it and it clatters on the varnished floor, and the matches spray everywhere. That felt good. He goes in the kitchen. The same fucking pots and pans, couldn't they bring their own? He makes some of them fly too and they clang nicely. Even the cereal dishes are the same. He throws one and it cracks and splinters real good.

He stands in the master bedroom, wondering what it would feel like to pull the big storage shelves right off the wall. He's wiping his face, realizing it's all salty wet, when the phone jangles.

Fuck! Could they have figured out where he is, and called the old number? It rings and he lets it. It keeps going, for two minutes. Finally it stops.

He goes out to the living room and there is his grandparents' oak dinner table. And there is Dave's painting of a rocky point with a pine tree, in a birchbark frame. He stands and looks at it. It's got that Dave look, like all his paintings. The dark blue water and the light blue sky.

The seaweed song is going through his head. He thinks again of the steamboat, the old man in the water. Something breaks inside him, and he starts to cry. Sits down on the floor and writhes in a soundless wail until the tears are all gone.

For some reason he wants to talk to his uncle. He pulls out Dave's cassette. "Songs for George." It has a phone number on it.

He dials it and knows right away it's Maggie saying hello.

"Is Dave there?" he says anonymously.

"No—I'm getting his calls, because he has a habit of missing them. Is this long distance?"

"Yes."

"Is that you, George?"

"Yeah."

"I thought Dave was with you. Didn't he get there yet?"

"I don't know. I'm not there."

"You're not there either? Well where are you?"

"I'm at the cottage." He can't seem to say anything that would help her.

"Oh! Well that's odd. Are you having a good time?"

"I don't know," he says.

"George, are you okay? What's happened?"

He forces himself to pull it together. "I'm okay. I'm here with my friend Carl. It's his cottage."

"Oh, so you're not at *that* cottage. I didn't think so. Well how is your grandfather? That's why David went."

"I don't know," he says.

"Oh, well, I think David's there now, in Calvan. Hoping to get there in time. What time is it there?"

"I'm not sure."

"It's after three here. I'm running late. I'm supposed to be in my car right now. You know me, always on the go." She sounds over-excited. "Did you want something, George?"

"Just to see if you're all right," he tells her and somehow it pulls him back into sync.

"If *I'm* all right? Oh, yes, certainly, of course! I just hate vacuuming."

"You have to vacuum?"

"Today is Saturday. It's vacuuming day. I'll get it done, and I'll be fine—you'll be glad to hear my voice."

"I'm already glad to hear it," George says.

"You're so nice. You're too nice. Not like your uncle. I didn't mean that. George, I have to go."

"Don't worry," he says. "About the vacuuming."

"Oh. Okay. I'll just get it over with. See ya."

George doesn't want to hang up. It'll be another failed mission. He hasn't even talked about anything. But he says bye and he hears her click off and then the dial tone.

He falls back on the big queen mattress, which has a thin old Moore bedspread on it. The old shelves that he didn't pull over catch the last light of the sunset; then they go dark and so does the room.

50

We have your canoe

IT'S LIKE A MOVIE OF THE BAY. A VIEW FROM HIGH IN THE night. The water is smooth as the top of a limo. A boat pulls out from the Moore dock; the lights bounce off the black lake.

We move in closer now. It's not the Elsinore; it's the one they had before, the cedar-strip. You can see Dave in it, and the other three kids, and Joseph, all bundled up in coats. Dave is at the stern, steering the Evinrude engine. He is about fifteen. They have that Kodachrome look.

The boat churns out into the bay, reversing to a stop between Henderson's Point and One Foot Island. You see Joseph dumping things, bottles and cans, sinking them, while nine-year-old Susan holds the flashlight. He's got a big cardboard box; he holds it under while everything fills up with water, and then lets go. "Sinking the crib," he calls it.

The boat speeds back to the dock and you see Irene standing there. The engine shuts off and it's so quiet you can hear everything.

"You forgot this," she says. "This was the whole point."

"I *sank* a teapot," Joseph tells her. "A big purple one."

"That was my new one," she says. "Oh hon." She's mad.

"It couldn't be," Joseph says, and the kids start laughing.

"You sank my new teapot," Irene barks. It echoes all over the lake, under the black sky.

"I'll get you another," he says, but then she starts laughing, and then all of them do, echoing on the water.

George *knows* this story. It's a classic. This is a good dream.

Then they're on the porch of the cottage, Joe and Irene, out to enjoy the view. Joe says to Irene, "No, pour it on the canoe, putz. It's not his canoe, we watched him steal it."

Irene smiles at him and says, "Fuck you, I'm pouring it on this dock. It'll burn better." She has a boy's voice.

So does Joseph. He says, "Asshole, give me the fucking can."

George sits up, wide awake. That wasn't Joseph talking. "Fuck you," he hears from the lake.

He runs down to the dock and it smells like gas. Some kids have got his canoe, Grampa's canoe; they're pouring gas into it from their boat, which is alongside.

George leaps into the canoe, yelling, "What the fuck are you doing?" But it's moving. They've tethered it to their boat. They're towing him out onto the lake, taunting him and high-fiving.

"Hey kid, want to go for a Halloween ride? HE WANTS TO! He wants to!"

George picks up the old anchor. Holding the end of the rope he swings the weight way back, and lets it fly. It lands in their boat and rattles on the floor. "Grab it, grab it," the tall kid yells, but George is too fast for them, hauling himself forward until he's on them.

"You don't do this," he bellows and he's in their boat, swinging Dave's paddle, bashing their heads. The tall kid crashes between the seats; the other kid is draped over the side. That leaves the one at the engine. He stands up. George leaps on him like he was a tree, pressing the paddle into the guy's neck. The kid topples over the engine, tries to clutch it to break his fall, and succeeds only in shoving it forward so the propeller pops out of the water, whirring now behind the kid's head as George pushes him back.

"You're done! You're done, right?" George says.

"Okay," the kid pants, as the bill of his backwards baseball cap is sheared off. "Okay, okay."

George backs off him. The kid sags onto the corner seat. George shoves the engine back into the drink.

They've gone in a circle. George jumps back onto the dock, and almost slips on the gasoline. "Steer your fucking boat," he says. The kid glides away, his friends starting to stir behind him.

"Hey kid! Guess what, we still have your canoe!" The tall one is holding the rope, dragging the canoe right beside them.

"Watch this!" the kid yells, and he strikes a match. Before he can throw it, the whole scene goes up in a big flare. Two kids dive out of the boat.

The rosy flare spreads across the water, lighting it up like a field of dry grain, then starts on the shore.

"No!" George screams. He runs up the steps; he can't let it get the cottage.

It's coming up after him. It takes up half the hill. George runs for the hose by the side porch, turns the tap on, yanks the hose around to the front of the cottage. He stands there and twists it, but nothing happens. Of course: the pump isn't on.

The first blast goes past him and he hears the cottage crack into flames.

The second blast lifts him through the air and pins him to the fireplace, while all around him the walls and ceiling split and scream in the flames.

The third blast melts his flesh, and he looks down and sees his blood running over the blackened bricks.

"I should have turned on the pump," he says, and then he sees a dead tree toppling through the air. It smashes against the chimney on which he's impaled, uprooting it from the earth like an old stump to reveal a hole. And George, hanging over it, is bleeding into the dark cavity.

Down he goes, a stream of him into the pit.

The spectre's arm

ON FRIDAY AFTERNOON I WAS IN THE CONFERENCE ROOM with the Plandor team, waiting for Murry Barr's interrogation. I was sitting there thinking, tomorrow we get the abortion. If I don't stop us.

Barr walked in, and I was appalled to see who was with him. My duplicating friend.

"I think some of you know Richard Ocher," Barr said. "He is one of our best and brightest, he has fortunately become available, and I've asked him to ride point as we drive the Plandor cattle the rest of the way to market."

Ocher sat down in the empty chair next to mine, his eyes turned on me with a strange unfocussed brightness.

Barr continued. "Richard will be working with Dave Moore and the client, to put together an executive summary of the pollution sites for use in the settlement talks which will increasingly monopolize my energies."

Ocher opened a Site Report binder and perched his pen on a legal pad.

Barr began to question the various paralegals on their reports. Impressively, most of them coughed up great ropes of fact.

He reached the Jauniss site, which was Larry Shrift's responsibility.

"You don't tell me what year pollution started," Barr said.

Larry mouthed off for five minutes, describing his trek through the research materials.

"Cut to the chase," Barr said. "Don't bog me down."

I had had enough. "Even if he does, it'll be the wrong chase," I told them all. "We don't care when pollution started."

They stared at me. Barr looked dumbfounded. "How else do we get policy years?" he said.

"Larry said that Plandor owned the site from the beginning," I said. "So they were polluting their own property. We don't cover that. *We exclude that.* We have to look at when pollution hit other people's property."

"Dave makes a good point," Barr said. But he looked like he was tired of walking this dog. "We need the non-owned property. What's your date on that?" he fired at Shrift.

"We don't have one. We just know when the dumping started, not when it spread off-site. It started in '63."

"Then we go with that," Barr said.

"You can't," I said.

Barr looked around the room and said, "Moore has had his head up his desk so long he thinks it's the real world."

Laughter splashed over the mahogany table. Ocher beheld me with joy.

"Well in the real world," I said, "don't courts recognize exclusions?"

"In the real world, courts look for the nearest deep pocket," Barr said calmly.

"So you're saying, buy insurance—it's a license to pollute." My voice betrayed the stress of taking on Barr.

"Who do you think directs the courts, Dave?"

"I would have said the legislature."

"And who owns the legislature. Now we've got a job to get

done here people, let's do it. Give me the Pasly site. Who has it?"

There was an aroused silence around the table. Everyone was looking at me. My face was red, like in high school when I tried to hide my pimples. This site was my personal hell. The one I couldn't master. I had ended up cribbing undigested facts out of the old memo. That was a week ago.

"I guess I do," I said.

"Okay. I'm looking at your report, I don't understand. Who owned the Pilon portion in 1943?"

I stared at him. "Plandor, I think."

"You think?"

I madly churned pages of the old memo. With Ocher next to me I felt like a wounded crow being watched by a turkey vulture.

"I disagree," Shrift piped up. "I ordered some of the EPA studies. Plandor never bought the Pilon portion. That's why they weren't sued by Charteroff." Shrift was good with facts. He couldn't reason, but he was fucking good with facts.

"Dave?" Barr said, tapping his fingertips together contentedly.

I had found something on the Pilon portion: it implied that Shrift might be wrong, but it referred to a footnote in another memo. Which I didn't have.

The door opened. Maggie was standing there. "I'm sorry to interrupt," she said. "There's a personal call for Dave. From Canada. It's an emergency."

Barr followed us out into the hall.

"Is this about your father?" he said.

"Yes," Maggie answered.

"I'm sorry. He's died, then?"

Maggie spoke up again. "No, but he's near the end."

"Well Dave," Barr said, "of course you have to do what you have to do. But this case won't be able to stop and wait for you."

Saturday. The Dallas-Fort Worth airport seemed to go on forever. I had hiked for a half hour to get to the gate where my connecting flight was supposed to go to Detroit. That's when I found out it was cancelled. I would have to wait till four P.M. to catch it at another gate several miles away. All this for a three-hundred dollar savings in fare.

I got there at two and bought some beef barley soup. I sat near the gate and watched the hours tick away. Four o'clock, that was when Maggie was supposed to be at the clinic. Only her clock was two hours earlier: I would be on the plane when she got there.

So here I was, in a terminal on a plastic chair, and she was going through with this, and I didn't even really know why. In the last few days I had become a seething mass of doubts, but I had kept silent because it didn't seem fair to talk her out of it after I had talked her into it. And what if I was wrong?

That thought survived another hour and then it just ran out of gas. This couldn't go down this way. I found a pay phone and got out my calling card. It wouldn't read so I had to enter a bunch of numbers, and when I got to hers, I drew a blank. *This is ridiculous*, I thought. *What is it?*

Then I remembered I had forwarded my calls to her number. I hadn't known how many days I would be away and I had wanted there to be a chance of people reaching a live person. So I dialled my number. It clicked and then it rang. And rang and rang.

I dialled information and got the number of the clinic.

"I want to leave a message, for Maggie Taylor," I said.

"We can't do that," the nice female voice said. "We have no way of identifying you, we don't take phone messages."

I argued and pleaded and got nowhere. They were protecting their clients from sabotage. They were doing a good job. I couldn't stop her appointed hour from coming.

Somewhere over the Midwest, time took that hour away.

It was 8:30 P.M. when I finally got out of the Cal Van at my parents' house. I found the back door unlocked. There were several notes from Irene on the dining room table. She had apparently been out three times today, and each time she had been afraid I would arrive while she was gone. The last note just said "Eight o'clock. Going to Joe with Greg and Doreen." The handwriting was almost indecipherable.

I saw her car keys on the table.

I went down to the little bathroom to pee. Joseph's shaving cup and brush were still sitting by the sink, ready for the morning that would never come.

I climbed the big Mossbank hill, turned onto Bombay Street. Halloween was being observed tonight. A few straggling kids were still out, working their way from house to house while adults stood watch on the sidewalk. The house decorations were much more elaborate than I remembered—they looked like school projects. Witches, life-size harvestmen, multiple pumpkins, and throngs of ghosts strung from the leafless branches. Baby boom parents were so ambitious.

I pulled a U and parked by the Narwood Bush. Overhead there was a mass migration of silver clouds. The hospital looked like it was sailing northward at a good clip, with a gibbous moon as escort.

What floor was it? Hadn't Joe been moved up a floor? I punched Three.

Most rooms were already dark—I could see lone figures in the beds, some TVs on. The nurses' station held two women, both busy.

Then I found it, a large, almost empty room, all the action in the far corner. Seven people were gathered around a bed, all haloed by a real floor lamp that some thoughtful person must have brought in. I could see their faces, lit up with concern for the figure in the bed. Even before I sorted them out individually, they had a sort of Moore-family look.

There they were, my people: there was Susan, a bright smile on her face. There was Greg, standing affably on the far side of the bed. Those backs belonged to Lorraine and Boris, leaning over the patient. And wasn't that Phyllis Robertson, wife of Joe's long-standing partner, with her arm around Irene? That left Doreen, Greg's wife. She appeared to be in Joe's clutches. She was bent in a willing way upon his chest. He was sitting up like some shadow-creature, the remains of his right arm pressing her to him while his good eye veered heavenward.

The visitors seemed like orbs of light circled around him, saving him a little longer from the darkness. And me, as I stood in the doorway I suddenly felt unprepared, inadequate to play my part. I would have liked to hold there awhile and try to get the hang of it.

But I'd been seen. The first to notice me was Phyllis; her rumpled face lit up with welcome and sympathy. Then Susan added me to her smile without saying a word. I stepped between Lorraine and Boris, feeling like the last pilgrim to arrive at the shrine, and Boris gave me a hug, while Greg grinned at me from across the bed. Why was everybody so happy?

Lorraine turned to me and whispered, "This has been going on for a while. We thought maybe he was scared, that he was trying to hang on. Now we think he's saying goodbye."

It was my turn. But as I came around the bed and the old creature peered at me, I felt as if now I was the shadow and he the light. It seemed that he could see the crooked heart I was carrying, the medal of my day. I leaned over him like the others had, only it didn't go the same way. They couldn't see the spectre's arm snake *inside* my embrace, fastening itself on my heart, the withered hand firm against me. The contact seared me; then it went off like a grenade and I was hurled away from him.

I staggered a moment and had to catch myself against the hot radiator.

"Wow! Quite a hug," I said, trying to simulate a good-natured chuckle. Everyone was thrown off rhythm—it would take them a moment to forget this and go back to the ceremony. But they would do it.

And I wouldn't. Because I had gotten the message. I wasn't like them. I wasn't a bright orb that he could cling to at the last.

All I could do was hover with the others, trying not to get in the light.

When they all went, when the old man zoned off again, when they hit the lobby, they were all too moved, too full, too used up to notice my malady of the facial muscles that wouldn't allow a smile.

All too blown away to care when I said, "I'm gonna walk."

"See you tomorrow," they said, believers all of them, and they went down the hallway, Irene glancing back, down to the parking lot.

Give me a reason

A MIST WAS SETTING IN AS I WENT DOWN THE HILL TO THE river and across the steel bridge by the old mill. My feet knew where to go. They carried me up the side street.

Sometimes only beer will do. Across Twining Road, the pub was glowing like the last jack-o'-lantern in the world. Shaking with rant and revelry.

Inside, the throng was almost impenetrable, but I fought my way through to the heart of the din, the bar at the back. Mike Tyson—a short version—was shouting to a very tall Ronald Reagan. I pushed between them and found the barmaid, decked out like Little Red Riding Hood, ready for my order. The first pint of Creemore I downed in one gulp—all it did was fire up my thirst. The second pint I took for a little stroll, cradling it against my body while I blocked with my forearm. I found a slot by the window where I could breathe, and poured the beer down steady.

The third pint I hauled into the big front room with the fireplace. Through a bunch of jocks whose idea of a costume was to tape hockey pucks to their heads, I saw a striking woman in a lacy white dress, hair pulled back in a bun. At first she reminded me of Bette Davis, but the forehead was finer, the nose longer and straighter. The lips were full like that Greek boy statue, the Hermes of Praxitiles. I moved closer to her and saw her eyes. They were huge and fathoms deep. The likeness that now dawned on me was uncanny. I couldn't resist her. I halted about a yard away, looking.

She had two guy friends with her who appeared too hip to bother with costumes, and thus had cannily avoided competing with her. Both sported standard-issue black dusters, shaved heads, and dewy features.

I had often cursed the way that mere youth, buttressed by fashion conformity, could give mediocre males access to women of real distinction. But this was going too far. This woman actually looked like Virginia Woolf, looked like she *was* Virginia Woolf. Or rather, Virginia Stephen, the fledgling writer fighting off marriage proposals. Her face exuded an intellectual beauty so rarefied that it was sensual. Even so, I wouldn't usually gape so openly. But tonight I did.

"Okay, you've looked," said the shorter male, who was quite husky. "Now park it somewhere else." His campy grimace to his companions said *I can't believe I did that*, but there was something hazardous in his eyes.

"We meet again," I said to her.

She looked askance at me.

The other male gave a shrill laugh and said, "Sorry, she doesn't know you."

"No, it's all right," she said. "Let's see what he's got."

I bowed and said, "I only wanted to say that you look so like yourself tonight."

"Why thank you!"

"The dress is perfect—I love the floppy collar. The hair is perfect. Your *eyes* are perfect." I hadn't meant to fawn over her like this.

She said nothing, but fixed me with the kind of smile that the truly classy can always produce when their goal is to confer favour without granting intimacy. It made me flustered. Suddenly I couldn't hide the fact that I wanted to connect with her. With *her*, not the character she was playing.

"I only meant that it was great—your costume," I said.

"What costume?" she said, and hooked her fingers through her friends' arms. "This *is* getting tiresome," she said, and they sashayed over to the bay window.

Okay, I'm rejected again, I thought, wandering back to the bar.

First my father has to doubt me on his deathbed. Could he not have chosen a better time? Then Virginia Woolf finds me tiresome. Does she not know my devotion to her works, my longing for her, my tooth-grinding over her unnecessary death?

I got a shot of single malt from svelte Red Riding Hood, downed it and ordered a double. "It wasn't the stones," I muttered.

"What'd ya say?" Mike Tyson asked.

"It wasn't the stones," I said louder, and entered the other room.

"What the hell does that mean," he bellowed.

His voice was bigger than mine, but not by much, and mine had more intensity: "It wasn't the fucking stones!"

I reached my lady friend. But Mike Tyson had followed me. He said, "Hey man, I don't like your attitude."

I said, "Okay, take your mask off."

He did. He was white but he looked kind of like Mike Tyson.

I said, "*Now* do you like my attitude?"

He raised a fist, held it for a moment, and then laughed. "Oh forget it," he said.

"That was deft," the wonderful woman said.

I thanked her, and asked her where her friends were.

"Oh, they're smokers," she said. "I made them go outside."

How interesting, I thought: Leonard was a smoker too. The plot thickened.

"What were you saying to that man?" she said.

"I was talking about you," I said. "I was saying it wasn't the stones that did you in."

"No?" She looked quizzical.

"It were Leonard what sunk you," I said in my best cockney. "Leonard, sure as the pint I had tonight."

"Who is Leonard?"

"Leonard. Leonard Woolf."

"I'm sorry?"

"Aren't you Virginia?"

"Oh! No, you have the right period, but the wrong country. I am dressed as Agnes MacPhail. I was a Member of Parliament. In Canada."

"You were?" This couldn't be right. I stared at her.

"I'm sorry," I said, "I'm out of order again." I started to walk away.

But she followed me, saying, "It's okay, tell me about it: what did he do to her?"

I halted, feeling embarrassed now. "He, um ... he told her, and this was right after they were married, that she couldn't have children, because she was a madwoman. Dr. Savage said it would do her a world of good. But Leonard didn't like that answer, so he went with two *other* doctors who agreed that she was crazy. None of them asked her what she was suffering from."

"Which was?"

"Abuse. Sexual abuse as a child."

"So what happened to her?"

"At the end of March 1941, she was hearing voices again. She put stones in her pockets, and she walked into the river. Some children found her body three days later."

"God, that's awful," she said.

She offered to buy me a drink but I said no thank you.

The crowd was stirring like a restive beast; I pushed through into the separate hubbub of the hall. There I saw a pay phone staring at me. Sick at heart, I dug in my jacket pocket for my calling card.

It came out, but so did something else that tumbled to the floor. It lay unfolded down there. Before I could reach for it, someone crossed in front of me; a Doc Marten tromped right on the photo. I squatted down and picked it up.

It was in sad condition. It had been riding around in my pocket since the end of summer. It had been folded and unfolded too many times. But you could still see Maggie, in living colour.

The weathered dock beside her was grey, the lake was blue with black creases in it. Where the sky should be, there was a shrouded vision of traffic, six-lane traffic. The L.A. freeway, stealing into Maggie's world because I had forgotten to advance the film.

The water laid its fingers on her chest. One pink arm reached to the dock. The dark hair was wet and shiny. The face was tear-stained. A defiant look in the eyes instantly told you a couple of things. First, that under that water she was not wearing a thing. Second, that she wanted to trust you but she didn't know why she should.

Give me a reason, her eyes seemed to say.

I folded it and put it away. I used my calling card and dialled the number.

"It's me," I shouted into the phone when she answered.

"Where are you?" she said.

I could hardly make out the words. I tented my jacket over the phone, and said, "Just lifting a glass."

"Are you all right? Is everything okay there?" she said.

Be careful, I was thinking. Don't sound like you're having second thoughts, because she probably went through with it.

"I'm wonderful."

She said something; it might have been about George.

"That's cool," I said. "So, I just wanted to know if you . . ."

There was a pause.

Fuck. Blew it. She's mad because I had to ask.

"What do you think," she said. "Yeah, I did what you wanted."
Then there was silence. She didn't seem to have a lot to add.

She had done it. She had done it. This was where I should
comfort her. The noise around me was deafening. I didn't
know what to say. I cleared my throat. I sagged against the wall.

But I still held the phone against my ear. After a while I
heard her say, "Why don't you go back to your drink?"

I couldn't make out the tone, but I could imagine it.

53

The Maltese statue

OUTSIDE, THE COLD AIR INJECTED ME WITH LIFE. "I want books, Hogarth Press books," I said. "Books for ballast. Where do they have books?"

The tide of my drunken steps soon carried me to the Public Library. I tried the door; it was open. I walked in, saw a clutch of very respectable-looking people in half-hearted costumes, and walked out again. "Not the place," I said, feeling like Dudley Moore in *Arthur*. "Not the place."

I turned right at the corner, thinking, I'll go to Joe's old high school. Maybe they have books. But two blocks along, I saw a stone mansion on the far side of the street. Arched windows glowed through silver spruces. "They'll have booksh," I pronounced.

The guy at the door was blond, sweet, absurdly handsome. He was dressed as Robin Hood. "Sorry," he said. "Nobody gets in without a costume."

"I am in costume," the lovable drunk told him.

"Really. What are you dressed as?"

"A shadow."

"Well you don't look like a shadow to me." A fairy joined the hero of Sherwood Forest. She leaned on his shoulder, grinning at him. Robin was ripe for the picking. "Whose shadow are you?" he said languidly.

"I'm a shadow of my former self," I said.

The girl laughed appreciatively. Robin was relenting. "Okay, well . . . who do you know—who are you a friend of? 'Cause I don't think I know you."

Really the guy was a perfect gentleman. Everyone was true to form tonight. "I'm a friend of Leonard, I'm with Leonard," I said.

"Oh, okay . . . he's not here yet, but go ahead, go in . . ."

The party was way too elegant, but it was crowded and the place was vast. Easy to get lost in. I took a glass of champagne from a passing waiter and ducked down a hallway. Another gorgeous couple appeared—in eighteenth-century French finery—and the bewigged male handed me a fat, smoking joint. I turned into the doorway whence they came. Near-darkness; casement windows giving on the wooded grounds; a faint yellow glow from candles inset in the walls. I groped next to the doorway, twisted a dimmer dial. The candles all flared to gold.

Books. Wherever you looked, thousands of them, all the way from the Persian carpet to the fifteen-foot moulded ceiling.

I took a deep hit, held it in.

Books. Old books, first editions some of them. And something else: statues. Little statues on the shelves—oh, they were bookends. What a fine idea. Bookends would surely sink.

So where would my favourites be? Halfway down the wall I found Dickens, lots of Victoriana, there sat *The Moonstone*, there was Tennyson. And then, would you believe it, a whole tier of Bloomsbury. Clive Bell, Forster, Strachey.

And here was Virginia, lots of her. And Freud—that's *right*, the Woolfs gave Freud to England. From their own Hogarth Press. And here at last was Leonard. Five fusty volumes: Leonard Woolf's own story in his own stolid, decent words.

What do I want? I wondered. I want Volume Two, that's where he sinks her.

Here it is. *Beginning Again*, he called it. What an imagination.

I hefted it. Not that massy. It was made from trees, after all. Trees float. Even monster pine trees. They call them logs. I had seen a book float once.

A bookend would be better. A statue. I looked on the shelf, but Virginia was nowhere to be found. Her books filled the space she should be in. At the opposite end, though, was a shiny black statue of Leonard, in a tight suit, looking solemn and stiff with a pipe in his hand.

Where was his wife? I tried up and down and around; but all I could locate was Sigmund Freud. I didn't want him with me; he was entirely too heavy.

So it was down to my esteemed comrade.

Leonard. Good to see that you, at least, are on the case. Come along, come into my sack. God you're heavy. You must weigh thirty pounds. Leonard the lead-footed. We'll have to make do without Virginia. We'll take you *and* your book.

It was a nasty show trying to stuff these objects into my pack while consuming a major joint. It merited a little sit-down.

Oh God, I thought when I came to. Now I'm really stoned. If I think about it at all, I'll get an asthma offer that I won't refuse, and I'll blow the whole plan. Don't *try* to breathe. Just breathe. And hoist the heist. Bearing the Maltese statue, we abandon the enemy mansion and slip into the night.

It's like London out here, a classic pea souper. Only it's orange. Miles of orange gas lamps in the fog. In the fine tradition of Edward Hyde, let us march. That's Frederick March to you, boy. Frederick . . . MARCH!

Marching for the deaf and dumb,
Marching for the rat,
For the mystic mislaid mother,
The mistitled bureaucrat . . .

The hills are lovely, slick and steep. There's Louise Croft's house. We should go in and see if she still lives there.

But we have promises to break.
And miles and miles before we wake.
Me and Leonard.

The lake is lovely too. What you can see of it in this fog. Let's not do this by the highway, let's have a little discretion here. Let's carry this weight a little longer.

A little marina up ahead. No power boats though—all very ecological. Canoes and sailboats.

Let's drag this here canoe—yeah this one: anybody got a problem with that?—over to the shore. Okay. Now, we'll float out there where the really big ones bite and we'll do the deed.

It's hard to get it in though. This shore is too slopy, too grassy, too smooth. Whooooops. Now we've done it. We're sliding down the slippery slope and it's so slick it turns us all into otters. Not much rock around here!

So. We didn't need the canoe. We're under anyway, well under, well done, undone most excellently. We're sliding right down to the bottom of this fucking lake. We really are. This plan has got legs of its own.

Like, guy, if we wanted to check the surface one more time, just check it for wildlife, I don't honestly know if we could!

It's wet down here! Shit. I wasn't ready. You have to *choose* the moment. Now I'm going to do the knee-jerk thing and res-cue myself. Can't help it.

I'm gonna shuck this stupid pack off—I was intending to do some reading in the canoe anyway, just for ceremony, and I can't even float up to the canoe with this damn weight on my back.

I intended to read a few words of Leonard's. In honour of Murry Barr, with his impressive grasp of facts.

In honour of Joseph, with his deep-springing love.

But most of all in honour of Maggie, who only wanted a chance to rise to the occasion.

Now that's why they say don't dress macho. These epaulettes, et tu Paul, or Saul, these things they are surely straps of the shoulder. Now where was I?

Epaulettes. Make me epaulettes on your floor, ON YOUR FLOOR! Oh. Right. Can't get the backpack strap over the epaulette: that's why we're on the ocean floor. It's not fair to Leonard. He didn't do anything. Well, he sunk her. Sank her. Sans care. Canker. Crank her, boys, she's stuck on the bottom. Leonard, help Miss Kendall with her handbag. Our flight is waiting.

You know, maybe it would be easier to just take the jacket off. *There's* a novel approach. Just unzip the sucker and divest ourselves of this sculpture. Pull down the zipper. But you can't, can you? It's stuck. And this sucks. A zipless suck. Or sink. Or sunk.

There, finally we got it. Zipper down. Time to shuck off this mortal coil. But you know, it's a small point and I don't want to belabour it, but, put very simply, I am just plumb out of gas. No energy. No zip.

And I can't remember the last time I breathed. Or saw anything.

But I hear something. I do. Music. Creeping by me. Irish music, by the instrumentation. I mean the French don't have Irish pipes, do they? And what are they playing—isn't it the song from *Scrooge*? The Alastair Sim version. My daddy loved it. Scrooge comes in to his nephew's party, all full of trepidation, and the maid smiles at him, and my dad blows his nose. What the fuck was it called.

Barbara Allen. It occurs to me it's an old English air. Odd that an Irish band should play an English air. Really, I suppose, an air is just an air.

But it is beautiful. It's getting to me. Very sad. But a lilt to the melody. And here they come, all the little horses. The kings and queens, elves and dwarfs, knights and ladies. But all so small. Still, a goodly parade. Well lit for the bottom of a lake.

This knight now, with the red cross. I know this fellow. Goes by the name George. Blond, a pretty lad. Seems to be making a collar. My collar. There he goes, dragging my collar, and my pants, oh yes, even my arms and legs. Leaving the pack behind. There he goes with me in tow, up the watery vale to the top of the world.

There he went, he took me to the ceiling. To the sky. To the air.

But he forgot something.

Because I'm still down here.

Watching him. I'm here with the plants. I wonder if the sun ever reaches down here. We could all use some.

54

Some Halloween thing

A VOICE CALLED THE NAME GEORGE.

I tried to lift myself off the ground, got my head up a few inches, crumpled again.

Cattle groaned, cars whished by, a dog barked in the distance.

I felt a hand on me, prying me up. Rolling me onto my back.

"It's you, Dave," Ed said. "I was hoping—never mind what I was hoping. What are you *doing* here?"

He pulled me to my feet, and held me up while I tried to get my balance. I was groggy, damp.

"You weigh a ton," he said. "Were you in the water?"

I looked around. The canoe was sitting by the shore, like a faithful horse. The sky was reddish.

"I may have been," I said. "What time is it? What day is it?"

"It's Sunday."

I started to shiver. "I think I'm cold," I said.

"You shouldn't be walking. You may have hypothermia." He picked me up and slung me over his shoulder. Around the shore we went, to the road.

"Stay here," Ed said. "I'll get the car."

It seemed to be dawn. The frogs were loud and my head was aching. What had I done? What was Ed doing here?

He pulled my jacket off and put a blanket around me. He said we should get me checked over at the hospital. He was going there anyway. In the car I thought I was going to be sick. I rolled down the window and said, "You may have to stop."

"Just let me know," Ed said.

I took my first look at him. He was dishevelled, tired—almost old.

"Thank you," I said.

"I've been up half the night," he said. "Searching for George. He's disappeared. Alicia saw him after school and then he disappeared."

"Some Halloween thing?" I said.

"I traced him to Jennifer Bull's house. I went to talk to her. She had seen him, but she didn't know where he went."

He made a weird noise and I realized that he was crying.

Ed turned into the hospital's circular drive. "Maybe Susan heard something," he said. "She's here. Your dad is on the brink."

We went through the sliding doors and my sister was standing there. In a little room beyond her, my mother sat with a blank stare.

"Dad's gone," Susan said. "He went this morning."

I leaned on the wall, too woozy to put all this in perspective.

"Ed," she said. "I got another call, right after you left."

Her features started to break up like a bad signal. She stepped over to him, grabbed his arms. "It was Ralph Guthrie."

She shook her head slowly, as if rejecting her own words. "There's been an accident at Bayne Island. A fire broke out. Gas spilled. Some teenagers in a boat. Burnt."

She looked down and then up again. Her eyes brimmed over. "Ed, the cottage burned too. All but the fireplace. The men went up to take a look."

She fell onto his chest and sang to him, "They found another body. A boy. In the cottage."

55

Abide with me

It was my worst visit with my mother, and my best. We kept meeting in halls and doorways and we would just hold on to each other.

We ate toast together, and slept a lot of the time.

At two in the afternoon there was sun in the hallway and she showed me some of my dad's sports jackets. She held them out and asked me if she should sell them and I said no. Don't worry about that yet.

I heard every member of the Stone family honoured with her favourite adjective: poor George, poor Ed, poor Susan—Alicia got one too. And that was fine. It seemed to take Irene's mind off her own plight. I thought maybe it was referred feeling; maybe it was herself she was mailing comfort to.

On Tuesday we got ourselves in a semblance of order and went to see the Stones. I hugged Susan a long time. She said, "How did we lose track of him?" But I still couldn't believe that George was gone.

It made no sense. How could he be on Bayne Island? What was he doing in some gasoline incident with local boys? Yet his wallet had been identified in the ashes. There was an investigation going on in Muskoka and his remains hadn't been released yet, which was ridiculous but somehow made it seem as if the result wasn't final. Meanwhile Ed was conducting his own Calvan investigation: where had George been and what had happened to him? Ed had talked to George's schoolmate, Jennifer Bull, again. Susan had offered up another piece of the puzzle, some house on Empress Street where she had busted George with some kids, and it smelled like dope. Strangest of all, some old stoner named Carl had shown up at Ed and Susan's house and told them more about those kids—a weird boy named Graham and a rich girl named Laine, who got George embroiled.

Our visit didn't last long. I only heard fragments from Ed, but I got the feeling he was putting a story together. Susan was barely responding to stimuli. Her look exuded a crushing guilt.

I kept thinking of George running along the dock and jumping in. With the John Lennon T-shirt on, into the cold water. "The T-shirt helps," he had told me.

There would be a service for him later on. But the first funeral we had to face, on Wednesday, was Joseph's.

I didn't have to do anything at my father's funeral except hold my mother's hand. And that was a good thing. Everyone sang "Abide with me." My mother and I didn't need a hymnary; we knew the words. My sister Lorraine and my brother Greg got up and read poems that had been favourites of my dad's. As Lorraine read "Along the Line of Smoky Hills," she seemed as innocent as a child, and I felt tears choke me. And then I knew that if I let go I would create my own Wailing Pew, I would just howl until I shook the building. Many upstanding people were in the rows behind us, secretaries and lawyers and farmers and relatives. The Chesleys, parents of my oldest friend, were here, and he was here too; Scott had somehow made it. I did not want to make a scene in front of these people. My mother seemed more under control; I tried to take my cue from her.

Ed was not, of course, presiding. He was there, ashen in a back pew with Susan and Alicia.

When it was over I went into the reception area and saw among the crowd strapping toothy men from my mother's side of the family, and more angular specimens from my dad's. For a few of those present, not in the loop, this was a tenable occasion: a man had died in his eighties, a successful, well-connected man. But for most of us there could be no cheer: George was gone too, this couldn't fail to be about that. And for me another one was gone, I had let another go as well.

I got a cup of water and moved through the crowd. A cousin on my mother's side took me in his grip and said, "Dave, my condolences. How is your mother bearing up?" The implication was, we men worry more about our mothers than we do about ourselves. This was a man I had never been close to, who had trashed me at a dinner in north Toronto years before when we were both in college, because I had long hair and didn't have a business plan. He was still trying to correct me.

I got away from him and came up to my dad's sister Rose. She took me in a bony embrace and just said, "Oh Dave." That was going to break me down so I squeezed her arm and walked on, past my friend Scott who sent me a small salute, and out the door into the back lane.

Maggie was standing there. She was wearing a black dress.

56

The red maple

"You're here," I said to Maggie.

A light rain started in my eyes.

She looked at me solemnly. I couldn't tell where I stood with her.

"I had to come," she said. "I think I was the last person to talk to George."

"How . . . could that be?"

"He called me, from the cottage. Right before it happened, I guess. Whatever 'it' was. He called you and got me."

I leaned against the wall of the next building. We were in a sort of stone hallway. Sunlight was coming over the edge and hitting us.

"I'm sorry I haven't called you," she said.

At last I could pull in some air. I stood free of the wall. "I've been so wrong," I said.

"I have so blown it," I said, and my personal rain started again.

She came closer.

"Don't comfort me," I told her. "I think I said that once before." I gave a strangled laugh.

She nodded and then said, "I lied to you."

I stood to attention, gazing at her.

Just then my mother burst out of the church door and looked around frantically. Then she seemed to get us in focus.

"Maggie!" she said. "This is awful—I can't—" and she astonished both of us by throwing her head on Maggie's chest and clutching her.

Maggie held her tight, saying, "That's okay, Mrs. Moore, that's okay."

My mother pulled back to look at her. "I'm so worried about Ed and Susan," she said. "They can't stay here. They can't be alone. I don't know what to do."

With an eye on me, Maggie said, "Why doesn't Dave drive them home? I'll stay with you. We'll go to their place and take care of them."

Not believing I couldn't hear the rest of what Maggie had to say to me, I went back in the church and steered through the throng, which had not thinned out. I could see my brother over by the window with a bunch of relatives from both sides of the family. I found Susan and Ed still in the sanctuary, Alicia holding Ed's hand. Standing with them was a beautiful girl about George's age with honey-blonde hair. She was saying something to them and it was making Susan and Ed tear up.

Lorraine was in the doorway; she whispered to me, "They're losing it." I told her our plan. She said she would hold things down at the church.

"Who was that girl?" I asked Ed in the car, as Susan sat stiff in the backseat, Alicia holding *her* hand now.

"Jennifer Bull. She came today on her own, just to express her condolences."

"She seemed really nice."

"She is. I think she may have been George's sweetheart."

We lapsed into silence and I tried to reconstruct the route to Jeremy Street from the downtown.

Back at the house there seemed little hope of getting alone with Maggie.

Ed and Alicia found a home in the little family room looking out on the backyard; Susan got a notion that what was needed was hot tea for everyone, and proceeded to fill a teapot from the kitchen faucet. Maggie gently took the teapot from her hand and said, "Why don't we put some water in the kettle?"

Susan sat at the table and I stood beside her with a hand on her shoulder. My mother came from the bathroom and helped Maggie deploy the china cups.

Things seemed to be moving towards order and calm, if those states can be in company with unbearable heartache, when the doorbell rang.

We heard Ed go to answer it, and then we heard him talking with some adult male. Ed came into the kitchen and said, "It's a man from Bracebridge."

"Has he got our George?" Susan burst out.

Ed furrowed his brow and Susan started to sob; my mother moved next to her and put her arms around her. "My baby," she crooned.

"Dave," Ed said, "can you help me? With him?"

Ed and I took the man into the living room, the fancy room at the front of the house with the blue and silver upholstered furniture.

He turned out to be the father of one of the boys who had been in the incident with George. He had driven down from Bracebridge to be at the funeral and talk to the Stones. I asked him questions and his story emerged. His ten-year-old son James had witnessed the whole thing, and at the crucial moment had dived into the lake and avoided the flames that engulfed the boat they were in. It had taken him a couple of days but eventually he had spilled everything he knew to his father. Three boys from the Portal Marina had followed George to the island and a struggle had ensued, which our guest described in detail. The bottom line was: not George but the oldest boy, a fifteen-year-old named Eric, had poured the gasoline and lit the match that sparked the conflagration. George had been trying to fight them off; then as James watched from a rock on the shore, George had tried to defend the cottage against the flames. Then rain had come, the first since August, in time to help the firefighters but not in time for George.

"I want to apologize so much for what happened to your son, and for the part my boy played in it," Mr. Lambert said.

Ed had sunk open-mouthed deeper and deeper into the couch; I stood with Lambert and thanked him for his extreme thoughtfulness and assured him that he could stay longer; but he was bound he would go. We exchanged the relevant contact information and I thanked him again.

When I got back to the kitchen, Maggie was arranging some cookies on a plate. The others were in the family room: I could see Susan stiff as driftwood on the couch, with Irene on one side of her and Alicia on the other. I took a cup of tea to Ed, who didn't look like he was going to hazard any travel anytime soon.

Then I returned to Maggie, and we went over to the kitchen window.

"You said you lied to me," I opened, praying that this could mean what I thought it could mean.

"I did," she said. "When you called me on Saturday night, I lied to you. I hadn't had the procedure."

I nodded, trying to find some footing on the razor's edge of this sentence.

"I got distracted," she said. "When George called me. I just never went to the clinic."

"Never," I repeated, nodding my head slowly.

"Until Monday. Then I did go."

I stopped nodding my head.

"But I ran out of there," she said. "I suddenly realized it wasn't your decision."

"That is completely right," I said, sucking in my first real oxygen in the last hour.

"No, I don't mean that," she said. "I mean I realized that when I agreed to have the abortion, it wasn't you forcing me; I was onboard. I couldn't put it all on you."

I nodded again. I couldn't say a thing; she was doing fine.

"It was my decision too," she said. "So I had to vote for it. But I couldn't."

I forced myself not to grab her and kiss her.

"I was already in their awful blue gown. They were about to stick me with a needle. I snatched my purse, ran to my car and got away. I left behind a perfectly good pair of slingbacks."

My mother walked by. She gave us a silent, graceful wave and headed for the front room. We turned back to the window, and seemed for the first time to see the propane grill on the deck and beyond it, a small maple tree with a few red leaves left. I felt Maggie's fingernails bite into my hand as, in a spasm of emotion, she said, "That tree. It's about the same age as George."

We both cried a little. Her hand stayed in mine as she said, "You know that awful game we were playing."

I thought. "The one where I got my way so I had to be nice to you?"

"Exactly."

"It was twisted."

"It was."

"We shouldn't play games anymore," I said.

"Not even when we're scared shitless?" she said.

I hooted briefly, then cut it off. I put my arms around her and inhaled the smell of her hair.

"Not even then," I said.